Not Cut Out to Be a Teacher?

Betty Weinberger

Messianic Family Publishers
University Park, Illinois

Not Cut Out to Be a Teacher?
Messianic Family Publishers
553 Irving Place
University Park, IL 60484
©2016 Betty Weinberger
All rights reserved.
Printed in the United States of America

ISBN: 978-0-9754836-3-3

Cover & Interior Design by Jonathan Lewis | Jonlin Creative

Cover Photo Credits
Woman: iStockPhoto.com/mediaphotos | Hair: iStockPhoto.com/ariwasabi
Necklace: www.iStockPhoto.com/CaronB | Background Texture: Kim Klassen

Handwritten inscription:

> 5/30/20
>
> To Janet,
> a friend of Dana & Joel, my children. Hope you enjoy & are blessed by my story.
>
> Love, Betty Weinberger
> dweinbe@gmail.com

Written from my heart with love for my children, Lael and Sarah, Joel and Dana; and my grandchildren, Chaim, Esther, Micah, and Leah, as well as the grandchildren yet to be born.

Also written to bless Claire, Cara, and Anja.

And written with a heart full of thanksgiving to Almighty God for giving me such a wonderful husband, David Weinberger.

CONTENTS

Part One: Work
...and to rejoice in his labor; this is the gift of God. – *Eccl 5:19*
Page 9

Part Two: Relationships
There be three things which are too wonderful for me, yea, four which I know not: The way of an eagle in the air; the way of a serpent upon a rock; the way of a ship in the midst of the sea; and the way of a man with a maid. – *Proverbs 30:18-19*
Page 113

Part Three: Fulfillment
Delight thyself also in the Lord; and He shall give thee the desires of thine heart. – *Psalm 37:4*
Page 237

This story takes place in the 1970's, 80's and 90's. You'll see references to tape players, land line phones, and life without the internet or smart phones. You'll come across some of the older terminology used in the special education field of those days. But the subject matter is not dated. This is the story of a girl searching for her place in life, in the work world, in guy-girl relationships, and most importantly, in her relationship with God. It is a fictionalized story based on real people, situations, and events. I hope you enjoy it.

Part One: Work

...and to rejoice in his labor; this is the gift of God. – *Eccl 5:19*

Chapter One

ELLIE WAS EXCITED. The new job she applied for several months earlier was finally becoming a reality. She could actually feel it, not in her bones but in her nervous system. She was all ready for bed except for setting her hair. She got out the usual four rollers and rolled up her medium length brown hair, with two rollers on one side and two on the other. Then she climbed under the covers.

10 o'clock wasn't bad, she thought. Actually pretty good for a 22 year old, at least from the many accounts she'd heard from friends. And then Ellie tried to fall asleep. Her father once told her that even if you can't fall asleep, just keep your eyes closed and rest and pretty soon you'll fall asleep. Ellie tried that until she had to open her eyes to see what time it was. 10:35! Oh no, it wasn't working. She wished she could rest her mind somehow. It kept replaying old scenes of her past jobs and past experiences that led her to this point in her life. Her college years, her student teaching days, her first job as a substitute teacher…how interesting it all had been, if only it was somebody else and not her!

Yikes, why was it that she could remember every detail of that horrible day so clearly! But there she lay, remembering. It was her third week of student teaching. Mrs. Cody, the master teacher she worked with, was strict and very effective with the children. She devised a sort of rap song, way before rap was popular, to review the various sounds of the alphabet.

Mrs. Cody was older but she was "cool." The fourth graders she taught were way behind academically, but they were very street smart and "cool." Ellie was the opposite. She felt so "uncool" that she purposely tried to never say a cool phrase because she just knew it wouldn't come out right. She resisted wearing bell bottoms until she got so used to seeing them, she finally started liking them and wearing them. And wouldn't you know, that was just about the time when straight legs came back into style.

Well on that day, in her third week of student teaching, Mrs. Cody asked her to lead the alphabet rap. With no time to think, no privacy to present her objections to Mrs. Cody, Ellie knew she'd have to do what she was asked to do. So feeling more uncool than ever, Ellie began to lead the alphabet rap. She could feel her face turning warm and red.

"A is for apple, a a a, arrow and alligator, a a a; B is for basket, b b b, barbeque, boat, b b b; C is for carrot, c c c , calendar, carpet, c, c, c, …"

It came out sounding pretty stiff, embarrassing, and weird, but she hoped the kids' voices drowned out her own. At least none of the kids laughed out loud. Straight from that experience of chanting rap, she had to jump into teaching a hard mathematics lesson. Her courage and confidence were already used up for the day, and just as she thought would happen, the kids acted up. The lesson was such a flop that Mrs. Cody had to take over.

Mrs. Cody surmised that a big reason for Ellie's ineffectiveness was her voice. "You've gotta get rid of that baby voice of yours, Ellie," Mrs. Cody said at break time. Ellie was shocked and humiliated, but she tried not to show it. She never did like the sound of her voice when she heard recordings of herself giving a speech. But for someone to imply that her voice was so strange she needed to change it—that was too much! She wondered how a person would go about changing their voice anyway.

Mrs. Cody continued. "Another thing is that you should never smile for the first few months of teaching a class. The students will take advantage of you, and that's just what they're doing." After that, Ellie went to the bathroom to splash cold water on her face to prevent her tears from popping out. Then she had to march straight back into the classroom and handle her reading group.

Amazingly Ellie made it through student teaching and received the grade of A. The college professor who supervised her must have thought she did a reasonable job. That helped, but Ellie was still filled with doubts. Would she ever make it as a teacher? Mrs. Cody's remarks to her on her last day still reverberated in her mind: "You're a lovely person, Ellie, but be open to other possibilities. Maybe you weren't cut out to be a teacher."

Now a new job was starting and it wasn't teaching! Ellie tried to be hopeful and stop thinking of her failures and get to sleep. She finally dozed off, when a sudden, loud r-*r-r-i-i-i*—*ng* woke her up again.

Ellie's heart began racing as she jumped out of bed to answer the phone, most likely a call from the school district about substituting. But her cousin Carol, whom she roomed with, had already picked up the call. And it wasn't for Ellie. Carol's boyfriend was calling. It was still night-time, 11:07 to be exact. But Ellie was up again. Too bad. But in a way it was good, because she was rescued out of a nightmare. However, the phone call re-awakened her to memories of another episode in her life which she preferred to forget.

How clearly she remembered those feelings of dread that would begin when she heard the telephone ring at six or seven in the morning. The secretary from the school district called about then to inform her that one of the teachers called in sick and a substitute was needed. The calls were so unpredictable. Sometimes she stayed in bed and no phone call came. She would start planning out what she would do that day when suddenly the phone would ring. It might even be as late as an 8 o'clock call giving her an assignment at a school at 9 a.m.! The extra pressure of rushing to get ready so fast was not a bit helpful. And then when she pulled into the school parking lot, her stomach would drop with that sinking feeling of fear and foreboding. How did she ever survive so many months of substitute teaching?

There was one particular day she remembered more than the others. She was assigned to sub in a first grade classroom. She felt relief and joy at being assigned to a first grade class again. She loved that age group. But as she was in the classroom preparing for the day, one of the boys peered through the window and yelled out gleefully to his friends, "Hey man, we got a sub today!" And then she heard whooping and hollering from a lot of voices outside her window.

Then, of all things, she began the day by smiling! Bad move. By the end of the day, the bulletin boards were being dismantled as various students took out the tacks and started jabbing each other. Ellie was so overwhelmed at how to bring back order into the room that she actually asked the kids for advice.

"What does your teacher do to control the class?" she asked. Amazingly, the students weren't afraid to tell her the answer.

"She whips us. The paddle is in the second drawer there."

Ellie opened the drawer and saw it, then closed it again. The day was almost over. Did she really make a mistake in going into teaching in the first place, she wondered.

But that was then and now was now. She was starting a new job. It was dealing with kids, but not exactly teaching. She had high hopes that it would turn out well. And somewhere in the middle of her musings, sleep came.

Chapter Two

ELLIE'S ALARM RANG and she sat up in bed and said a prayer. She was glad the day was finally here. Since Monday was a holiday, she had a long three day weekend for the tension to build. As she washed and dressed for the day, Ellie tried to calm herself. She put some yogurt in a bowl for breakfast, along with a blueberry muffin. Fifteen minutes later, she put half of the yogurt and half of the muffin back in the refrigerator. She was still a little, or a little bit more than a little, nervous. She packed her lunch, put on her coat and left for her new job.

Ellie got to the Monroe Avenue Center faster than she thought she would. She headed to the main administration building where she was to report for her first day of work. She decided to leave her plastic bag lunch in the car. Then came her usual debate, that all important decision of whether or not to wear her hat. Hats weren't in style that year, but her ears and throat were so sensitive to the cold. She put her hat on, then took it off and fluffed up her hair. But as she reconsidered the frigid February temperatures, she put her knitted floppy pink hat back on and locked the car.

Even with the hat on, she was shivering. She had on her new winter coat with down lining. She also had on a new pair of jeans and a new, warm, forest green turtleneck. She was told to dress very casually, since the job included things like cooking, doing dishes, and giving the children baths or showers. Ellie was dressed warmly enough, so she figured her shivering must have been from anxiety, the typical new job syndrome.

The man who hired her, Mr. Pulanski, met her at the door. "Hi Ellie, come on in."

"You're Mr. Pulanski, right?"

"Wow, you're pretty good at remembering *and* pronouncing Polish names," he said. "But just call me Mike."

"Oh ok," Ellie said. "My mother's side of the family is Polish, so I'm pretty used to names like Pulanski."

"Great," Mike chuckled. "Take off your coat and have a seat. It's nice and warm in here. Would you like a cup of coffee?"

"No thanks," Ellie said.

"Ok, I'll just give you a little more information about your job and then have you fill out a few more forms.

"We've assigned you to work in house 25. Before letting you loose there, let me give you a little more of the background on the Monroe Avenue Center. I know you probably heard a lot already at the orientation talk. But I'd rather risk boring you by telling you the same things again, than take the risk that maybe you didn't hear some of the important things you'll need to hear."

"Sure," Ellie said. "I'd be happy to hear as much as possible about my job before I start. I really want to do a great job here."

"I like your attitude Ellie," Mike said. "As you probably know, the Monroe Avenue Center is composed of group homes, ten for children and twenty for adults. You'll be working in one of the children's homes.

"Each home houses eight residents who are severely or profoundly retarded. Along with the severe impairments our children have in their brain function, they also have severe lacks in their adaptive skills. They need a lot of help just to function in everyday activities we take for granted.

"Of course, there's also a balance that every case manager needs to keep in mind. You can't do everything for the children. You'll have to balance helping the children with teaching the children. Wherever possible, the children are to be taught to do as much for themselves as they can.

"I know you'll keep this teaching aspect uppermost in your mind, since you are a teacher. Yet I notice your degree is in elementary education, not special ed. But I know you're a very bright young lady and you realize you won't be teaching these children any calculus or constitutional law."

Ellie smiled even though Mike's jokes weren't too funny. But she knew he was trying to be nice to her, so she played along. She wanted to make a good impression.

Mike continued, "You'll be teaching them how to eat without stealing each other's food, how to wash themselves, how to hold a crayon and color on a piece of paper…"

Mike went on with his list, but Ellie's mind was still on his first point, *how to eat without stealing each other's food*. She was a little surprised and shocked to hear that. That wasn't exactly how she imagined it.

Meanwhile Mike was going on with his list, "… how to clean off the tables and carry their dirty dishes into the kitchen, and even how to use the toilet."

How to use the toilet! Ellie gasped, but only in her mind. She didn't want to show her ignorance or repulsion to Mr. Pulanski. But she wasn't sure if her eyebrows rose slightly or her eyes twitched or if her body gave some kind of clue at her shocked reaction. But it didn't seem like Mike noticed anything.

He went on, "Many of these children also have other problems. Some of them are blind or hearing impaired, and some have severe behavioral issues. But our specialists have developed effective programs for most of these behavior problems. And if there's a child with behavior problems in one of the houses, we try to have at least one male case manager on the job during each daytime shift. Did we talk about what shift you'll be working on?"

"No," Ellie said. "So far I was just asked what my preferences were."

"Yes, I see it on your application. You said you'd prefer a daytime shift. As you know, we have three shifts. The morning shift starts at 6 am and goes until 2:30. On that shift the workers wake up the children, get them dressed, prepare breakfast, do morning activities, and finally handle lunch."

"Yes, that's the shift I'd prefer," Ellie said.

"Unfortunately, there's no opening on that shift. It *is* the most popular shift. But there's also another daytime shift, from 2 till 10:30. And we found we can use you best on this second shift in House 25." Ellie nodded, trying to look neutral and not show her disappointment.

Mike went on. "Now there are many advantages to second shift. It's much more relaxed, with a lot more home-type activities. The shift starts with some afternoon activities and then goes on to dinner preparations. After dinner there are some winding down activities for the day and then bath time and bed time. How does that sound?" Mike asked.

"It sounds very nice," Ellie said.

"Good, I think you'll really like it. The third shift is the night shift. The night workers come in at 10 and work until 6:30 in the morning. They do more of the house cleaning, but are also available if there is a problem in the night."

As Ellie filled out more forms, she was trying to adjust to the thought of getting home from work at 11 at night. And she couldn't stop thinking about what it would be like to work with older children who weren't toilet trained yet or who would steal each other's food. Finally she and Mike were ready to walk to house 25.

Chapter Three

THE COLD WIND was actually refreshing to Ellie now. It acted as a great tension reliever as she and Mike walked briskly to the house. But much sooner than she expected, they were there. The number 25 was painted right on the door.

Mike knocked with a loud firm knock and then walked in. That was the way people entered around here. A knock would politely let the people inside know someone was coming in, but at the same time it didn't give them too much warning. Knowing that at any moment a specialist could just walk in made the case managers more diligent to treat the residents with patience and kindness all the time.

Ellie looked around. There were a lot of sights and smells to take in. This was to be Ellie's work environment for the next few months or maybe even years of her life. She plastered an outward smile on her face as a whole merry-go-round of emotions went spinning around in her head.

She was shocked to see how tall two of the boys were. Grant was almost six feet tall. He was a nice looking young man, about seventeen years old, but with an expression on his face of a much younger boy. He was smiling and kind of laughing to himself at what seemed to be some private joke. He kept repeating a crazy phrase over and over again in a funny, high-pitched voice, "running out of steam at the zoo." It seemed Ellie's smile wasn't really *plastered* on her face like she thought, because somehow one of the case managers noticed her bewildered expression and tried to reassure her. "Oh don't pay any attention to Grant. He's off on one of his rants."

At that, Grant laughed out loud and started running around and repeating even louder, "running out of steam at the zoo, running out of steam at the zoo, …"

Ellie would find out in a few days, after working in house 25 for a while, that if Grant heard some phrase that caught his fancy, he played with it and repeated it over and over, having a lot of fun with the words. It *was* pretty funny, but right now Ellie thought it was just plain odd and even a bit scary.

The other tall boy was not so pleasant-looking. He had crossed eyes, a shaved head, and buck teeth. His name was unusual, Mahfta. He was about fifteen years old. He did not speak at all; he just made babbling sounds like a baby. The sounds weren't so cute though, when they came out in the lower voice range of a teenage boy. Ethyl, the case manager, introduced Mahfta to Ellie.

"Ellie, meet Mahfta."

"Hi Mahfta," Ellie said.

Then Ethyl talked to Mahfta and held both his hands as she exuberantly said, "You're a sweetie, aren't you, Mahfta? Isn't it exciting for you to meet Ellie?"

Mahfta just smiled back and gurgled more sounds.

"I know you might think I'm strange," Ethyl told Ellie, "but Mahfta is one of my favorites here."

Ellie smiled because Ethyl was right. She *did* think it was quite strange. Ethyl seemed very stylish in the way she carried herself, with clothing and make-up to match. She had on two or three pretty rings, a dangling bracelet, and a necklace. She of all people didn't seem the type to love such an unusual boy as Mahfta. Ellie admired Ethyl for her love and care for Mahfta, but she wondered if she could ever be compassionate enough to love him so much.

Then Ellie saw Lawrence. He was a small boy with Down syndrome and he, like Mahfta, had very crossed eyes. She was surprised to find out he was thirteen years old. He just sat on the couch and licked his hands and bounced back and forth. The smell from his constant drooling and licking his hands was very unpleasant, even repulsive, so Ellie had to move away at first. She'd need time to get used to Lawrence.

Ellie didn't have time to worry about whether she'd like this new job yet, because her senses were overloaded. All these impressions of the children in the house came on her in just a matter of minutes. It was all so new, so different, and a bit bewildering!

Suddenly Ellie's eye caught a beautiful sight, the cutest little girl standing in a corner by the window. She looked like a doll. She had beautiful brown skin and her black hair was done up in several braids. She looked like she was about three years old. She just stayed in that corner and swayed from side to side. Her eyes were a lovely brown, but they didn't seem to focus directly on anything. She had a beautiful smile on her face.

"This is Wendy," Ethyl said. "She's eight years old." Ellie was amazed.

"Yes, she sure looks like a three year old, doesn't she?" Ethyl said. "We all watch over her, don't we guys?" she said to Grant and Lawrence and Mahfta. Grant picked up that phrase and said, "Yesiree, we all watch over Wendy. Oh yes." Then he started running around saying, "Oh yeah, we all watch over Wendy. Yee-ah! Watch over Wendy…"

Ellie didn't know if Grant was joking around or really understood what Ethyl said, but she liked Ethyl's method of talking to the children normally, as if they really could understand.

The other case worker just walked out of the kitchen with a bag of M&M's. He went to Mahfta who was now sitting on the couch and said, "Good sitting Mahfta," and gave him an M&M. Mike then explained to Ellie that most of the children were on a "good sitting" program. They were rewarded for sitting quietly on the couches. This helped the house stay in order when the workers had to prepare dinner or take care of other residents.

Just then Angel came out of the toy room and sat on the couch. She was a chubby fourteen year old girl. She looked like a teenager in size, but not in her dress or her behavior. She had a short afro, was barefooted, and wore a blue and white checkerboard sack dress. She had a huge smile on her face. "Good sitting Angel," she was told, and given two M&M's.

Mike reminded the first shift workers that Ellie would be staying till 6:30 that day and the next. "I want her to see a little bit of what both daytime shifts are like," he said. "But after tomorrow she'll officially start working the second shift, from 2 till 10:30." After reassuring Ellie that he could see she'd fit right in, he left.

"Don't worry, Ellie," Matt said. He was the case worker who handed out the M&M's. "You'll get used to the kids here in no time. Wait till Lisa comes back. She'll be a lot of fun for you to talk to. She's the highest level girl in our house. I'm going to pick her up now from her arts and crafts class. Usually she has her class in the afternoon, but today they changed it to the morning."

"Where does she have the class?" Ellie asked.

"It's on the second floor of the administration building. And today Lisa Lynn and Benton are there too. We have a local dentist who comes out here once or twice a year, so two of our kids had appointments today. I'll be back with the kids for lunch. See you later," he said and then left.

"Did you want me to do anything now, Ethyl?" Ellie asked.

"The best thing you can do now is to stay out here with the kids and just get to know them. And try to keep them out of the kitchen." Then Ethyl disappeared into the kitchen to begin the preparations for lunch.

Ellie was glad no adult was out there watching her, because she felt a little awkward figuring out what to say or do with the children. She decided to talk to them like Ethyl did, as if they knew what she was saying. She started with Grant.

She didn't make much progress getting through to the youngsters, but she was starting to feel more comfortable around them. Grant did answer her questions, but in such a funny way, she didn't know if he really knew what she was asking or not. Wendy didn't even look up at her when she talked to her. Lawrence looked at her with his big brown eyes, but continued licking his hands and bouncing. And Mahfta and Angel just sat. Angel did seem to have good eye contact with Ellie and she smiled, enjoying the attention of somebody talking to her. She didn't and couldn't talk back, though.

Soon Matt returned with Lisa, Lisa Lynn and Benton. Lisa was very talkative, just like Matt said. She walked in the house joking with Matt. She thought she was one of the staff and she tried to imitate them. But the things she chose to imitate from the staff and her teachers were often their complaints and sarcastic comments. It was cute and funny in a way, but it was also a little irritating to see her acting so uppity. She had Down syndrome too, like Lawrence, but was much more advanced. Whereas Lawrence functioned at about the level of a one year old, Lisa was more on the three or four year old level. She could talk and understand basic concepts.

"So who you?" she asked Ellie in a bold and confident way.

"I'm Ellie and I'll be working here in house 25."

"Oh yeah? Who says so?" Lisa asked in her normal bossy tone.

"Well, I was hired by Mr. Pulanski," Ellie said.

"Who??" Lisa asked

Matt helped out. "She means Mike. That's his name, Mike Pulanski."

Then Ellie decided to meet Lisa on her own territory. "Why, was I supposed to be interviewed by you too?"

"Ha, yeah!" Lisa said, greatly enjoying the compliment, and she became Ellie's friend.

"What's your name?" Ellie asked Lisa.

"Jaypeel," Lisa said.

"What? Jaypeel? I thought your name was Lisa."

"No," Lisa said, a bit irritated. "Jaypeel!"

Ellie looked at Matt for an explanation. "Oh, we call Lisa 'JPL.' She likes that. Since we have a Lisa Lynn here too, we could get mixed up having two Lisa's. So somebody started calling Lisa, Just Plain Lisa. And the other Lisa we call Lisa Lynn. Pretty soon Just Plain Lisa got shortened to JPL."

Then Matt whispered to Ellie, "Lisa loves that nickname. She thinks she's the coolest one in town to have a nickname like that. Don't ever call her Lisa or you risk a cold shoulder!"

"Hey, you talkin' about me?" JPL asked in a high and mighty way.

"Just explaining to Ellie how you got your nickname."

"Yeah, I got a nickname and don't you forget it!" JPL said in her bossy but half-joking sort of way, pointing her finger at Ellie to emphasize each word.

"Ok Lisa, I mean JPL!" Ellie said on purpose. And Lisa actually laughed.

"JPL, come to the table and quit your jabbering. Can't you see lunch is on the table?" Ethyl said.

"Mmmmm, hamburgers!" JPL said, and walked quickly to her seat at the table.

Everyone had one hamburger with a little bit of ketchup on a bun. They also had some tater tots and applesauce. Lawrence probably had the same thing, but his was all mashed up. His tongue was so thick he had a hard time chewing food, so he had to have his food mashed.

Ellie found it very fascinating to watch the children eat! JPL and Grant were about the only ones who held the hamburger like a sandwich and took bites of it. Mahfta just grabbed the top bun and stuffed that in his mouth. Then he took the hamburger and stuffed that in his mouth. Then he took the bottom bun. He grabbed several tater tots and stuffed them in. Then he grabbed Lisa Lynn's tater tots and started eating them

"No Mahfta!" Ellie said and ran up to stop him. But he already ate the tater tots and had his hand on Lisa Lynn's hamburger. So Ellie opened up his fist and pulled out the hamburger and put it back on Lisa Lynn's plate. It wasn't too damaged. And Lisa Lynn didn't seem to mind. She giggled.

Ellie stayed next to Mahfta and stopped him just in time from grabbing his own applesauce with his fingers. She put his spoon in his hand and helped him eat the applesauce properly.

Ethyl and Matt were bringing out the drinks from the kitchen. When they came out, Matt said, "So Ellie just got initiated into mealtime at house 25."

Ellie laughed. "I never saw anything like it before! But why isn't Wendy eating anything?"

"Wendy needs to be fed," Ethyl said. "Why don't you feed Wendy, Ellie?"

Ellie was beginning to feel like she would really like working in this home atmosphere with the children. It was a little hard to get used to, these odd behaviors from children so old. But it was so much homier and friendlier than a classroom.

After cleaning up from lunch, the first shift workers started watching the clock. They were ready to go home. They'd been there since 6:30 that morning. The second shift workers came on duty and everyone talked and introduced Ellie. There was a half hour overlap of each shift, so that the workers leaving could bring the next shift up-to-date on the day's happenings. But on this day everyone seemed more interested in discussing the big coat sale at Carson's. Matt made fun of the girls talking about shopping for coats, so he clicked the TV on to a soap opera.

"If somebody knocks on the door, Ellie, the TV goes off. They don't want us watching it during the day."

Ellie was surprised Matt put on the TV even though it was against the rules. Soon she would see more examples of how the staff in the homes got around many of the "rules" made up in the administration building.

Chapter Four

TWO GIRLS IN THEIR TWENTIES were on duty in house 25 on the second shift. Add Ellie to the mix and it was three girls in their twenties.

"I guess there's no one with behavior problems in this house," Ellie said.

"Why do you say that?!" Diane asked incredulously.

"Well, Mr. Pulanski, I mean Mike, said that if there were some bigger kids with behavior problems, they would have at least one guy on each shift."

Diane grunted a little cynical laugh. "Yeah, that's the way it's supposed to be in the ideal world. You'll learn pretty soon that houses don't run the way that the people in rose-colored glasses in the administration building think they should."

Marie, the other worker, added, "Too true! They break their own rules whenever it's convenient. Like if they don't have enough male workers hired, they just ignore their rule about having a guy on each shift."

"Who is the behavior problem in this house?' Ellie worried.

"Mostly Grant. He can 'go off' on a tirade at odd times. See that fire extinguisher there? See that dent in it? Grant threw it through the window last month and just missed dropping it on Wendy!"

"Really?!" Ellie was very surprised. "Did you have to get a new window?"

"Definitely. The second new window we've gotten!" Diane said. "The handymen they hire here can work for a window company when they leave this job; they have to board up so many windows! Right now I think house 18 has a window boarded up."

"That's right," Marie agreed. "One thing I have to admit, though, is that they get the new windows put in pretty quickly. Usually it's just the next day. I think that's because they don't want the parents to see windows boarded up whenever they come out to visit."

"Well how did you control Grant after that happened?" Ellie asked.

"It happened on first shift and Matt was there. He tackled Grant to the floor and asked Ethyl to call for help. Then Ethyl came and sat on Grant's legs while Matt controlled his upper body, till another guy came to help. They eventually calmed Grant down and gave him a bigger dose of his tranquilizer medication."

"Wow, how often does that happen?" Ellie asked.

"Thankfully not that often. I have a theory that Grant 'goes off' when he gets pushed too far. It always seems to happen on first shift and some things that Grant never does on our shift, he does on first shift. Once they were bragging about how they got Grant to clean all the bathrooms and put two loads of clothes in the washer. It's hard for us to get Grant to just wipe out the sink in one of the bathrooms, much less to clean all three, including the toilets! I don't know how they do it, but sometimes I think they push him too far."

"Oh," Ellie said. She sure hoped Grant wouldn't 'go off' on their shift. First graders sticking each other with thumb tacks seemed so tame compared to this!

"Are you working here tomorrow Ellie?" Diane asked.

"Yes, I'm supposed to work from 10 in the morning till 6:30 like today."

"Oh, I wonder if you can just work the regular second shift with me," Diane thought out loud. "Marie is taking tomorrow off, a vacation day. It's her daughter's birthday."

"Well, Mike told me to work 10 to 6:30, but I guess we can ask him."

"I'll call him now," Diane said. So she did and she came back with the news that Ellie could start her official second shift hours tomorrow, from 2 till 10:30 at night.

Ellie felt it was a compliment that Diane asked her to work as a full-fledged worker with her the next day. *She must think I'm competent at this job,* Ellie thought. She didn't want to disappoint Diane, so Ellie determined to work really hard on this first day to show Diane she was right in trusting her.

"Do you want me to help get the afternoon arts and crafts set up?" she asked eagerly. Diane and Marie both looked at each other and laughed out loud. Marie spoke first.

"Listen, Ellie, there's something we need to tell you. House 25 doesn't run the way the administrators think it should run. They mean well, and they're great people, don't get me wrong. But some of the programs they cook up for us are so, so, I don't know, how would you describe them Diane?"

"They're so irrelevant to our kids here, they're so unrealistic, idealistic, and basically absurd!" Marie and Diane laughed. Ellie was perplexed and a little nervous. She hoped she wouldn't get caught in the middle of this tension between the home workers and the administration.

"You see Ellie," Marie said. "It's us and it's them. It's kind of like us against them, but not really against. It's more like they're not with us and we're not with them. See, they're not here with the kids eight hours a day. They think up some cute activity so they can report it to the parents or the state, and they don't realize what's involved in actually implementing it."

"What *is* involved in an arts and crafts time?" Ellie asked a little innocently.

"They have these lesson plans written up for each child," Diane explained. "Angel is supposed to learn how to use scissors. Lisa Lynn is supposed to practice scribbling with a crayon. Mahfta and Lawrence and Wendy are supposed to scribble on paper with someone guiding their hands. And Grant and JPL go to a higher level arts and crafts class."

"That really aggravates me," Marie interrupted. "The two kids who might actually be able to do something with arts and crafts don't even do it here with us! They take the easy ones to teach there at the administration center!"

"That's too bad," Ellie said. Then she took the risk of disagreeing with Diane and Marie just a little bit. "But wouldn't it be fun to try some of this with the other children?" She didn't realize it, but some of the "teacher" was coming out from her again.

"Fun? Well, why don't we try it and then you can determine for yourself if it seems fun for them *or* for you?"

So Marie and Diane opened one of the cupboards in the kitchen and got out four big crayons and a pair of safety scissors. They also took out several sheets of paper.

JPL came up to the cupboard demanding to know "What's up?"

"So it's Miss Curious is it? What do you think is going on, JPL?" Marie answered.

"Huh?" JPL said, having no idea of what to guess.

Diane explained, "Don't worry, JPL, we know what we're doing. Ellie just wants to draw some pictures with Wendy, Angel, Lisa Lynn and Lawrence."

So JPL took it upon herself to round up the group mentioned and bring them to the table. Angel came laughing her funny nervous laugh, running and flapping her arms as she raced by. Everyone in her pathway had to watch out because she could really slap a person hard with her large, powerful arms (though she never meant to)!

Lisa Lynn and Lawrence came when JPL called, but not Wendy. JPL ended up half carrying and half dragging Wendy, who was neither happy nor sad, but oblivious to everything that was going on.

Ellie guided Lisa Lynn to a chair. Lisa Lynn was about seven years old. She had long, curly blonde hair, and a full beautiful face, though she wasn't at all fat. Her personality seemed very delightful and playful. Ellie felt her heart already turning toward Lisa Lynn as one of her "favorites," but she didn't want to pick the nicest and cutest child to be her favorite. She always liked to go for the underdog that no one liked very much. But try as she might, she couldn't prevent her heart from reaching out to Lisa Lynn in a special way.

So as Marie and Diane watched, Ellie sat each child in front of a piece of paper and a fat crayon. She also had the safety scissors next to Angel's paper. Then suddenly, seemingly out of nowhere, Mahfta appeared at the table and started to stuff a crayon into his mouth. As Diane ran up to take away the crayon, his other hand grabbed the paper and he tried to stuff that in his mouth. His arms were so long and lanky, his reach was unbelievably far!

"No Mahfta," Marie yelled, as she rushed to help Diane get Mahfta out of the area.

"Oh," Ellie said, "I'm beginning to see your point."

But she decided to persevere and try the arts and crafts session anyway. She told Lawrence to sit still and wait for her, and she cleverly removed all paper and crayons away from his reach. She decided to start with Wendy. At that moment, Grant came running in from the toy room laughing. Angel, who was holding her scissors, got startled, screamed, and ran out of her seat, arms flapping with the scissors.

"Drop the scissors, Angel," Diane called out. Angel obeyed. She dropped the safety scissors. Then Grant picked them up and ran to flush them down the toilet.

"Oh no," Marie said when she heard the toilet flush. "Grant probably flushed the scissors down the toilet."

"Why would he do that?" Ellie asked.

"You have to know Grant. He's got an obsession with neatness. If something is out of place, he's been known to pick it up and flush it down the toilet."

"Wow," was all Ellie could say. Her hopeful enthusiasm for arts and crafts was slowly fading. Now Wendy and Lisa Lynn and Lawrence were the only ones left at the table. So she gave Lawrence a chubby red crayon and helped him draw a circle. Then she put two eyes in the circle and a nose and a smile. It seemed like Lawrence appreciated the one-on-one attention he was getting though he didn't seem to grasp what he was doing. But Ellie could perceive that he liked it, so she continued.

Soon Lisa Lynn got up out of her chair and came to watch. She liked seeing the smiley face and so Ellie said, "Let's put some hair on this face, Lisa Lynn. I'll help Lawrence draw some nice long curly hair like you have and this can be you." Lisa Lynn smiled, giving the impression that she understood what Ellie was saying.

For all the mishaps that happened at the start of arts and crafts, Ellie thought it went quite well. Even though Wendy wandered away from the table and back to her favorite corner almost as soon as the session started, Ellie was encouraged. Just to be able to somehow connect with Lawrence and Lisa Lynn was a big step for her in getting comfortable working with these children. The rest of the afternoon was a bit boring, so while she and Marie and Diane took the children one by one to the bathroom and did some laundry, Ellie's mind started filling up with ideas. She was thinking of ways to make the children's lives more interesting. She was thinking of better methods of doing arts and crafts. She was thinking of bringing some children's books to read out loud to the children.

Dinnertime came and went. Ellie stationed herself close to Mahfta and made sure he didn't steal anybody's food. She observed what was happening with the other children. And she began thinking of ideas for making mealtimes better too. She was actually looking forward to the next day, when she and Diane would be working together. She wouldn't just be an extra third person who could sit next to Mahfta and do arts and crafts with one child at a time. She would have to keep an eye on all the children and help with all the household duties of the second shift workers.

At 6:30 Ellie said good bye to Marie and Diane, and each of the children by name. Lisa Lynn and JPL seemed kind of sad that Ellie had to leave already.

"Hey, you can't leave yet," JPL said, "your shift not over."

Diane good-humoredly explained to JPL, "Sorry Miss Bossy, but Ellie's not working the usual second shift today. It was her first day and she worked part of the first shift and part of the second shift. Tomorrow she'll be a regular second shift worker."

"Good," JPL said and Ellie chuckled. The children already liked her! Her heart felt light as she walked out the door to her car.

Chapter Five

ELLIE'S COUSIN WAS GETTING DRESSED for work the next morning. She was surprised when she saw Ellie walk past her open bedroom door at 6:30 in the morning.

"I thought you didn't have to be at work till 2 o'clock today!" Carol exclaimed.

"I don't," Ellie answered.

"Then why in the world did you get up so early?" Carol wondered.

"I guess my body is just used to getting up early," Ellie said. She didn't want to tell Carol about her mind swishing with ideas for the day at work. She thought Carol wouldn't understand her excitement at finally finding a job that she thought she'd like, because Carol seemed so successful with just about everything she tried.

Carol was very nice, and it wasn't that Ellie didn't get along with her; it's just that they were two completely different people. Carol was the type of person who was in style, popular, and very successful in her job. She got her master's degree in special education and now had a job as assistant director at a workshop for mentally handicapped adults. In fact, the workshop she worked at was called the Monroe Avenue Workshop. It was part of the same organization as the Monroe Avenue Homes where Ellie worked, although a few miles away. It was actually Carol who found out about the job opening in the children's home and encouraged Ellie to apply for it.

Carol's family lived seven hundred miles away in Virginia. But Carol applied for the job at the workshop in Ellie's home town because her fiancé lived very close to it. So when Carol moved into town, both families thought it would be a good idea for the two cousins to share an apartment.

However, Ellie spent more time visiting back home with her brother and her parents than she spent with Carol. Ellie's family lived just twenty minutes away. In fact, Ellie was looking forward to going there this very morning to see if she could find her Children's Literature book. She wanted to find some suggestions for good books to read to the children in House 25.

After Carol left for work, Ellie made herself a bowl of oatmeal and a piece of whole wheat toast. Then she showered, got dressed, grabbed the car keys from off her dresser, and headed home. She still called her parents' house "home" and called her apartment "my apartment." She knew her dad would be on his way to work, but she hoped she'd at least be able to see her mother and brother. As she neared her house, she saw her mother walking the two blocks to her uncle's restaurant. Ellie pulled the car up next to her mother and received the warmest motherly smile.

"Ellie! Nice to see you! What are you doing here?"

"I don't have to be at work till 2 o'clock, and I wanted to look for one of my college books at home."

"Oh, too bad I won't be there. Ask Daniel to get the boxes down for you. Don't try to do it yourself."

"Ok," Ellie said.

"There's a funeral luncheon at the restaurant today and Uncle Stanley asked if I could help make the coleslaw," her mother said pitifully. "But how I wanted to hear all about your new job!"

"I think I'll have time to stop and talk to you while you're shredding the cabbage, Mom," Ellie said. "First I'll go and look for my book and try to catch Daniel before he goes to school."

"That sounds great Ellie. See you later!"

"Bye," Ellie said, and drove one more block to her old house.

Daniel was in the kitchen, eating a bowl of granola and reading a book from his History 102 class. He was in his first year at the community college.

"Ellie!" he exclaimed. Daniel was happily surprised to see his sister pop over so early in the morning. "What are you doing here now?"

"Hi Daniel. What time do you have to leave for class?"

"I have another half hour," he said.

"Good. Nice to see you! I wanted to look for my Children's Literature book that I used in my senior year at college. It has a list of some of the best children's picture books, and I want to get some from the library to take to my job."

"So how is your job? Talk fast. I want to hear all about it."

"I think I'll really like it. It was a little weird at first. But the kids started growing on me."

Ellie proceeded to describe a lot of what happened on her first day at the job. Daniel noticed how one phrase kept coming up over and over again in Ellie's rendition of the story—*home atmosphere*. She kept repeating it at different times in different sentences, telling Daniel just how much she preferred this *home atmosphere* to a classroom atmosphere.

Finally Daniel said, "Ellie, that job sounds pretty close."

"What do you mean, 'pretty close'," Ellie asked suspiciously.

"Pretty close to the perfect job, I mean. Because I know what the perfect job would be for you."

"What?" Ellie asked, ready for a smart retort. Daniel was very fond of teasing Ellie and she sensed he was about to do it again.

"The perfect job for you would be to get married and have your own family and take care of your own kids in a real, genuine, authentic *home atmosphere*."

"Ha," Ellie laughed. Then she surprised him by saying, "I'm surprised how perceptive you are." She didn't get angry but actually admitted, "You're right, Daniel. I totally agree with you. I'd love that kind of job. But of course I can't go around applying for such a job, can I?"

"I guess not," Daniel said. He was sorry now that he teased Ellie. She was so sincere and honest with him. She wanted to get married and have her own family and she was honest enough to admit it, at least to him. He really hoped she would meet the right guy soon. He added, "I don't know what's wrong with the guys around here. They're crazy not to be interested in you, Ellie."

"Thanks Daniel," Ellie said. "Do you think you could take all those boxes off the top of my box of college books, so I can look for my Children's Lit book?"

"Sure," Daniel said, glad that he could appease his conscience by helping Ellie in some way. He had a bad habit of teasing her, then regretting it a minute later. He reproached himself for doing it again, and just when she was so hopeful about this new job.

Unfortunately, Ellie's box of books was on the very bottom of a stack of four other boxes. When she finally opened it up, her Children's Literature book was not there.

Ellie was disappointed, but glad she came home and saw Daniel, and after that, her mother. By the time she was finished talking to her mother and helping her shred some cabbage, she felt quite happy and refreshed. She satisfied the longing she had to share her first day at the job with her family. Her next stop was the library. She decided to use her own judgment in picking out picture books.

Chapter Six

ELLIE WALKED INTO HOUSE 25 with a canvas bag that included 5 picture books as well as her lunch. She put them in the kitchen cupboard that was designated "safe storage" for purses and other personal belongings. Soon the first shift workers left, and Ellie and Diane were left to hold down the fort.

"Well, Ellie, the first part of the afternoon is long and boring. But things will get more hectic around dinner time and bath time. My advice is to relax and save your energy now," Diane offered. Then she took her own advice, grabbed a magazine and sat on a couch.

JPL came up to Diane to look at what she was reading. "None of your business, JPL," Diane said in a teasing way. "Anyway, you're not interested in recipes for vichyssoise, are you?" Ellie wondered why Diane said that. It wasn't the type of magazine that had recipes. Ellie guessed she just didn't want to be bothered by JPL.

"Hey JPL, I have a book you might be interested in," Ellie offered. She rushed to the kitchen and took down her bag of books. She grabbed the one about blueberry pancakes. The rhymes were so much fun in that book and the pictures were so colorful and funny. When JPL saw it, she said, "Huh! Baby stuff!"

"No it's not, JPL! I like this story! It's for all ages! Don't you want to look at it with me?"

"Baby stuff," JPL said, acting like she was insulted that Ellie even suggested reading it with her.

Ellie said, "Ok, I guess I'll read it to Angel or Lisa Lynn."

Angel was on one of the couches by herself and Ellie sat right next to her. Angel had the biggest grin on her face. She was so glad Ellie sat next to her. Then Ellie asked Lisa Lynn to come and sit on the other side of her and she would read them a book. Lisa Lynn smiled and came over but didn't sit down. She just stood and looked at the book as Ellie began reading.

"A one and a two and a pancake for you," Ellie read aloud, as she pointed out the mother frying up the pancakes. "A three and a four, and we need a lot more." Then Ellie showed the girls all the kids that started coming into the kitchen wanting to eat pancakes. Lisa Lynn looked very interested, but Angel kept staring at Ellie and didn't seem to grasp the concept of a book. At least Ellie felt satisfaction that Angel liked the attention of someone reading right next to her. But now Ellie concentrated on reaching Lisa Lynn with her storytelling skills.

"A five and a six, let's make some more mix," Ellie read as she pointed out all the ingredients each of the children were carrying so their mother could make more pancakes. The next page had no words, just a picture of a stack of pancakes on the table that reached the ceiling, and about ten children around the table eating happily.

Then before Ellie read the last two pages, she said, "I'll start from the beginning again and read it all the way through so you can hear the nice rhymes better. Then the ending will be more dramatic." Ellie noticed JPL peeking toward her from the doorway of the activity room. She seemed to be listening. Ellie read a little bit louder:

"A one and a two and a pancake for you.
A three and a four and we need a lot more.
A five and a six, and let's make some more mix.
A seven and an eight, the pancakes are great!
A nine and a ten, and let's do it AGAIN!"

She finished the book and asked Lisa Lynn if she liked it. But since Lisa Lynn didn't talk, Ellie was encouraged by her smiles (and also by JPL's secret enjoyment of this "baby book").

Diane smiled at Ellie's sincerity in trying to 'reach' or was it 'teach' the children in house 25. It was very noble of her, she thought, but a little too much. She told Ellie it was time to take four of the non-toilet-trained children to the bathroom. They each took two.

Afterwards Diane was surprised to see Ellie going to the kitchen cupboard to get the crayons and paper. "Ellie," Diane warned. "There are just two of us here today. If you do arts and crafts with some of the kids, I'll be watching the other ones. I won't be there to pull the crayon out of Mahfta's mouth or …"

"Thanks Diane," Ellie said politely before she finished her warning. "I'm thinking of just trying one at a time today."

"Ok," Diane agreed reluctantly and was more than a little perplexed at how persistent Ellie was.

Ellie had medium success drawing simple pictures while guiding Lawrence's hands again. He didn't seem too aware of the face they drew or the house, but it gave Ellie something to talk about to him and he also seemed to like the personal attention. Ellie was very pleased that JPL and Lisa Lynn came by to watch her, so she tried to make her comments and pictures entertaining for them too. She made some funny expressions on the faces and made cute interesting houses, as cute as they could be with her limited artistic skill and the awkwardness of moving a thirteen year old boy's hand around to make the designs.

Later she worked on dinner preparations with Diane. Diane seemed a little colder toward her today than yesterday. Ellie didn't want to come across as a know-it-all, doing all these projects with the children that Diane didn't want to do. But she didn't know how to do it without annoying Diane. She determined to try to get along with Diane as best as she could and work together for the good of the children.

Diane directed Ellie and told her where to sit and who to help at dinnertime. It worked out very well. Diane sat next to Mahfta and Benton.

Both of them had been known to steal other people's food, so Diane usually sat them together. That way, if they stole, it would be each other's food. And they did steal, but it usually worked out evenly. Ellie fed Wendy and kept an eye on the other children too.

After dinner it was bath time. Ellie cleaned up the dishes, with JPL helping her put them in the dishwasher. Lisa Lynn stayed around the whole time too, just enjoying being around Ellie. When they were finished, Ellie saw Angel sitting on the couch already, all nice and clean and in her pajamas. Lawrence and Grant were also finished and sitting or walking around.

Diane didn't tell her to stay out there and watch the children, so she thought she'd help Diane finish the bath time routines. It seemed that just Lisa Lynn and JPL were left, so she took them to the back bathroom. As she went to the closet to get the towels and wash cloths, she heard Diane yell from the other bathroom, "Ellie, is that you? Don't leave the other kids alone out there. I'll wash Lisa Lynn and JPL."

"Oh," Ellie said, a bit embarrassed. She went to the back bathroom and told the two girls that Diane would help them and then she went out into the living room. She didn't see Angel. "Where's Angel?" Ellie asked Grant.

"She's in the kitchen, get-tin- in- the- su-gar- jar-the –su-gar-jar –the-su-gar-jar" Grant said in a sing-song happy sort of way, like it was a great delight for him to report that happy event. Ellie never knew if she should believe him or not, but she ran to the kitchen and there was Angel with her hand in the sugar canister, eating the sugar straight out of her hand!

"Angel!" Ellie exclaimed. Angel was startled. And just like her behavior the last time she was startled, she dropped what she was holding, in this case, the whole container of sugar! She screamed and ran out of the kitchen, flapping her arms in fear and terror. She slapped Ellie on her way out, but not on purpose! *Wow, is she strong,* Ellie mused. Even though the slap hurt her, she was more concerned about what Diane would think of her. She didn't know she should have been out there watching the children. But now she knew!

Ellie wanted to clean up the sugar mess before Diane saw it. So she got the broom and dustpan, swept it up, and threw it in the garbage disposal while running the water. She wasn't that familiar with a garbage disposal, but she did know that she didn't want Angel going through the garbage can, scooping up handfuls of sugar! The sugar canister was plastic, so it didn't crack. She rinsed it out and wiped it. As she was looking for more sugar to put in it, Diane walked into the kitchen.

"What are you looking for?" Diane asked.

Ellie confessed, "Angel got into the sugar. I just finished cleaning it up and now I'm looking for more sugar for the canister."

Diane was surprisingly calm and understanding. "Don't worry, Ellie. That wasn't the first time for Angel and the sugar. I keep telling first shift to keep the sugar in the top cabinet and not in the canister. Let's not refill it. Or better yet, let's hide the canister."

Ellie laughed, but Diane was serious. "I mean it! Why leave it around to tempt Angel?"

"It seems perfectly logical to keep it out of reach," Ellie agreed. So they hid the canister in back of the garbage bags in the closet. And the second day in house 25 was winding down. By the time Ellie left at 10:30, all the children were in bed and Ellie had a sneaking suspicion that maybe she and Diane would get along after all. Maybe that mistake of leaving Angel unattended turned out for the good. She sure didn't expect such a positive, sympathetic response. Diane actually seemed to like Ellie better when she wasn't trying so hard to be perfect.

Chapter Seven

THE NEXT DAY when Ellie got to work, both Marie and Diane were already there. "That's great all three of us will be on today," Ellie said cheerfully.

"Yeah, when it rains it pours," Diane said in a disparaging sort of way. "Sometimes it's just two like yesterday. But today when all three of us are here, wouldn't you know that's the day our volunteer is also coming in."

"Oh, I didn't know we had volunteers coming in," Ellie said.

"We do, and it would be a big help if the administration would let *us* decide their schedules. But no, they want it written two weeks in advance, when we don't even know what days we'd need somebody and what days we wouldn't."

"So who is this volunteer?" Ellie asked.

Marie started to say, "We call her Little Miss...." But she stopped midsentence because Diane was shaking her head and raising her eyebrows, signaling Marie to stop. Ellie noticed this, though Marie and Diane weren't aware that she noticed.

Then Diane continued, "Her name is Sarah. She's a high school student at some little Christian high school where her parents teach, I think. She just started a couple weeks ago. Anyway, it'll be hard to find enough work for her to do when she gets here, with all four of us here!"

"Maybe she can take some of the children for a walk with me," Ellie offered.

"That's a great idea," Diane said. "You and Sarah can pick up JPL from arts and crafts, and you can take Lisa Lynn and Mahfta and Benton with you."

"Here comes Sarah now," Marie announced.

Ellie didn't know if they resented Sarah for volunteering, or if they were just upset that she came on a day they didn't need her. But Ellie was happy to have Sarah's help in taking the children for a walk.

The first thing Ellie noticed about Sarah was that she wore a skirt. That was unusual for someone working in the group homes. She had on a light brown corduroy skirt that she wore with a pretty maroon sweater, brown tights and boots. Ellie never really knew anyone who wore every-day skirts like that and still looked in style. Ellie liked that style and wished she could feel confident to dress like that, but she didn't think she could pull it off without looking weird and old-fashioned. Sarah had light brown hair that was so thick and luxurious, she could probably make whatever outfit she wore look cute and normal. Sarah was different all right, and Ellie wondered why her co-workers reacted to Sarah's coming in such an unusual way.

Soon after Sarah arrived it was time to pick up JPL. Ellie and Sarah worked together to get Mahfta, Benton and Lisa Lynn dressed in their winter coats, hats and mittens. Mahfta was so excited to be going outside, he was smiling and jumping up and down. It was a cute but unusual sight, a tall teenage boy jumping up and down, gurgling and drooling, excited to be going out for a walk. It made Ellie happy she was taking him.

They stepped outside and closed the door behind them. But before they got too far, they noticed that Lisa Lynn didn't have one mitten on. "I'll run back and get it," Ellie told Sarah. So Ellie quickly went back in and retrieved the mitten. But what she overheard Diane and Marie talking about made her stay a minute longer than she intended.

"Why didn't you want me to tell Ellie about Little Miss Perfect?" Marie asked Diane.

"Because I worked with Ellie all day yesterday and she's kind of like Sarah herself! I don't know if she's one of *them* or if she's one of *us*. But the way she wants to do all these programs for the kids makes me think she's closer to one of *them!* She just might be another Little Miss Perfect herself!"

"You don't say!" Marie was surprised.

"I found out she has a teaching degree. There's a chance she has her eye on a job in administration. I really like her though, but I'm still not sure if we can completely trust her. So we better be careful what we say around her."

Ellie quickly and very quietly left. So they didn't trust her; that was sad to hear. Yet she was glad it was not Sarah who overheard those comments. Sarah probably would have been very hurt to hear how they referred to her as Little Miss Perfect.

As soon as she quietly shut the door, Ellie started running to meet Sarah. "I'm coming," Ellie yelled, and to her surprise, Mahfta almost ran right into her. It seems that Mahfta got away from Sarah and she started chasing him to bring him back. Was she ever glad to see Ellie grab onto Mahfta's hand!

"Mahfta, slow down," Ellie said. "We're not going back home yet."

Mahfta was tall and had long lanky arms and legs for running and grabbing, but he was very compliant. As soon as Ellie had hold of his hand he stopped running and came along willingly. And it was a good thing he did, because next Benton started running. As Ellie held onto Mahfta, Sarah was free to catch Benton. Benton was thirteen, like Mahfta, but he was a smaller boy, skinny and short. Ellie thought he was so cute. His brown eyes were so expressive and joyful. But hyperactive was an understatement to describe Benton's behavior. He was always moving around, even when he was sitting. He didn't sleep long during the night either, she was told, because on more mornings than they could count, first shift workers would find him at work in his bedroom very very early. He would take off his sheet, and twist it into a rope and hang it onto his curtains, which he also twisted into a rope, as well as his clothes from his drawers and whatever else he could find. Ellie couldn't picture what they meant, but it sure sounded amazing!

But for now, Benton was also easy to round up and bring back to the little group of walkers. Lisa Lynn stayed put and just laughed at all the comical antics going on around her. Now with Ellie holding Mahfta's hand and Sarah holding on to Benton, they were safe. Ellie grabbed Lisa Lynn's hand too, but more to show love and concern for her than to keep her from running away. Sarah said, "Whew, you got back just in time Ellie!"

"I guess so! But don't feel bad about what just happened. I'm told it's a common malady around here. What a treat to have you helping me. What if I was by myself? I just started working here two days ago!" Ellie said.

"Really?" Sarah said. "I started about two weeks ago. I was only planning to work one day a week, but after I told my parents how much I think the kids here could use my help, they thought I could come more often."

"That would be great," Ellie said. "I guess you'd have to arrange that through the administration office."

"Yes, I thought I might have a chance to do that today. Hey, do you think I could ask now, when we go there to pick up JPL?"

"That's a great idea. But I have a question. You said your parents thought it would be good to come here more often, but what about your high school?"

"Well," Sarah started, "my parents are kind of my high school teachers. I'm being homeschooled by my parents. Homeschooling is still not officially legal in our state, but a lot of people are finding out about it and want to do it."

She was about to explain but Ellie just jumped in with a "Wow! That's interesting! I never heard of such a thing!"

Sarah then got to explain how her parents set up a small private Christian high school. "Though homeschooling isn't legal, private schools are. So since my mom and dad both have their teaching degrees, and since dad also is a lawyer, they went through all the red tape to establish our private Christian high school. Three other families from our church have their children in our high school, and we just get together 3 mornings a week for classes. The rest of the time the parents teach their children at home."

"Wow Sarah, does that ever seem good! I got my teaching degree one year ago and did some substitute teaching. The schools are in such bad shape! A parent teaching their own children sounds so right. That's what I'd love to do with my children!" Ellie said.

"Oh, I didn't know you were married and had children," Sarah said.

"I'm not and I don't," Ellie said.

"Oh," Sarah laughed.

Ellie continued. "I could imagine a parent teaching their kids the elementary school subjects, but to teach high school subjects sounds pretty challenging. Are your parents able to teach you geometry, a language, and things like that?"

"Yeah, but they don't actually have to know all the subjects themselves. We use this curriculum that some Christian missionaries use to teach their own kids, you know, when they're not able to go to a local school."

"How did your parents ever find out about such things? And then how did they ever know how to do it and set it up?"

Sarah's answer confused Ellie. "God really equipped mom and dad to be the perfect people to set this up. It's funny they have all these credentials in just the right fields, law and teaching!"

Ellie's brain was making connections now, at the mention of missionaries and God's involvement in the whole thing. She took a step backwards in her enthusiasm and began to be a little wary of where this discussion could lead. It sounded like Sarah could be part of one of those Christian fundamentalist groups she had heard about. And she did not want to encourage Sarah to try to convert her!

By now they were at the main building, and there was JPL waiting for them in the foyer. JPL was very happy to see two of her new favorite workers. She greeted them in her usual bossy style, "Hey, what you doin' here?"

"We happen to be working today! Would you like to walk home with us?" Ellie asked. JPL just laughed.

"Oh," Ellie remembered, "Sarah has to talk to Mike for a minute first. She wants to sign up to come and work here more days."

"You mean every day!" JPL said. Now Ellie and Sarah laughed.

Sarah went to see Mike and was out in about three minutes. "Well, it's been approved. He said I can come whichever days I want!"

"That's great!" Ellie said.

Benton was getting hard to control. JPL thought she'd take matters into her own hands. She acted like she was his big sister and grabbed his hand and said, "Calm down, man, quit acting like a coo-coo crazy guy." Ellie wondered where she picked up that phrase. Benton kept moving around and it seemed JPL was just annoying him more.

"Let's start walking," Ellie suggested.

They left the building with JPL holding Benton's hand. As they walked he became easier to control and Ellie breathed a sigh of relief. JPL so much wanted to act grown up, like a big sister, so Ellie let her. She thought it was good practice for JPL to take care of her "younger brother" Benton.

Now with JPL in on the conversation, Ellie and Sarah stuck to simpler topics. Ellie knew JPL liked Sarah, so she purposely asked Sarah, "Have you ever read a picture book about making pancakes, with a rhyme kind of like 'one and a two and a pancake for you'?" Ellie reasoned that if Sarah put in a good word for the book, maybe JPL would also give it a chance.

"Yes, I remember it! I loved that book," Sarah said. "My parents liked the pictures and rhymes so much that they checked it out of the library for us at least once a month for a while."

JPL just listened. Ellie hoped she would be open to reading a book with her later. She knew JPL would like it, and she knew it would also help her cognitive abilities develop more. She could hardly wait till they got home to see if her subtle little trick worked.

It did! When she got out her bag of books, JPL said, "Which one should we read today?" Ellie was so happy... until Diane decided to tease JPL.

"What's this, JPL? You don't think that's baby stuff today?"

Ellie's hopes sank as she witnessed the quick change in JPL's attitude. JPL defensively said, in a rather mean way, "Baby stuff, for babies like Wendy, not me! Not me, Diane, not me!"

Diane laughed, but Ellie didn't. She tried very hard to control her frustration with Diane.

So again, Ellie read a book to two of the children, while JPL peeked at her from the doorway of the activity room. Today she picked Wendy and Lisa Lynn. Wendy's reaction was even more disinterested than Angel's was the day before. Wendy was in her own world and didn't even seem to appreciate the attention of sitting next to Ellie or having something different happening around her. But Lisa Lynn (and JPL) enjoyed it. So did Grant. He picked up a few new phrases and had a lot of fun with them. He especially liked saying, "Woody was a wooden woodpecker in Walter's toy box." But he usually got tangled up in some of the words and would just laugh out loud in a funny high-pitched laugh. Then he'd start all over.

Overall, it was a very good day for Ellie at house 25. It turned out to be very helpful and fun to work together with Sarah. And she was still determined to keep on with the struggle of getting JPL interested in books. Another day would mean another try.

Sarah's parents were planning to pick her up at 7:30 that evening, but at 7:15 her mom called. Sarah explained afterwards. "Our car is acting up, so my dad's gonna try to fix it. If he can't, my mom will borrow our neighbor's car and pick me up. She's not sure when. So I'll just stay until whenever that is."

"Where do you live?" Ellie asked. When Sarah explained, Ellie said, "That's probably just ten minutes away from my apartment. I can take you home at 10:30 if you want to wait that long." Sarah called her mom and the plan was approved.

Chapter Eight

DIANE AND MARIE told Ellie she could leave a half hour early, at 10 instead of 10:30, since she had to take Sarah home. Ellie didn't know if they were being nice to her or if they just wanted to get rid of her and Sarah. But she accepted the offer and she and Sarah walked out together.

"It was fun staying longer today and getting to talk together about some of those arts and crafts ideas," Sarah said.

"I enjoyed it too. It was so much more fun to do the craft activities today since you were enthusiastic about it too. The other days I felt like I was treading on dangerous territory."

"What do you mean?" Sarah asked.

"Well, Diane and Marie don't like to do it and so they don't like to have me do it. They feel intimidated, like I'm acting as if I'm better than they are. And I really do see their point. If there are only two workers on the shift, it's pretty hard to have one of the staff tied up with just one child, doing some coloring, while the other one has to watch all the other kids. And when I tried to involve three or four of the kids, I told you what happened, didn't I?"

Sarah remembered, "That's when Mahfta started eating the crayon, then the paper, then Angel ran away with the scissors and dropped them and Grant flushed them in the toilet!"

"Good memory," Ellie said.

"How could I not remember such a crazy scenario?" Sarah chuckled. "So yes, I can see Marie and Diane's frustration. But at the same time, it seems like the kids just sit around doing nothing most of the time and so do the staff. And it seems like doing something different would help the staff as much as the kids," Sarah said.

"I know!!" Ellie said, a little too loudly. She was so happy to have someone put her own thoughts into words. But she didn't know if they were far enough away from the house to speak without being overheard. Of course it was still winter and the windows of the houses were closed, but you never knew if someone might have stepped outside to smoke.

Ellie continued in a more hushed tone of voice. "I agree with you so much, Sarah. I think it would really help the staff. The day can be so long and boring if you don't at least try doing something different with the kids once in a while."

"I know," Sarah said. "And even if the kids can't do much themselves, they can at least watch *us* making things. I think some of them would be pretty interested to do that. I know I used to love watching my mom make decorations when I was younger. She'd have me help her in some small insignificant way and I actually thought I had a huge part in making the thing!"

"Me too!" Ellie laughed as she unlocked the car.

As Ellie started driving, Sarah said, "It sure was fun working with you, Ellie. You have such normal common sense, it seems."

Ellie chuckled.

"And I've been thinking of that conversation we had on our walk today. It was so great to hear how excited you were about our homeschooling. It made me feel better about it."

"What do you mean, *feel better about it*?" Ellie asked.

"Well, it's not easy to be so different from everybody else. I had a lot of friends in my grade school class, even though there were a lot of things that weren't good about it. My parents gave me a choice before we started homeschooling and I told them that I wanted to do it as much as they did. Even now, I think it's the best way to go. But it's not perfect. I kind of feel isolated now, and like I'm losing my friends."

Ellie felt sorry for Sarah. "Don't your parents allow you to be friends with your old friends anymore?" she asked.

"No, it's not like that. I still call them once in a while and I go over to their houses and we talk. But it's not the same. They're going through their highs and lows in high school and I can't relate to what it's like for them. And the opposite is true too. They can't relate to my life very much either."

"Oh," Ellie sympathized.

Sarah continued, "They're starting to make new friends too. I talked to my parents about it and they knew I needed to get out more. That's why we all agreed on trying out this volunteer program at Monroe Avenue."

"That sounds like a good thing you all decided on," Ellie agreed.

"We were all praying about how I could get more fellowship," Sarah explained, "and then we met a lady at our church who works the night shift here. She started telling us about the kids she works with and I started getting very interested."

Ellie didn't jump in with a comment immediately, although her brain was taking it all in and processing it. The phrases Sarah used were so uncommon to her. She wondered just how a person goes about praying for more fellowship. And she wondered what sort of group in this day and age would use words like *fellowship* anyway. She started getting even more suspicious that maybe Sarah was from one of those Christian fundamentalist families.

Ellie's slow response made Sarah continue with her ramblings. "At first I was quite scared when I got to house 25. The kids were stranger than I expected. When I heard Grant saying his crazy phrases, it was a little unnerving. And the other workers seemed a little stand-offish to me. But one time I heard a teaching on not giving up. The preacher said one time he attended a group that was kind of different and a little bit intimidating to him, but he determined not to drop out. He told himself to attend at least seven times before he made a decision. And it turned out he met his wife in that group!"

Ellie found Sarah's dialogue very curious and thought-provoking, even though she noted another religious reference, this time to a preacher. Ellie didn't say anything out loud, but was more than happy to keep listening.

Sarah continued, "So I decided to try this volunteer thing for at least seven weeks. And even though it felt like the staff was treating me like an outsider, I decided to persevere. Then I began to fall in love with some of the kids, and you know what happened today. I volunteered to come in more often."

"That was brave of you," Ellie said truthfully.

"Thanks Ellie. I was so encouraged to meet you today. I know you're older than I am, but I already feel close to you, like we understand each other or something. I'd like to volunteer on days when you're working."

"That's fine with me. Well, actually, more than fine. You really made a difference in my day too, Sarah. And I think we can help the kids more if we have each other to work with."

After a short pause of silence, Ellie asked, "Do you mind if I ask you a question, Sarah?"

"Sure, why would I mind?"

"Ok, I was wondering why you weren't satisfied with the friendships of the kids from those three other families you were homeschooling with."

"Well, just because somebody agrees with you in the theoreticals of Christian homeschooling, doesn't mean you click with them completely. Do you know what I mean?"

"I think so," Ellie said.

"See, one family just has one boy who is very academic. He's not mean or conceited or anything like that, he is just so into his studies that he hardly talks about anything else. The other family has two girls quite a bit younger than me. They're very pretty and a little flirty with this other boy, Matthew. Matthew is very nice, but his love is sports and he's really good at almost every sport he plays. And the two sisters are also pretty athletic. We all get along fine during the school day, but I'm more of a person who likes deep conversations. So we don't hang around with each other much outside of school."

"I can totally understand that," Ellie confided. "I'm kind of a serious person myself. I used to have two good friends in college, and we used to go out and have coffee and talk deep into the night. I really miss them. We talk on the phone now and then, but it's just not the same. It's kind of like how it is for you, Sarah, when you try to visit your old friends from grade school. We're all into different things now, with different people and different jobs, and it's just not the same."

"But Ellie, now maybe we'll become close friends," Sarah said hopefully.

"Yeah it seems like we think alike about a lot of things at work, but I don't know if you'd feel so close to me if you knew my religious views," Ellie said cautiously.

"Really?" Sarah asked. "I'd be interested to hear them."

"It's hard to know where to start," Ellie began. "I guess I can say that I'm kind of a mix between Jewish and Christian, and yet I'm really not either one."

"That's interesting. So are your parents Jewish and Christian?"

"My mom is Christian," Ellie answered, "but she only goes to church a couple times a year. And my dad is Jewish, but he doesn't do much about it. We do go to our relatives' house sometimes for Passover or Hanukkah. But that's about it."

"That's interesting," Sarah said. "I think it's neat you celebrate Passover. I always wanted to."

"Really, why would you want to?" Ellie asked.

"Because Jesus celebrated it and I think it would make me feel closer to Him and understand more about Him if I celebrated it too."

"That's funny it would mean something to you, because it doesn't mean that much to my father, and he's Jewish! He kind of thinks of it all, the story of Moses and everything, like a collection of Jewish fairy tales. He really doesn't believe in God at all."

"That's interesting," Sarah said. "But that's better than being lukewarm at least."

"What do you mean *lukewarm*?" asked Ellie.

"The Bible says God would rather have us be hot or cold towards Him, not lukewarm. He says that if we're lukewarm He will spit us out of His mouth."

"That's strange," Ellie said. "What kind of person would you say is lukewarm?"

"I guess somebody who, unlike your father, says they do believe in God and yet they don't do much about it."

Ellie was quick with her retort. "But I believe in God, and I think that's a whole lot better than my father not believing in anything." Her emotions seemed to be kicking in to a fighting mode. Ellie could feel her face getting warm and probably turning very red, as well as feeling her heart starting to race.

Sarah was amazingly quick in her reply as well. "The Bible says that the devil believes too and he trembles."

"That doesn't make sense," Ellie complained. "How could the devil believe?"

"The devil knows who he's fighting against and he knows the greatness and power of God. He believes all right, and he even trembles about it. But he sure doesn't change his ways."

"Well, what is a person supposed to do anyway?" Ellie asked a little aggressively. "If a person like me believes there is a God, but there's no right way to Him, and that you can know Him from a bunch of different angles in a bunch of different religions, Jewish, Christian, Eastern, whatever, how can I find a church like that?"

Sarah stayed quiet. She was a bit surprised at Ellie's fiery reaction. Ellie took a breath and went on. "My parents suggested that I go to the Unitarian Sunday School class when I started asking them questions about religion. And I did go there during my last year in high school. Actually I made up a prayer there. It was one of our assignments. And since then, I've been saying that prayer every day. But the class was just for high school kids so after I graduated, I didn't feel comfortable going there anymore. I'm not a one-size-fits-all type of person. I don't think there is a church for a person like me."

Sarah gathered her thoughts and replied. "I didn't exactly mean to find a church. I guess what I think a person should do is to study and research and pray and do everything he can to know more about God and what's true and what isn't. If a person knows that God is real, they should realize how super important it is to know about Him and find out what's true and what isn't."

"I agree with you on that one, Sarah," Ellie said, calming down a little. "Actually, I am doing my own research. But it might not be the type of research you were thinking about."

"I hope you'll feel free to tell me about it," Sarah said, "but here's my house. Let's continue this conversation sometime soon."

Ellie pulled off in her car and both girls were left feeling hopeful and yet unsure where this friendship would go.

Chapter Nine

IT WAS ELLIE'S day off and she slept in. She couldn't stop thinking about her conversation with Sarah. She wished she had Sarah's phone number so she could call her and continue the discussion. In a way she wanted to see how shocked Sarah would be when she told her about her visits to the Krishna temple in the city several years ago. And what about her latest adventure of going with a group of friends every few months to hear a yogi speak on finding God? She felt maybe it was a mean streak in her wanting to shock somebody as protected as Sarah. Or maybe she just wanted to know for sure if Sarah could relate to her just as she was without trying to convert her.

Ellie really disliked the Bible groups on her college campus and its members who kept trying to recruit her. Some of the people seemed ok, but some of them seemed arrogant, just like the slogans on their banners. She remembered one group who had a table giving out free cups of hot chocolate around Christmas time. The banner at their table said something like "Jesus is the ONLY way." And the heading she read on a pamphlet they tried to give her said "ONE WAY." Ellie thought it was so haughty for people to think their way was the only right way. And when some brave soul actually cared to confront these Jesus people, Ellie remembered hearing pretty heated arguments instead of love coming out of the encounters.

Yet somehow, something Sarah said to her struck a chord. She realized it when she tried to say the daily prayer she prayed every morning for the past several years. She kind of combined two traditional prayers, joining them together in her own sort of way. It was part of a project she worked on during her Unitarian Sunday School days. As she said it this morning, she felt like it was kind of cold and sterile.

"Avinu, Malkenu, Our Father our King, Blessed are You, oh Lord our God, King of the universe, and You're also my Father. Our Father which art in heaven, hallowed be Thy name. Thy kingdom come, Thy will be done in earth as it is in heaven. Give us this day our daily bread and forgive us our debts as we forgive our debtors. And lead us not into temptation or hard trials, but deliver us from evil, because You have all the power in the world, because Thine is the kingdom and the power and the glory forever. Amen."

Following her prayer, she started her relatively new spiritual exercise of trying to meditate for at least 5 minutes. When she began this practice several months ago, she found herself looking at the clock almost every minute. But now, after several months of meditating, she became very adept at estimating when 5 minutes went by without even looking at the clock except at the very end. Yet try as she might, she still couldn't empty her mind.

Was she really researching God as much as she should, she wondered. Was her daily prayer and 5 minutes of meditation sufficient? Sarah had a good point when she said that if God is real, it would be really important to get to know more about Him and what's true and what isn't. Could those Jesus people be right that there is only one way to God, through Jesus? That seemed too far-fetched. Many other religions made a lot of sense too. She decided it was time she started reading the Bible for herself. That way she could give answers when Sarah came up with her gems of wisdom that were hard to refute. There was one problem though. Ellie didn't have a Bible.

How to go about getting a Bible was what she was focused on while she scrambled herself one egg with a piece of lunchmeat cut up in it. After she put butter and jelly on her toast and got out the ketchup for her egg, she looked for something to read while she ate. The first thing she saw was the stack of picture books she brought to work the other day, so she started to read some of those. She realized she couldn't concentrate on anything too heavy anyway. Her mind kept repeating the same question over and over: *Where should I get a Bible?*

She definitely didn't want to ask Sarah, even though she knew or at least she suspected that Sarah's family had a box of Bibles they kept on hand for any new convert. She didn't even want Sarah to know she was interested in reading the Bible. However, if she were to purchase one herself at one of those Christian bookstores, she'd have to step out of her comfort zone.

As soon as she finished eating, she drove to the strip mall where a Christian bookstore was located. As she walked in and saw the walls of books in different categories, she knew it wouldn't be an easy task to find a simple Bible. She saw children's books and went to look at them for a while. It was like finding some old friends in a scary place. There were some pretty cute books. But she knew she was just distracting herself. The saleslady was busy with someone else so Ellie knew she better get busy searching for a Bible. Otherwise, the saleslady might finish with her other customer and then try to convert her when she found out Ellie never read a Bible before.

She finally found the Bibles, but even then it wasn't easy. There were so many translations! Another salesman appeared out of nowhere. He was not at all intimidating but was a very friendly college-age young man. "Trying to decide what translation to get?" he asked simply.

"Yes," Ellie responded.

"Well, I can give you my thoughts if that would help."

"Sure," Ellie answered.

"It depends a lot on who you're getting it for. If it's for an older person, we have large print versions here. If it's for some friend who wants an easier translation, the Bibles on this shelf would be good. And then there's the standard King James, which a lot of churches swear is the best translation. But I'll let you look for yourself, unless you have any other specific questions."

"No, but thanks. That was pretty helpful."

Since Ellie really wanted to do the research the right way, she chose a King James. She saw pens for sale at the check-out counter, and she, being a teacher, was a pushover for a new pen. She thought it would be nice to get a new red pen and underline all the words that Jesus said in the Bible.

"A King James Bible and a red pen…you must be a teacher," the saleslady commented with a chuckle.

Ellie laughed and answered, "Sort of." She was grateful to get out of the bookstore without having anyone confront her after all.

Ellie drove home and started her research immediately. That's the type of person she was. If she had an idea, she was quick to put it into practice. She knew enough about the Bible to know that the story of Jesus began in the New Testament, so that's where she started. After reading the genealogy of Jesus, she got to the Christmas story. She found it strangely comforting, reading about Jesus being born in Bethlehem, straight from the pages of the Bible. She read a couple of chapters, but didn't come to any of Jesus' words yet.

Then the telephone rang. It was Monroe Avenue Center calling, asking if she could come in today, her day off. Diane called in sick and Marie asked for the day off because her daughter was sick. There were two people substituting in house 25 in the meantime, but neither of them really knew the children. Ellie agreed to go in, but she told them it would be about an hour before she could get there.

Ellie was disappointed she didn't have the whole day off, but she also had a feeling of fulfillment in knowing she was really needed at house 25.

As soon as she walked into the kitchen of House 25, Ellie looked in the cabinet where the staff phone numbers were kept. She jotted down Sarah's number.

She walked to the closet to hang up her coat and change from her boots to a comfortable pair of gym shoes. As soon as one of the two women working in the house saw her, she put on her coat and announced she was leaving. "We're so glad you're here," she told Ellie. "I think your kids were missing you. It's hard on them, you know, as well as us, if we're all strangers to each other."

"Yeah, I guess it would be," Ellie said. Lisa Lynn was already at her side and Angel came smiling right towards her. Then Angel just stood there next to her. Ellie was glad she came. The substitute worker was glad to leave.

"I guess it'll just be you and me then," Bertha said. She was a middle-aged woman who seemed friendly and competent. "I'm supposed to be in house 17. I just started two weeks ago and I barely know the kids in my own house, much less your house here!" she said.

"I'm new too," Ellie told her. "I'm surprised how short-staffed they are lately. I've only been on the job for three days so far."

"But at least you know these kids!" the woman said. "How about if I make the dinner and do the clean-up, and you can take care of the kids," she suggested. "Since you know them, I think it'll be easier that way."

That didn't seem exactly fair to Ellie, but she agreed. She had a hard enough time being in charge of the children, so she didn't try to take charge over a forty year old woman too. Ellie started by toileting all the children who needed that reminder and assistance. Thankfully, not one of them had an accident. That was a big relief—especially since she got there so late! It seemed that no sooner was she done toileting the children than supper was on the table.

"Don't put the food out yet," Ellie tried to warn the woman who was helping her. But she was too late.

The food was on the table and Mahfta saw it and ran over and grabbed food from two plates and started eating. Ellie ran up to him and sat him down and made sure that he was away from any other plates. She decided she'd let Mahfta eat first and then keep him out of the area. That would be the easiest.

So while the substitute helper stayed in the kitchen keeping the food warm and starting the clean-up, Ellie supervised Mahfta and tried to figure out a plan for the rest of the meal. Just then JPL walked up to Ellie and asked, "So what's the big deal here? Where's the rest of the food?"

"It's coming. Mahfta is just eating first and then we'll keep him away as the rest of us eat. Hey, JPL, do you want to be my helper? Our new worker doesn't know the kids here, but you do."

JPL smiled boastfully as Ellie continued. "Can you sit by Wendy and feed her? And I'll put Benton at your table on the other end. Do you think you can watch so he doesn't steal Wendy's food?"

Was JPL ever excited! "Yesiree!" she shouted. "I'm staff today!"

"Yep, you'll be staff today. Do you want to eat your supper with me when I take my break later?" Ellie asked her.

JPL was beside herself with joy. "Sure," she said in her bossy grown-up tone. "I'm staff. I eat with you later, on break."

Ellie smiled to herself. She was building a rapport between herself and JPL. And she was gaining confidence in her ability to handle these eight special needs children.

Ellie supervised the other tables while keeping Mahfta far away from the dining room. Whenever he wandered too close, she would take his hand and say, "Mahfta, you already ate, now let the other children eat. I'll give you a snack later if you're still hungry." She wasn't sure Mahfta understood her words, but she thought he probably understood the general gist of what she meant, which was: "Stay away, Mahfta, but Ellie still likes you."

When dinner was over the substitute worker stayed in the kitchen to put food away and wash the dishes. Ellie and JPL ate their dinners in the dining room while still keeping an eye on the children in the living room. Most of the children just sat on the couch, watching the antics of Grant and Benton. Grant walked around picking up toys and putting them away and talking all the while he was doing it. In a voice kind of imitating one of the first shift workers, Grant was repeating, "Toys put away at the end of the day…toys put away at the end of the day." Benton was trying to build something with one toy next to another, but Grant kept taking it down and Benton kept taking them back and building. Ellie was happy it kept everybody entertained for a good long time, but poor Benton was getting so frustrated.

She had hoped she could try reading to JPL today, when Diane wasn't here to make fun of her. But now she knew she couldn't risk doing something like that, when she had to work with a substitute. So right after she and JPL ate their dinners, she decided to start bath times. She'd get the supplies ready and she hoped her co-worker would be done in the kitchen by then and help with the baths. Bertha did appear out of the kitchen, right when Ellie needed her.

"Oh, glad you're done in there. Want to help start baths with me now?" Ellie asked.

"Sure, I'd be happy to. But would you mind if I first made a personal phone call? I'll try not to be long."

"Ok, I'll get started on a few of the baths right now," Ellie said. "You can keep an eye on the kids out here while you're on the phone."

As Ellie was getting Wendy ready for a bath, JPL raced back to find her and said, "Somebody's here!"

Ellie rushed out and saw her co-worker in the living room talking with a young woman in a pants suit and high heels. Ellie figured she was from the administration, since no one would come to work in one of the houses dressed like that.

As soon as Ellie came within her view, the stranger said, "Oh hi, you must be Ellie. Sorry to barge in on you like this, but I tried calling and was just told one of the children must have pulled the phone off the hook."

Ellie chuckled at the creative lie someone must have told.

"Anyway," the friendly administrator continued, "it seems that your house will be short-staffed again on Sunday. And quite a few houses will only have two workers that day, so we won't be able to pull an extra staff from another house to help, like today."

The administrator continued. "Since you're scheduled to work Sunday, I wanted to know if you'd feel comfortable working if we just got one of our volunteers to work with you."

Ellie immediately said, "If you could get Sarah, I'd really feel comfortable. I've already met her and she's a great worker."

"That's who I was thinking of. She wrote on her volunteer form that she'd be available on short notice if we ever needed her. I'll give her a call and if I can't get ahold of her I'll let you know, and we'll come up with Plan B. But hopefully it'll all work out."

"Ok, that sounds good to me," Ellie said. "Bye."

As Ellie went back to the bathrooms, she chuckled to herself to see her helper was now actually helping! She was bathing Angel and had Lisa Lynn sitting on the floor waiting for her turn next.

The older woman started to warm up towards Ellie. She seemed quite relieved Ellie didn't tell the administrator that she was on the phone with a personal call.

"Don't get me wrong, Ellie," Bertha said. "It's not that I don't like kids. It's just that I don't know these kids here. I subbed in another house last week and when I walked into the kitchen, this boy threw a jar of mayonnaise on the floor right in front of me! The glass shattered and I almost stepped on it. That would've been a problem, since I was barefooted!"

"Oh, that's scary," Ellie sympathized, although she wondered why anyone would go barefoot in the house in February.

"So I don't like to get too close to kids I don't know. You never know what to expect from some of these kids, you know?" the lady continued. "And for some reason, whenever a sub is needed from our house, they send me."

"Hmm," was all Ellie could think of to say.

It was a busy day, but things got in better order with the two of them working together. Soon the children were all tucked into bed, and a little later a very tired Ellie walked to her car to head home.

Chapter Ten

ELLIE WAS ABLE to do her wash on Saturday, as well as other chores and errands that had been building up during the week. She really missed having two days off in a row and was kind of emotionally drained thinking about going back to work on Sunday. Then she started worrying that Sarah might not be able to work with her. After all, it was a Sunday and Sarah was from such a strict family of church goers. What if she couldn't come and Ellie had to work another whole day with a sub?

Finally Ellie decided to stop brooding about possible scenarios. She had Sarah's number and would just call her as soon as she got home from the laundromat. But by the time she stopped to get groceries, it was almost dinner time and she was famished. The phone call would have to wait until the evening.

When the phone rang at 6:30, Ellie was pleasantly surprised that Sarah was calling *her*!

"Hi Ellie. I hear we're working together tomorrow," Sarah began.

"You mean you can do it? I mean, you can really skip church and come to work on a Sunday?" Ellie exclaimed.

"No problem. Church gets out at eleven in the morning. So I can even have dinner with my family before going in to work. I'm actually calling to see if you'd like to come over and have dinner with us. Then we can drive to work together. That way my parents and brothers can leave earlier to see a movie they wanted to see and I can ride to work with you, if you don't mind."

"Hmm," Ellie said, being caught off guard. She thought it would be a little awkward having dinner with the whole family. But she was so happy that Sarah was going to work with her. And Sarah needed a ride. So Ellie agreed, trying to sound enthused about it all.

Ellie reserved the evening of her day off for reading more of her Bible. She finally got to the pages where Jesus spoke. She laughed out loud when she saw that the Bible she purchased had all of Jesus' words printed in red already! So much for the red pen!

It turned out that the words printed in red took up page after page after page. It would have been hard to underline all those words after all. But it was very interesting. Ellie knew she always liked Jesus. Her mother believed in Him and Ellie loved going to the church at Christmas time and seeing the almost life size statues. There were statues of baby Jesus in the manger, Mary, Joseph, the shepherds, the three kings and even a few animals. She smiled to herself as she pondered that soothing memory.

She was really glad she was having this Bible reading adventure alone. She didn't have to force herself to think of answers to questions or anything like that, because nobody knew she was doing this.

Her cousin Carol was hardly ever home these days, what with her wedding day approaching and the planning becoming more intense. Although Ellie normally didn't like being alone, she was glad it worked out like this for now at least. She wanted to process her own thoughts about the Bible without anybody else influencing her for or against it. She thought she might share it with Sarah, but she wasn't even sure about that.

On Sunday, Ellie headed to Sarah's house. Sarah's two younger brothers both answered the door. "I guess you're Ellie, right?" the older one said.

"Yes, that's who I am all right!" Ellie assured them.

"You're not how I imagined you'd look," the younger boy said.

"Oh no, how did you imagine I'd look?"

"Well, I read a book about an Ellie one time and she had glasses and was kind of, um, well, chubby, and you don't look like her at all."

"Oh. So is that good or bad? Do I pass your inspection?"

"Sure, I think you'll be a great friend for Sarah!" the younger boy named William said.

"And for all of us!" Adam added. "After all, any friend of Sarah's is a friend of ours!"

Ellie laughed and followed the boys into the house. Sarah welcomed Ellie with a hug. It was genuine and warm and Ellie felt strangely at home with this family.

At the dinner table William asked Ellie what time her church let out.

"I don't always go to church, William, because there's kind of no church for a person like me. I'm a real mix between a Christian and a Jew, and I also believe in some things from other religions too."

"Oh, so do you believe in Jesus and the Bible?" Adam asked.

"Maybe Ellie would rather keep her spiritual life to herself for now, Adam," his father wisely said.

"No, I don't mind answering Adam," Ellie said. "Yes, I do believe the Bible and Jesus, but I don't think Jesus is the only way. I think some of the other religion's books and bibles are true too."

"Well, at least you believe the Bible," William said. "You know what that means!" William said it as a statement and not as a question, as if Ellie and everyone should automatically know what that means.

"Um, no, I don't think I know what that means. What does it mean, William?" Ellie asked.

"Well if you believe the Bible, it means you can come to our Bible Study meeting here on Tuesdays!"

"Well, thanks for the invitation. I'll think about it," Ellie said.

"When you know the secret, I know you'll want to come," Adam stated. "The secret is —-we always have chocolate chip cookies!"

"Oh too bad, I'm allergic to chocolate," Ellie said. Then she added, "Just kidding!"

William and Adam laughed at Ellie's little joke, which made Ellie happy.

Ellie was thankful the discussion got steered away from religion at that point. The dinner was very tasty, chicken with gravy and mashed potatoes, buttery green beans with garlic and pepper, and homemade bread. Jell-O with whipped cream was served for dessert. Ellie felt warmth she hadn't expected from what she thought would be a strict religious family.

Sarah offered to clear the table and put away the leftovers as the rest of the family left for the movie theater. Ellie was more than happy to help her.

"I'm packing myself some of these leftovers for my lunch, or rather dinner," Sarah said. "You're welcome to do the same, Ellie."

"Thanks, but I have a sandwich and apple waiting in the car. It's my usual lunch, and I still call it lunch because I eat it at work, even though I eat it at supper time. I'm still not used to working evenings on second shift," Ellie confided.

"It must be hard to get used to," Sarah agreed. "I don't usually work the whole shift, so I don't know how that would feel, I mean getting home at eleven day after day. But I'm glad to do it today. It'll be fun. It was fun the last time we worked together till ten."

"Yes it was," Ellie said. "Sarah, your outfit is so cute, I was wondering if you're sure you want to wear it to work?"

"I don't know. I was wondering about that," Sarah said. "Maybe I should change."

She changed from her pretty skirt and sweater vest to a denim skirt and sweatshirt. Ellie was amazed how easily Sarah wore skirts and didn't look so weird and different as Ellie thought she would look if she started wearing skirts all the time. She'd have to ask Sarah where to get nice skirts like that. She wanted to ask Sarah so many things. There was certainly something different about her and her family.

Chapter Eleven

IT WAS FUN driving to work and walking into house 25 together. Ellie was looking forward to doing so many things today, since she and Sarah would have the house to themselves in a way. But her number one goal for the day was to be able to convince JPL to look at some books with her.

All the children seemed very happy to see both Ellie and Sarah. But JPL was nowhere around.

"Where's JPL?" Ellie asked.

"She's on a home visit this weekend. She should be back after dinner tonight. It's her birthday weekend," one of the first shift workers told her.

"Oh, is today her birthday or was it yesterday?" Sarah asked.

"Neither. Her birthday is on Friday, but her family can't come out then. Her father is some business executive or something and has to go to London next weekend."

Ellie was quite disappointed that JPL was gone this particular day! She was happy JPL had time with her family, but of all days for her to be gone! Now she knew she couldn't try reading to JPL today. But very shortly another idea started brewing in her mind. She'd be working with Sarah all day. What a time to begin their plan of making decorations for the house during arts and crafts. And they could begin by making decorations for JPL's birthday coming up on Friday!

Sarah was excited with the whole idea too. They brainstormed, trying to think of what to make.

"Well, it *is* still winter, so we can make snowflakes," Sarah said.

"Great idea, Sarah! That's a good start. But I wonder if there's something special JPL really likes. For once I wish Diane was here. She's been here long enough to know if there's any special interest JPL has."

"Why don't you call her and ask her?" Sarah suggested.

"She'd probably think I was strange to bother her on her day off," Ellie thought out loud.

"Maybe, but maybe not. I think she might be glad to be included in the planning, and then maybe she'd be more supportive of the decorations, instead of making fun of them," Sarah replied. It was a convincing argument, but Ellie was still undecided.

Ellie and Sarah worked together very well. That is, they did their jobs very well, but the children didn't do as well. Mahfta and Wendy had accidents. It took a while to clean them up. After they were cleaned, their clothing had to be soaked and laundered. While they were together in the laundry room Ellie started asking Sarah just what happens in a Bible Study. They were talking a little too long when all of a sudden they heard a loud crash.

They ran out together. A lamp was knocked over, but nothing was broken and no one was hurt. As far as they could piece the story together, it seemed that Angel was walking around holding a ball. Grant scared her and she screamed and threw the ball. The ball hit the lamp and it fell with a loud crash. Ellie and Sarah were more shaken up than the children, because they both felt guilty for talking together so long in the laundry room.

"Let's do some arts and crafts out here now," Ellie suggested. "One of us can work on it, and the other can watch the children."

"That should be fun," Sarah said. "Should we just start with the snowflakes?"

"OK, let's start with them, but keep thinking of something JPL would like."

"What about calling Diane?" Sarah reminded Ellie.

"Hmm, maybe," Ellie said, still not totally convinced.

Ellie started folding white paper and cutting out shapes. Then she opened it up and showed Lisa Lynn how it came out to be a snowflake. She even held Lisa Lynn's hand with the scissors and tried to give her a part in making the snowflake. Mahfta tried to grab it, but Sarah got him in time.

Next Sarah made one with Angel. Grant came around to watch for a while, but he didn't want to make one. Ellie asked him, "Grant, do you know what JPL is interested in?"

Grant replied, "I don't know." As he started to walk away, he repeated in a funny higher pitch, "I just don't know. How should I know? I just don't know, how should I know..."

Sarah and Ellie laughed. At least Grant seemed to understand their question, but too bad he didn't have any ideas.

Ellie said, "Maybe I should just go and call Diane."

Sarah was quite positive that this would be a great idea.

Ellie asked, "Don't you think she'd be upset if I bothered her on her day off?" Ellie knew more about Diane's attitude toward them than Sarah did, but she didn't want to tell Sarah. So Sarah continued to insist that Ellie call.

"Ok, I'll try. I might be asking for trouble, but I'll try."

It turned out that Sarah was right and Ellie was wrong. Diane was happy to be asked. She didn't know right away what JPL was interested in, but she said to give her a few minutes to think about it and she'd call them back.

Ellie wasn't too confident she'd really call back, but she did!

Diane said this was JPL's sixteenth birthday and her family must have told her about it weeks before. For several days after they told her, all she could talk about was that she was going to be sweet sixteen and that she was going to get sixteen roses. Eventually she forgot about it and quit talking about it all the time. So Diane suggested that maybe some red flower decorations would be good. JPL wouldn't be able to tell if they looked like roses or not. As long as they were flowers and they were red, she'd think they were roses.

Ellie was excited, not only for the new idea, but for the fact that Diane was part of the planning! Diane seemed very much behind the idea of having a birthday party and decorations for JPL on the real day of her birthday. Now Ellie wouldn't have to dread what reaction Diane would have when she sprang the idea on her. Between Diane and Marie, Diane was the stronger personality. So if Diane was behind something, Ellie thought Marie would very likely follow along too. And they were all three scheduled to work on Friday, the day of the birthday.

Ellie and Sarah wanted to make as many of the snowflakes and roses as they could on Sunday afternoon, so JPL could see them when she returned later in the evening. They found 4 sheets of red construction paper and decided that would be enough to make at least 16 roses. They made a few before dinner, and planned to continue after dinner.

The dinner time menu was hamburgers. The food came pre-packaged. There were frozen burgers to cook in the oven. Buns and chips were in the cupboard. There were also boxes of jello, pudding and cake mixes that the staff could mix up for dessert. Ellie had an idea. Since JPL really liked hamburgers, she'd save the hamburgers for the birthday dinner. They could make Friday's dinner menu today, which turned out to be fish sticks, corn bread and baked beans. Sarah made the salad and prepared a box of vanilla pudding for dessert.

After a very nice uneventful dinner, Sarah and Ellie cleaned up and got back to the decorations. They were wondering where to put them, to keep them out of the reach of Mahfta's long, lanky arms.

"I know," Sarah said. "Let's tie the snowflakes to string and hang them from the ceiling."

"That's a great idea!" Ellie agreed.

So they enlisted the help of Grant who was at least six inches taller than either of the girls. He stood on a chair and they handed him the scotch tape and snowflakes. Ellie felt so fulfilled that Grant was doing something useful and the home was feeling like a real home and family.

The house already looked so nice and cheerful, with about twenty big snowflakes dangling from the ceiling. Now they wondered where they could put up the red flowers. Ellie thought if they stuck them to the outside windows, no one would be able to tear them down. The only question was, would scotch tape be able to stick to cold outdoor windows. Sarah ran out quickly with a piece of scotch tape to test the idea and she motioned a thumbs up. It stuck!

So Sarah and Grant went outside with flowers and tape. Ellie asked Lisa Lynn if she wanted to go out with them to watch. Her answer was a smile. Ellie took that as a yes, and got her dressed in coat, hat and mittens and sent her out to watch. Ellie pointed from the inside where she wanted the flowers to be. She thought each of the four windows could have four flowers on it. Then JPL could practice counting to sixteen every time she counted the roses.

Grant dropped one flower in the dirty blackish snow, so Ellie pulled some red construction paper scraps from the garbage and managed to cut out one more flower. She called Lisa Lynn to come to the door to get the flower and hand it to Sarah. Lisa Lynn actually understood what Ellie said and took the flower and gave it to Sarah. Ellie had tears in her eyes when she saw Lisa Lynn handing the flower to Sarah. It would seem to most people like a little thing, like a tiny, tiny, insignificant thing, giving a paper flower to an eight year old girl to hand to someone else. But Ellie knew it wasn't just a little thing. It was big. Lisa Lynn was involved, she was helping! To Ellie, it was the beginning of making house 25 a home. With the children working to help and doing what they could do and bonding together with each other and the staff, it seemed more like a family.

The job was done, but it was getting pretty dark outside already. They would have to wait till tomorrow to really see how the flowers would look in the daytime, with the sun shining through the windows.

The house was peaceful for a while and Ellie and Sarah had another chance to talk, while everyone was together in the family room.

"I guess you don't know many other Jewish/Christian mixed up religious people like me," Ellie said.

"No I don't. But my father works with a Jewish man and we've been praying for his family for years."

"Really?" Ellie exclaimed. "Why would you pray for them?"

"We're praying that they'll be saved, you know, accept Jesus."

"But what if they think they're already in the right religion for them?"

Sarah explained that her father told her that the Jewish man named Ed and his wife Lorraine didn't seem too sure their religion was the right one.

Ellie said, "Ed and Lorraine?! Those are my parents' names. Where does your dad work?"

"My father's a lawyer at Blake and Hargrove, and Ed is an associate in his law firm. It seems like Ed went back to school later in life and now he's a second year associate in the firm."

"Sarah, I think Ed is my father."

"You're kidding! Then we've been praying for your whole family, Ed, Lorraine, Nelly and Daniel. But I wonder why you weren't mentioned."

"Sarah, you must have gotten the names wrong. Probably Nelly was meant to be Ellie, because everything else is true. My brother is Daniel!"

Sarah was stunned, and so was Ellie. Now they both felt awkward. Sarah thought she revealed too much too soon. How would Ellie feel about somebody praying for her when she didn't see anything wrong in the way she believed?

At the same time, Ellie was wondering how Sarah and her nice family could be so arrogant as to think they knew the truth more than anybody else. Sure the Bible was growing on Ellie and she loved reading about Jesus. But that didn't mean He was the only way to God. Other people might get the same feelings when they read about Buddha or Krishna or some other holy book. Besides, even if Ellie decided to choose the Christian religion, that wouldn't give her the right to pray for everybody to make the same choice.

Lost in their thoughts, neither of them said anything for a couple of minutes. And a couple of minutes of silence are usually much longer than one would think. Finally Ellie broke the stalemate and said, "We better start bath time, it's getting pretty late."

As they rounded up the children into the bathrooms, they heard a knock at the door. JPL returned. Her father and mother came in with her, carrying some of her stuff. JPL had her hands full. She was carrying a bouquet of sixteen roses and her face was almost as red as the roses! She was rosy-cheeked from the cold and she was so very proud to be sweet sixteen with a bouquet of roses all her own!

"Happy Birthday JPL!" Sarah said. "We decorated our house here for your birthday!"

"And there are red roses on the windows for you too," Ellie said. "It's too dark to see them now, but you'll see them tomorrow."

JPL could hardly digest what they told her. She was concentrating so hard on holding her roses and telling everybody her big news. "I'm sweet sixteen," she boasted. Sarah and Ellie were so happy for JPL.

She had a big day and was very sleepy. As soon as her parents left, she was the first one to take a shower. With Ellie and Sarah working efficiently together, they got everything done at a good time and in good order. Lisa Lynn was such a big help, bringing them washcloths and towels for Wendy and Lawrence and being available to fetch any other simple thing that was needed.

Ellie wished Sarah was on staff with her, as her job seemed so fun and easy today. However, it wasn't the kind of easy that just happens naturally. They had to carefully plan out their strategies. They thoughtfully arranged which children they had in the bathrooms with them and which children they could leave out on their own. It was like the fox, the hen and the basket of corn riddle. The fox couldn't be left with the chicken, since he'd eat the chicken, and the corn couldn't be left with the chicken, since the chicken would eat the corn. But it wasn't about the fox and chicken now, it was about not leaving Grant with Angel, or not leaving Angel with the sugar, or not leaving Mahfta with anything. So they figured out a plan and it worked.

Finally the children were asleep, the house was clean, and it was almost time for the night shift worker to report for duty.

Chapter Twelve

ELLIE AND SARAH were admiring the roses on the table, hoping they'd stay safe till the day of JPL's party. The bright red roses looked especially beautiful with twenty white snowflakes dangling above them. "Wasn't it a great day?" Sarah asked with a very sleepy enthusiasm.

"It sure was," Ellie wholeheartedly agreed. "You're so good working with special needs children, Sarah. Do you think you'll major in special ed?"

Sarah's answer surprised Ellie. "We're still not sure I'll be going to college."

"Are you serious? Is it because of the cost?" Ellie asked.

"No, it's not just the cost. It's because we're still not sure that's God's plan for my life," Sarah said. "Who knows when I'll get married and when I do, I want to stay home with my children. And we're not sure if a degree would be helpful to me or not."

"Wow," Ellie exclaimed. "But it seems like it's just the thing to do, going to college I mean. People don't even think about it these days. It's just like it's taken for granted or something, unless of course, you just want to work as a cashier in some store or in a factory."

Sarah laughed. "No, I don't really want to be a cashier. And actually my family still doesn't know if I should ever get a regular job."

"But you're sort of working here," Ellie reasoned. "Wouldn't you want to keep doing this and actually get paid for it? Then you can save your money and it can help when you have your own family?"

"I know what you're saying, Ellie, but my family is trying to re-think all these things our culture takes for granted. We want to re-think everything by what the Bible says. And the Bible says women should be keepers at home."

"Really? It says that? Maybe that's why I can't find a job that I really like. Boy, Sarah, when I talk to you I have so many questions. Things I never even thought about before! I mean, I had so many questions to ask you before we even got on this new topic! Not going to college? Not getting a regular job? Wow, my mind is spinning."

Sarah laughed. "Well, I have an idea. Why don't you come to the Bible Study? You can bring up any of these concerns and we can explore together just what the Bible says about them. It doesn't mean you have to believe it. But you did say you believe the Bible, as well as other books, so you might as well see what it says about some of these issues."

"Ok, I'll think about it. But I'm not promising anything," Ellie said. "Hey, I think I see your dad pulling up. Thanks again for coming in to work with me today! It sure was nice for me."

"And me too," Sarah agreed. "Call me to let me know if you'll be coming on Tuesday."

Ellie walked to her car, the day's events whirling around in her brain. Praying for her family for years! How could a nice family like that, one she felt so at home with, be so proud and self-righteous! Not sure about college or if a woman should work?? What an interesting and strange thought and what an interesting and strange family. They were so nice to Ellie, every one of them, and yet so haughty in their thinking that their way and their religion was the only right one. Ellie felt a strange draw to go to this Bible Study. And at the same time she felt fearful and repulsed by the thought of it.

Sarah's father drove into the parking lot where Ellie was parked and rolled down his window. Before Sarah could stop him, he said, "Oh Ellie, remember William invited you to our Bible Study? I just wanted to let you know it starts at 7 o'clock. If you'd like to come, you're welcome to come to our house about 5 and have dinner with our family beforehand."

"Thanks," Ellie said. "Sarah already reminded me. But thanks for inviting me to dinner too. I'll call Sarah and let her know what I decide. Bye now."

Ellie walked to her car with a heart that was pumping fast. She was overwhelmed with all that was happening. She drove home reviewing all that had happened that day and tried to process it. She was so glad she worked these weird hours, because when she got home, her cousin would probably be asleep.

Chapter Thirteen

ELLIE GOT READY for work on Monday with eagerness and a little trepidation. She had gone shopping in the morning and gotten three things she was really excited about: some rope, three bags of flowers, and a book. She had the idea that since Benton really liked stringing up curtains and clothes all over his room every morning, he might be happy to have his own rope. Ellie creatively thought that if she bought some nice quality rope and some plastic red flowers, she could give them to Benton and get him to decorate the activity room for JPL's birthday. He knew how to attach things to curtain rods and bed posts like an expert, so maybe he could do something in the other rooms too. She found all that she needed at a discount store, which had bags of a dozen plastic roses on sale for a dollar a bag. She got three bags.

But even more intriguing was the book she found at the store. It was a children's picture book called *Roses for Lisa*. The story was so cute. Lisa was about to be twelve years old. She longingly watched different people in her life get a bouquet of roses in the past year. Her sister got roses from her fiancé, her mother got roses on Mother's Day, her grandpa gave her grandma roses on their anniversary, and her aunt got roses when she had her first baby. It turned out that on the day of Lisa's birthday, all these people decided to get Lisa a dozen roses. None of them knew that the other people were planning to do the same thing. So on Lisa's twelfth birthday, she got four dozen roses. Ellie found it amazing that there was a book like this! A book for JPL about another girl named Lisa who got roses for her birthday! The only thing that wasn't perfect was that the Lisa in the book was turning twelve, not sixteen. Ellie thought maybe JPL would actually accept this book as a birthday present. And Ellie was planning to show it to Diane today and enlist her support in giving it to JPL. Ellie just hoped Diane would be excited too.

But she had no need to fear Diane's reaction, because when she got to work she found out Monday was Diane's day off. It would just be Ellie and Marie. Ellie now had to decide how much to confide in Marie about her plans and ideas.

Marie arrived late, just as the first shift workers were leaving. Ellie was glad it worked out that way. Now she could explain to Marie about the decorations without everybody else putting in their two cents worth. The first shift workers acted a little suspicious of the plans and decorations, and they moved the bouquet of roses to the top of the refrigerator. That was a good idea, Ellie thought. That way they'd last till the day of the party. But the first shift workers also said Benton was eying the snowflakes all morning and they hoped he wouldn't climb the tables and mess with them.

Ellie understood their fears and concern. It could be a big waste of time to make decorations and then have a big mess on your hands if they all got torn down. Maybe somebody could even get hurt climbing on the tables trying to get at them. All sorts of situations could happen because of these dangling snowflakes. Yet it didn't seem right to refrain from putting up any decorations. If they didn't take little risks like this, the children would live boring lives in safe, sterile environments. One day would be the same as the next day, week after week and year after year. And besides, Ellie wasn't that worried about Benton pulling down the snowflakes because she thought her secret gift would more than satisfy him.

Marie seemed fine with Ellie's explanation of the decorations and the party, especially when she told her that it was partly Diane's idea. But she seemed startled as Ellie explained why she bought a rope for Benton to play with.

"You want him to do what with that rope?" Marie asked.

"Well, you know how he winds up his curtains and sheets into ropes and then hangs clothes and stuff on them? I mean I saw him do little bits of that here and there, but according to first shift, it seems like almost every other morning they find some weird creation in his bedroom."

"I've seen it, Ellie. I worked first shift here a couple times and it really is crazy what Benton does!"

Ellie replied, "Wow, that's what I heard. So anyway, that's why I thought of buying him a genuine rope. He won't have to make his own rope by rolling up sheets and curtains. Maybe he'll be really happy and creative when he gets to use a real rope. Then I found these bags of roses and thought they'd make great decorations for JPL's party. And then I put the two ideas together and thought maybe Benton could string up these roses and actually do some useful decorating for JPL's birthday week.

"And how would you explain that to someone with the IQ of a two year old?" Marie asked.

"I'd just show him and give him an example," Ellie calmly answered.

Marie laughed. "I like it. Why not try it? It'll be interesting whatever ends up happening."

Ellie laughed too and was much encouraged

After the children were toileted, Ellie began her experiment. She showed Benton the rope and flowers and asked him if he wanted to put them up and decorate the activity room. He didn't act interested in the least and seemed to not understand anything that Ellie was saying. Ellie fully expected a reaction like this. Next Ellie opened one bag of flowers and then she unwound some of the rope. She got on a chair in the activity room and tied one end of it to the curtain rod. Then she tied one flower to the string and gave the free end of it to Benton. He seemed happy when he realized he could tie knots and string things up. She gave him a flower and asked him to tie that to the string. He didn't seem to grasp the concept, so Ellie tied another flower. Since he always did his work in his bedroom when no one was around, she thought she would leave and give him freedom to do his work. So Ellie left the activity room and went out to talk to Marie about the party.

"I switched the menu around so the kids could have hamburgers the day of the party," Ellie explained.

"Great idea, Ellie," Marie agreed. "JPL loves hamburgers. And let's save the chocolate cake mix for the party too."

"Hey, that sounds great," Ellie said.

"Speaking of JPL, she should be through with her arts and crafts class in five minutes. Do you want to pick her up or should I?" Marie asked.

"I'd love to go and take a few of the kids out with me for a walk," Ellie requested.

Ellie and Marie decided it would be good to take out Lawrence and Lisa Lynn. Lawrence walked very slowly, but he needed exercise badly. He spent practically the whole day, every day, sitting on the couch, bouncing lightly and licking his hands. Ellie washed his hands before they left and put some mittens on him. The walk there was peaceful and uneventful. Ellie talked out loud to the children, just like a mother would talk to her baby who didn't yet understand her words. She pointed out different things outside and also talked about the Bible study and Sarah's family and the book she bought for JPL. She thought that just talking to the children as if they understood what she was saying would somehow help their communication skills. After all, it seemed to really help babies who were talked to a lot.

JPL was waiting for them when they got to the center. As they walked back, Ellie told JPL about having Benton decorate. JPL didn't quite understand Ellie's complicated explanation, so Ellie changed the subject. All of a sudden, Lisa Lynn plopped on the sidewalk and sat down. She refused to get up and walk. "Lisa Lynn, what's wrong? Are you tired? We're almost home." Lisa Lynn just laughed, a bit impishly. Ellie didn't know what to do. She urged Lisa Lynn to get up. "Come on, get up, Lisa Lynn," Ellie said again and again. Finally she asked JPL, "Did she ever do this before?"

"All the time," JPL said cockily, showing off how smart she was.

"How do they get her back up?" Ellie wanted to know.

JPL didn't answer. She just grabbed Lisa Lynn's hand and roughly pulled and said, "Get up and walk. You know better." And after a little more pulling, Lisa Lynn got up.

Ellie felt quite humbled by that experience. She didn't know as much about the children as she thought she did!

When they got back, Ellie was excited to find out how Benton's project was going. Marie forgot all about it, so they went to check on it together. What a surprise they got! Benton was happily stringing things up, but not the way Ellie had hoped! Somehow he tied up washcloths and towels and mittens and scarves and toys all over the room in intricate knots. He looped his rope of many colors over and over in circular fashion, and attached it to chairs and furniture and curtain rods. The bags of flowers were up too, but not the nice individual roses. Benton attached the whole plastic bag up, unopened. There was one muddy boot and Wendy's winter jacket too! The room looked horrible. It was Ellie's second failure of the day.

Marie was sympathetic to Ellie. "Don't be too hard on yourself. You tried. And Benton is having the time of his life! Actually, if we had a camera I'd love to take a picture of this. Why it's a masterpiece!"

Ellie realized Marie was right. Benton was having the time of his life and he was creating a great work of art, in his own way.

"When should we clean it up?" Ellie asked.

"Let's wait till the kids are in bed. Let Benton enjoy his new toy and his new artwork."

Ellie happily agreed. The rest of the day went fairly well, and Ellie still thought this was the best job she had had so far. But her confidence level at having found the *perfect* job was waning just a little. As she walked to her car, after a very full day at house 25, she was surprised her thoughts went immediately to the Bible Study the following day. It seemed like a neat coincidence that she was off on that day and would be able to attend an evening event like that. She wondered just what a Bible Study would be like.

Chapter Fourteen

ELLIE WANTED TO FIND a skirt to wear in case she decided to go to the Bible Study. She couldn't decide whether she should go or not, so she thought if she just went shopping and stopped thinking about it, she might get the answer.

But before she left she read more of the Bible. She was amazed at the wisdom in the words of Jesus—like the great advice He gave about praying. He talked about not bragging about how much you pray, but doing it in secret and God will reward you openly. She also liked the great saying that if you love those who love you, how great is that? That's easy. Everybody can do that! But to love your enemies, that's the thing to aim for. And then there was that one verse that Ellie was very surprised to find. It kind of agreed with what Sarah was saying that Jesus was the only way to God. Ellie read that Jesus said no man can know the Father except the Son and he to whomsoever the Son will reveal Him. That seemed to say that nobody can know God without having Jesus reveal God to him. That was a lot of stuff for her brain to chew on. And she wasn't even halfway through the first book, the book of Matthew, yet!

But she wanted to get to the stores at 10 a.m., right when the mall opened. It might take a long time to find a good outfit. So she stopped reading, got her water jug for the car, collected her coupons, and left. She checked all the possible stores, first checking the two stores she had coupons for. She didn't see any of the nice longer skirts like Sarah wore. There was one that fit Ellie really well. But it was made of a fancy polyester material and it was black with tiny white flowers on it. It seemed like a nice skirt to wear to somebody's wedding, with a fancy white blouse or maybe a black top and white pearl necklace, but it wasn't the type to wear to work or to a Bible Study. Ellie kept debating in her mind whether to buy it or not. She decided against it.

She went home for lunch and then set out for some of the discount stores in the afternoon. She found some durable every-day skirts made out of the right material, cotton or corduroy. However, the colors and patterns were so wild and bright. She couldn't picture herself wearing a cherry red skirt or a skirt with giant yellow and orange daisies. She felt so pathetic and immature, still trying to find out what style was really "her."

She started looking at the tops and found a very nice black sweater, not too heavy and bulky, yet not too dressy. She thought maybe that would make a nice outfit with the black skirt with white flowers she saw in the morning. She was mad at herself for not buying that skirt! She made the same mistake a couple of times before, not knowing whether to buy or not to buy. She only hoped the skirt would still be there when she went back to purchase it. What relief Ellie felt when she found it still hanging where she left it!

Ellie was surprised how much time she wasted in this shopping trip. She still didn't have the answer, but when she thought of just staying home, she knew she'd be disappointed. She wanted her life to go somewhere, not just stagnate. So she had to do something, even if it was such an unexpected thing as going to a Bible Study. After all, it was an important part of her research, she convinced herself. So she put on her new outfit and was quite happy with her image in the mirror.

When Ellie arrived, Sarah answered the door. And surprise of surprises, Sarah was wearing blue jeans and a nice snowflake sweatshirt. *Oh no*, Ellie thought, feeling so out of place already. She stumbled out the words, "Oh, I thought people would get dressed up for a Bible Study, umm, like maybe sort of like for church."

Sarah quickly reassured her. "They do. I mean some of us do and some of us wear jeans and more casual clothes. But I'm planning to change before the Bible Study. "

Ellie took off her coat and Sarah exclaimed, "Wow, Ellie, that's a really nice outfit! Where did you find that skirt?"

Ellie felt relieved that she must have looked half way acceptable or in style or at least dressed appropriately for the evening. Sarah continued her explanation, "I'm wearing jeans because I thought we could go ice skating for a few minutes before dinner. Mom said dinner won't be ready for another forty-five minutes and there's a frozen pond right behind our house. Do you like to ice skate?"

"I do," Ellie said. "I really like it. Of course I just do it for fun. I don't know any fancy moves or anything."

"Great," Sarah said. "We have some skates that I think would fit you. And you can borrow a pair of my blue jeans. We seem pretty close in size."

Sarah had her own room. She had two younger brothers, but she was the only girl. Her bed had a pretty patchwork quilt on it. Sarah said she and her mother made it themselves. She also had one tall set of bookshelves, and it was filled with books. It was quite impressive. Sarah's Bible seemed right at home on the shelf, right next to some history books and biographies.

There were some framed pictures of flowers on the wall, simple sketches done in watercolor. Sarah explained that she painted two of them herself and her youngest brother did the third one. There was also a picture of Sarah as a little girl on her dresser. And there was a poster with a scripture verse leaning against the wall, waiting for Sarah to find the right spot for it.

"It was my birthday a couple of weeks ago and some of my gifts are still piled up over there," Sarah pointed out. "I'm trying to decide where to put up that poster. And this box here is a skirt my aunt bought me. Here, let me show it to you."

"Wow, it's really cute! Do you like it?" Ellie asked.

"I like it so much that I actually bought one just like it before she gave that one to me," Sarah chuckled. "I was planning to return it to the store, but it's awkward, because my aunt didn't give me a receipt. Hey Ellie, would you like it?"

"Are you serious?" Ellie asked.

"Of course. You said you liked it, didn't you?"

"I love it," Ellie said. "I can pay you for it."

"Don't be silly. It'll be my early birthday gift to you."

"Thanks," Ellie said whole-heartedly. Yet inwardly she began feeling very awkward, knowing she wouldn't be so gung-ho on the Bible Study and wondering if Sarah would still want to befriend her then.

They joined Sarah's brothers outside and the time flew by way too fast! They skated and played funny simple games invented by Sarah's youngest brother, William. He was seven and thought it would be fun for everybody to have a race going ten skates forward and then ten skates backward. They would have to keep changing from forward to backward till they got to the other side. Then he thought of a game where everyone skates in a circle and one person is outside the circle. Then the outside person has to try to skate to the inside of the circle, while the people around the circle have to time their skating to block him from going in. It didn't work out too well. It was as easy as anything to get into the middle of the circle, but everyone was playing along and laughing very hard. It was such a ridiculous game, but so much fun!

Supper time neared and they all went in. "Let's get dressed for the Bible Study before we eat," Sarah suggested. "That way, we don't have to rush to finish eating, and if someone comes early, we'll be ready."

Ellie thought that sounded like a good plan. They got dressed and came down just as Sarah's mother was putting the last pot on the table. Sarah's father prayed, just like the last time she was there. She felt a little more comfortable this time, since she was kind of prepared and expecting it. Then Sarah's mother explained what the different dishes were and everyone served themselves. There was a delicious stew with chicken, carrots, potatoes and peppers. There was also homemade bread and a beautiful salad. Everyone had a glass of water next to their bowls. It was a very pretty table, even though the glasses didn't match and the pots sat on worn-out pot-holders on the table.

"My favorite meal!" William exclaimed. "And chocolate chip cookies for dessert!"

"But we have to wait for dessert till later, when we can share it with the Bible Study people," twelve year old Adam reminded William.

"Oh yeah," William said.

"That's good you're not too disappointed," Ellie complimented William.

"Oh, I love Bible Study days!" William informed her.

"Oh you do? Do you all participate?"

Adam explained, "Not really. But William likes to get me to spy with him during the meetings."

William excitedly added, "Yeah, we sneak up on the group, without anybody seeing us."

"That does sound like fun," Ellie thought. "Does anybody ever catch you spying?"

"No, never!" William said proudly.

"William, they probably know, but they're too nice to tell us," Adam said.

"No, I don't think they know. I would be able to tell from the look in their eyes if they saw us, and I never saw any indication of that," William insisted.

Ellie smiled to herself as she heard this seven year old boy throw out phrases like 'I never saw any indication of that.'

"No indication of that, William? What about the time that one guy winked at us?" Adam reminded him.

"He was just blinking," William said. "Remember we cut up all those onions that day and the onion smell was still in the air and people were blinking a lot that day."

"Oh," Adam said, trying to keep a straight face.

"Hey Ellie," William said. "You said you were Jewish last time you were here. Did you know that there's this other Jewish family we pray for every day?"

"I know. I think Sarah told me about that," Ellie said.

Sarah looked embarrassed. She didn't want William to bring this up. She quickly tried to steer the conversation in a different direction.

"I thought we should tell Ellie what happens in a Bible Study."

"Good idea," her father said. "We've had a lot of different kinds of meetings in the last three years. Sometimes we go through one of the books of the Bible one chapter per week. Or if somebody has a particular issue they want to bring up, we talk about that. We all share our thoughts about it and we try to find out what the Bible has to say about it."

"What kind of issues have you talked about lately?" Ellie asked.

"Some of the college guys wanted to talk about what the Bible has to say about dating. So that was what I planned on tackling today."

"That sounds interesting," Ellie said. "I wouldn't have thought the Bible speaks on that subject."

"It does, but not directly. We find verses that can relate and then we talk about what they imply about dating and boy-girl relationships."

Ellie was very interested in what the Bible had to say about guy-girl relationships. But she was still a little annoyed that they thought Jesus was the *only* way and skeptical about how they thought their interpretations were the *only* ones that were correct. So she blurted out, "But don't you have to be careful you're not just going by your own interpretation and reading things into the passage?"

Immediately afterwards she regretted what she said. Sarah and her family were being so nice to her and here she was antagonizing them. Quickly she added, "I'm sorry."

"No need to apologize. All your concerns are good ones. You'll add a lot to our group, Ellie!" Sarah's dad said with meaning.

Just then the telephone rang. It was one of the college guys saying that their group couldn't be there that evening.

"Too bad," Mr. Kirby said. "That just leaves us and Kevin and your two young friends from high school," he said to Sarah. "Maybe we should hold off on the dating topic. What do you think, Sarah?"

"Yeah, I think we should hold off," she agreed.

"Now I have a question for Ellie. If you don't mind, how about if we discuss the question 'Is Jesus really the only way to God?' Sarah told me a little bit about your beliefs. Would you be ok with us studying that topic? You don't have to let anybody know your beliefs if you don't want to. Or you can join in the discussion and comment and debate as much as you want."

"That sounds very interesting to me," she replied.

A few minutes after they finished eating, a young man named Kevin and two younger girls from Sarah's high school arrived. They went straight into the family room where Mr. Kirby was waiting for them. Sarah and Ellie joined them.

Mr. Kirby had everyone turn to John 14:6. He had everyone read it out loud in unison. "Jesus saith unto him, I am the way, the truth and the life; no man cometh unto the Father but by me."

Next Mr. Kirby asked, "So does anyone think this is another way of saying that Jesus is the only way to the Father?"

Ellie answered. "It seems like that's what it's saying, but it's so strange. If Jesus said that, why would all these other religions still say Jesus is a great teacher and a great prophet and all that? If He's really saying that He is the only way, that would be the same as saying their religion is all wrong."

"Anybody want to try to answer Ellie's question?" Mr. Kirby asked.

Kevin was quick to volunteer. "Great question, Ellie. My guess is that these other religious leaders want to appeal to as many people as possible. They want to say they also believe Jesus is great. Then people who were brought up in Christian homes would still be attracted to this new religion and yet they wouldn't have to give up their old beliefs. I think a lot of these leaders don't know about all these verses or they interpret them in different ways or maybe they even misquote some verses on purpose."

"Very true," Mr. Kirby said. "And if it's just one verse, it's very easy to think it can be overlooked. That leads me to another question. If people didn't know about this passage, is there any other verse in the Bible that might say the same thing if they came across it?"

Ellie herself knew the other verse she just read in Matthew, but she would never say it. She didn't want anyone to know she was reading the Bible on her own.

Sarah said, "I'm thinking of that verse that says Jesus is the door and any man who tries to get into the sheepfold any other way is a thief and a robber."

Ellie wondered out loud, "Why would Jesus compare such a person to a thief or a robber? Maybe he's really just looking for God."

Kevin replied. "You're right, Ellie. Some people might be sincerely seeking God by trying some different paths. But I think if we read the verse in context, Jesus is referring to those who say that they themselves are the Messiah and want others to follow them. And they would be sort of like thieves who would be robbing God of the glory and worship due to Him and trying to get it for themselves."

Ellie was quite impressed with the depth of Kevin's and Sarah's knowledge of the Bible. It sure seemed like they were logical, well thought-out and very believable interpretations.

"But," Ellie began, "all this only makes sense if somebody already believes the Bible to be true. What if somebody isn't sure? How can they know if the Bible is true and if they can believe these quotes in the first place?"

Mr. Kirby began, "Great questions, Ellie. There is a lot of evidence these days pointing to the truth of the Bible. The nation of Israel is one of them. The Bible prophesied that a nation would be born in one day and that God would never turn His back on the Jewish people and He would one day restore them to their land. And that's just what's happening. It's really a miracle. There's no other known culture, where a language that hasn't been used in a thousand years or more, gets revived. There's also not many other examples of people groups like the Jewish people, who were so hated and fought against and killed, yet somehow managed to survive and even thrive."

"Like the pogroms and the Holocaust," Ellie said.

"Exactly. Has anyone in your family been affected by any of those, Ellie?" Mr. Kirby asked.

"Not that I know of directly," Ellie answered. "But I know we've been affected indirectly."

"How?" they all wanted to know. Even Sarah's younger brothers were hanging around listening.

"Well, I know some of my relatives changed their names around the time of the Holocaust. Even though my relatives were in America, they were a little scared they wouldn't be able to get jobs if they had Jewish names. My aunt and uncle used to be the Goldbergs, but they changed their name to the Gilberts. And my aunt's first name was Rachel, but she changed it to Rhoda to sound less Jewish. Even my name, Ellie, was chosen because I was named after my great aunt Elisheva. But my parents made my official name on my birth certificate Ellie, so it wouldn't sound Jewish."

"Oh no," William said with concern. "Your aunt better change her name again. The name Rhoda is in the Bible too and people might find out she's Jewish!"

"Good thinking, William," Kevin said. "But Rhoda is in the New Testament, and people usually don't think that part of the Bible is too Jewish."

"That's true but they're wrong," Mr. Kirby said. "But that topic is for another night."

"Before we close, can I make a suggestion?" Kevin asked.

"Go ahead," Mr. Kirby said.

Kevin was one of the interns in Mr. Kirby's law office. "Since we were talking about the Jewish people, I was reminded of this Jewish guy named Ed at the law firm. Can we pray for him and his family to be saved?"

Ellie was almost sure Kevin had no idea that Ed was her father. And somehow, she didn't seem to get as upset at his suggestion to pray for her family as she did when Sarah revealed that her family had been praying for them. Ellie was very impressed to see a young man with such a heart for doing what he thought was right and being so concerned about other people. She was also struck to see a young man being interested enough in spiritual things to actually come to a Bible study! And she was remembering how Kevin responded to her comments by saying things like, "You're right, Ellie" or "Good question, Ellie." He called her by name and he made it sound so warm and friendly, as if they'd known each other for a long time already.

Mr. Kirby defused the awkwardness of Kevin's suggestion by saying, "Why don't you and I pray, Kevin, since we both know Ed personally?" So the two men stayed a couple of extra minutes in the living room to pray, while the rest of the group drifted into the kitchen for the chocolate chip cookies.

Kevin came in and grabbed a couple of cookies, but had to leave early. Ellie was disappointed. Before he left, though, he made it a point to come and tell Ellie how glad he was that she was part of the group. "I like your sincere questions," he said.

Ellie left Sarah's house with a mind that was reeling and a heart that was full of hope. She wished to someday marry a man like Kevin, but probably one with a more balanced spiritual point of view similar to hers. As much as she liked the Bible Study and felt the discussion exhilarating, she still couldn't see herself becoming one of "them." She couldn't change her years of doubt about the Bible into belief in just one night. And ironically, even though she didn't tell anybody there, she would be going to the opposite of a Bible Study the very next day!

It just so happened that the Indian guru she liked to hear was speaking the next day at the university convention center about an hour away. And she was able to do it because Wednesday was another one of her days off. She thought maybe God arranged it like that, just so she could go to hear this lecture.

Chapter Fifteen

ELLIE WATCHED FOR the little white car her college friends had. They weren't close friends now, but they used to work on a lot of projects together in their elementary ed classes. She sat in the back seat and listened quietly as the other three girls discussed some of their experiences with the guru. Being officially declared "disciples" of his, they bowed to him and got specific advice from him for their lives.

One girl began telling an interesting story. She said she was wondering at one time if she could make her husband her guru. That way she would just do whatever he said and it might make for a very secure marriage. But the guru told her that wouldn't be a good idea. He said her husband's pride would get in the way and he'd start taking advantage of his leadership. It seemed to Ellie an odd question in the first place, yet nevertheless, very interesting to hear about.

When the yogi's lecture began, things about the whole evening seemed to bother Ellie more than usual. She always felt a little awkward, being one of the few people there who didn't bow to the Yogi. But today she felt even more repulsed when she saw so many others bowing to this man. And the talk wasn't filled with such wisdom as she was hoping for. However she was glad she came. She really needed to ask the guru a question about Jesus.

She waited in line with the twenty or so people who also wanted to ask for his advice. Ellie was timid but determined and when her turn came she boldly asked, "Do you believe Jesus was a great man?"

"Yes without a doubt," he said. "He is on par with the some of the greatest men and teachers in the world. Not many have matched him in purity. There's a lot you can learn from him."

"Then why do you think Jesus said that He was the only way to the Father?" Ellie continued.

"That was true. He was the only way to God, but just for his disciples. Everybody has to go through somebody. You don't have to go through him. You can go to God through Jesus, if you choose, or you can go through Buddha or through me or through some other guru," he replied.

"Oh I see. Thanks," Ellie said, letting the person behind her have his turn to ask a question.

On the way home, Ellie was shaken up. The guru's answer didn't satisfy her. She was shivering. She didn't know if it was from the cold or from nervousness, but she spotted Molly's blanket and asked if she could borrow it.

Molly said, "Oh no, that's my meditation blanket. It has certain vibes, and I have to be very careful with it."

Ellie saw the contrast between this group of 'friends' and the friends at the Bible Study. She stayed pretty quiet all the way home. But her mind was anything but quiet.

By the time she got to her bedroom that night, she made a decision. The guru said you can go through Jesus or through him or somebody else. Well, she didn't trust the guru or any of the other religions' gods. But she did trust Jesus. The guru himself told her she can go through Jesus. And she would just take him up on that!

She knew that for two thousand years, ever since Jesus came, a whole lot of people had chosen to die for their faith rather than reject Jesus. Why would so many people die for something that wasn't true? She knew that no one could deny that Jesus was a great man. This was too uncanny. If Jesus were just a great prophet from one particular religion, why would so many people from all religions agree He was a great man? It didn't make sense. He was great and everyone knew it. And how could a great man lie? He couldn't. If he lied, he wouldn't be considered great. She knew now in her heart that she trusted Jesus. If He said He was the only way to the Father, she believed it. She believed it so much that she prayed an unusual prayer that night, straight from her heart.

"Dear Jesus, will you be my guru? I want you to teach me and I want you to be in my life. Help me to know the truth. I don't really want to believe these Christian fundamentalists. But they make sense and they're so loving. You have to help me, Jesus. I don't know what else to say, so I'll say Amen."

She went to bed smiling and wasn't shaking anymore.

Chapter Sixteen

THE NEXT DAY, before Ellie went to work, she called Sarah. When she told Sarah the news, Sarah was overjoyed. "I won't tell my family unless you want me to, Ellie. Would you want me to wait so you can tell them yourself?"

"Well, I'm not sure I'm ready for that yet. It's a little scary, like I feel in a way that it's saying I was wrong and you were right and it's a little humiliating. I don't know. I know it's kind of humbling and good, and I know I shouldn't be embarrassed, but...."

"Ellie, I really understand what you're saying. You're actually very good at putting your thoughts into words," Sarah said encouragingly.

"Thanks, Sarah. In a way, I think I'd be brave enough to tell your mother, but nobody else yet."

"That would be great. Dad and the boys went target practicing today anyway, and Mom and I are here by ourselves now."

"Will your Dad still be gone if I stop over right before work?" Ellie asked.

"Oh definitely. Dad and the boys make a day of it and go out to lunch on the way home and go look at models at the toy store and all kinds of things."

"Ok, I'll come about quarter after one," Ellie decided.

Ellie told Sarah and Mrs. Kirby all about her search for a Bible and her secret research of starting to read Matthew in the New Testament. Then she told them about the guru and his answer and her nervousness and the meditation blanket. They both listened with rapt attention.

"So then when I got home I made my decision and I prayed and asked Jesus to be my guru."

Sarah and her mother both smiled. Mrs. Kirby exclaimed, "That's great! Your prayer is so interesting, so from the heart! I'm so glad you formed your prayer your own way. It was wonderful!"

Sarah agreed. "Ellie, I love your story. Would it be ok if I told Dad and the boys?"

"I'm not sure if you should or if I should just wait a while and do it myself. No, I think you should just do it, ok?"

"Great! Thanks! It would have been hard to hold it in."

Then Mrs. Kirby continued. "It would be great for you to give your testimony sometime in the future. I'd love for people to hear your story. It's such a good example of how you don't have to pray some stiff stereotyped prayer to accept Jesus as your Savior. You just have to pray from your heart."

Ellie agreed, "I think I'd like to do it someday when I'm more ready and brave, but not for a while yet."

Mrs. Kirby asked, "Does your father know anything about this? Did you ever tell him you met the daughter of the man he works with or that we were praying for your family?"

Ellie chuckled and coughed and managed to answer. "No, I didn't really tell him anything yet. I think I'd still be a little scared to do that."

"That's easy to understand," Sarah said.

"Sure," Mrs. Kirby added. "In fact, it's probably wise for now to just enjoy your new life and grow in the truth for a while before sharing it with someone else."

Ellie was so happy to receive this understanding and support.

Then Mrs. Kirby gave Ellie some suggestions for starting each day with some prayer and Bible reading. She told Ellie how she herself liked to pray out loud while she took a walk every morning. "Of course I just pray quietly when I'm passing people, but I actually try to time my walk for times when the kids won't be walking to school."

"That's true," Sarah said. "Mom learns the bus schedules for our neighborhood each year, just by watching. And then she walks either before the buses come or after all the kids are picked up or between the two different pick-up times."

"That's a good idea," Ellie said. "I like to walk too. But now I better leave to get to work on time."

"Yeah it's getting late," Sarah agreed. "See you Friday at JPL's birthday party!"

"That should be fun," Ellie said. "Bye."

It was a routine day at work, with no big disasters and no extra cute or memorable incidents. But somehow nothing on this day seemed routine to Ellie. She drove home thinking of the next Bible Study meeting and thinking of Kevin. She was also thinking about the fact that now she was 'one of them.' And she also had room in her brain to start thinking again about tomorrow's birthday party.

Chapter Seventeen

ELLIE SLEPT IN the next morning. When she woke up, her heart was pounding fast. She was so excited, so filled with hope for her life and a new trust in God and love for Him. She decided to get dressed quickly and go for a walk and pray. She needed the physical exercise and she was excited to try a prayer walk, like Sarah and her mom suggested to her. But it turned into a prayer jog at times. She had so much nervous energy that she started her walk by running two whole blocks. Then she began a heart to heart conversation with God her Father.

"Father God, thank you so much that You're my Father, like a real father and I can talk to you. Thank you for Sarah and the whole Kirby family and how they prayed for me and my family all these years. Help me to keep learning and know how to pray.

"O God, You know how I really want to get married just like my brother Daniel said. And I sure don't want to marry just anybody! But that guy I met at the Bible Study, Kevin, he seemed so nice. Lord I want to marry somebody like him, some man who loves God and who is nice and kind and smart and has a purpose in his life. Maybe he's the one for me, or maybe You have somebody else, but I'm so happy, God, that now I can tell you this desire of mine and it really feels like it's already starting to be answered!

"And thank you for this job I have. I really like it, I like the kids and I feel so useful and sort of even loved by them. And the staff is starting to be nice to me and wow, Father, so many things are happening in my life now and I'm so thankful to You! Help me calm down and have a good day and help us have a really nice birthday party for JPL.

"And please help me to be able to teach the kids different things. Please, Father, help me to teach JPL to like books and not think they're babyish. And help me to teach Benton to do some useful things with his rope tying and stuff. Ha, it's funny, Lord, that I'm asking You to help me teach! I thought maybe I wasn't cut out to be a teacher, but now I'm not too sure. Oh, Lord, I just need Your help in everything! Even in understanding myself! Wow, I'm so happy I can ask You all this!"

And Ellie was indeed so happy and overwhelmed with everything that was happening that she had to run again. It felt good to get all that fresh cold air in her lungs and the sun shining on her face. It was a cold but beautiful sunny day, a great day for JPL's sixteenth birthday!

Ellie felt so refreshed when she came back in. She thought this would be a good way to begin every day of her life, walking and praying. She read her Bible, then showered and dressed. She took extra thought of what special thing she should wear for the big birthday party.

The skirt! She saw it still folded in the bag in which Sarah gave it to her. She laughed to herself as she remembered it was already a double birthday skirt. Sarah's aunt gave it to her for her birthday, and then Sarah gave it to Ellie as an early or late birthday gift. Why not make it a triple birthday skirt and wear it for JPL's birthday? She thought her white turtleneck shirt and beige sweater vest would look perfect with the earth tone flowered skirt. She put on the new outfit and it did look almost perfect. She ate a late breakfast and got ready to pack her lunch.

Even though the staff was allowed to eat the food that they fixed for the children, Ellie didn't like to do that. The food was so institutional-tasting. She really preferred bringing her own lunches. But she changed her mind for today. She thought maybe today, for the birthday dinner, she would eat the hamburger meal there and also the birthday cake. Maybe she should make something homemade to bring for the dinner too.

She opened her refrigerator, and saw the dozen boiled eggs in a bowl. Ellie liked to have them handy for a quick breakfast or snack. A blueberry muffin and a hard-boiled egg were one of her quick breakfast combinations. Then she had an idea. *Hey, I can make deviled eggs. But that's a terrible name for them! What should I call them?* She started to make them anyway and think of the name later. Then she remembered the big bag of frozen corn on the cob she got last week. She opened the freezer and found that her cousin opened the bag and already had one. She counted how many were left. It was nineteen, more than enough! That would be a fun addition to the meal, a corn on the cob and a fancy birthday egg for everyone! And that's when Ellie realized she had a new name for deviled eggs, *fancy birthday eggs*. By the time she was finished with the food, it was time to go. She got in her car and almost drove away when she remembered the book. *Roses for Lisa* was still not wrapped, so she grabbed a tube of wrapping paper and the book and ran back to her car. Off she drove.

Ellie didn't think she was speeding, but somehow she got to work five minutes earlier than usual. As she walked in, Marie met her at the door and said, "Hi Ellie, you might as well keep your coat on. You have to work in house 18 today, they're short-staffed."

"What?" Ellie asked, not able to digest the news so quickly.

"Somebody called in sick in house 18 and there's only one other worker scheduled. So they called our house since we had three people scheduled today. And the rule is that the person with the least seniority has to cover in the other house."

"Oh," Ellie said. Her face dropped but she didn't want to show how crushed she was at this news. She said as cheerfully as she could, "I made some special birthday eggs for the birthday party. I'll put them in the refrigerator."

Marie was only half-listening, mostly involved with conversations with the first shift workers who hadn't left yet. Ellie refrigerated the eggs, put the corn in the freezer and left. She thought she'd call Sarah and tell her where the stuff was later. As she walked out the door, Sarah's mother was just pulling away and Sarah was walking in.

"Where are you going, Ellie?" she asked.

"I have to work at house 18 today. They're short-staffed."

"Oh no, too bad! Too bad! It just doesn't seem right!" Sarah said.

"They always call the houses that have three people working and the one with the least seniority has to go," Ellie explained. "But Sarah, at least you'll be there and you can make the party successful! Maybe you can come and pick up this book for JPL after I wrap it. Maybe you can take one of the kids for a walk with you and I can give you the book."

"Ok," Sarah said.

"Oh," Ellie remembered, "and I made some special birthday eggs that are in the refrigerator and I brought a bag of frozen corn on the cobs. I put them in the freezer. So you can get them out for everybody for the birthday dinner."

"Oh Ellie, this is too sad! You made all that stuff and now you can't stay. I'm so disappointed and I know you must be even more so!"

"Yeah," Ellie said gloomily. She was glad she could be herself with Sarah. "Well I better go. See you later."

She tried not to cry, but one tear managed to escape her eye as she walked slowly to house 18. When she got there, she planned to head straight to the bathroom and try to pull herself together.

Chapter Eighteen

A FRIENDLY WOMAN who seemed to be in her early thirties greeted Ellie in house 18. She was so relieved to have Ellie's help because Harold needed to be taken to the toilet and Leslie just had a big accident.

"Would you mind taking Harold to the bathroom while I clean up Leslie?" she asked.

"Sure," Ellie said, even though she still had her coat on.

Harold was a cute little boy, about seven years old. After Ellie put him on the toilet, she went out to hang up her coat.

"Ellie, I forgot to tell you," her co-worker shouted. "You can't leave Harold by himself!"

"Ok," Ellie answered and rushed back to the bathroom. She found that Harold had already used the bathroom, but somehow missed the toilet.

Ellie first got Harold out of the toilet area and into the sink area. She cleaned him up, wishing Lisa Lynn were here to hand her a clean washcloth from the closet and some underwear. But she managed to clean up the little boy and then went back to tackle the toilet area clean-up. She put on some rubber gloves and got a bucket with soapy water from the laundry room. She closed the bathroom door, so no other children would get in till the place was cleaned. She was on the verge of tears, but successfully managed to hold them back again. She did cry out to God as she cleaned ever so carefully, trying to keep her "triple-birthday skirt" and her white sleeves clean. "Oh God, help me. Help me have the right attitude. Please help me."

The clean-up was quite therapeutic for Ellie. She felt better after that. She realized the party was supposed to bless JPL and not herself. So she went back to work with resolve to make it a better day. After the toileting, Ellie asked her co-worker if she would mind if Ellie took some time to wrap the birthday book for JPL. She explained the whole story of why that book would be perfect for JPL.

It seemed the other woman was a Christian, because she said, "The Good Lord must have found that book for you, Ellie. You know JPL's real name is Lisa, don't you? And you know how she's been going all around the center talking about her roses for weeks now, don't you?"

"Yes I heard about that. But how do you know JPL?" Ellie asked.

"Oh, she's in arts and crafts with two girls from our house here. When I go to pick them up, there's JPL. She's the little ringleader of the class, and there she was bragging about her big birthday coming up and her roses! I'd say it was almost two weeks straight she was doing that!"

Ellie laughed. Then the doorbell rang. Ellie thought it was Sarah, so she answered it. What a surprise when she saw Marie standing there.

"Ellie, I'll work here today. You planned this birthday party and you need to be there!"

"Really Marie? I can stay here if you want."

"I don't want!" Marie insisted. "How could I see JPL crying and everybody sad because Ellie can't come to the party?" she said.

"Wow, that's sure nice of you Marie!" Ellie said. "Thanks!"

As she got her coat out of the closet, she started talking to God again, silently. *Wow, God, You're so good to me! Thank You, thank You, thank You!*

Ellie hadn't gotten around to wrapping the book yet, but she was glad she didn't. Now she'd have a chance to show it to Diane first. She wanted to enlist Diane's support for convincing JPL to accept it.

Ellie walked with a quick cheerful gait back to house 25. When Ellie arrived, Diane asked her if she wanted to leave her coat on and go get JPL from arts and crafts. "Sure," Ellie said. "Should Sarah come with me and we can take three or four of the kids?" Ellie asked Diane.

"That would be great!" Diane agreed.

"Oh, before we leave and before JPL gets back, I wanted to ask your help with something, Diane."

"Sure," Diane said, feeling complimented that Ellie was asking for her help again.

"You seem to have a lot of influence with JPL and I was wondering if you could put in a good word for this book I'm giving her for her birthday. I didn't wrap it up yet, so you can take a look at it while we're gone. If you could, maybe you can somehow convey to JPL that this book isn't a baby book, but it's a book for older girls like her." Ellie hoped she phrased her request in a gracious way. After all, it was Diane who was teasing JPL about liking baby books.

Diane didn't take offense at all. She was honored that Ellie, who graduated from college as a teacher, was asking her for her help. "Sure Ellie, I'll try my best," she said.

Ellie handed her the book. Then she and Sarah headed out the door with Mahfta, Benton, and Angel. They were a good group to take together, as their walking speed was quick. Ellie didn't want to risk taking Lisa Lynn today, just in case she had an episode of stubbornness and sat down on the sidewalk. And Lawrence and Wendy were very slow walkers. She never took Grant yet. She was still a little too nervous to do that. But just as they reached the front sidewalk, Diane called out. "Can you wait a minute? Grant said he wants to go along."

"Ok," Ellie answered. She hoped it would go all right. And it did. Grant was happy to be walking and just talked to himself a lot of the time in a jolly sort of way.

As long as everyone was behaving, Ellie took the opportunity to ask Sarah, "Whatever made Marie decide to replace me? She said something about not wanting to see JPL cry or something, but JPL wasn't even there yet."

Sarah laughed. "Marie was probably imagining what would happen if you weren't there at the party. She said she forgot all about it at first.

Actually, it was very interesting what happened. Diane came in so enthusiastic about the day. She asked where you were and when she found out you had to work in house 18, she acted dumbfounded. She couldn't believe you'd be called out on this big day of the party you planned. She said she'd go and replace you. Then Marie volunteered and said that since Diane helped plan the party too, she should stay and Marie would go. It was amazing to see how they were both so eager to get you back here for the party."

"Wow, I can't believe it," Ellie said.

"Praise the Lord," was Sarah's response.

Ellie just answered, "Yeah."

Then they reverted to talking to Grant and the other children. Grant seemed excited about the party too. "Sixteen roses for her sixteenth birthday," he kept repeating.

When they got to the arts and crafts class, JPL had a party hat on. It turned out that they celebrated her birthday in class. They had cookies and punch. Ellie was disappointed. She hoped JPL wouldn't be too tired of parties to celebrate again.

But she needn't have worried. JPL was only too happy to be the center of attention for as long as possible! Ellie told her she wouldn't have to have a piece of the birthday cake, since she already had so many cookies and was probably tired of desserts already. But JPL asserted, "No way! I love happy birthday cakes!"

Grant started mimicking that line, "I love happy birthday cakes!"

When they returned to the house, Diane motioned Ellie to the laundry room. She shut the door and said, "That book, Ellie! I can't believe you found a book like that! It's perfect! I'm planning to tell JPL that if she doesn't want it, I'll keep it!"

Ellie laughed. She was delighted with Diane's enthusiasm. Diane said, "I hope you don't mind, but I wrapped it for you."

"Oh thanks a lot, Diane. When do you think we should give it to her?"

"How about later, sometime after the birthday dinner?" Diane suggested.

Ellie agreed. Then Diane said, "And I have a question for you. I bought a bag of these big-sized red balloons and I don't know what we should do with them. Any ideas?"

"Hmmm. We know our kids wouldn't be able to play many games with balloons. Hmmm," she said again. Diane waited patiently for Ellie to think. Diane didn't have any creative ideas about the balloons yet, either.

Finally Ellie said, "Well, I have a thought. Maybe we should just blow them up in the kitchen and then bring them all out at once. It'll be a big dramatic thing for them to see sixteen big red balloons appearing all at once in the living room. We can bring them in after dinner or after the cake and just let the kids play with them or watch or whatever. We can bat them back and forth to each other and that way they might get the idea."

Diane brightened up and agreed, "That sounds fun! And now maybe I should go and make the cake mix with JPL. I bought some letters and flowers to decorate the cake with too!"

"Great!" Ellie exclaimed. The phone started ringing so she ran to answer it. It was Marie asking if she could bring a few children from house 18 over for the birthday cake after dinner. "Why not?" Ellie said. "That'll make it even more special!"

The exhilaration of planning this big birthday party in house 25 was contagious! Now house 18 would be involved too! It almost seemed like a real family giving a birthday party for their child, and the neighbor children were coming later for the cake.

As Sarah and Ellie were out in the living room with the rest of the children, they heard JPL and Diane fussing at each in the kitchen. "Ellie, can you come here a minute?" Diane called.

"Yeah, come and tell Diane my name," JPL said in a sarcastic tone of voice.

"We were getting out these candied letters for the cake and I was showing them to JPL," Diane explained. Ellie saw the letters on the counter all ready to go on the cake as soon as it was frosted. **HAPPY BIRTHDAY JPL.**

"That looks so nice, JPL, what's wrong with it?" Ellie asked.

"Where's my name?" she demanded.

Ellie pointed out the letters, ***J P L.*** "That's not my name! That's not my name!" JPL cried.

"Oh, do you want us to put the name Lisa on the cake?"

"No, not Lisa, JPL!" JPL insisted.

"Oh," Ellie quickly had an idea. "You want us to spell your name the way you usually spell it, like this?" Then she put out the letters, **L I S A.**

"Finally you got a brain!" JPL said.

"That's not nice to say," Ellie said, "because there are really two ways to spell your name, and Diane was spelling it one of the other ways." Then Ellie turned to Diane and with a knowing wink she explained. "Oh Diane, JPL wants you to spell JPL, like this."

"Good thing you were a teacher," Diane said. "It would be a shame if the party girl was sad and crabby on the day of her big party because no one knew the right way to spell JPL!"

"Yeah," Ellie said.

"Yeah," JPL echoed.

A semblance of peace returned to the kitchen and the anticipation of the party returned.

Chapter Nineteen

THE SMELL OF the freshly baked cake wafted through the house. Grant, Lisa Lynn and Angel all peeked into the kitchen at various times. Too bad no one thought of the problem of the frosting having to be put onto a cool cake, not a warm one. The three young ladies debated about whether to put the cake outside to cool off or in the refrigerator or freezer. The freezer was agreed upon. They all hoped it would cool off the cake in a short amount of time.

When the cake came out of the oven, the hamburgers went in. The supper meal was being prepared and the sixteen big red balloons were being blown up in the kitchen. Pretty soon, all three of the staff and five of the children were crowded into the small kitchen, watching it fill up with balloons. JPL, Lisa Lynn, Grant, Angel and Benton watched this unusual happening with extreme interest.

Lawrence still sat on the couch, Wendy bounced around in one of her favorite dining room corners and Mahfta just wandered around. If he did wander close to the kitchen, someone was sure to lead him in the other direction.

How the balloons would stay in the kitchen till after dinner was the next big problem. Diane had the best idea. She rushed to the activity room and made a huge clatter as she poured out all the toys from the giant cardboard toy box. She left the toys all over the floor, and she dragged the box into the kitchen. Then she stuffed most of the balloons inside the box. Next Ellie found a sheet to drape over the box to hold the balloons down. They shoved the box as far away from the food and ovens as they could.

At last it was time for the birthday dinner. Sarah brought some white plastic table cloths from her church to put on the tables. She also pulled out a package of red napkins from her purse. JPL was so happy she started getting a little prideful. "My birthday is so special," she bragged.

"Yes it is," Sarah agreed. "But everyone's birthday is special. And your sixteenth birthday is an extra special one, because you're growing up to be a beautiful young lady."

"Yep," JPL laughed, agreeing completely.

Sarah continued, "But we have to remember to make everyone's birthday special, JPL. Maybe you can be on the birthday committee of house 25 and make sure we do something extra nice for everybody's birthday, okay?"

"Sure," she said.

Sarah stood on a chair and brought the vase of roses down from the top of the refrigerator. She decided to trust JPL to carry it to the table. JPL walked cautiously, with Sarah walking right next to her. Sarah guided her in setting it right in the center of one of the tables.

The tables looked so nice for such a short time. Diane remembered to bring a camera to capture the scene before it got destroyed. Mahfta pulled the tablecloth off one of the tables, but happily it was not the table with the roses. All it had on it were the red napkins and silverware.

The table with the flowers was carefully guarded. "We need some security police to guard this table," Ellie said. "Can you guard it, Grant?"

"We need security police!" Grant repeated. "Call the police, call the police!" he repeated. He was funny and irritating at the same time, but he did guard the table. When all the children were seated, the table with JPL and the flowers as well as Grant, Lisa Lynn and Ellie was pretty safe. Diane ate with Mahfta and Benton. Sarah fed Wendy and had Angel and Lawrence at her table too. All the children except for Wendy and Lawrence had a lot of fun eating the corn on the cob. And the birthday eggs were a big success too, especially in JPL's opinion. She loved them!

After dinner, Diane and Sarah toileted the children, while Ellie cleaned up with JPL's assistance. JPL helped so willingly that Ellie wished every day was her birthday! Then they took the cake out of the freezer and frosted it. They left the letters and decorations for Diane to put on, since she was the one who brought them.

The table cloths were shaken out and then put back on the tables. Sarah took out the second package of red napkins from her bag. Ellie and Diane moved the couch to kind of act as a gate, blocking the dining room area. Marie called and said her group was ready to come over. The decorated cake was put out on the head table, with the vase of roses. Ellie brought candles in her purse just in case they didn't have any, and she was glad she did. When Marie came over with three girls and one boy, the place looked so beautiful!

"Oh no," Marie teased. "I think I'm in the wrong house. This house is too fancy! Where is house 25?"

JPL and Grant both took her seriously and said, "This is house 25!"

Everyone giggled and the festivities began. No big thing, just the happy birthday song, blowing out the candles, serving the cake to everyone, and the constant struggle to clean up spills and stop cake stealing. The balloon box was then dragged into the living room. While all the children followed the box there, Diane quickly cleaned up the tables and put the roses back on the refrigerator.

All the balloons were dumped out of the box at one time and then Ellie and Sarah started throwing them into the air and batting them to each other. Some of the children got into the act and started throwing balloons themselves. Others just watched. Even Lawrence was so distracted, he watched without licking his hands! Wendy wandered to a closer corner to bounce and watch at the same time. It was a lovely sight to see. Huge red balloons and a house full of children playing. Inevitably one balloon after another bit the dust and popped. Ellie, Sarah, Diane, and Marie all worked together to get up every piece of popped balloon before someone put it in their mouth. The jolliness of this one and only game lasted a good half hour.

Then Marie and her crew had to leave. "Ellie, this was the best idea house 25 had in a long time," she said before she left.

As the house quieted down, Ellie told JPL she had a present for her. Then Diane said, "JPL, listen to me. I saw the book, I mean the present. It is so nice and so special that if you don't want it, I'll take it. And I mean it! I want it!"

"No you don't," JPL said. "Where is it, where is it?"

Ellie was thoroughly satisfied with the good word Diane put in about the book. She herself wouldn't have used the same technique, but she had to admit, it seemed to be working!

JPL opened the gift and her eyes got wide. "It's about me! It has my name on it!"

And sure enough, she recognized her name, LISA, on the cover of the story, *Roses for Lisa*. Since the main character had a dozen roses, JPL actually thought it was a story about her own birthday! Even though the twelve year old girl in the story had a long brown pony tail and no bangs, and JPL had very short hair and bangs, she still insisted it was a picture of her.

Ellie read the story to JPL. She changed all the *Lisa's* in the story into *JPL's*. JPL sat right next to Ellie and Lisa Lynn crawled next to her on the other side of the couch. Angel stood in front of her the whole time, watching Ellie's face as she read aloud the story.

"ROSES FOR JPL

JPL loved flowers.

All kinds.

Daisies and marigolds and tulips.

Lilies and petunias and pansies.

But her favorite flowers were roses.

When Charles asked JPL's sister to marry him, he gave her roses.

JPL looked at them longingly. Her sister took note.

When her father gave her mother roses for Mother's Day,

JPL looked at them longingly. Her mother took note.

When her grandfather gave her grandmother roses for their anniversary,

JPL looked at them longingly. Her grandma took note.

When Aunt Esther had her first baby, Uncle Harold gave her roses.

JPL looked at them longingly. Her aunt took note.

So when JPL turned twelve years old, her sister, her mother, her grandma, and her aunt all had a great idea.

But no one told anyone else.

Finally it was JPL's birthday.

JPL got flowers.

JPL got more flowers!

And more flowers!

And more flowers!

They were all her favorite flowers—roses!

JPL got four dozen roses!

She looked at them longingly. Everyone took note.

JPL was happy."

How still JPL sat and looked at the pictures and listened. She wanted the story read again. So Ellie was happy to oblige. She wanted it read a third time. Ellie didn't complain. Then JPL wanted to hold the book, so Ellie handed it to her. JPL smelled the book. She opened each page and smelled it. She felt the smooth silky pages. She took off the dust jacket and was amazed that the exact same picture was on the book itself! She just delighted in the book. Ellie was satisfied. The day was a success.

When the children were in bed, Diane and Sarah and Ellie debriefed about the day. They relaxed as they joyfully shared their feelings and thoughts, recounting the events of the day. But some thoughts Ellie kept to herself. She had more grand ideas. Now she could start bringing in more books. Maybe she could bring in a book with pictures of all the different flowers. She could teach JPL just what a marigold and a daisy and a lily were. She could get permission to plant some flowers in the yard there. She could teach Angel how to look at a book. Since Angel liked to look at faces, she could find a book with close-ups of faces. She could teach….

Her mind drifted. She laughed to herself as she realized how many of her thoughts had to do with teaching. Was she cut out to be a teacher after all? She still didn't know. But she knew this job was a pretty good fit for her now. She knew God would guide her in her life. She knew Sarah and her family would be great friends and help her grow in her knowledge of God and His ways. And she knew she could talk to God about everything, big and small, even asking Him for the right husband for her.

"Ellie, did you doze off?" Sarah was asking her.

"Oh, sorry, I wasn't paying attention. I thought I was daydreaming, but maybe I was night-dreaming."

They all laughed.

"Were you asking me something?" Ellie asked.

"Yes," Diane said. "I wanted to know where you got that book. I want to get my own copy."

Sarah added, "I want to know too. I was actually planning to ask you the same question. I want to get one and put it in my hope chest."

"In your hope chest?" Diane asked. "What do you mean?"

"Well, I have a hope chest where I put all the things I'm saving for when I get married and have my own family. And I want this book to be in there, so that when I have my own children, I can read them this story and then tell them all about my year working at Monroe Avenue and about all of you and about JPL and her birthday and everything."

Diane just shook her head. She definitely was not making fun of Sarah. She just never heard of such a thing before. Imagine, a sixteen year old girl already thinking about saving things for her own children!

It was a new way of thinking for Ellie too. Though she never heard of such a thing before either, she was thrilled to hear Sarah's plan. She thought it was a brilliant idea. She liked how Sarah thought, and she hoped that someday she would be able to think things like that too.

Part Two: Relationships

There be three things which are too wonderful for me, yea, four which I know not: The way of an eagle in the air; the way of a serpent upon a rock; the way of a ship in the midst of the sea; and the way of a man with a maid. – *Proverbs 30:18-19*

Chapter One

ELLIE WALKED TOWARD house 25 and smiled as she saw the one lonely tulip that bloomed. It had been over a year since she hatched the plan to plant flowers and make House 25 look more like a cozy family home. She remembered her dream of teaching JPL the names of different flowers and maybe even teaching Lisa Lynn to learn colors. She pictured the scene in her mind.

"Lisa Lynn, can you show me the red flowers?" After Lisa Lynn would point to it, Ellie would say, "Very good! You're smart! Now can you point to the yellow flowers?" At which point, Lisa Lynn would point to the yellow flowers and Ellie would say, "Wow, I can't believe it. That's really great!" And Lisa Lynn would get a huge smile on her face. In the meantime, JPL would be bragging. "Of course those are red tulips, what else would they be?"

If that really happened, it would be wonderful, even though Lisa Lynn was almost ten years old and JPL was seventeen. Who knows how much the flowers would have helped stimulate the lives of these mentally challenged kids? But the impatiens Ellie planted last summer were devoured by rabbits. And so far this year, only one tulip appeared. There were no buzzing bees and no fluttering butterflies. Only rabbits!

But in the life of House 25, even the pesky rabbits were a thing to be thankful for. They had become a funny cause of fun and excitement. Whenever one of them was seen, Grant would start running around the house laughing in his silly way and saying in a high pitched scream, "Bugs Bunny! Bugs Bunny!" He acted like he was scared, then he laughed hysterically. This would cause the staff to come look out the window at the cute bunny. Eventually someone would make sure JPL and Lisa Lynn saw it. The other children were oblivious to the screams and laughter and interesting sights outside. Sometimes Angel would appear at the window with the crowd that was looking, but never seemed to grasp the concept of looking out the window. She just smiled a huge smile and stared at everybody else who was looking out the window. Even if someone tried to turn her head and encourage her to look, her eyes stayed looking at the person who was trying to help her. This was how it was at House 25. It was unique. But it was home.

March usually brought with it the hope of spring, but this year spring did not bring much hope to Ellie. She didn't even know if she'd be at her beloved House 25 when summer arrived.

Ellie was getting so attached to this house and the children that she was angry… angry at the administration. Somebody in some high-up position came up with what they thought was a brilliant new policy. They wanted to move all the children and re-arrange the houses. They wanted all the lower level children together, all the higher level children together, and a special house for the autistic, blind and deaf children. How Ellie mourned this happening. It wouldn't be like a family anymore. Higher level children couldn't act like older sisters and brothers helping the staff and the lower level children in their homes. JPL and Lisa Lynn wouldn't be in the same house anymore. They almost seemed liked sisters. How could somebody just make an executive decision and separate them so easily? If all the lower level children were together, how could somebody take a walk with them? Who would go along to help?

What would happen in a lower level house to make life interesting? Who could provide humor and conversation and bring joy and variety to a day of toileting eight children? Ellie was happy when different things occurred to delay the final implementation of the grand plan of re-shuffling the children.

Ellie talked about this to her parents and was quite surprised how her dad got so interested. He suggested that Ellie go back to school for her master's degree in special education. He told her that then she could be one of the specialists who would have input regarding the new policies. Ellie thought this was a great idea. She thought God must be putting His stamp of approval on it, because her dad was so involved. He was generally very sympathetic to her problems, but not very talkative. Ellie hardly had to think about the suggestion. Right from the start she wanted to do it. Sarah was taking classes at the university now too. That made the idea even more appealing. So Ellie was now taking one morning class each semester.

Her cousin who shared her apartment the previous year had gotten married. Since then, Ellie moved back home with her parents and her brother. This probably helped her father understand her situation better. At dinnertime on Ellie's days off, he enjoyed hearing some of the cute, funny stories involving the kids from House 25.

Ellie was a little tired today, since it was one of the days she woke up at 6 o'clock to go to her 8:45 class. Being tired made it easier to be a bit gloomy. She was glad that this was her last day of work before her two days off. As Ellie hung up her coat, she was thinking about the joys of getting to bed when she got home.

Lisa Lynn spotted Ellie before she even closed the closet door. She immediately came over so she could just hang around Ellie and follow her around. Ellie smiled and warmly hugged her little admirer.

As soon as Diane saw Ellie, she said, "Ellie, glad you're here today. We need you to go to the carnival with us."

"What?" Ellie asked, quite taken aback by this unusual comment.

Diane explained that she and Todd, the new guy working second shift, were going to the carnival after work.

"We'll be meeting Marie and her daughter there!" Diane added enthusiastically. "You never want to go out drinking with us, Ellie, but you can't say no to a carnival. We all want you to come!"

"Hmm, sounds nice. I'll think about it," Ellie replied.

"What's to think about?" Diane said. "Don't you like carnivals?"

"I used to like them," Ellie replied. "But I haven't been to one for quite a while."

"All the more reason to come," Diane said.

Ellie chuckled. She could see how much this meant to Diane. She didn't want to act with a "holier than thou" attitude. She knew she should reach out more to her co-workers. So after about a minute of ponderings, Ellie answered Diane. "Yeah, ok, I'll go."

"Hey Todd, Ellie said 'yes.'"

"Great," Todd said. "You girls can leave your cars here and we can all go together."

"Nah," Diane said. "I'll want to go straight home in my own car."

"Me too," Ellie agreed.

"Ok. We'll meet up in the parking lot."

Ellie wished Sarah was working today, but she knew Sarah had to really cut back on her volunteer hours since she started taking classes. Ellie would have loved to have Sarah's company at the carnival. But alas, there was no one for Ellie to confide in before the unexpected carnival trip took place. She was all alone in trying to sort out her feelings.

Ellie had gotten past the point of enjoying carnivals. The rides made her dizzy and it wasn't as much fun as when she was younger. Yet it seemed like the right decision to go. What she would actually do at the carnival, she did not know. Should she go on the rides? Who would she go on the rides with? What would they talk about?

Ellie went through the work day in a daze. She was nervous and very much dreading the end of the work day. She didn't have much in common with the people she worked with except for the job and the children. They'd probably think Ellie was weird if she just talked about the job.

Then she had an idea. She could sort of act like a baby sitter and friend to Marie's daughter and hang around with her. It wouldn't be all that fun, but it would be better than the other options she thought of. What if Todd asked her to go on a ride? She forced herself to stop thinking about it. She might lose her courage. Before she knew it, the work day was over.

Diane, Ellie and Todd all caravanned to the carnival in their own cars. It was a pretty cool evening and Ellie was quite surprised that the carnival was scheduled so early in the spring. But the town wanted to have a carnival to celebrate their hundredth anniversary.

There were plenty of parking spaces at 10:45 pm, and they all managed to park close to each other. As they headed to the carnival grounds, Todd asked, "Who wants to go on the Ferris wheel with me?"

Diane frowned. "Todd," she exhorted, "don't forget we have to meet up with Marie and her little girl."

"Oh sorry," Todd said.

He really seemed to be a nice guy, Ellie thought. He was gentle with the children and friendly with Ellie and the staff. But Ellie was not interested in him as a boyfriend. However, every once in a while she got the feeling that he might be interested in her that way. Ellie definitely did not want to go with him on the Ferris wheel ride.

Soon Marie came running towards them. "Hi Diane, Ellie, Todd," she said, a little out of breath. She was laughing and stumbling, maybe a little drunk, Ellie thought.

"Where's your daughter?" Ellie asked.

"Oh, we got here early and she met up with her friend's family. After going on all the rides at least twice, they decided to leave and they invited Katy to sleep overnight."

"That was nice of them," Ellie said out of mere politeness. What she really thought was, *Oh no, that's too bad.* Now there was no little girl to befriend, Marie was drunk, and Todd had asked her and Diane to go on a ride with him. Marie plopped down on a bench and seemed to want to sit down for a while.

"Well, who wants to go on the Ferris wheel with me?" Todd persisted.

"I don't really like Ferris wheels," Ellie said, "but if you and Diane go, I guess I'll try it again."

Diane laughed and they all ambled over to the rides. They all just assumed Marie would wait for them on the bench, but she followed along to the ride.

When they got in line for the Ferris wheel, all three girls were ahead of Todd. The carnival worker buckled the girls in and told Todd three was the limit per seat. Todd went by himself. Ellie was happy the way that worked out, until Marie started laughing and burping on the ride. Her burps and laughter were making Ellie feel nauseous herself. But Ellie kept laughing and tried to conceal her uncomfortableness.

After the ride, Todd was stopped by some of his friends, and Diane and Marie went to get a drink. Ellie headed for the bathroom. She was feeling very nauseous and thankfully made it to the bathroom in time. When she came out, she just stood awhile by herself. A stranger walked past and said with a thick foreign accent, "You don't look so good."

Ellie smiled and said, "Yeah I know. I'm going home." She didn't know if he understood her, but he seemed satisfied and left. Now she wondered what she should do. She was still pretty dizzy and wanted to go home, but she didn't feel like hunting down Marie and Diane and Todd. Yet she knew they would all be wondering where she was.

Pretty soon Todd spotted Ellie and trotted over to her. "What happened to you? You look so pale."

"I got too dizzy from the ride and got sick in the bathroom."

"Poor Ellie," Todd said. "Let me drive you home."

"Uh, thanks Todd, but I think if I just sit down awhile, I'll feel ok to drive myself. Can you find Diane and Marie and tell them what happened?"

"Sure, but don't leave till I get back," Todd said.

With his long legs, Todd did a super-fast jog to find Diane and Marie. He told them Ellie was sick and he was taking her home. Then he quickly reappeared at Ellie's side.

"Come on, Ellie. I'll take you home."

"But what'll happen to my car?" Ellie asked, a little too weak to resist Todd's offer.

"Just leave it here," Todd said. "I can give you a ride to pick it up tomorrow."

"Is it ok to leave it?" she asked.

"Sure, I've done it myself," Todd said. "The police know a lot of people get too drunk to drive home and they'd rather have them leave their cars here than drive them when they're drunk."

Ellie was too sick to protest, so she followed Todd to his car. She was starting to shiver. "Do you have a jacket or blanket in your car I can borrow?" she asked.

"No, sorry Ellie," Todd apologized as they climbed into the car. "But scoot close to me and I can keep you warm," he offered.

"Oh no, that's ok. I'm not so cold now that we're out of the wind," Ellie replied. She was pleased with herself for thinking of that excuse so fast.

When Ellie saw the railroad gates going down she whispered, "Lord, help me."

Todd asked her how she was feeling.

"A little better," Ellie said. She didn't want him to get closer to keep her warm or anything.

"That's good to hear. You'll be better even before you get home. I know you're a strong woman, Ellie. You're such a nice person. I really admire you."

Ellie smiled shyly, not knowing what else to do.

"Are you getting cold again?" Todd asked.

"No," Ellie said. She actually was cold, but she sure didn't want Todd to know.

"Your poor hands are shivering," Todd said and he gently grabbed the hand closest to him and lovingly rubbed it.

Ellie just gulped and looked ahead. She was never in such a predicament before.

"You have such nice small hands," Todd said. "You are very beautiful, Ellie."

"Thanks," Ellie grunted with a forced smile. He had her hand. If she pulled it away, she knew she'd hurt Todd's feelings. But she really didn't like him, at least not that way.

Help Lord, Ellie prayed silently. Then she got an idea: start talking.

"So what made you decide to work at Monroe Avenue Center, Todd?"

"I love helping people," he said, still holding her hand. "My sister-in-law works here, so when she knew they had more openings, she told me. I needed a job, I applied, and I got it."

"Oh, that's neat. Did you ever think of going into special ed?" Ellie asked.

"Not before I started working here, but now I'm thinking about it."

"What do you think about the new policy of moving all the kids to new houses soon?" Ellie asked.

"I think it'll be good," Todd said. "That way JPL can be with more kids like herself and have more friends and advance faster."

Ellie knew he was sincere in his answer, but she didn't agree with him. However, she didn't want to talk about her own ideas, so she stayed quiet about them. They talked about the kids till the train ended and finally Todd let go of Ellie's hand and started to drive again.

"Thanks so much, Todd," Ellie said as they pulled up to her house. "I really appreciate this."

"I can pick you up for work tomorrow," Todd offered.

"Uh thanks, but I'm off tomorrow and my mom can give me a ride to pick up my car," she replied.

Ellie thought she was in the clear now, but Todd grabbed her hand and kissed it before she could get out.

"Thanks again," she repeated awkwardly as she shakily scrambled out of the car.

"Bye, Ellie, see you at work in a few days. Rest up."

"Ok, bye."

Ellie was glad no one in her family was up. She got ready for bed and then thanked the Lord very, very much that she was home, safe and sound in her own bed, all covered up, safe and snug. Then she pulled the blanket over her head and said in a quietly loud whisper, "Yikes!"

The dizziness from the Ferris wheel ride wore off already, but Ellie found herself still shaking from the emotional stress and confusion. She wanted to talk to somebody, but unlike Sarah, Ellie was not used to talking to her parents about things like boyfriends. Since she was off the next day, she planned to call Sarah and see if she could come over and talk.

As Ellie's mind drifted between worry and sleep, her thoughts and prayers merged. Why couldn't it be a Godly guy like Kevin that asked her to go to the carnival? Why didn't Kevin ever tell her that he admired her? Why couldn't it be Kevin who tried to hold her hand? And what should she do at work now that Todd started to show he liked her more than just a co-worker? "Help, Lord," she said over and over. And then she let out another "Yikes!"

Chapter Two

SARAH INVITED ELLIE over for lunch. So after Ellie's mom dropped her off at the carnival to pick up her car, Ellie headed straight for Sarah's house. Only Sarah and her mother were home.

Ellie had planned to tell Sarah what happened when they were by themselves, but she just couldn't wait any longer. Besides, she trusted Sarah's mom and it seemed somehow appropriate to talk to her about things like this. After all, at the Bible Study they talked and prayed about marriage and relationship issues.

"Actually, I was intending to talk to only Sarah. But I'm so shaken up, maybe I should just start talking to both of you right now, if you don't mind," Ellie blurted out.

"Why should we mind?" Sarah's mother asked.

"I don't know. It might spoil your lunch."

"Ellie, you're family," Sarah's mom said. "Now that we know you're shaken up about something, we wouldn't be able to enjoy our lunch *until* you filled us in on what's bothering you."

"Thanks," Ellie said, and then she plunged into her story. With rapt attention, they listened to the replay of last night's drama. Sarah kept saying, "Oh no," over and over as Ellie recounted each disappointing detail of the carnival scene.

Sarah's mother was the first to respond after the whole story was told.

"I can see why you're so confused, Ellie. You don't want to hurt Todd's feelings, but you really are not interested in him. And you're wondering just how you can avoid hurting his feelings and yet let him know you're not interested."

"Yes, yes, yes," Ellie replied, so happy that she was totally understood. "And to add to the mess, I have to go back to work with him!!"

"Ellie, I think you don't realize your rights in a relationship. You know you don't have to let anybody hold your hand if you don't want them to. And you don't have to think of an excuse. You are fully justified if you tell them you don't want to hold their hand."

"Really? That's good to know," Ellie said. "But he didn't ask me. He just did it. What should I have done? What would you do, Sarah, if you were in a situation like that?"

Sarah's mother and Ellie both patiently waited for Sarah to think of her response. Finally Sarah said, "I'm glad to say it never happened to me. But I guess I would say something like, 'Um, I don't really feel right to have you hold my hand.' Well, maybe not that exactly. Wow, I don't know. I just don't know. It sure is hard to think of how to say it in a nice way."

Sarah's mom reassured the girls. "Don't be afraid of just saying it, however it comes out. You can just say that you don't want them to hold your hand. Sometimes you have to be blunt to be understood by some people, unfortunately."

After a nice talk and a very tasty lunch of chicken salad sandwiches and apple slices, Sarah's mother started clearing the table. "I know you girls probably want to talk by yourselves for a while. I'll clean up here and you two can go for a walk."

"Thanks!" they both said together and made themselves laugh as they grabbed their jackets.

"Your mom is sure easy to talk to," Ellie said.

"Yeah, I don't know what I'd do if I didn't have her to talk to. But your mom seems very nice too, Ellie."

"Oh, she is. But I never talked to her about boyfriends and things like that. You remember, don't you, that in our family, I'm used to there being things we just don't bring up, like religion?"

"Oh yeah," Sarah recalled.

"But now that it's just us, I wanted to tell you more of my thoughts. It's so frustrating that the guy I like, who we all know is Kevin, doesn't want to hold my hand or give me compliments or anything like that. But it seems like he likes me and we have so much in common."

"I know," Sarah agreed. "I think he really enjoys being with you. And when you sang that song together at the Bible Study with the beautiful harmony, it sounded heavenly."

"Thanks, Sarah. What do you think is going wrong here? Kevin graduated college, has a good job and it seems like he wants to get married, doesn't it?"

"I think so," Sarah answered in the tone of voice that conveyed her own confusion at Kevin's relationship with Ellie.

"I'm so tired of being confused, of getting my hopes up then having them dashed. I think I'll have to pray for some type of breakthrough. I really want to. If the answer is yes, let it be yes, and if it's no, let it be no."

And then Ellie added in an uncharacteristically loud voice, "I am just so tired of this nothingness. Reminds me of a crazy jump rope rhyme we used to use when I was in first grade. "Fudge, fudge, call the judge, mama's got a brand new baby, It's not a boy, it's not a girl, it's just a newborn baby…"

They both laughed. Then Sarah said, "That's some crazy rhyme, Ellie."

"Yeah," Ellie agreed. "I never really understood it because it really doesn't make sense. Not a boy and not a girl, ha! But it sure fits with this situation, doesn't it? It's not a yes and it's not a no."

"I know it's no fun wondering about that for so long, Ellie. We have to pray. Pray, pray, pray, and let's see what the next Bible Study brings," Sarah suggested.

"Yeah, we'll find out soon enough. The next one is tonight, just five hours away! I better leave so I have time to do my laundry first. Thanks so much for being here for me, Sarah."

"Oh sure, for me it's just an adventure to hear about your escapades. It's you that has the hard part of living them out!"

"Yeah, too true," Ellie agreed.

Chapter Three

ELLIE WORE A NEW PAIR OF JEANS and her favorite pink sweater to the Bible Study. She was quite happy that her hair was looking pretty nice that day. On her drive over to Sarah's house, Ellie poured out her sadness and her frustration as she prayed to God out loud. Of course it was Kevin that her prayers centered on, but now Todd was becoming a big concern too. She felt so much better after praying, yet as she parked and walked to the house she got pretty nervous again.

Sarah's family and Kevin were the only ones there so far, and it was a nice easy entrance. Sarah's younger brothers and Kevin were all talking together and all of them acted genuinely happy to see Sarah.

"Hey, Sarah," Kevin said, "I think you'd be interested in what I was just telling Sarah's family. There's going to be a Passover Seder at a local church in two weeks. Since you're Jewish, I thought you'd like to go. In fact, I thought it would be great if our whole Bible Study group could go!"

"That does sound exciting," Ellie answered. "Tell me when it is, so I can arrange to have the evening off."

"I want to go too," William said eagerly.

"Sorry, William, that will be during the week of Easter and that's when we always go to Grandma's," Mr. Kirby said.

"No!" William said, not rebelliously, but more as an exclamation of grave disappointment. "I wish the people who made our calendars didn't make Passover so close to Easter!"

"William," his father said, "Passover and Easter are sister holidays. That's why they're so close together."

"You mean they're about the same thing, like Passover is the Jewish Easter or something?" William asked.

"Sort of, but it's a little more complicated. There was a time when Passover wasn't even on the calendars because some church leaders didn't want people to celebrate it. They even persecuted people who did celebrate it," Mr. Kirby explained.

"That makes me boiling mad, Dad," William said.

Mr. Kirby told Ellie and Kevin how William hates to hear of persecuted Christians. "He really does seem to boil over in rage about it."

"Hey William," Kevin said, trying to lighten up the situation. "Boiling reminds me of the story of how boiling eggs for Easter came about."

"How?" William asked a little suspiciously.

"Don't you see, William, the Jewish people were boiling mad that Passover wasn't on the calendar. So they decided to boil some eggs. Then they decided to color them in real dark and mad colors, like black and purple and colors like that."

William laughed.

"But then it gave the people who celebrated Easter a new idea," Kevin continued. "Coloring eggs in nice light colors could be a thing for their tradition. And that's how it got started."

"Oh sure," William said, pretty convinced it was a joke, but not really certain.

Ellie normally was rubbed the wrong way by Kevin's corny humor, but this time she was ok with it. She saw that it did help cheer William up.

"Anyway, Passover will begin on April 8th, and the Seder will start at 6 p.m.," Kevin informed them all. Just then a group of two guys and three girls walked in, all arriving at the same time. Sarah's father announced that everyone was there. He suggested that Kevin make his announcement about the Passover Seder again, now that the whole group was assembled.

Although everyone seemed excited about the event, only Ellie and Kevin seemed able to go. Ellie was wondering if God was answering her prayers in this way. She and Kevin would be going to a Passover together, all by themselves! And he *seemed* happy about it.

Ellie tried to concentrate on the study, but her mind kept going back to the Passover event. However, midway into the study, something happened that changed everything. Someone knocked on the door. Sarah answered it and seemed very happy to see someone who used to come to the Bible Study before her family moved away. It was a girl named Margo.

"Look who's here!" Sarah announced.

"Margo!" some of the other girls yelled out. "What are you doing here?"

"I'm on spring break and so I came to visit my aunt and uncle for a few days," Margo replied. "I thought I'd take a ride here just for the fun of it and see if the Bible group is still meeting. I saw all those cars outside and am I right? Is it actually going on right now??"

"Yes it is, Margo," Kevin very joyfully yelled out. "It's so great to see you!" He then hugged Margo, followed by the others who were so happy to see her. Ellie just watched.

Margo was a beautiful girl, long blonde hair and all. She was smart, stylish, and very confident in her abilities to talk and socialize. She sat next to Kevin, who got another folding chair and put it in the empty space right next to his own chair. She made some great observations on the topic they were studying, very insightful and thought-provoking. Ellie remained quiet for the most part, but inside she was anything but quiet. All kinds of emotions were bubbling up within her.

After the study, there were snacks and as usual, an opportunity to play ping pong in the basement. Ellie liked ping pong. She and her brother had a table in their home and she got pretty good playing against her brother. But today it seemed that Kevin and Margo were sort of having a tournament with each other.

Sarah explained to Ellie, "Margo was a champion ping pong player here about two years ago, before her family moved away. She and Kevin used to have great matches."

"Oh," Ellie said with a smile that she definitely did not feel. She watched as she saw Kevin's face light up like she never saw before. As the last game in the round ended, with Margo winning, Kevin led Margo straight toward Ellie.

"Hey Ellie, did you get to talk to Margo yet?"

"Not yet," Ellie said. "I heard you used to come to this Bible Study a few years ago."

"Yes I did. Then I started college downstate and just came back on my breaks. But since then my whole family moved about a hundred miles north of here, to a little town called Castleton. I'm sure you never heard of it."

"No, I don't think I have," Ellie said.

"Anyway, so now I don't even get here on my breaks too often, except on rare occasions, like today, when I came to stay with my aunt and uncle for a few days."

Kevin slipped away as Margo and Ellie were talking. "So what are you majoring in at college?" Ellie asked.

"I'm a pre-pharm major."

Ellie was confused. "You mean pre-farm, like agriculture or something?"

Margo laughed. "No, I mean pre-pharmacy, with an emphasis on physiology and anatomy."

"Oh, that's a little above my comprehension. How many years will you have to go to school?"

Margo told Ellie that she didn't know if she'd just get a master's degree or go all the way for a doctorate in Pharmacy. Then Margo very politely asked Ellie if she went to college.

"I graduated with a bachelor's degree in elementary ed," Ellie said. "But I'm back in graduate school part time now, working on a master's in special education."

"That's interesting," Margo replied. "So since you're going part-time, I assume you're teaching full time."

"Not exactly teaching," Ellie confessed, a little embarrassed to admit that she was not a success at teaching. "I'm working in a residential setting with special ed kids."

"That's really neat," Margo said. "My college roommate has a sister who's special ed and she's the cutest little thing. She's really eleven years old, but she looks like she's only about seven."

"I know," Ellie agreed. "A lot of the kids I work with look so much younger than they really are."

Just then Kevin returned with a little dessert plate on which he placed one chocolate chip cookie, a piece of pineapple, and two crackers with cheese.

"Here Margo, I got this to re-fuel you so we can continue our tournament," Kevin said cheerfully.

"So you had an ulterior motive for this act of kindness?" Margo retorted playfully.

Kevin laughed a hearty laugh.

Ellie did a forced chuckle and then was rescued by little William, who asked her if she wanted to play a game of ping pong while the table was free.

"Sure," Ellie said, and left Kevin alone to talk with Margo.

"I'll be with you in just a minute," she told her little friend, "after I use the bathroom."

While in the bathroom, Ellie looked at herself in the mirror. Her hair had gone flat and now her face was all red. Poor Ellie couldn't hide her feelings too well with her sensitive skin turning red so easily whenever she felt stressed. So she brushed her hair, then touched a few drops of water on it with her hand, to take away the dry electricity. She was able to puff it up a little, which she thought made it look much better than having it flat and electric, sticking to her head and falling in her eyes. She also splashed cold water on her face, trying to take away the nervous redness. She pulled herself together with a deep breath and went out to play ping pong.

Ellie was a favorite with Sarah's younger brothers. She purposely missed some easy shots, so they could get more points. She was very insightful and made sure she won some games and let them win some games. That way they didn't think she was babying them. It was easy to see that William loved playing with Ellie.

Soon Kevin and Margo came by the table to cheer them on. Ellie pretended she was enjoying this, but actually, she couldn't wait for the game to end.

"That was great fun, William," she said. "But Margo doesn't get here too often so we better let her and Kevin continue their tournament."

William had a frown on his face indicating that he really didn't agree with Ellie's reasoning, but for some unusual reason, he didn't speak out. For that, Ellie was tremendously grateful.

Right before Margo left, Ellie overheard Kevin asking her if she would be in town on April 8 for the Passover.

"That sounds wonderful, but I'm afraid I won't be here till then," Margo replied.

"Well too bad," Kevin said. "How long will you be here?"

"Only three days," Margo said.

"How about a tennis game at the park, if the weather keeps up like this?" he asked.

"That would be fun, Kevin," Margo answered. Ellie slowly drifted away, as the conversation between Kevin and Margo continued.

What a change from her thoughts an hour ago. Now Ellie thought God was answering her prayer by saying that Kevin was not interested in her. But after Margo left, Kevin came up to Ellie and said, "So Ellie, it seems like it'll be you and me going to the Passover together."

"I hope I can go. I'm pretty sure I can get the time off," she said.

"I'll pray that you do," Kevin said sincerely.

Of all things for him to say! Now Ellie didn't know what to think!

Chapter Four

ELLIE SPENT THE FOLLOWING DAY trying to relax and catch up on homework as well as sleep. But the events of the previous two days kept interfering with each activity. The next day when she drove back to work was no different. So many thoughts were swirling around in her brain all at the same time.

Uppermost in her mind were the events involving Kevin. After many hours of thinking and re-thinking about it, she came up with a conclusion that was easy to live with. She knew Kevin was attracted to Margo, but she also knew Margo was a very popular girl wherever she went. She figured Margo probably had several guys who were good friends of hers at college. Margo probably didn't think twice about Kevin's shower of profuse attention on her. She must have been used to it. So Ellie began to feel sorry for Kevin. She didn't want him to get hurt or make a fool of himself. She was convinced nothing serious would come of his friendship with Margo. And she was equally convinced that once Kevin got to know her, Ellie, he would really, really like her. True they already knew each other a little, but only a little.

What's more, Ellie thought once she got to know Kevin, she would really, really like him. She already did, of course, but there were a few things that irritated her about him, like his corny jokes and his being carried away with his attraction to Margo. His attempts at jokes were a minor detail; she did get a little embarrassed for him whenever he made one. His attention to Margo was a bigger thing, but she liked him too much to make a big deal of this temporary attraction.

And then there was the upcoming Passover to daydream about. Ellie didn't have much brain space left to think about Todd, but she knew she better. She needed a strategy. How should she act towards him? What should she say? She didn't give herself enough time to dwell on the Todd topic, and hence, she arrived at work before any answers came into her mind.

The weather turned very balmy that day, and Ellie loved the smell of the fresh spring air. She decided she would take some of the children out for a walk as soon as she could. Maybe the fresh air and exercise would help her think of a good way to approach Todd. At the very least, it would give her a little more time before she had to interact with him much in the house.

"What a nice day it's turning out to be," she said to the staff chatting in the kitchen. "Why don't we open some windows?"

"What a novel idea! You mean winter is actually over?" Charlene, one of the new first shift workers, asked. "I think I'll stop and get some plants for my window box. Would anybody mind if I left now? All the second shift people are here already."

"I don't mind," Ellie said, "but can't you get in trouble leaving early?"

"Ellie, don't you worry your little head about me," Charlene laughed. "Nobody's gonna bite my head off for leaving twenty minutes early."

Everyone else laughed, seemingly at Ellie's expense. There was always a slight tension between first and second shift workers anyway. So Ellie didn't let their teasing bother her too much.

As she walked into the playroom, she was greeted by her second shift co-workers, Todd and Diane.

"Hi guys," Ellie said. "I think I'll take some of the kids out for a walk."

"Who do you think you'll take?" Diane asked.

As Lisa Lynn came up to shadow Ellie for the day, Ellie said, "Of course I'll have to take Lisa Lynn!" Then she hugged her little friend. "And let's see, who else should I take? Maybe Mahfta, Benton and JPL." She knew this was a big undertaking, but it was such a nice day. She wanted as many of the children as possible to be able to enjoy it. Taking JPL along would be a big help.

"JPL isn't here now," Todd said. "She's out with the group of upper level kids that she'll be moving in with soon."

"Oh," Ellie said, disappointed. "Well, maybe I better not take Mahfta if JPL can't come and help."

"Take Mahfta," Todd said. "I'll go with you. And we can take Angel and Grant too. That way Diane can stay home with Lawrence and Wendy."

"Ok great," Ellie said, trying to sound normal and casual. In reality her brain was saying: *Gulp... Todd and me on a walk together... Well, nothing like confronting the issue right away...I have to let him know sometime that I'm not interested in him, and the sooner the better...I think!?*

"First I wanted to open up some windows," Ellie said. Todd used the time to take Mahfta and Benton to the bathroom.

Even before the first shift workers left, Ellie and Todd were out walking with five of the children. They headed to the little playground in the center of the Monroe Avenue Center. None of the children really liked the swings or the slides, but it was a place to go and there were benches to sit on. Sometimes there were other children and staff out, and it was fun to visit with them or even just watch. But today Todd and Ellie had the park all to themselves.

Grant was happy just pacing back and forth, waving his hand in front of his eyes, looking up at the trees, and saying some nonsensical sentences. It sounded something like, "Whee, come out to the vision." Benton happily twisted a swing round and round and round and then let go. He was actually smart enough to move out of the way when he let go and watched the swing spin wildly around. Mahfta, Angel and Lisa Lynn were happy to just sit on the bench, after what to them seemed like a long walk. Ellie had a goofy, awkward smile on her face as she watched the children and worried about what Todd would say.

"Say Ellie," he began, without wasting much time. "I sure counted it a privilege to take you home from the carnival. It looks like you're feeling back to normal again."

"I am. Thanks, Todd. And I really appreciate your taking me home then."

"But Ellie," Todd continued, "I wanted to tell you that even if you weren't sick, I was hoping I could take you home."

"You were? What do you mean?"

"Ellie, I like you. I think it would be great to get to know you better, to do things together after work, you know?"

"Oh, thanks Todd, but I don't really like to do things that late."

"No problem," Todd said. "I totally understand. How would you like to do something next Monday? I saw on the schedule that we'll both be off."

Ellie was a fast thinker. She was able to think a bunch of thoughts and still answer Todd in a reasonably timely manner. Some of her thoughts were:

I can tell him I have classes in the morning and then plan to do something with Sarah, who I'll see at school.

But then I'd have to make excuses for all the things he asks me to do.

It's better if I just say something now to stop the whole chain of questions.

"Well, Todd, I don't think we better. I really like working with you, but I don't want to do anything outside of work."

"Ellie, I know some people don't like to date people they work with. I know it can be pretty awkward. But we'll probably be assigned to different houses soon, you know, with all the changes coming up. I know they need a lot of guys to work in the behavior home and I was already asked to consider working first shift in the boys' behavior home."

"I didn't know they offered you that job, Todd. First shift would be really nice to have. That shows they must have a high opinion of you."

"Yeah, I guess it is sort of an honor that they offered that to me. If I take the position, then maybe we can date and you don't have to feel awkward."

Now even fast-thinking Ellie was stumped. She had no idea how much Todd liked her. She didn't know what to say. Just then Mahfta started running, so Todd ran after him.

When he brought him back, they both saw that Mahfta was running toward JPL. She was walking to the park with the group of young people she would soon be moving in with.

"Hi JPL," Ellie called out.

"Hi yourself!" JPL answered sarcastically. She seemed to be acting a little more uppity, being with the higher level group.

Another boy in the group added, "Hi yourself, ape man!" All his friends laughed.

The case manager walking with them said, "That's not a nice thing to call people, Julius."

Julius said, "Hi yourself, lamp head."

The laughter of his new friends encouraged him, and the case worker just smiled and shrugged at Ellie and Todd. "This group is getting a little swell-headed," she apologized.

Ellie said, "Or maybe a little too lamp-headed."

"Good one, Ellie!" Todd laughed.

Mahfta started running again and JPL went after him immediately. But now her big sister bossiness had an edge of meanness about it. "Get back you big baby," she said as she pulled Mahfta's wrists and brought him back

"Thanks, JPL," Ellie said. "But I don't think you have to pull on Mahfta's wrists so hard. He usually comes back pretty nicely for you."

"He better if he knows what's good for him," she said, looking for the laughing support of her new friends. But they weren't paying much attention to JPL at that point.

Ellie and Todd both looked at each other with concern. "I sure hope this big switch-over doesn't happen," Ellie confided.

"Don't worry, Ellie. Everything will be ironed out as time goes on. JPL's just feeling her oats, like the old saying goes."

"I'm not so sure," Ellie said.

Ellie and Todd soon herded the children together and started walking back home. The opportunity for Ellie to tell Todd she wasn't interested in him was over.

Why did I miss this chance? Ellie chided herself. *Lord, help me to think faster. I just didn't know what to say.*

The awkwardness in the house continued all day. After baths were done and the children were in their pajamas, Diane told Todd and Ellie that someone from the administration stopped over when they were out walking. They dropped off some forms for them to fill out, with questions that would help them determine the placement of the staff when the big move took place. They all looked at the forms together.

"What type of children do you feel you are most effective with? What was the most rewarding part of your day at work today? What was the most frustrating part of your day at work today?"

"Pretty interesting questions," Ellie said.

"Interesting?!" Diane exclaimed. "They want us to write an essay for each one? I don't like these questions. I wish it was multiple choice."

"I like them," Ellie said. "I'd rather write out my own answers and be able to explain myself better."

Todd surprised Diane with quite an unusual response. "I just want to make sure my answers are different from Ellie's. We don't want to be assigned to the same house."

"Ok?…" Diane said, in a questioning tone, hinting that she wanted to hear more of an explanation, but none was offered.

Ellie's heart sank a little. She realized Todd was assuming she would go out with him as soon as they were assigned to different houses.

When the children were bedded down for the night, Ellie, Todd and Diane filled out their forms. Then the night shift arrived and the very long day was over. Ellie was so glad Todd's car was in the shop and his brother came to pick him up. What a great rescue from what would have been a very awkward walk to the staff parking lot.

Chapter Five

ELLIE ARRIVED AT WORK the next day determined to tell Todd how she felt. In fact, she even practiced what she'd say *out loud* as she was driving to work.

"Todd, I don't mind if they assign us to the same house. You're very good with the kids and you're a great co-worker. It's just that I don't want to go out on a date, because I only believe in dating a fellow Christian."

At least the upcoming move had one point in its favor. It gave Ellie a good way to make her views known to Todd, without hurting his feelings too much. It was true what she said, she thought, because Todd was really a good co-worker. As Ellie stepped out of her car, there was Todd parking his car. *Yay,* Ellie thought, and walked over to wait for Todd.

Unfortunately, seeing Ellie waiting for him raised Todd's hopes so much he smiled hugely. *Oh no,* Ellie thought. *Lord, help me.*

"Hi Ellie, thanks for waiting for me. You look so bright and fresh today."

"Thanks, Todd. Glad you got your car back."

"Yeah me too," Todd said.

"Hey Todd, about working in the same house together, I wouldn't mind if we got assigned to the same house, cause you're really a good co-worker and I enjoy working with you. But I just don't want to date because I only want to date somebody who's a Christian." Ellie couldn't believe she said it already! And just like she practiced!

"A Christian?" Todd asked. "Well guess what? I *am* a Christian, even though I know I don't act like it sometimes."

"You are?" Ellie asked. "Um, I wonder what you mean by 'Christian.'"

Now Todd was confused. "What do you mean *what do I mean about it?*"

Ellie tried to explain. "I mean, well, are you a Christian because you were raised that way, or because you were born again at one time or what?"

Todd answered, "I'm a regular American Protestant who goes to church a few times a year. I believe in God and I try to do what's right. But I'm honest and I admit I don't live up to all I should do, but I keep trying."

"Hmm," Ellie commented.

"What do you mean *hmmm*?" Todd asked.

"I mean it's pretty interesting to hear about your religious views. But it makes me think of a lot more questions. I guess we can continue this conversation later," Ellie suggested as they walked to the door of House 25.

Todd didn't take the hint. He kept talking as they walked in. "Well let me ask you a question. What kind of a Christian are *you*?"

Poor Ellie was quite embarrassed to be asked this question by Todd as they passed through the kitchen where two of the first shift workers were standing. As they made their way to the closet to hang up their coats, Lisa Lynn came up to get her greeting and hug from Ellie. That effectively stopped the conversation for a time and was a big relief to Ellie.

As the first shift workers left, the telephone rang. It was a recorded message sent to each house reminding the staff that the Exercise with Zany Zach show would be shown at 3 o'clock. Ellie liked the center's new TV policy. They had their own station from which they piped in different shows for the children, usually one a day but sometimes two. Often the shows would be shown in the late morning during first shift, so when there was a showing during second shift, it was a real treat. Ellie thought that would be a great time to finish her conversation with Todd. Only the two of them were working today and it would be the perfect time to get this over with.

At 3 o'clock the children were all seated, standing or pacing around in the living room. Only two of the children could understand what

Zany Zach was saying, but two or three more actually looked like they were watching. Angel, as usual, was just gazing at Ellie or Todd as the show came on. The usual corny host of the show, Zany Zach, didn't grate on Ellie's nerves as much as usual today. In fact, she was very grateful for his jolly voice, corny antics and lively music. Ellie and Todd sat in the adjoining dining room where they could see the kids, but still talk privately.

"So should we continue our conversation now, Todd?" Ellie asked.

"Yeah, so what kind of a Christian are you, Ellie? You don't seem like a fanatic to me."

"Well, I'm a born again Christian. Did you ever hear of that?" Ellie asked.

"Sure I heard of it, but I don't know exactly what it means," Todd replied.

"Well, I think it basically means that if a person was born into a Christian family and maybe baptized as a baby, it doesn't really count unless he makes the decision on his own to follow Christ."

"So is that what describes you? You were born into a Christian family and then decided on your own to follow Christ?" Todd asked.

"Well, not exactly. My father is Jewish and my mother is from a Christian family but neither of them ever really practiced their faith. So I was raised in a home where we didn't talk about religion too much. My father did go to the synagogue on Yom Kippur sometimes, and we celebrated Passover with another family several different years. My mother took us to her church on Christmas and Easter. And that was the extent of our family's religion until I was in high school. Then my parents enrolled me in a Unitarian Sunday School so I could find out about the world's religions."

"Interesting background, Ellie!" Todd seemed impressed. "So at the Unitarian Sunday School did you decide to pick the Christian religion out of all the religions in the world?"

"Actually, the Unitarian experience didn't help me very much at all in figuring things out. It was when I met Sarah and started talking to her that I found out what I was searching for all my life." Ellie was looking down as she explained this, as it seemed too intimate to explain such deep things while looking into Todd's eyes.

"Sarah?" Todd asked. "You mean the Sarah who volunteers here?"

"Yep, that's the Sarah."

"So are you saying you won't go out with somebody unless he's what you call a born-again Christian?" Todd asked.

"Yeah, I guess that's what I mean."

"So if I decide on my own to accept Christ and stay in the Christian religion, then I'll be born again and then you'd be able to go out with me?" Todd concluded as a question.

"Well yes and no. First of all, it involves a lot more than just a quick decision or some quick words. You really have to be sincere and really want to know God and really believe that Jesus died for your sins and rose again and is alive now. So if somebody did that, then yes, I would be able to go out with them if I wanted to."

"So how would I find out more about this if I was *sincerely* interested in knowing more?" Todd asked, emphasizing the word *sincerely*.

Ellie wasn't sure if he was playing around with her and pretending to be sincere or if he really was. "Well, you can come to the Bible Study I go to. It's at Sarah's house and her father leads it."

"Sounds really interesting," Todd said. "Do you still go to it?"

"I try to, whenever I can. It's in the evening, so sometimes I'm working here and can't go. But I can write down the address and the dates of the next few meetings for you if you're interested."

"I am interested," Todd said.

"That's great," Ellie said, though she didn't feel as enthusiastic about it as she let on to Todd. "But there's one more thing I think I should tell you. I'm not going out with anybody now, but I *am* interested in somebody. We're good friends and I don't know where it will lead, but since you asked me out, I think you deserve for me to be honest with you."

"Ho ho," Todd said, putting the accent on the second *ho*. "So there's another guy. Ha, the mystery is solved. Ellie has another guy she's interested in. Well," he paused for a teasing effect, "I guess that then, *if* I ever do show up at the Bible Study, you'll know it's not just because of you. It would show that I'm really *sincere* about it."

Ellie laughed. "Yeah, I guess so," she agreed.

The rest of the day was a little awkward, but not too bad. Ellie was definitely tired when she got home. In fact, she started feeling scratchiness in her throat.

Chapter Six

BY THE TIME Ellie woke up, she had a full-fledged sore throat. She hated sore throats, but was grateful she had a good excuse to stay home from work. She slept, she read, she gargled, she drank tea, and she ate her mother's comforting and delicious chicken soup. She tried not to think about work or about Todd, but she was not successful. After two days off, Ellie felt well enough to go back to work.

She couldn't remember if it was Todd's day off, but she hoped it was. When she pulled into the parking lot, though, she saw Todd's car. Then she saw House 25 with a boarded up window. Her curiosity got the better of her, and she hurried herself into the house.

"What happened?" Ellie asked as she rushed in.

"Grant went off yesterday," Diane said, "and he's acting weird again today. Be on guard."

As Ellie went to hang up her coat, Lisa Lynn ran up to her and hugged her.

Then Benton came close laughing and twisting a T-shirt with fast spastic movements. He was glad to see Ellie, which she understood by his laughter and coming close.

Out of the corner of her eye, Ellie saw Grant running wildly around the playroom. Soon he came into the living room and started making sounds like a jungle monkey. Todd decided to rein him in with a harsh command. "Grant, sit down and be still!" Then he added a couple of curse words.

Ellie knew Grant didn't react well to harshness, so she moved out of the room with the three children that were nearby. As soon as they moved away, Grant ran to the dining room and put his fist through another window. Todd jumped on him and asked for help to hold him down. Diane ran in from the kitchen and sat on Grant's legs.

Ellie just watched, then rounded up all the other children and went into the playroom and closed the door. She happened to see the expression on Todd's face when he tackled Grant. It was fierce. She didn't know he had that in him. She thought he was so gentle with the kids. Yes, she knew the situation was serious and called for quick action. But the look on his face was so different, so weird, so out of character, or so it seemed. It was like he was enjoying this new role of fierce, aggressive hero. It was a sobering moment for Ellie. It kind of scared her to see Todd like that.

Suddenly her feelings changed. Instead of feeling so sorry about her role in hurting Todd's feelings, she felt justified in not liking him. She remembered what her father told her once. He didn't talk much, but sometimes he said things that were really profound and helped her in her life. She didn't remember what triggered this comment, but she remembered her father saying that you can't really know what a person is like until you've seen them in a lot of different situations. That was so true. This was a new side of Todd that she never suspected before. That look on Todd's face and the curse words…she wondered if Todd was angry with her and taking it out on the kids. Then Ellie started wondering how Kevin would have handled that situation with Grant.

Soon the nurse came and gave Grant an injection to calm him down. She treated his hand that went through the glass window, which thankfully just had minor wounds. Grant became pretty dozy for the rest of the day. In less than an hour after the window was broken, the maintenance man came and boarded it up. And two hours after the incident, Grant was being moved to House 18, the "behavior" house. House 18 was beginning to be home to a group of older boys who had various outbreaks of destructive behavior. The change was starting to happen. Ellie was sad about that, yet glad for the immediate benefits of Grant being gone and the other children being safer.

Another unexpected benefit to Ellie was that the administration transferred Todd to House 18. They needed more men for the second shift and they greatly prized having someone on staff who already knew Grant. Todd and Grant left together that very afternoon. Ellie felt a little guilty about feeling happy that such a bad thing happened. But she couldn't deny that that's how she felt, happy and relieved.

Everyone was a bit shaken up at House 25 that day, children and staff alike. Any little thing that happened at supper that day made Ellie and Diane a bit slap happy, as kind of a relief from the stress. Mahfta walked up to Angel and took a hamburger right out of her hand as she was about to put it in her mouth. She swung wildly with her hands, as was her usual custom when afraid or upset, and knocked the hamburger out of Mahfta's hands. It landed on the floor where Benton picked it up and ate it. Ellie and Diane both had to force themselves to stop laughing and get the children in order once again.

Hamburgers, oven fries, corn, and lettuce and tomato salad were followed by angel food cake for dessert. Kitchen clean-up and bath-time were followed by an hour or two of calmness and then the night shift came on duty. Ellie headed home.

Chapter Seven

IT HAD BEEN an exhausting day, physically as well as emotionally. Ellie slept well that night. Her mother had to wake her up the next morning when a phone call came in from Mr. Pulanski, the assistant director of the Monroe Ave. homes.

"Hello Ellie, sorry to call you so early."

"Oh, that's ok," Ellie said a little uncertainly.

"I wanted to tell you that the board made a decision to move the children from House 25 to their new locations today. Since Grant is already transferred to the behavior house, and since JPL is well-prepared to move to her new higher level house, we decided to move the other six today as well."

"Oh, that's a surprise," Ellie said.

"Yes, it happened a bit suddenly for your house, I guess. But it's all for the good of the children you know. Don't you agree?"

"To tell you the truth, I'm not a big supporter of this move. I really liked when each house had different levels of children and it was more like a real family," Ellie boldly shared.

"I hear you," Mr. Pulanski said. "But I'm sure you can see there were some pitfalls too. You were there when Grant went off, I believe."

"Yes I was. I saw it happen. And I do realize it was a dangerous situation for most of the other younger and less mobile kids," Ellie conceded.

"I'm glad you can see that," he said. "Anyway, with your background in elementary education and also with your current pursuit of a special ed degree, we want to make you a shift leader in one of the homes. You'll be transferred to House 10. The children there will be a bit lower in their abilities and they can use your expertise."

"Oh," Ellie said. "Should I go to House 10 today then?"

"Yes, the children will be moved on the morning shift and by afternoon House 25 will have its new residents living there."

"Oh, ok," Ellie said. "It'll be hard to get used to, but I suppose it might be harder for the children themselves."

"Maybe," he said, "or maybe not. It might actually be harder on the staff. These kids get to know so many different staff members on all three different shifts, you know. This happens for them year after year, and soon they get used to changes. You'll be surprised that many of them will seem unaffected. But I know some will feel it more than others."

"I guess so," Ellie said.

"Well, Ellie, I know you can be a big help in this situation. We're counting on you to lead the way in House 10."

Ellie chuckled and said thanks. But as soon as she was off the phone, she muttered, "Oh brother!"

Ellie's brother happened to hear her and said, "Did I detect a call of distress going out to your very helpful brother?"

"No," she said. "But guess what? The big move is actually starting to happen. The kids will be moving to their new houses this very morning."

"Too bad, Ellie. I think they should have taken your advice and left things as they were."

"So do I," Ellie said. "And guess what else? They made me a shift leader in a house with kids who are a little bit of a lower level. I wonder what that means."

"I think we both know what it means. Too bad, Ellie."

"Yeah, too bad."

Chapter Eight

THE FIRST THING Ellie checked at House 10 was the new schedule. She breathed a sigh of relief when she saw that she would still be off on April 8, Passover!

Her two co-workers seemed nice enough, but it was still hard to leave her old group. And meeting the new children made it harder still. Most of them were teen-agers who weren't fully toilet-trained. Most of them were not that pleasing to look at. But she remembered how Mahfta and Lawrence were also hard to love at first, and then they grew on her.

Yet her first toileting experience in this new house almost turned her stomach. Barbara was a teenager with short dark hair. She could have been cute if she had an expression on her face other than just a glassy stare. She was in the middle of her menstrual cycle and when Ellie checked on her progress in the bathroom, she saw Barbara's long, dirty fingernails filled with the blood she was clawing on her sanitary napkin. Ellie helped Barbara to wipe herself and then brought her straight to the sink where she tried to wash her hands and scrub her fingernails. There was no fingernail scrub-brush around, but at least Ellie got Barbara to claw into the bar of soap and swish her hands in a sink full of warm water. Barbara was resistant to all this and she didn't display any emotion, which made it even harder for Ellie to warm up to her.

There were two cute little boys, little in size at least, though in age they were also teenagers. Ellie wondered if it was easier to warm up to them because they were smaller and cuter than the others, or because they did show a little emotional reaction to various encounters throughout the day.

Ellie loved to take the children outside for walks, largely because she herself liked going for walks, so she thought they would like it too. She took Barbara and the two boys out. Today, however, she had another motive for taking the kids outside. She was hoping she might run into somebody from House 25, like perhaps Lisa Lynn or JPL or Benton.

Soon she spotted another group walking, and she recognized Angel. Angel seemed to be the highest level girl in that group and thus was given a lot of attention. Ellie thought that just maybe the move would be a good thing for Angel.

"Hi Angel," Ellie called out. Angel looked and saw her and starting running toward her.

"Come back, Angel," her new caregiver called. But Angel didn't listen. She ran to Ellie and just stood there smiling.

"Sorry," Ellie said to the guy who was taking care of her.

"No problem," he said. "I guess you two know each other."

"Yes. Today is my first day in a new house and I guess it's Angel's first day in your house too," she added. "Do you have any of your old kids in your new house?"

"I'm happy to say that I do. I actually know three of the kids."

"That's nice," Ellie said. "In my house all the kids are new to me."

"That's rough," the new guy said. "But it looks like your kids are getting impatient and so are mine."

"You're right. I better go," Ellie said, as they both took off again in different directions. "Bye Angel!" she called out as she left.

Liz and Bob, Ellie's new co-workers, already knew each other. They had worked together in one of the houses before, and actually knew two of the new children. They seemed quite easy to get along with and did their jobs well, which involved cleaning the house after the children were in bed. In fact, they worked amazingly efficiently. They worked together cleaning the back bathroom and then stayed there to talk. When they came out, they both seemed a little giddy and more relaxed. Ellie wondered if they were doing drugs or something. She was pretty innocent about things like that. So she just enjoyed their happy-go-lucky banter until the night shift person came on duty.

Chapter Nine

GOING TO WORK the following day was a different feeling for Ellie. She used to like her job. Today she wasn't so sure. She went on her regular morning prayer walk, since she had no early morning classes. She prayed about the job and she prayed about the Passover coming up with Kevin. Tomorrow was already April 8!

As she began packing her lunch, which would really be her supper meal at about 6 o'clock, her telephone rang. It was Kevin!

"Hi Ellie, busy now?"

"Just packing my lunch and getting ready for work," she said.

"Well, glad I caught you. I thought we'd figure out what time we should leave tomorrow. The Passover Seder starts at 6, and they say not to be late. So I figured if I pick you up at 5 that should put us there by 5:30. How does that sound?"

"Sounds good," Ellie said. "You can either come in to meet my family, or else I can just be watching for you and come out when I see you pull up."

"Oh, I'll come to your door. Maybe I can meet your brother. Maybe I can convince him to come to the Bible Study sometime."

"That would be nice," Ellie said. "So I guess I'll see you about 5 tomorrow."

"Yeah, and have a good day at work today," he said.

And that was that. Kevin would actually be coming to her door to pick her up! That would be a first. The first guy that ever picked her up, the first guy that ever came to her door, and more importantly, the first guy she ever really liked.

After the phone call, Ellie was more light-hearted than she had been before the phone call. Now work didn't seem so bad. More interesting things might happen today and then she'd be able to share them with Kevin the next day.

So Ellie went off to work in a surprisingly happy state of mind. She almost pulled into the House 25 parking lot. Her driving was sort of on automatic pilot while she daydreamed of different conversations she could have with Kevin the next day. As she re-oriented herself to her new surroundings, she found the House 10 parking lot.

Today was Bob's day off, so she and Liz were responsible for all eight children. They divided them up and Ellie got Johnny. She hadn't dealt much with tall Johnny the day before. It was mostly Bob who took care of him.

Johnny was the most baby-like of all the children. His mentality might have been less than a one year old. With very handsome natural features, Johnny could have been an attractive teen-ager, were it not for the strangeness of his expressionless face. He had well set brown eyes, thick brown hair, a fine sized nose and mouth, and a slender yet seemingly strong body. But from the look on his face you could tell that he did not comprehend much of anything. He had a continual smile which conveyed more of a feeling of blankness rather than happiness. That look on someone in the prime years of life made him look very unusual.

Ellie wondered how many of these children could have been in better shape had they had more loving, consistent care when they were younger. True, their minds might never have reached beyond the toddler stage of understanding. But perhaps their demeanors would have been different, friendlier, happier, and more cooperative.

Annette and Kathy were also in the new house. Kathy had Downs Syndrome, was a bit chubby, and had a hint of a smile on her face, not much, just a hint. Annette on the other hand had an almost constant frown. Neither of them talked. Actually none of the children in house 10 talked. The autistic boy used a little sign language for simple things. At least that was what Ellie was told. But she never did see much more than a little sign asking for more dessert once in a while.

There weren't a lot of gross toileting episodes that second day, but the day was still hard to get through. It was long and dull and very discouraging. Ellie and Liz talked about the mistake they thought the administration made in switching the children around like that. It was fun talking once the children were in bed. After a while they both started to clean the various bathrooms. And once again, when Liz came out from the back bathroom, she acted more silly and dreamy, and Ellie just couldn't get back into any good conversations with her. Ellie really suspected that Liz was taking or smoking some sort of drugs. She did smell an unusual smell. She'd have to ask her brother what marijuana smelled like and what the signs were of someone smoking it. Of all situations for Ellie to be in, being the shift leader when something like that was going on!

Chapter Ten

IT WAS APRIL 8, her day off. The morning began as an overcast, gloomy day with a light drizzle. It should have been an easy morning to sleep in, and Ellie wished she could have. But her mind was too active to lull back to sleep. Problems at work seemed far away right now. All her thoughts centered on Passover. She knew she'd be up late on this first night of Passover, so she tried keeping her eyes closed for a while yet. But she finally gave in and got up.

As she walked into the kitchen to start some water boiling for her tea, she saw Daniel. He smiled and said, "Today's the day."

He knew and she knew that he knew, but both of them knew she didn't really want to talk about it much. Ellie was thankful for Daniel's kindness. He seemed like he was really trying to restrain himself these days from teasing her so much. Her father was getting ready to leave for work and he knew a little, but not as much as Daniel. So he said, "Ellie, today your boyfriend's taking you to a Passover Seder at some church, right?"

"Yeah, but he's just a friend, Daddy, not a boyfriend."

"Well he's a friend and he's a boy, so in my book that equals boyfriend."

Ellie chuckled a little and knew that would be the end of it. She was glad, at times like this, that her father was not much of a talker.

Ellie decided to wash her hair in the afternoon instead of in the morning, since it looked best right after it was washed.

The morning and afternoon went by ever so slowly, but finally 3 o'clock came and Ellie began to get ready. She liked to seem very natural, fresh and spontaneous, but to get this effect took a lot of planning. Since Kevin planned to pick her up at 5, she decided to wash her hair at 3. Then she could let it dry naturally and by 4:30 it should be perfect. The only thing she didn't plan on was that her nylon would get a run as she was putting it on, and she wouldn't be able to find her other pair. The run was a small one just ever so slightly below the knee. If she wore a skirt that was slightly longer than the one she planned to wear, she knew she would be safe. But that was stressful. She had carefully planned out what she would wear and now it was back to square one, with just a half hour to go. She finally picked out an orchid colored blouse and a navy blue and orchid patterned skirt. It seemed nice and springy in color and appropriate for the Passover-Easter season. Daniel used to tell her that the color of the blouse reminded him of an Easter egg.

At last she was dressed and ready to go. Even her hair turned out perfectly. In ten minutes, Kevin would arrive. She sat down on the couch and picked up the Bible to find some verse to calm her down. She read through some psalms, but when it was 5:15, she could hardly concentrate.

Her mother was in the kitchen preparing dinner for the rest of the family. Ellie could tell how excited her mom was to meet Kevin, because she wore some of her nicer clothes and her hair was freshly brushed and all in place. The phone rang and soon Ellie's mother called out, "Ellie, Kevin's on the phone."

Oh no, Ellie thought to herself. *He's not even on his way yet!*

"Hi Ellie. I'm sorry I'll be a little late. I started working on a new project at work and I completely forgot about Passover tonight."

"Oh no," Ellie said, forcing herself to laugh lightly.

"I know, pretty scatter-brained of me. I think I can be at your house at about 10 to 6. Would you be able to watch for me and come out to the car?"

"Sure, no problem. See you then."

Ellie's frame of mind made a quick return to reality, though she had to briefly pass through a short dark valley of disappointment before she got there. *How could he forget about the Passover dinner tonight when it was his own idea! How could he think so little of me as to make me late for this big event that I was so looking forward to!* But she couldn't afford to think such negative thoughts for long. She had a Passover to go to.

One good effect of Kevin's forgetfulness was that now Ellie didn't have to pretend to be cool and collected because she really wasn't so nervous any more. Now she didn't have to try to cover up her infatuation with Kevin because now she wasn't so infatuated. She was temporarily quite upset. As she saw Kevin's weaknesses more clearly, she could tell that they did bother her.

Though she was frustrated with Kevin's absent-mindedness, she knew Kevin was still a nice person and more than that, a godly man. She didn't exactly know what she would say or whether or not she'd be honest with him. After all, she didn't really want to make him feel bad. Yet somehow she knew she would be able to communicate with him better than ever before. She knew she could be more of her real genuine self and not be walking on eggshells trying to be who she thought Kevin might like her to be.

Her father and brother both got home before Kevin arrived. "What are you still doing at home?" Daniel asked.

"Oh, Kevin was delayed at work, so he's on his way now," Ellie replied, trying to sound unaffected. She chose not to tell anyone yet that it was Kevin's own forgetfulness that caused the delay.

Soon she saw Kevin's white car pull up to her house. "He's here. Bye. See you later."

The whole family came to the door and waved to Kevin and Ellie as they pulled away.

Chapter Eleven

ELLIE AND KEVIN arrived about twenty minutes late. They had to park two blocks away. As they got within a half block of the congregation, they started hearing the music. It was joyful and exciting. It sounded like horns, guitars and some keyboard. They walked fast, both of them quite excited but not saying much. When they got inside, they heard the music coming from the basement area, so that's where they headed.

The tables were pretty much full already. Kevin saw the older couple who told him about this event, but there was just one empty seat at their table. Finally Ellie spotted a table with two empty seats. Ellie was sad that they probably missed a lot of the music. She was thankful, though, that with everybody still singing, no one paid too much attention to two people arriving late. The table with the two seats had mostly young people in their twenties like themselves. They were welcomed with smiles and song sheets. When the music ended, the rabbi or pastor or whoever the leader was, began to speak. The clarinet player walked over to their table and politely began to remove his clarinet case from the floor next to Kevin's chair. Kevin realized that one of these "empty" seats was really his.

"Oh, I'm sorry. I must have taken your seat."

"No problem," Ben said. "You can stay here. I'll find another seat."

"No, I don't want to make you do that," Kevin said. "I'll find another seat. Ellie, you don't mind, do you?"

Ellie wondered what she was supposed to say. Of course she minded. No matter how nice these people were, they were strangers. What she ended up saying was, "Sure, that's fine."

Meanwhile Ben insisted that Kevin stay there and he would find another seat. Ellie hoped Kevin would accept this kind gesture. But unfortunately, Kevin out-insisted him.

Just then a kind lady, watching the little scene, brought up an extra chair and said, "I think there's enough room here for all of you young people to stay together."

Now Ellie was seated right between Kevin and Ben. She was a bit preoccupied with her own thoughts for the next several minutes. She couldn't fully digest all the wonderful explanations of what the Passover elements meant and how they pointed to Jesus. But the music took her out of her own little mental games. At every important juncture in the Passover Seder, there was another song. Ben would get up and join the musicians and they would play a song like *Passover Lamb*. The songs were amazing. The words and the melody matched the emotions so accurately, they actually brought tears to Ellie's eyes. The way the young people sang the songs reminded her so much of the Bible Study Group at Sarah's house. These were real, genuine, from-the-heart Christians.

Before the meal, which happened right in the middle of the whole Passover experience, the pastor gave an explanation of Messianic Judaism. She never heard that word before. She knew about Orthodox, Conservative and Reform, but not Messianic Judaism. The pastor explained that Messianic Jews were Jews who believed in Jesus the Messiah, or Yeshua, which was His name in Hebrew. He said that Jews who believe in Jesus aren't some aberration. They aren't turncoats who rejected Judaism and converted to Christianity. They are still Jews, Jews who have found their Messiah. He said it was totally Jewish to believe in Jesus. After all, Jesus was Jewish, and He fulfills all the prophecies pointing to the Messiah in the Old Testament or Hebrew Scriptures.

Now Ellie wondered if that's what she was. She was Jewish and she believed in Jesus. Did that mean she was a Messianic Jew? It was an exhilarating thought, but new and strange. Ben seemed very impressed that Ellie was Jewish and he invited her and Kevin to come to one of their regular Sabbath services the following Saturday morning.

Ellie's first thought was, *That would be fun. Another opportunity to do something with Kevin!* Almost immediately she realized that wasn't a good reason for going. She actually was very curious to find out what a Messianic Jewish service would be like.

"Thanks for the invite," Kevin said. "We'll think about it. What do you say, Ellie?"

"I'd really like to go," were the words that seemed to pop out of Ellie spontaneously. Though Ellie had to be at work at 2 o'clock on Saturday, she knew she'd have the whole morning free.

"Well, maybe you'll see us here in a few days," Kevin told Ben.

When the meal was over the pastor started explaining the next event of the Seder. The children were informed that the time had come for them to search for the hidden matzah. How interesting that explanation was! Just like Jesus was wrapped in a clean white linen cloth and buried, so was this matzah. The matzah was wrapped in a white linen napkin and then hidden, which was sort of like burying it. Then it was sort of "resurrected" by being found by the children. Each table had their own hidden matzah and each child that found it was given a reward. One of the guys at Ellie's table hid the matzah in his girlfriend's purse, letting it stick up a little so it could be seen. The kids were very animated and fun to watch. After it was found, this matzah, which represented Jesus, was used as part of the communion.

It was amazing to Ellie. She said out loud, "Amazing! I can't believe it!"

"What do you mean?" Kevin asked.

"I've been to Passovers before and we did these same things and it all seemed kind of weird. But now it makes sense! All these things do point to Jesus! Incredible!"

Ben heard the exchange and was super excited at Ellie's realization.

"Yeah me too," he shared. "We used to go to Passover at a friend of ours home when I was young and none of it made sense to me. But now I love it! This is my third Passover as a Messianic Jew and every year it seems I learn something new."

"So what did you learn this year?" Ellie asked.

"Let's see. I learned that this table can seat more than eight people very comfortably."

Ellie laughed. She really liked this group of people.

At the end of the Passover Seder, Ben joined the other musicians again. They played such lively Jewish melodies that many of the people got up to dance. They did circle dances, like the hora. It looked like so much fun, but Ellie was afraid to join in. Kevin was always adventurous though, and when he insisted that they try, Ellie was easily persuaded. It took her a while to catch on to the steps, but it took Kevin an even longer while. Kevin stepped on her toes a couple of times, but she didn't mind. She didn't remember when she had this much fun. It was like experiencing spiritual joy in a real, physical way, as Ellie described it to Sarah a few days later.

Soon all the festivities were over. Ben walked both Ellie and Kevin to the door and gave each of them a brotherly hug. Ellie thought that was so nice of him. When she commented on the beautiful bright night, Ben told her that Passover is always on the evening of the full moon. So many new things Ellie found out about Passover that night!

As she and Kevin drove home, they discussed their plans to go to the Saturday morning service in a few days. Kevin offered to pick Ellie up, but Ellie told him she had to work that day so she should probably drive herself. She hoped Kevin would offer to drive her anyway and then drive her to her job, but he didn't. Ellie didn't let this bother her tonight. She was still on a spiritual/emotional high after the wonderful Passover Seder.

Chapter Twelve

THE FOLLOWING MORNING before Daniel left for school, he stopped to talk to Ellie.

"So how was the Passover? Did you and Kevin have a great time or what?"

"It was wonderful, Daniel. Remember all those things that seemed so weird to us whenever we went with Dad to his cousin's house for Passover? Well, they did all those same things, but they explained them so well. They all point to Jesus. It made so much sense. It was so neat! And then there was the dancing and music!"

"Dancing? What kind of dancing?" Daniel wondered.

Ellie explained a little more and then told her brother that she and Kevin would be going back to the Sabbath service on Saturday morning.

"Wow Ellie. You're buying into this thing hook, line and sinker! Is Kevin picking you up again?"

"He offered to, but I have to go to work after the service, so I told him I better drive," Ellie told him, with her disappointment showing through.

"I'm free on Saturday. Why don't you let Kevin pick you up and then I can pick you up from that church or whatever it's called and take you to work?" Daniel offered.

"Really?!" Ellie asked. "Umm, sure, ok, thanks."

And that's why Kevin pulled up to Ellie's house at 10 in the morning on Saturday. He actually came to the door and rang the doorbell. Ellie's mother and father said hi and wished them a good time. Daniel was still asleep.

They had an easy time talking in the car that morning. "This should be fascinating," Ellie said. "I wonder how a Messianic Jewish service will be different from a church service or a synagogue service."

"I know. I'm quite curious myself. Pastor Weisman gave such a good explanation at Passover; I think it'll be neat to hear him preach."

"I agree," Ellie said. "I don't know if he's called a Pastor or a Rabbi. I heard people call him both. I'm really looking forward to hearing the music again. It was so joyful the other night, not exactly like hymns or contemporary Christian choruses."

"I liked it too. How would you describe the music, Ellie?"

"I'd say it was an odd blend of joyful lively songs, yet in a minor key," Ellie answered.

"Good description," he agreed.

They arrived five minutes before the service started. And they were not disappointed. The music and the preaching were all they had hoped for, maybe more. Ellie was fascinated to hear the Old Testament explained in such a way that made sense to her for the first time in her life.

After the service Ben joined them and invited them to stay for the oneg.

"What's an oneg?" Kevin asked.

"That's a Jewish word that refers to a meal or treats on the Sabbath. Come on down to the basement and see for yourselves."

They went down and were welcomed by some of the other young people they met at their Passover table. They got some food and joined them.

The conversation was stimulating, but soon one of the guys challenged Kevin to a ping pong match. Kevin couldn't resist these challenges, so off he went. Ellie was left talking with Ben and two other girls.

Ellie had to leave earlier than the others to get to work on time. Her brother was probably on his way to pick her up. She said good bye to

Kevin, who very pleasantly wished her a wonderful day at work, then went on playing ping pong. Ben walked her up the stairs to the door of the building.

"Do you go to another congregation on Sundays, Ellie?" Ben asked.

"No, not really. I've been visiting a few different churches with some friends from my Bible Study group, but haven't gone anywhere regularly, if that's what you mean."

"Well, I'd like to invite you to consider coming to Broken Wall regularly," Ben said.

"Thanks. I'll think about it."

"Do you like it here or is there anything that makes you hesitate to come back?" Ben asked.

"No, I really like it here," Ellie replied. "The music is great, it seems like it's from the heart. It's neat to hear a clarinet in the group. It seems like it goes deeper than the traditional organ and guitar, if you know what I mean. I mean I like the Christian songs we do at our Bible Study, but some of them are kind of um, I don't know how to describe it."

Ellie was impressed that Ben didn't lose patience with her. He waited, looking quite interested. So she continued. "Well, some of the hymns are good, but so sort of syrupy, sugar sweet, like high ideals but hard to mean them from the heart. Do you know what I mean?"

"I think so," Ben said.

"But this Jewish music, like 'I cried unto the Lord with my voice' or that other song 'I love the Lord cause he hears my voice' they're kind of more real, easier to relate to and easier to actually feel the words as you sing."

"That's great. I try to play with feeling, though I'm bad on memorizing the words."

"That's understandable. You can't sing and play clarinet at the same time."

Ben laughed, then pursued his original question. "So Ellie, if you like it so much, how is it that you're not sure you want to come back?"

"Oh, I want to come back. But you asked me if I want to come regularly, like every Sunday, or I mean Saturday. I never did anything like that before, that is, except for going to school or to work on a regular basis."

"Well even if you don't go here regularly, it's important to attend some fellowship on a regular basis," Ben said.

"It is? Why?" Ellie asked.

Ben began answering, but all of a sudden Ellie got nervous she'd be late to work. She tried to politely end the conversation, but Ben didn't take the hint. Finally she said, "Ben, it really makes sense what you're saying, but maybe we can continue this discussion some other time, because I've got to get to work in twenty minutes. My brother should be outside right now waiting for me."

"Oh sure," Ben agreed. "Sorry to keep you."

"No, it was great talking."

"So I'll see you whenever you can make it back here," Ben said.

"Probably next week," Ellie replied. "Bye."

Ellie saw Daniel right away. He was parked almost directly in front of the front door.

"So this is the place," Daniel said. "Interesting."

"You should try it sometime, Daniel," Ellie said.

"Maybe. So tell me what it was like."

Ellie told Daniel what she thought she could, without turning him off. He wasn't even a believer yet, and she didn't know how he felt about his Jewishness. She only shared a little about the service, and talked more about the music and the people and the oneg.

Ellie knew it was a bit unusual for Daniel to offer to do this for her. He just got his driver's license, so she thought maybe he just wanted a chance to drive her car. Or perhaps she thought he was really trying to be nice and help her get to know Kevin better. But now she thought there could even be a third possibility. Maybe he was really interested in this Messianic Jewish thing. Ellie really hoped it was the third reason.

Before she got out of the car at Monroe Center, Daniel asked, "Do you mind if I use your car today? I'll be here at 10:30 sharp to pick you up."

"Sure, just drive carefully," she said and laughed to herself as she walked into House 10.

The day at work was uneventful. In fact, it was quite dull. Maybe it was the obvious result of being assigned to this low level house, Ellie thought. Or maybe it was just the sharp contrast it produced, following right on the heels of a blessed Sabbath service and fellowship. At any rate, it was very hard to get through the eight hour work day. The end of the day brought the drifting smell of marijuana smoke into the house again from the back bathrooms. The way Daniel described the smell, like a fireplace kind of smell that's more woody with maybe a tiny bit of incense smell, made Ellie think it really was marijuana. Ellie began to be genuinely scared she might lose this job if she didn't report what was happening. Why was her life bringing her so many challenges lately? She told God she thought He was giving her more than she could handle.

When she got home, her mom was waiting for her. "Kevin called. He said if you're not too tired you can call him when you get home."

Ellie's heart started racing fast with excitement. She didn't want her mom to know how excited she was, so she took her time brushing her teeth and getting ready for bed. Her mom went straight to bed after she gave Ellie the message, but Daniel was hanging around the kitchen looking for a snack. By the time Ellie was ready to make her phone call, Daniel had retreated to his room with a bowl of cereal. Ellie dialed Kevin's number.

Chapter Thirteen

"HI KEVIN, MY MOM told me you called."

"Yeah, thanks for calling back. I thought it would be great to touch bases with you about what you thought about Broken Wall, if you're not too tired. Too bad you had to work this afternoon."

"I know," Ellie said. "And I'm not too tired. I'm excited to share what I think about Broken Wall. I really like it! I feel so comfortable, kind of 'at home' there. What do you think?"

"I like it too," Kevin said. "And no offense to you, but I was wondering if you think it's maybe a little too Jewish?"

"What do you mean?" Ellie asked.

"I mean, do you think they want everybody to just worship on Saturdays as the Sabbath and do Passover and all that? Do you think they're adding the old legal system to today's Christianity?" Kevin asked.

"I don't think so," Ellie replied. "I love the teachings. I never really understood the Old Testament before, but I love the way that Pastor Weisman explains things. He really shows how the whole Bible fits together, the old stuff and the new stuff."

"Yeah, I agree," Kevin surprisingly said. "I guess I'm just reacting to what some of my other Christian friends are saying to me. They're warning me not to get sucked into that legalizing Old Testament stuff. They called it Judaizing. Anyway, I wanted to check in with you and see what you thought."

"I'm honored that you want my opinion," Ellie honestly said. "I don't think they're doing any dangerous legalizing stuff there. I can't believe people would say things like that. I really like it there. I was talking to Ben as I was leaving today and he told me to consider making Broken Wall my regular church."

"Ha ha, he told me the same thing. But I'm surprised he called it a church. He told me he doesn't like to refer to it as a church but as a congregation."

"Oh you're right, he did say congregation," Ellie laughed.

"That's what I mean by Judaizing, like I'm thinking, can't he even bear to say the word *church*?" Kevin exclaimed.

"I know it can seem like that," Ellie said. "But now that you reminded me, I remember Ben told me that if you said it was a church to a Jewish person, he would be less likely to come. And part of the vision of Broken Wall is to show Jewish people that it's totally Jewish to believe in Jesus and that you don't have to give up being Jewish."

"Hmm, that makes sense. I didn't hear that myself."

The conversation continued to flow so naturally, that soon Ellie started sharing her dilemma about the pot smoking at work. Kevin agreed it could be grounds for people being fired. He didn't know how Ellie should handle it, but he suggested she pray about it and he would too and they could talk again tomorrow. They talked for fifty-five minutes!

Ellie went to bed happy that night. Funny, she thought, now she was glad she had so many challenges in her life because it gave her so many things to talk to Kevin about.

Chapter Fourteen

ELLIE JUST HAD one more day of work left before her two days of being off. She wracked her brain thinking of some activities to plan to make the day more exciting. The children in House 10 were so much less responsive than the House 25 gang. Maybe she could bring the CD of Christian music she just ordered and play that during the long afternoon. And if the rain stopped, she could take some of the children for a walk.

Liz and Ellie were the only ones on duty. It was a Sunday and the weekends were usually short-staffed. The CD idea worked well. Liz said she liked it because it reminded her that it was Sunday. Ellie was glad it was having a good effect on Liz. But the rain didn't stop. The children didn't have umbrellas and even if they did, Ellie wasn't sure they'd know how to handle one.

In the evening, when the children were in bed, Liz started telling Ellie that she was welcome to share their stuff whenever she wanted to. Ellie told her she didn't smoke and she didn't do drugs. Liz said, "Good for you," as if she really meant it. Then she went on to tell Ellie how she made a mess of her life because of her drug habit, and now she owed the dealer $200.

"It's such a mess, Ellie," she continued, "and my daughter is in the middle of it. She's just eight, and her father is one of the dealers. He says if I ever don't pay, he'll take Janelle away from me. And believe me, he'll do it."

"Oh no," Ellie said. "Does he get to see Janelle often?"

Liz let out a cynical laugh. "He doesn't care two beans about Janelle. He never even sends her a birthday card. He just uses her as a weapon to get to me. I beg you, Ellie, can you manage to loan me $200? I'll be all right on pay day, and that's just 4 days away. I'll pay you right back, I swear."

Ellie was dumbfounded. She never hung around in circles like this before. She didn't even know what marijuana smelled like till a few days ago when her brother described it to her. And to think of a little eight year old girl stuck in the middle of it all! Ellie's heart hurt for Liz and she agreed to lend her the money.

"But wait a minute, Liz," Ellie told her. "I'm off tomorrow and Tuesday."

"I need it tomorrow," Liz insisted.

"Do you want to pick it up from my house?" Ellie asked. "I should be home most of the day, and if I'm gone out for a while, my mom should be there. I can leave the money in an envelope for you with my mom."

"Oh no, Ellie, I'd be too embarrassed to take money from your mother. Can you just meet me in the parking lot here at 10 minutes before 2? I'd be so eternally grateful."

"I guess so," Ellie agreed reluctantly. Liz immediately gave her a hug and Ellie saw tears in her eyes.

But a few minutes later Liz said she wanted to go out for a smoke. When she came back in, she was again under the influence of something. Her mood did a dramatic change.

Ellie was greatly disappointed to see Liz like that again. She wondered if she did the right thing. She knew it was right to protect Janelle, but should she be giving Liz $200? Would she just be helping her to stay hooked on drugs? She was very tempted to call Kevin when she got home and ask his advice. But it was Sunday and she wouldn't be able to call till 11, when she got home. Since Kevin had to work early Monday morning, Ellie resisted the urge to call him. "Maybe tomorrow," she said out loud to herself and to the Lord as she drove home. She was praying out loud, talking to God, rolling out her thoughts and confusions. She was pretty sure she made another wrong decision.

Chapter Fifteen

ELLIE HAD CLASSES Monday morning. She knew Sarah had a morning class too and hoped they'd be able to take a break together. She had so much to talk to her about.

Ellie arrived early, since she wanted to go to the library first. She needed to read the textbook that was assigned to her education class. She was reluctantly going through the motions of being a good student, but she was very cynical about the whole education curriculum. It didn't seem to be very practical. She ventured on a somewhat silly experiment to prove that the classes she was taking were not very substantial and that the whole course of study was irrelevant fluff. She decided she would not buy one single book during her masters' degree program. She would try to get by with finding some books in the library and taking good notes in class. She could prove her point and save a lot of money. So far it was working. She was getting all A's.

After class she went to the cafeteria where Sarah sometimes ate a snack and studied. Ellie was so glad to see her there.

"Sarah," she called.

Sarah looked up. "Ellie!" she exclaimed. "I was hoping you'd be here. Do you have time to talk?"

"I sure do. I'm off today. And what's more, I've got so much news to tell you!"

"Me too," Sarah replied. "But you first."

"Thanks! I'm so excited to tell you that things are picking up with my friendship with Kevin!"

Sarah's eyes sparkled with joy for her friend's good news. "What?? Tell me about it."

"Well, I told you about Passover and how Kevin didn't even seem to care if he sat by me, right?"

"No, you hardly told me anything about Passover, remember? You just told me I would have loved the dancing and then you said you'd tell me all the other juicy details later."

Ellie laughed and said, "Oh yeah! It's hard to believe I didn't even tell you about that yet! So much has happened since we talked last."

Ellie began a very interesting monologue, which was much shorter than it could have been. She found herself zipping along quite fast through the Passover story, because she was so eager to get to the part about the phone call.

Sarah was all ears. When Ellie told her about calling Kevin back at almost 11 p.m., Sarah was quite impressed. "I'm so glad to hear that, Ellie," she said. "Finally he seems like he's starting to appreciate you. And I'm happier about that than you know."

"What do you mean?" Ellie wanted to know.

"I was feeling so sorry to have to tell you that Dad wants to stop the Bible Study."

"What!" Ellie exclaimed.

"He wants us to move closer to my grandparents," Sarah explained.

"Oh no, Sarah. I'm shocked. Your whole family is moving?"

"Yes. I'm sort of shocked too. Plus I was scared to tell you because I didn't know how you'd react. You know it would mean not having a regular place for you to see Kevin anymore. But now I'm so glad to hear you're doing other things with him. It makes me feel better."

"You're such a good friend, Sarah!" Ellie said. "But I thought the Bible Study was an important ministry for your Dad."

"It was. I mean it is! But he's been talking on and off about this move for a long time. When we were at my grandparents' house at Easter, he knew it was time. We saw how hard it was for them to just do normal things now, like cooking and cleaning. Their house is getting a bad smell, you know, the smell of a closed-up house, no fresh air, a bunch of clutter. It was pretty sad to see."

"Wow, too bad."

"I know. But at least I'll still be able to see you often here at school."

"For sure," Ellie replied. "We'll have to be intentional about it and make definite times to meet and stuff. Anyway, I'll probably be here a lot more, since I might be going to school full-time and quitting my job soon."

"Really? Why?!" Sarah was surprised.

Ellie told her about the drug use at work and how scary it was to her because she was the one in charge. "Actually, my father suggested I quit my job and go to school full time. And he doesn't even know about the drug stuff going on there. He just knows how frustrated I've been since working in this low level house. And now that he's almost done paying off his own school loans from law school, he says he can afford to pay for me to go back. So I can finish working on my master's."

"Those school loans sure take a long time to pay back, don't they?" Sarah asked.

"Yeah, but remember, he went back to law school later in life. He was already married and my brother and I were already born. So he's doing pretty well, considering."

"Oh that's true. I forgot," Sarah said.

"And I'm doing a silly experiment to save more money too. I'm trying to get by without buying any books and just find the books I need in the library. Oh, and I make sure to take good notes in class and stuff."

"Oh no, Ellie. That doesn't sound like you. Why are doing such a thing?" Sarah asked with concern.

"Well, I'm so frustrated with the whole education curriculum. It seems it's all opinion, nothing solid, just one theory after another. And some of the theories are so outlandish! And then when I student taught, I realized how all the things I learned didn't really help me that much."

"That's interesting," Sarah said. "I know that at Monroe Center we both saw how the specialists didn't understand the kids as much as the workers who worked first hand in the houses with them. It kind of showed that all that schooling didn't teach the specialists what they needed to know after all."

"Yeah. And most of the people who work in the houses don't have any college at all, just a high school diploma!"

"I didn't know that," Sarah said.

"Yep," Ellie confirmed. Then she added, "I do realize I did learn some good things, like how to teach phonics for example. And I admit I'm a little too cynical of a person. But I believe so strongly that common sense is needed much more than the educational theories they teach today. That's why I want to prove it by not buying any textbooks and still trying to get great grades. I do want the credential and I do want to get a good job in the special ed field."

"I know," Sarah said. "But promise me that if you start floundering in some class because you really need the book, you'll reconsider this experiment."

"I'll try not to be foolish about it, Sarah. After all, I realize that if I failed a class that would mean I wasted all the money I spent on registering for that class. Besides, my transcripts would be ruined, and who would want to hire me then," Ellie reasoned. "So I'll be careful, Sarah. But back to your news. How can your family just up and move like that? That'll be so hard on you and your brothers, not to mention the Bible Study group."

"Well, you mentioned that you thought my dad really liked doing the Bible Study. And you're right. He did. He does! He loves it! But he said it's a good time to move because all the college kids now have good churches they're connected with and now you found that Messianic Jewish church."

"That's sure wonderful how he's concerned about each of us," Ellie said. "He is right. I love the Messianic Jewish church, as he called it. I'm going back next week too and so is Kevin! And by the way, they don't like to call it a church."

"That's odd," Sarah said.

"Not really, when you understand the reasons." Then Ellie went through the explanation of what a Messianic Jewish congregation is. "You should come with me sometime!"

Sarah replied, "I'd love to, it sounds so exciting! And I'd love to try that Israeli dancing sometime too. But my family likes us to keep going to church together."

Ellie didn't say anything. She actually felt sorry for Sarah. It seemed like her family was stifling her growth. Yet ironically, she thought they were the best example of a family she ever saw.

Ellie and Sarah both talked so long, they ended up buying their lunches and eating together. Actually, Ellie treated Sarah and bought her lunch, since Ellie was the one who still had a job and money. And they talked and talked till they actually finished the French fries that they thought they were through with!

"Look at the time," Sarah exclaimed. "I better call my mom and tell her I'll be late. Where's the nearest pay phone, Ellie?"

Sarah scampered off, and Ellie prepared to leave too. She had to meet Liz in the parking lot at 1:50.

Ellie got there early and waited for Liz, who also arrived a little earlier than expected. After giving Liz the money, Ellie headed home. She studied for a few more hours and then went into the kitchen to help her mom get supper ready. When Ellie's mom was asking about her day, Ellie was answering with half her mind. The other half kept thinking, *Should I call Kevin tonight?* It was her day off and she could call him in the early evening. After all, he did want to know how it went for her at work.

Ellie ate supper with her family and just as they were finishing, the phone rang. Unbelievably, Kevin called her!

Chapter Sixteen

"HI KEVIN," Ellie said enthusiastically. "Can I call you back in fifteen minutes?"

"Sure," Kevin agreed.

Ellie hung up the phone and explained to her family, "I can clear the table while I talk to Kevin later." She hoped they would take the hint and clear out of the kitchen.

"I have a better idea," Daniel said. "Let's try to get the dishes done in fifteen minutes."

So Ellie, her mom, and Daniel took up the challenge and actually did it. Ellie was so happy to have the kitchen to herself when she called Kevin back.

"How did it go at work yesterday, Ellie?" Kevin asked. "Did you collect any more evidence?" He was trying to be half humorous, but also serious.

Ellie chuckled a little. She still found Kevin's humor a bit lacking. "Unfortunately, I have all the evidence I need now. Liz confessed to me last night and even asked to borrow $200 from me. It seems that she owed this drug dealer money. And what's even more serious is that this guy who she buys the drugs from is the father of her daughter. And he keeps threatening to take her daughter away from her if she doesn't pay up."

"That doesn't make much sense, Ellie," Kevin said. "If he's on drugs too, what kind of a case would he have to take away her daughter?"

"I don't think she means that he'd go through court or anything. She implied he'd do something like kidnapping her as she walks home from school or something. And he'd do it not because he wanted her, but just to get back at Liz."

"What a tangled up situation. What did you say?"

"I didn't know what to say, but in the end, I agreed to lend her the money. And I already met with her today in the parking lot."

"How did that go? Did anybody see you?"

"I don't know. Why do you ask?" Ellie wanted to know.

"Did you ever think that it might look suspicious, I mean meeting in a parking lot and exchanging money?" Kevin suggested.

"No, why?" Ellie asked.

"Well, that's how a lot of drug deals are made," Kevin informed her.

"Oh no, you're scaring me now. Do you think somebody might have seen me?"

"Sorry, Ellie, I didn't mean to scare you. I'm sure it'll be fine. Do you think you can trust her to pay you back?"

"I'm pretty sure I can," Ellie replied. "But anyway, this episode made it clear to me that I don't want to keep that job. I'm planning to give my two week notice and quit, and then go back to school full time for my master's."

The phone conversation continued for an hour and went very well. Ellie and Kevin talked about Sarah's move, Messianic Jewish theology, and Kevin's day at work. They even made tentative plans to start attending the Broken Wall midweek Bible Study, after the Bible Study at the Kirby's came to a close. But the last thing they talked about was the most fun for Ellie.

"I have an idea for the last Bible Study at Sarah's place," Kevin said. "I heard this great new Christian song, *Friends*. I have the tape and I'll play it for you when we drive to Broken Wall next time. It's about parting with friends who God is calling away to a different chapter in their lives. Anyway, I think it would be a great surprise if you and I learned it. Then we can sing it together for the Kirby's at our last meeting."

"That sounds like a great idea! I can't wait to hear it."

"Well, if you can't wait, I can play it now and you can hear it over the phone. Just a minute, let me set up my tape player near the phone."

Ellie melted when she heard the song:

> "…I can't believe the hopes He's granted, means a chapter in your life is through.
> But we'll keep you close as always
> It won't even seem you've gone
> 'Cause our hearts in big and small ways
> Will keep the love that keeps us strong
> And friends are friends forever
> If the Lord's the Lord of them
> And a friend will not say "Never"
> 'Cause the welcome will not end
> Though it's hard to let you go
> In the Father's hands we know
> That a lifetime's not too long
> To live as friends."

The tears welled up in her eyes as she heard the touching lyrics and melody. She thought about the love she felt for the whole Kirby family and how they were responsible in such a big way, for her coming to the Lord and finding joy and purpose in life. She loved Sarah. She had become her best friend. And what's more, it was through the Kirby's that Ellie met Kevin!

Some of the tears dropped out of her eyes and some were stuck back in her throat. She was trying to hold back her emotions for the sake of the phone call.

She couldn't believe how the tide had turned in her friendship with Kevin. They were talking on the phone so often now, attending the same congregation together once a week and soon to be twice a week. And on top of that, Kevin wanted to sing this song with her! What a blessing! How could she keep this joy to herself, when she had to keep it as a surprise from her best friend and confidante, Sarah?

Before the song ended, Ellie managed to collect herself and say with heartfelt enthusiasm, "I'd love to do that, Kevin! What a magnificent song! I love it!"

She went to her room to read and turned on the Christian radio station, hoping to hear that song again. But she didn't hear it that evening.

Before she went to bed, she took out her college catalog and mapped out the classes she would have to take in order to complete her degree. She was getting quite excited. Just then the phone started ringing again.

Chapter Seventeen

IT WAS SARAH. She was calling to inform Ellie that her grandfather had fallen and broken his ankle. He had to stay off his feet for several days, then get used to using a walker. Sarah's mom and brothers were packing up to move in with the grandparents for a few days. They were leaving in the morning.

"Too bad," Ellie said.

"I know," Sarah agreed. "We won't have to move right away. But it's got my Dad and Mom pretty jumpy now. Dad is already calling up some rental properties in the area."

"You're kidding!" Ellie exclaimed. "How soon do you think you'll move?"

"I don't know. But I'm guessing we'll have to take turns staying with my grandparents for a while now. And since my Dad doesn't like us to be separated, he's super motivated to get moving pretty fast."

"Won't it take some time to sell your house though?" Ellie wanted to know.

"I guess so, but the real estate person is coming over tomorrow already."

"Wow," was all Ellie could say.

"So Dad wants to have one last Bible Study before things get too hectic," Sarah continued. "He wants me to ask you what days you're off next week."

"That was so sweet of him, to make sure I could be there," Ellie said. "I'm off Tuesday and Wednesday."

"Great, Dad was hoping we could do it Wednesday or Thursday. So Wednesday it will be!" Sarah announced. "And by the way, can you do me a favor and call Kevin and tell him?"

"Ha ha. That's doing *you* a favor?" Ellie asked, when she knew it was really the other way around. Sarah probably knew it too.

When they hung up, Ellie decided to call Kevin right away. If he still wanted to do that song, they'd have to start practicing as soon as possible.

Chapter Eighteen

ELLIE COULDN'T BELIEVE IT! Kevin actually was coming to her house! Since she had the next day off, she suggested they rehearse that evening. Kevin agreed and said he could arrive at 7.

Ellie was a little nervous about what her father would say. She didn't want him to say anything about boyfriend/girlfriend type things. Her dad was just about to go get gas and a car wash and she hoped Kevin would arrive when he was gone. But when she looked out the window, there he was already!

"So you must be Kevin," her father said. "And is that your violin?" he asked.

Kevin laughed. "Sort of. It's actually my guitar."

"That's what I meant," Ellie's father chuckled. "Have a good practice. I'm on my way to get the car filled up and get a car wash. I don't like Ellie to run low on gas, and she'll be using the car tomorrow."

"That's really nice of you," Kevin said. "See you later."

"You really have a nice dad," Kevin told Ellie.

"I know," Ellie said. "He does a lot of nice things like that. I think he shows his love that way, since he's not so good at talking with me."

"Is he a believer?" Kevin asked.

"No, so far I'm the only one in the family. But I think my brother Daniel is getting close."

"That's great!" Kevin said, genuinely excited. "I'd love to meet him. Is he home?"

"Sure, I'll introduce you," Ellie said as they walked into Daniel's room.

Before any introductions were made, Daniel popped up from his desk and greeted them. "Hey man, you must be Kevin. I'm Daniel. Nice to meet you. I heard a lot about you."

"Likewise," Kevin said. "I hear you like to play chess."

"Yeah, I'm a bit of an addict."

"When we're finished practicing, would you have time to play a game with me?" Kevin asked.

"That'd be great," Daniel said.

Ellie was half happy and half not happy about that. She was glad Kevin was reaching out to her brother, but disappointed that he seemed so very eager to do it. Kevin, as well as the whole Bible Study group, prayed regularly for Daniel to accept the Lord. Ellie prayed for Daniel every day too. She wanted him to know the Lord more than anybody. She wanted Daniel and Kevin to become friends too. But why did it have to start on this day, one of the first times Kevin visited her at home? She was frustrated at Kevin's behavior and also disappointed in seeing her own selfishness revealing itself in this whole situation.

The practice was all she dreamed it would be. They listened to the song and practiced with the recording. Ellie made a few mistakes with the words, so they spent time listening and writing out the words as fast as they could. Then they toyed with the idea of changing some words to be more specific to the Kirby family. They actually made each other laugh with their suggestions, even though they both meant for their words to be serious. In the end, they just agreed to go with the lyrics as originally written. The melody and words were so touching and the harmony they sang was so beautiful. Ellie's heart was full. While she wasn't ready to call it quits yet, Kevin suggested they stop there so he can have time for a good game of chess with Daniel. Ellie didn't share her reluctance to quit. She of course didn't want Kevin to know just how much this meant to her.

Ellie knew Kevin loved games and loved competition. Playing with Daniel was no big sacrifice for him. He thoroughly enjoyed himself. Daniel got out a big bowl of potato chips and a dip that he just made with sour cream and onion soup mix. Ellie didn't know what she should do, whether to watch the game or pretend to be busy doing something else. So she did a little of each, coming back every once in a while to see how it was going.

The evening was a big success in the end. Kevin, Ellie and Daniel all had a great time, and Ellie realized later that the game between the two guys made it much better. She felt much less awkwardness in relating to Kevin in front of her parents when Daniel was in the mix too.

Chapter Nineteen

THE DAY OF THE LAST BIBLE STUDY at the Kirby house was bittersweet. Ellie was super thrilled to be teamed up with Kevin for the surprise song. At the same time, she was very sad that this, her first group of Christian friends, was breaking up and one of her favorite families was moving away. Yet she was also quite content with her growing involvement in the Broken Wall community, with mature believers her own age. So putting everything together, Ellie felt real sadness, but also a little guilty that she didn't feel even sadder.

Ellie once heard that music helps bring out the emotions. And sure enough, when she and Kevin began their surprise duet, *Friends,* the words really got to her. She started feeling the deep place the Kirby's had in her heart. They were irreplaceable friends and they were leaving her life. She began crying at the very start of the song and they had to stop and begin again. Ellie and Kevin's music created a memory that would be etched in many people's minds for years to come. Almost every eye got watery and love could actually be felt in the room. It was the beginning of a wonderful evening, with testimonials being given by almost every young person there. Ellie was amazed to hear all the ways the Kirby's reached out to help different ones at crucial stages in their lives.

Ellie and Kevin drove home together in Kevin's car. "That was a great meeting," Kevin remarked.

Ellie agreed and then asked, "What was Mr. Kirby talking to you about for so long?"

Kevin excitedly answered, "Oh, it was sort of an answer to prayer for me. He's looking for someone to fix up his house, you know, paint it, keep up the lawn and stuff like that, so he can sell it easier."

"So what do you mean that's an answer to prayer? Were you praying for a way to help the Kirby's?"

Kevin laughed. "No, not exactly. I really am more than happy to help out the Kirby's. But to answer your question, I've been praying about buying a house myself and getting it fixed up. I want to invest my money in my own home instead of paying rent every month. And though I was looking for a smaller house than the Kirby's, more of a fixer-upper that I could afford, I figured there's a chance Mr. Kirby can give me a good deal on his home. And if not, at least I'm happy to make some extra money in painting and mowing in the evenings. With the extra money, I'll be able to make a down payment on a fixer-upper of my own sooner rather than later."

Ellie digested the information and just basked in the joy of the moment, riding with Kevin and talking about life together.

When she got home, her daydreams began. *Would the Kirby home one day be the home that she and Kevin moved into when they got married? Wouldn't that be something? The home of her first real Christian friends becoming her home....*

Chapter Twenty

AS TIME WENT ON, Ellie's last day of work at Monroe Avenue Center dawned. Liz was working with her and pay day was the day before. Liz missed paying Ellie back when the first pay day rolled around. So Ellie hoped Liz got her check from yesterday cashed and would be ready to pay her back today. She hoped Liz would remember on her own, without Ellie having to remind her.

Ellie tried to think of a way to bring it up. She began, "It's hard to believe it's my last day here."

"You're smart to get out now," Liz agreed. "It's not getting any better."

"I really liked it when I started here," Ellie confessed. "Our house seemed like a family. There were always some kids we could talk to and they could talk back and understand and help out."

"That's not like this house," Liz said gloomily.

"I'm glad I already found a part-time job, to help with my expenses while I finish school," Ellie said. She hoped Liz would get the hint that Ellie wasn't rich and she could use the $200 now.

But Liz just said, "Oh yeah? What kind of work did you get?"

"I'll be teaching an evening GED class two evenings a week."

"Good for you," Liz congratulated Ellie.

The evening ended with no talk about Liz paying back the debt. Ellie was too timid to ask her directly. She realized she probably made a mistake lending Liz the money in the first place. She'd just have to chalk that up to another learning experience in life.

Chapter Twenty-One

THE SUMMER WAS HOT AND HUMID, but wonderful nonetheless. Ellie had classes four mornings a week. All her afternoons were free to either do school work or help Kevin. One evening of the week she and Kevin would go to the Broken Wall Bible Study. Two evenings of the week Ellie would teach adult learners at the local community college GED center. And Saturday mornings would begin with a prayer meeting and worship service at Broken Wall, followed by the oneg and usually some sort of get-together with many of the single people there.

It was a great group of people. Ellie was usually with Kevin, Ben started dating Candace, and Connie was becoming a good friend to Ellie. Three or four other girls and one or two other guys were also part of the group.

Candace lived close to Ellie and often asked for a ride to services. She was going through a divorce and she and her two school-aged children attended Broken Wall. Connie, however, lived an hour away. But so heartfelt was her love for the Jewish people that she drove all those miles, not only to attend the weekly Sabbath service, but also the Tuesday evening Bible studies.

The Kirby's had moved about 60 miles away. It was on the other side of the city and the drive involved going right through city traffic. It usually took an hour and a half to get there. Their house was close to the train station, so Sarah usually took the train to the city university which she and Ellie attended. Sadly, Sarah wasn't taking summer classes so Ellie hardly saw her all summer. This only made their phone conversations that much more appreciated!

Ellie woke up thinking of Sarah. She knew Sarah was an early riser and usually drove to help her grandparents in the afternoons. Ellie knew her own mom was helping at the restaurant today and Daniel was off at his summer job at the golf course. It would be a great time to call and talk, with a semblance of privacy.

"Ellie!" Sarah exclaimed over the receiver. "I was just thinking of calling you!"

"That's great. I love when that happens. Now I know I called at a good time," Ellie said.

"So how are you? What's going on with you and Kevin these days? How is school? How's your GED class going?"

"Everything is going pretty well, Sarah. Kevin is really being conscientious taking care of your old house. He gets to work early and then takes a two hour lunch break and comes out to work. He says it helps him to do some physical work in the middle of a day of sitting in his office and doing sedentary work."

"That Kevin, he always makes such good sense, doesn't he?" Sarah laughed.

"Yeah, he's pretty smart, well more like wise according to the Bible," Ellie added.

"I agree," Sarah said. "But how's it going with you and him? Do you see each other a lot? Do you still talk on the phone as much as you used to?"

"Actually, since I have my afternoons free, I go out to your house one or two days a week when Kevin's there. I make us both sandwiches and we eat lunch and talk and then get to work. I offered to help with the mowing and he's taken me up on the offer."

"Oh Ellie, that's so nice of you. I should tell my dad to pay you something too!" Sarah thought out loud.

"No, that would be embarrassing. If Kevin wants to offer me some of the money, that's one thing. But I don't want him to think I'm doing this for money. I'm doing it because I want to help Kevin and selfishly, I want to spend time with him and get to know him and have him get to know me."

"That's a great idea, Ellie. Do you and Kevin seem to be getting closer?"

"I think so. We're really enjoying going to Broken Wall together and talking about the sermons and our impressions and things. Oh, I wish you could come sometime. It's so interesting and so moving. I really feel the Holy Spirit presence there."

"I wish I could too," Sarah admitted. "But Dad wants us to go to church together and Saturday is our work day. He loves the Jewish people, as you know, and he knows Jesus was Jewish. But he's not so convinced that Jews should worship separate from Christians. After all, he says the middle wall of partition was broken down."

"I know," Ellie said. "But then whose side of the wall are you gonna gravitate to? Should everyone move over to the Gentile side of the wall and go to churches and sing hymns and stuff? Or should everyone slide over to the Jewish side of the wall and celebrate the Biblical feasts and play Jewish style worship songs?" Ellie very enthusiastically shared this picture that they had just recently talked about at a Broken Wall Bible Study.

"That's a good question, Ellie," Sarah said. "But what I think Dad means is that we should all merge together somehow."

"That sounds good in theory, Sarah, but in reality there are a lot more Gentiles right now in the church than Jewish believers. If this merge happened, I think the Jewish elements would be sort of lost in comparison. Well, actually, it has already happened. There have been Jewish people down through the centuries joining the church, and the church has stayed pretty much in the Gentile style of worship."

"Maybe so," Sarah admitted. "But if believing in Jesus is the main thing, does it really matter what the style of music or worship is in a service?"

Ellie said, "I think it does. It says in the Bible that the Jews who believe will be grafted back into their own olive tree. Then it says that Gentiles who believe are more like wild branches and they will be grafted in for the first time. So it seems like it really should be a Jewish olive tree with a Jewish style of service."

"That's interesting, Ellie. I should tell my father that example. But I hope you don't think I'm arguing with you."

"No, not at all. This is fun for me. I'm actually able to put these things I've been listening to and thinking about into words and it helps me too," Ellie said.

"Where is that in the Bible, Ellie, so I can tell my dad?"

"Sorry, I'm not too good at citing passages and verse numbers. I think it's somewhere in the New Testament," Ellie said.

Sarah laughed. "I think I knew that much. I'll look it up in the concordance. It's so fun talking to you. I really miss you, Ellie. Do you hang around with a lot of the people at Broken Wall now?"

The answer to that question was yes, but Ellie didn't want Sarah to feel that she had been replaced. So she paused and answered, "Yes I do, Sarah, but you are still my best friend. The other two girls, Candace and Connie, are really nice. But Candace is in such a different stage of life than I am, it's hard to relate. She's going through a divorce and usually when I'm with her, so are her two kids. So we can't get very deep in our conversations."

"Well I'm sure she really likes having you as a friend," Sarah said.

"I hope so. Sometimes I feel like such a kid myself. She's actually just six years older than me, but I feel like a teenager in comparison with her. I hardly have any experience with guys and my life has been pretty tame."

"But Ellie, your life is so much more exciting than mine," Sarah said. "Remember how I used to tell you I felt kind of isolated doing homeschool high school, even though I believed in it? Well now I feel even more isolated… since we moved, that is."

Ellie didn't know what to say. She agreed with Sarah. She thought Sarah was too isolated and she felt sorry for her. But Ellie didn't want to say anything against Mr. or Mrs. Kirby. Finally she diplomatically said, "That's probably because its summer and you're not taking classes. And also, I know that any type of move is a hard thing to do. You didn't have any choice, since your family had to move to be with your grandparents."

"You're right. I'm sure it'll get better in the fall. And I'm really looking forward to coming out next week for your birthday party."

"My what?"

"Oh no Ellie. I'm so sorry. I wasn't supposed to tell you!"

"Is somebody planning a surprise party for me next week? I hate surprise parties. I'm glad you told me. Tell me what you know about it," Ellie said.

"Oh no, I don't know if I should. Do you really want to know?" Sarah asked.

"Please, Sarah. I really don't like surprise parties. I'm happy somebody thought of giving me one and wants to make my birthday special! But please tell me. Otherwise, I'll be in suspense and just dreading the day."

"Well, how about if I just tell you where and when so you can be prepared?" Sarah offered.

"Sure," Ellie said.

"It'll be at our old house. Kevin said the kitchen and living room are done, so we can use them for the party. He'll lure you there by telling you he left something there, when you're on your way to some place together. I think he'll ask if you want to go out for ice cream on your birthday evening or something."

"Wow, thanks a lot Sarah. I think God wanted you to tell me that. What if I thought Kevin was actually asking me out on a date, when it's only a ploy to get me to the party?"

"Oh, I see what you mean," Sarah said. "I'm glad I was able to help."

When Ellie hung up, she changed from being disappointed that Kevin wasn't going to ask her on a real date to encouragement. She realized it must be Kevin who was organizing the whole surprise party. He didn't know she hated surprise parties.

Chapter Twenty-Two

ELLIE WAS ANXIOUS yet optimistic about the different type of afternoon she had planned. She had to do a paper for her special ed class on one of three topics. She chose the topic of taking a special needs child out into the marketplace, and recording the different types of reactions she received from the public. She wanted to take Lisa Lynn, but because Lisa's family was actively involved in her life, it would be harder and take much longer to get the permission paperwork done in time. On the other hand, Benton, her other favorite, was a ward of the state. His parents gave up custody of Benton at birth and the state was the only one responsible for him now. She could get permission to take Benton on a home visit or shopping expedition much quicker. So that's what she did and this was the day scheduled for the field trip.

It was a strange feeling going back to Monroe Avenue Center. Benton was now in House 8. Angel was in the same house with Benton. When Ellie walked in, she excitedly said hi to Angel. Angel seemed to have just a spark of recognition for Ellie, but was frightened at the same time. Maybe she didn't understand why Ellie was gone and now she was back. Benton saw her and seemed to smile, but went on with his present occupation of twisting an old undershirt into a tight rope. Ellie spoke to him, "Hi Benton. I'm here to take you on a nice little trip with me. You can take that shirt with you in the car if you want to."

The second shift worker got Benton's shoes on him and told him to behave for Ellie. "I hope it goes ok for you, Ellie. Don't let go of his hand in the store."

Ellie laughed. "I'm sure not planning to!" And then she grabbed Benton's hand and walked to the car.

Benton was happily looking out the window of the car as Ellie drove to the shopping mall. She had decided to just walk around the mall and not go into any actual store. That way there would be less chance of losing Benton in between aisles of clothing or toys or gadgets.

As soon as Ellie and Benton stepped out of the car, everyone eyed her and Benton. He wasn't acting very hyper yet, though his eyes were constantly moving and his little squeaks could have caused people to turn. Then Ellie heard a little girl speak to her mother.

"Mom, look at that white lady with the black boy. I wonder why she's holding his hand when he's so old."

Oh what a foolish mistake I made, Ellie realized. When she was working at Monroe Avenue, the black and white issue was quite inconsequential. The children had such unique personalities, problems, and behaviors, that color was hardly noticed. But now in the outside world she remembered how noticeable it was. She wondered if she could actually satisfy her assignment requirements now. How could her experiment tell her anything about society's reaction to special needs kids out in the community when all the attention would be on a white lady taking out a black child?

She walked into the mall with Benton. He seemed a little overwhelmed, with his head going from side to side very quickly and his arms wanting to move fast but being held down by Ellie holding tightly to his right hand. His left arm was going in sort of a spastic movement, but very awkwardly since it wasn't matched with the right arm. He would have liked to be twisting a shirt or a sheet. Ellie didn't know how to calm him down.

She sat on a bench with Benton and tried talking to him like she used to talk to the children, even though they didn't really understand what she was saying. "We're here at the shopping mall. See all these stores? Let's take a walk and I'll tell you about all the stores we'll be passing." Ellie found that talking helped her organize and plan out a strategy.

After walking around for a while with Benton still acting so strange, Ellie decided to leave and drive to the park for a while. Though she knew Benton could run, she knew he wasn't too fast for her. So when she found a nice shady spot at the park with very few people nearby, she let go of Benton's hand. He didn't run. He just started moving his body, especially his arms, in twisting motions. Then he walked and picked up a weeping willow branch and began to twist it. He started to finally relax and find release and maybe even contentment and satisfaction. Ellie was glad to see this. She had planned this outing because she thought she could fulfill her assignment requirement and also help one of her children have a nice adventure. Now it was finally happening. Benton was enjoying himself.

Ellie noticed a few more people staring at her and Benton at the park every once in a while. She didn't know if it was Benton's behavior or his color that caused so many stares. She let Benton romp in the fresh air of the park for another half hour, and then drove him back to the center. As she walked back to her car from house 8, she saw a staff worker she recognized walking with Lisa Lynn and another resident. Ellie jogged down the sidewalk to meet them.

"Hi Tamara," she said to a former co-worker who worked in the house next door to hers. "Hi Lisa Lynn!" she said to her Lisa Lynn.

Lisa Lynn smiled, but kept holding Tamara's hand. "I love Lisa Lynn. She's my baby," Tamara said.

"Oh, I'm so happy Lisa Lynn is in a home where she's loved!" Ellie said.

"Don't you worry about that!" Tamara assured her. "She's my girl! Anybody upsets Lisa Lynn, they have to answer to me."

As Ellie walked back to the car, she was very unsure about her plans to apply at the center for a job as a specialist when she graduated. Her heart was not into that work anymore. It seemed like Mike was right. It was harder on the staff than on the children. The kids seemed to flow with the tide, not making lasting bonds with the staff. Maybe it was because of their low mental capabilities that allowed them to remember only the staff of the present and not the past. Maybe it was because, try as they might, they couldn't make Monroe Center homes like a real family. Ellie was very glad her life had meaning in it now, apart from her job. But it still hurt to see her kids hardly recognizing or responding to her anymore.

Chapter Twenty-Three

SATURDAY MORNING FOUND ELLIE giving Candace and her children a ride to Broken Wall. Kevin said he was taking the day off from services in order to be at the Kirby's old house when the roofers came.

Ellie was glad to have the company of Candace and her son and daughter that morning. Ellie told Candace about her fiasco with Benton that just happened, and Candace greatly encouraged her.

"Ellie, you should tell your teacher what you did and how the color issue colored the results," Candace began.

The kids in the back seat laughed. "That's funny, the color colored it! But tell us more about Benton. Isn't he the boy that used to tie up curtains and sheets and things?"

"Just a minute," their mother said. "I need to finish my thoughts to Ellie. Anyway, as I was saying, you can tell your professor what happened and also tell her how your former students or whatever you call the kids you used to work with, didn't seem to recognize you or appreciate you so much. It seems like a great paper for a special ed course, telling about how this system of group homes is working for the kids."

"You're right, Candace! That's a great idea! And then I wouldn't have to think up another plan for a paper. I'm pretty sure I'll be able to do a great job on a topic like that. I would love to share my impressions and insights about the Monroe Avenue Center. I wonder if I should mention it by name."

"I don't think it would hurt. But then again, maybe word would get back to the center and they'd give you a bad reference. Anyway, there are not that many group homes around, so your professor would probably suspect that's the place you're talking about anyway. So you might as well leave the name out of it. It would probably be safer," Candace added.

"Are you through with your thoughts, mom?" Candace's daughter Cindy asked.

"Ok, I guess so. Ellie, do you feel like telling them again about how Benton's room was found each morning?"

Ellie told the stories so well, that by the time they got to the congregation, the kids were excitedly talking about how they wanted to volunteer at Monroe Center when they were in high school.

Ben pulled up right next to them and they all walked in together. Ben and Candace and the children were planning to go out for ice cream and eat it at the park after the oneg. They invited Ellie to come along. Since Kevin wasn't with her, Ellie happily agreed.

At the park the kids almost gave away the "surprise." Eleven year old Cindy asked, "Hey Ellie, will you and Kevin be coming to this same Dairy Queen on Wednesday?"

Ellie played dumb. "What did you say? Do I ever come to this Dairy Queen?"

Candace came to the rescue. "Cindy, that's a strange question. Ellie lived in this area for over twenty years and I'm sure she's been to this Dairy Queen dozens of times before."

"That's true," Ellie said.

Cindy realized her mistake and said, "Oops, sorry. I guess that was a dumb question."

Her brother agreed. "It was dumber than you think."

Ellie saw Cindy giving her brother the finger-on-the-lips shush sign, as well as a big frown.

Ellie went home that evening with the full intention of working on her idea for the paper that she and Candace talked about. But a call from Kevin interrupted that plan.

Chapter Twenty-Four

NATURALLY, KEVIN WANTED AN UPDATE on the Broken Wall service that he had missed. He also mentioned to Ellie that he'd be working at the house on Sunday. She agreed to meet him there and help with the mowing again. So noontime on Sunday found Ellie packing a couple of tuna fish sandwiches, apples and potato chips and driving over to the Kirby's.

As they were eating, Kevin asked, "Do you remember that book you mentioned yesterday over the phone?" When Ellie responded with a perplexed look Kevin reminded her, "Remember you said several people from Broken Wall were reading it and they thought it was so good?"

"Oh yeah," Ellie said.

"I was just listening to the Christian radio station before you came over and I think I heard it mentioned," Kevin explained. "Was it called *Appointment in Jerusalem*?"

"Yes it was! Thanks for reminding me. I wanted to order myself a copy."

"Well, if you get it you can let me know how it is. Then if it's good, maybe I can borrow it."

"Sure. I'll let you know after I read it. Are you planning to come to the Tuesday night Bible Study?"

"Yes, as a matter of fact I was hoping I could ride with you," Kevin said. "My car will be in the shop, getting the air conditioning fixed. Is it possible you can pick me up from work?"

"Sure, no problem," Ellie said. "It's a bad summer to be without air conditioning in your car."

"Believe me, I know! Thanks a lot, Ellie," Kevin said. "I'll be watching for you about 6:30. How does that sound?"

"Good. That'll give us plenty of time to get there," Ellie assured him.

"I'd like to treat you to ice cream for all the help you've been giving me. I was wondering if you'd like to go out, maybe on Wednesday evening, to the Dairy Queen? My car should be done by then."

"That sounds nice, especially since Wednesday just happens to be my birthday."

"You're kidding!" Kevin said, trying to sound authentic. But Ellie saw through his charade.

Ellie laughed out loud to herself as she mowed, thinking of the ice cream and the surprise party. How thankful she was that Sarah told her about it. She would have built up the invitation to the status of a real date if she didn't know the truth.

As Ellie was putting the lawn mower back in the garage, Kevin was shaking out his paint drop cloth. The neighbor lady crossed over the lawn and said to Kevin, "You sure have a good girlfriend. Such a hard worker!"

"Ellie is a hard worker all right and I'm so grateful for her. But she's just a good friend, not a girlfriend," Kevin explained.

"Well she's a girl and she's your friend," the woman said, not too original of a statement, but Ellie laughed thinking it was the same thing her father said about Kevin.

"Well, then maybe I should call Ellie my good buddy," Kevin responded.

Now what was that supposed to mean, Ellie wondered. *Does he really want no one to think I'm his girlfriend that now he doesn't even want to say the word 'friend'?*

Ellie was hot and sweaty and a bit depressed as she drove home that afternoon. She did do a lot to help Kevin and all he wanted to do to thank her was to take her out for ice cream. Yet even that wasn't for real. But if he planned this surprise party, he must be thinking of her as a very special person in some regard. Ellie wondered if he liked her but just didn't realize how much yet. Or she thought maybe he was just too scared to make a commitment.

Ellie's prayers would be straight from her heart that night. She really needed God to show her the truth. Was she just throwing herself at Kevin, helping him whenever she could? Was he just taking advantage of her? What was really going on anyway? "Oh God, help me," she said out loud in the midst of her musings. She would have a serious time of prayer that night, she promised herself. But before she talked to God, she decided she needed to talk to Sarah.

Chapter Twenty-Five

ELLIE WAS GREETED by a note in the kitchen when she arrived home:

"Gone shopping. Back around 6. Will pick up some Chinese food on our way home. Love, Us."

"Hurray!" Ellie said out loud. Though she was looking forward to the Chinese food, she was mostly thrilled that her parents were gone and no one in the house would hear her private conversation with Sarah. She couldn't wait to call Sarah, but she was too hot and sweaty to do it right away. She drank a big glass of water, then washed and refreshed herself and put on clean clothes.

She was frustrated with herself for wearing some of her nice summer t-shirts when she went out to mow. She couldn't bring herself to wear her older work clothes, even though she wouldn't think twice about wearing them to work in her own yard. As she tossed her dirty, sweaty clothing into the laundry basket she got mad at herself. There was one more good outfit out of circulation for the next few days. She wondered if it was worth it to put on such a good front for Kevin. She needed advice. She couldn't wait to call Sarah.

"Oh Sarah, I'm so glad you're home! Do you have time to talk?"

"Sure. I'm just relaxing and reading a book. What's going on with you these days?" Sarah asked enthusiastically.

"Pretty much I guess. My GED classes are ok, but I sure don't like working in the evenings. That's the one thing about Monroe Avenue I didn't like, having to work second shift. So getting back to evening work again isn't my favorite thing. But I must admit it's quite fun to teach English and math and basic skills like that, to people who really want to learn and pay attention."

"I guess so," Sarah responded. "It probably is especially nice for you compared to your student teaching or substituting days."

"It sure is. I don't have to worry about discipline. But I do feel a bit intimidated teaching adults. There's this one guy in class, a big older truck driver. He's very nice but I feel so weird teaching him, because I think I make him feel small having to learn things from somebody like me."

"What do you mean 'from somebody like you'?" Sarah asked.

"I mean a young person like me, so naïve, with not that much real experience in life, having to teach a man who's a man! I mean he has a big job and he seems pretty tough and I always feel a little awkward having him diagram sentences."

"That's funny. So why do you have him diagram sentences?" Sarah wanted to know.

"Just a minute, Sarah, Daniel just walked in."

"Say hi to whoever you're talking to," Daniel shouted as he ran in. "I'm just here to pick up my tennis racket. Doug is waiting in the car for me."

"Neat. It's Sarah. But be back by 6 if you want Chinese food," Ellie told him.

"I might be a little late, but be sure to save some for me. And tell Sarah hi from me," Daniel said as he raced back out the door.

"Sorry Sarah. Daniel just came in to pick up his tennis racket. He said to say hi to you from him."

"I know. I heard it all," Sarah laughed.

"I guess you did. It was loud enough! But back to diagramming sentences. I learned it in elementary school and it helped me so much in learning English grammar. And it even helped me in high school and college when I was learning other languages. Anyway, that's why I like to teach it."

"You should show me someday," Sarah suggested. "Sounds like you're a really good teacher."

"I wish I could believe you, Sarah," Ellie said. "I didn't have such a good experience with Benton a couple days ago."

After Ellie told Sarah that saga, she finally got to the main topic she wanted to talk about in the first place. Sarah actually brought it up.

"So Ellie, how long am I gonna have to wait to hear how it's going with you and Kevin?"

"I'm so glad you're interested! Do you still have time?"

"Of course! Your call is one of the highlights of my day. Are you still helping him around our old house? Is he still going with you to Broken Wall?" Sarah asked.

"This week he missed the Sabbath service, because the roofers were coming to work at your house. But he had been going with me pretty regularly before then. Anyway, I drove with Candace and her kids. It just so happened they needed a ride."

"That was nice. At least you weren't too lonely."

"No I wasn't. The people at Broken Wall are so nice. I really wish you could come there sometime, Sarah! Remember that guy named Ben I told you about? Well, he's now going out with Candace. He's so nice, even to her kids. They invited me to go with them for ice cream after the oneg."

"You mean you ate at the oneg, and then went out for ice cream afterwards?" Sarah asked.

"I know that's pretty funny, but that's what we did. We all purposely skipped the cookies and desserts so we could have ice cream. I think it was Ben's idea, mostly for the sake of Candace's kids. We got ice cream cones at the Dairy Queen and took them to the park across the street to eat. It was fun. Candace's daughter Cindy almost gave away the secret party for me. She asked if that's the ice cream place Kevin and I will be coming to on Wednesday. But I kind of played dumb."

"Whew. Glad you didn't give it away or I would've been in trouble."

"But Sarah, I'm so glad you told me about it!" Ellie said.

Then she proceeded to tell Sarah about her day with Kevin and his invitation to go out with her for ice cream on Wednesday.

"I might have gotten my hopes up and had the completely wrong idea of Kevin actually asking me out on a date if you hadn't told me this was a set-up."

"Well then I'm really glad I told you."

Ellie then went on with the more important story of what transpired when the neighbor lady came out. Sarah was all ears as Ellie got to the climax of the story.

"…so then Kevin said, 'No, she's just a friend.' Then the lady said the same line my dad likes to say, 'Well she's a girl and she's a friend, so I'd say that's a girlfriend.' So then Kevin says, 'Well maybe I should call her my good buddy then.'"

"What?!" Sarah said. "What did he mean by that?"

"That's what I was wondering. What do you think he meant, Sarah?"

"It seems like he really didn't want the lady to think you were his girlfriend, so he decided he better not even call you a friend, just a good buddy."

"That's just what I thought! Now I'm really low again on this crazy roller coaster of emotions. But then I wonder if he was just saying that to throw me off. If he went through the trouble of setting up a surprise party for me, he must think of me as someone pretty special, in some way at least."

"Oh Ellie," Sarah said with concern. "I'm afraid to tell you it wasn't Kevin who set it up. It was Candace and her kids."

Ellie's heart and head began reacting. She got nervous. She felt her face turning red. She felt embarrassed that she thought it was Kevin and it really wasn't. She felt ashamed of her adulation of Kevin and she felt so vulnerable and naïve for putting a positive spin on everything he did. She even felt foolish in front of Sarah, her best friend and confidante.

"Wow, Sarah, I feel so dumb. How could I think it was Kevin, especially after the way he treated me this afternoon?"

"Ellie, quit thinking that! Kevin is the one who should feel bad! He's been giving you mixed signals all along. He likes you to help him. He loves to talk with you. He agrees with you on so many things. He calls you so much and is interested in your life. Yet he seems so scared to call you a girlfriend. Any girl would jump to the same conclusions you did!"

"So what do you think I should do?" Ellie wanted to know. "Just assume he doesn't like me in that way and not do so much with him anymore?"

"I don't know. You can't just drop him as a friend. But helping him so much and riding with him and talking to him so much… I don't know. What if he really does like you? I think you definitely need to pray about it."

"But I have been," Ellie explained, "and I don't know how to hear from God exactly. It might be my fault. One minute I ask God to show me if Kevin is really interested in me or not. The next minute I pray that he *would* be interested. I know the Bible says we can't be double minded when we pray. But I can't help it. I want to know but I don't want to know. I don't know what to do," Ellie concluded.

"Well, how about if I pray with you? I mean I can pray here by my house tonight and tomorrow and you can pray wherever you are tonight and tomorrow. Then we can talk again tomorrow evening and see if God showed us anything," Sarah offered.

"That sounds great Sarah. You're the best friend in the world! But tomorrow is Monday and I teach GED from 7 till 9. Would it be too late to talk to you about 9:30 when I get home?" Ellie asked.

"That would be fine! It might even be the best time. At that time my Dad and Mom are usually in my brothers' bedroom reading one of the Sugar Creek Gang books together for about an hour. That way I'll have privacy when we talk."

"That's neat! Can you please pray that I'll have privacy at that time too?" Ellie pleaded.

"Sure," Sarah assured her. After they prayed briefly together, they hung up.

Ellie's parents came home at 6:45 with two big bags of Chinese food. "Sorry we're late. The Chinese restaurant was really busy. Is Daniel home? We got so much food," Ellie's mom said almost as one sentence.

"No, Daniel's not here yet. He's playing tennis with Doug. He said he'd be a little late but to save some food for him," Ellie answered. "By the way, what were you shopping for? I don't see any bags."

"Ellie, you should know better than to ask a question like that on a week like this," her mother light-heartedly scolded.

"And don't look in the car till we take the bags out later," her father warned.

Ellie's spirits were lifted by her parents' excitement of getting her some birthday presents. They ate a very pleasant supper together.

"Does anybody want to split the last egg foo young with me?" her father asked.

"Remember Daniel's coming, dad," Ellie reminded him.

"Oh yeah. I'll just have more of the sesame chicken then."

Before Ellie left the table, her mom asked her, "What time will you be gone tomorrow?"

Ellie hoped her parents weren't planning any kind of surprise party for her. All these unusual questions and hidden packages were making her edgy. One surprise party was enough. Actually, maybe even one was too many!

"I have classes from 8:30 till noon. Then I'll probably stay and work on my paper in the library for an hour or so. I'll probably be home about 2. Then I'll be leaving at 6:15 for GED."

"You sure have a full day, tomorrow," Daniel commented as he walked in. "But what I want to know is, how did it go with Kevin today? Did you eat lunch together? Did you do anything special after you mowed?"

"It went pretty well," Ellie said. "We didn't do anything afterwards today, but he did invite me out for ice cream on Wednesday, my birthday."

"Now that's a great birthday gift for you, Ellie," her dad said, "a date with your boyfriend."

Ellie just smiled. She didn't try to explain things any further to her family. She knew her father wanted to make her feel good, but his statement really hit her hard that day.

Chapter Twenty-Six

WHEN ELLIE GOT BACK FROM SCHOOL, her mom was the only one home. She said hi and then just kind of followed Ellie with a somewhat silly smile on her face. Ellie knew something was up but she didn't know what. She assumed it was some other birthday surprise. When Ellie got to her bedroom, she paused.

"What's this ribbon on my door for?" she asked suspiciously.

"You'll see when you go in," her mother answered.

"I don't see anything," Ellie said, looking around a little confused.

"Keep looking," her mom said. "There's a surprise in here somewhere."

Ellie saw it and squealed. "My own phone! I can't believe it! Is it connected and everything?"

"Yes, the telephone company was here this morning and put in the extra phone jack. I hope you like it! Daniel said to get you a white one to match the white trim on your windows and closet. He said pink or turquoise were more for little girls."

Ellie laughed. "White is perfect! I love it!" And she hugged her mom.

"Now you don't have to worry if Kevin calls you late in the evening and we're still up watching TV. Now you'll have privacy."

"Thanks, Mom. What a great gift!"

"I'll get back to my cooking," Ellie's mom said. "I'm making some apple pies for a treat today."

"Wow, you're almost making me think today is my birthday!" Ellie said. "I hope I can concentrate on my paper, smelling the pies in the oven."

Ellie had talked to her teacher in the morning. Professor Joyce very much encouraged Ellie in the idea Candace suggested for her paper. So with her teacher's approval behind her and her own zealousness to write on the topic, Ellie happily and fervently worked all afternoon. She tried to convey the positive elements as well as the problems she encountered regarding the group-home idea for retarded children. But she knew she stressed the problem side a little too strongly. She thought it was probably because she never saw the old institutions which used to house mentally challenged people. She knew that the group homes were a giant step forward from these institutions.

She remembered Angel's sack dresses that came from one such institution. Angel spent her first thirteen years in a place like that. The fear that Angel exhibited when she was caught with the sugar was so evident. Ellie wondered how Angel was punished in those places. Whatever they did to her had a lasting effect. Ellie could still recall some of those incidents when Angel's face looked terrified and she would practically fly out of the room, arms flailing and voice screeching. Angel probably had many bad experiences at the old mental asylum, as people used to refer to those places. Yes the new system was so much better, but it was far from perfect. Probably no place was as perfect as a child's own home and family would have been.

The afternoon of productive writing really helped Ellie. She was tired of thinking about the mystery and disappointment of Kevin over and over. He loves me, he loves me not, he loves me, he loves me not… Eventually she stopped her writing, put everything away, and knelt by her bed and prayed. She did the same thing earlier that day before she went to class. She couldn't wait to share her thoughts with Sarah later in the evening.

Ellie wasn't very hungry for supper, but she was easily tempted to take a big piece of apple pie. Her mother usually whipped up a pint of whipped cream to go with it. Ellie got it out from the bowl in the refrigerator and topped her pie with a very generous dollop of it. Then she made herself a cup of instant coffee. Since her family wasn't ready for dinner yet, Ellie brought her GED materials to the kitchen table and reviewed her lesson plans as she ate. She washed her dish and her cup, grabbed her car keys and books and left.

She prayed again on her way to her GED job, and she prayed on her way home from GED.

"Dear Father God, I'm so tired, so exhausted. It's too hard to keep going through these emotional highs and lows I'm going through. I think I'm really ready for you to show me the truth.

"Please, Father, in Jesus name, show me if Kevin is interested in me as a girlfriend and possible wife or not. I'm finally ready to know the truth. I think I can take it whether it's a yes or a no. I just want to know. If there's some kind of fleece I can put out, some sign to ask for, show me. I don't want to be presumptuous and ask for some big sign or something miraculous or something. Please somehow show me. And please somehow confirm it to me, so I don't make a mistake.

"I really like Kevin and I think if he really knew me he'd like me a lot. But I get so mad at him too. It seems like he takes me for granted. Please, God, show me the answer, show me how to pray and please help me when I talk to Sarah. Help us both hear from You. Thank you, Lord…"

Ellie was excited her workday was over and she could now call Sarah. When she entered her room, she saw her very own white telephone and headed straight to it.

Chapter Twenty-Seven

"HI SARAH, is this a good time to talk?"

"Yep, perfect. How about for you? Is it a good time for a private conversation with me about Kevin?"

"Is it ever! Guess where I am?" Ellie asked.

"At home I guess. What do you mean?" Sarah asked.

"I'm sitting on my bed in my room and talking to you on the new telephone my parents had installed for me today as an early birthday present!"

"Wow, Ellie, that's great!"

"I know. I really appreciate it. Except for the fact that my mom said that now I can talk to Kevin whenever he calls in the late evenings. Except for that reminder, it was a great surprise."

"You never know, Ellie. Maybe he will call regularly and God will show us that he is the one for you," Sarah said hopefully.

"Maybe," Ellie said. "But the more I thought and prayed, the more I think that I'm really ready now to know the truth. If Kevin isn't interested in me as a girlfriend, I'm ready to accept that."

"So what do you think God was showing you, Ellie?" Sarah asked.

"I think He was showing me that I will know the truth soon, because He knows now I'm ready. The more I prayed the more ready I felt. I really want to know the truth. I'm really exhausted emotionally."

"That's great, Ellie. I kept thinking of the scripture that says the truth will set you free."

"Really? That's like a confirmation. When I know the truth, I'll feel good about it, free. I really want to know for sure and get a confirmation on the answer, Sarah," Ellie confided.

"That would be great. Things are always better if you get it from the mouth of two or three witnesses I think. Anything else you felt during your prayer time?"

"Well, I was wondering what you got," Ellie said.

"I'll tell you, but I don't want to contradict what you got, so if you're done telling me, I'll tell you."

"Oh there is one more thing, Sarah. I'm kind of feeling led to ask for a sign or a fleece or something. I thought maybe you'd have an idea."

"An idea for a sign to ask for, you mean?" Sarah asked.

"Yes," Ellie answered. "Did any such idea come to you?"

"I did have an idea, but I was struggling all through the day wondering if that was my idea or if God inspired it."

"What was it?"

"Well you know how Kevin asked you out for ice cream but you're really not going out for ice cream?"

"Mm..hmm," Ellie replied.

"Well maybe if you or if I kind of jokingly asked Kevin if he can go through with his promise of buying you ice cream, we can see how he reacts. If he agrees to it willingly, it's possible he's really interested in you, just a little scared of going too fast. If he hems and haws about it, then it probably means he'd feel awkward going on sort of a date and try to get out of it."

Ellie chuckled. "That's pretty clever. I think that's a possibility. Let's think about it. I don't know if I'd be able to figure a way to say it nonchalantly or if you should say it. We'll have to have a signal and let each other know if one of us did it already, so the other one won't do it again."

"Yeah it would sure be embarrassing if we both did it!" Sarah laughed. "Let's think."

"I can't think of any signal, can you?"

"I have an idea," Sarah said. "Since the ice cream place is called Dairy Queen, why don't we have this for a signal? If I get a chance to ask him first, I'll say, 'Hey Ellie, by the way, my brother found the missing queen from our chess set.'"

"I don't get it," Ellie said.

"What I mean is, if I say that line, it means I already popped the question to Kevin. The word 'queen' is like the queen in Dairy Queen and it should remind you that yes, I asked him the question about taking you to Dairy Queen for ice cream."

"Ok, I see, and then I'll know not to ask him. But I won't know the answer he gave, right?"

"Right. It'll just be the signal that one of us has already asked him, so the other one better not ask him the same question. But it won't tell what his answer was. We'll have to talk about that later, in private."

"Great, I think that might work. I'm excited to try it out. Maybe God guided us to this plan, Sarah," Ellie said. "But on the other hand, if God really guided us, it wouldn't be through a lie."

"But Ellie, my brother did misplace the queen about a year ago and he found it!" Sarah assured her.

"Oh neat! Now we just have to think of what I can say if I have to give you the signal? You know, if I happen to ask him first? I can't say my brother found the missing queen."

"No, but you can say, 'Sarah, I heard your brother lost his queen from his chess set. Did he ever find it?'"

Ellie replied, "Great! I like it! Oh, I hope I like the answer we get. Thanks so much for praying with me, Sarah, and for just being there for me to talk to!"

"My pleasure. As I said before, your life is so exciting it's fun to be part of it. It's you that has the hard part of living through it."

Ellie laughed and felt much better as they hung up.

Chapter Twenty-Eight

TUESDAY WAS A HARD DAY to get through. Ellie just had one class at school, then a long afternoon to get through before the Tuesday night Bible Study at Broken Wall. She would have to leave a little earlier to pick up Kevin from his office in one of the nearby suburbs.

She was more restless than usual in the afternoon. She tried to keep busy, doing schoolwork and helping her mom with the ironing.

"What should we make for supper?" her mom asked.

"Hmm, how about something that's not too complicated? I have to leave about 6:30 for Bible Study."

"Oh, it's Tuesday already, isn't it? Are you picking up Kevin or is he picking you up?" she asked.

"I'm picking him up at work," Ellie said. "The air conditioning on his car broke and it's in the shop today."

"Hope they fix it for him real soon. He's a nice guy, isn't he Ellie? Are you two getting serious about each other?"

"I don't think so," Ellie answered. "We're kind of happy just being friends for now."

Ellie felt convicted. That wasn't the truth. She wasn't "happy" just being friends. But maybe she would be if they were genuinely friends and not just "buddies." She sort of rationalized herself out of feeling guilty about the lie. But she really didn't convince herself.

Ellie wasn't used to sharing deeply with her mother about topics like religion or boys. And now at this big crisis time it was not easy to change.

"How about hamburgers and frozen tater tots for supper?" Ellie suggested, hoping the topic of Kevin would fall by the wayside.

"That sounds good to me. Do you have time to make them? I have a couple pounds of ground beef in the fridge."

"Sure," Ellie said, glad for something else to keep her busy.

Ellie left at 6:15 to pick up Kevin. He was standing outside his office waiting for her. The conversation thankfully stayed on a very safe topic, Daniel. Kevin started it by asking Ellie how Daniel was doing.

The Bible Study was as insightful as usual. It was practical too. And the prayers afterward were very comforting. Ellie went up for prayer at the end and asked the rabbi to pray for her. She told him to pray for an unspoken request. She was glad she heard about that option. That was a safe way to get needed prayer and yet not have to bare some confidential information. Ellie felt God would really protect and guide her now that she got prayer for it from her pastor.

Ellie liked talking to Ben and Candace afterwards, but she missed seeing Connie.

"I wonder why Connie's not here. I hope she's alright," Ellie worried.

"I just talked to her today," Candace said, "and she seemed fine. I'm not sure why she's not here. Something must have come up for her."

Ellie felt so close to the people at Broken Wall. They were becoming like family. She and Kevin, along with Ben and Candace, were the last ones to leave. Candace's kids were at a friends' house that evening.

Kevin and Ellie drove home talking about the Bible Study, the people there, and other odds and ends. Ellie figured Kevin didn't want to skirt too close to the topic of Ellie or her birthday and give away the surprise. And Ellie definitely did not want to get too deep into personal conversation with Kevin at this time when she was so mixed up and unsure about her own feelings.

"Have a great birthday morning and afternoon, Ellie," Kevin said as he dropped her off. "And I'll see you tomorrow evening about 7 o'clock for ice cream."

"Thanks," Ellie said. She was surprised that she was already losing confidence that Kevin liked her. Her mood was subdued. She thought maybe the answers to her prayers were already kicking in.

Chapter Twenty-Nine

"HAPPY BIRTHDAY ELLIE!" her father called out as Ellie made her way to the bathroom at six in the morning.

"Thanks Dad," Ellie said. She really didn't like to talk so early in the morning, but she appreciated her dad's greeting before he headed out to work.

Daniel had set up a bowl on the table with Ellie's favorite cereal in it, along with half a banana and a knife. There was a note leaning against the bowl.

"Just because I won't be up at the crack of dawn like you, don't think I forgot about your birthday! Sorry I couldn't leave the milk out for you. Well, I could have, but I thought you really wouldn't appreciate sour milk left out all night. Anyway, happy birthday!"

Ellie chuckled. What a nice family she had. As she got out the milk her mom came into the kitchen.

"Happy Birthday, Ellie! Would you like some scrambled eggs?"

"Thanks Mom, but look what Daniel left me. I think I'll just eat his gift."

Ellie kind of got out of the habit of taking a prayer walk since she began to take early morning classes. But she purposely got up a half hour earlier than usual this morning so she'd have time for that walk. It wasn't that she stopped praying. She prayed in the car on her way to school. But that just didn't seem as deep and connecting as praying on a walk.

She was glad she got up early to walk, even though it was predicted to be the hottest day of the year. The heat and humidity were already pretty stifling. But Ellie was glad to be outside again on a prayer walk.

"Dear Father God, I'm trying to really imagine You here with me on this walk. Help me today, God. You know what's happening. There's this big surprise party for me, but I'm not too happy, I'm almost miserable. Well not really. I have so many good friends, really great friends. And I have such a nice family too. And thank you God so much for Sarah.

"But You know I want to really get married and have my own family and You know how I was thinking it might be Kevin. I thought I really was in love with him and maybe he was with me. But now I don't know. What I'm feeling more and more is that he's not in love with me or even interested in me in that way even a little tiny bit.

"Oh God, you know what I need. You know how I need Your help today. I don't know what to say. I want to know the answer, but I hate to hear it if the answer is he's not interested. But if he's not, I really want to know it. This is hard, but I know it's time. Help me, God."

Then Ellie walked a while without praying anything. She didn't know what else to say. Then she jogged, then she ran, then she walked. Then she remembered something.

"God, I remember how the Holy Spirit is supposed to intercede for us in ways we don't know. Please Holy Spirit, intercede for me because I don't even know how to pray anymore. Please help me. I pray in Jesus name. Amen."

Ellie felt much better after her prayer walk. She felt like she expressed her heart to God and she could feel real hope that He would answer her and help her in her life. She felt less anxious and more encouraged. She got a little sweaty from her jogging and running, so she freshened up a bit and changed shirts before taking off for school.

The day had begun. And somehow Ellie managed to get through it. She wasn't hungry for supper, and she thought that worked out well, since there'd probably be food at the party. She put on a new pair of cut-off jeans, a birthday gift from her parents. She washed and ironed her favorite yellow and white striped T-shirt. That outfit looked perfect with her new brown sandals. Her hair was actually long enough to be put into a sort of pony tail with a silver barrette.

She sat close enough to the living room window so she could see when Kevin's car approached. She practiced in her mind the line she would say to Kevin at the party. "By the way, Kevin, when are you going to take me out for ice cream like you said?" She'd say it in a joking kind of way, but it would still be a good enough test to see Kevin's reaction. She hoped she wouldn't have to say it though. Yet she didn't have a lot of confidence in Sarah bringing it up. Sarah meant well, but Ellie couldn't picture Sarah being bold and crafty enough to actually carry out the plan, even though she thought it up herself.

Soon Ellie saw Kevin's white car coming down the road. "Bye everybody, Kevin's here."

"Have a great time," her mother and brother said together. Her father waved.

Ellie walked out of the house. And to her dismay, the little white car didn't stop for her. It wasn't Kevin after all. She wasn't too good at identifying the different car models; she usually got by just watching for the right size and color. But now she felt foolish and didn't want to go back inside to tell her family. She was quite relieved when a minute later another little white car pulled up and it actually was Kevin.

Chapter Thirty

"HI KEVIN. Thanks for doing this for me for my birthday."

"My pleasure," Kevin said. "I hope you don't mind stopping at the Kirby's old house first. I left a tool there that I need to pick up."

"Ok," Ellie agreed.

When they got there she thought she'd see a bunch of cars, but all she saw was Sarah's car.

Ellie thought she'd tease Kevin. "Should I just wait in the car for you?"

Kevin was quick. "No, you can help me look. I'm not sure where I left it."

As they both walked in, a whole crowd of people popped out of the bedrooms and kitchen and shouted "Happy Birthday, Ellie!"

Ellie actually *was* surprised. Where was everybody parked, she wondered.

"I, I don't know what to say. Thanks!"

She spotted Connie. "Connie, thanks for coming all the way out here! I was worried when you didn't show up at Broken Wall yesterday. Were you sick?"

"Sorry to worry you, Ellie, but I figured I'd stay home from Bible Study this week, since I wanted to use the car to come out here today for your party."

"Thanks, that was sure nice of you," Ellie said. Then she saw Sarah.

"Sarah, did you drive here all alone?"

"No, my dad is working on some project in the basement for a while. He'll join the party later though."

"Who thought this whole thing up?" Ellie asked, even though she knew the answer.

Candace told her that she and Cindy brainstormed the whole idea. Soon Daniel walked in carrying 3 boxes of pizza. A few minutes later Ben walked in with a cake he picked up from the supermarket bakery. There were chips and dip, vegetables, cans of soda, a jug of apple cider, and even a coffee maker with the inviting aroma of freshly brewed coffee in the air.

Ellie thought she wouldn't like the surprise party, but it was really a wonderful experience for her. She was glad it wasn't a real surprise, but parts of it were a nice surprise anyway. She realized she was loved and she had great friends. Then she noticed a little card table with gifts on it.

She almost hated to spoil the evening by playing the little trick on Kevin tonight. She decided she wouldn't bring up the question, and if Sarah did it, that would be fine. If Sarah didn't do it, that would be fine too.

All the windows were opened and there were three fans working. With the sun going down, it was quite pleasant in the house. People ate while sitting at various places on the floor. After the food, Ellie opened her gifts. She got another beautiful skirt from Sarah's family. Ben gave Ellie a little Star of David with a dove that could be pinned onto a coat or sweater. He always tried to support the congregational book and gift table. Candace and her children bought Ellie a variety of school supplies. Ellie was a little anxious when it came time to open Kevin's little package. It was the size of a necklace or even a ring box. But it turned out to be a cute, very small candle that smelled like vanilla.

Soon the games started up. Ellie joined the group playing Password. Kevin decided to join that group too. Kevin surprisingly said, "Ellie, let's be on a team." Ellie was having a great time. She and Kevin played against Connie and Joanne.

Around 9 o'clock the wind started picking up. Everyone headed outside to feel the refreshing cool front coming in from the North. Suddenly thunder was heard and lightning was spotted. There was no rain, but the most beautiful lightning storm Ellie ever witnessed began.

"This is better than seeing fireworks!" eleven year old Cindy said to Sarah. "And my brother is missing it because he went to a movie with Freddie's family! Serves him right for missing Ellie's birthday!"

Ellie overheard that little conversation between Cindy and Sarah and had to smile to herself. Conversations ebbed and flowed, people drifted here and there, and Daniel and Kevin ended up talking together under the fiercely swaying branches of the willow tree. Ellie was sitting nearby with Connie, when Connie decided she better leave. She had a long ride back home. It was dark and Ellie stayed put for a while, wondering if she should interrupt Daniel and Kevin and join them. Then she overheard an interesting conversation.

"So this is the place that you've been fixing up," Daniel commented.

"This is it," Kevin answered. "Actually Mr. Kirby took very good care of the place when they lived here. But he did have a full time job as well as a family and his Bible Study work, so a few things slipped by."

"I would guess so," Daniel said. "Are you thinking of buying this place, Kevin?"

"I don't know yet. I'm toying with the idea. I wanted to buy myself a fixer-upper for cheap, and fix it up slowly. I thought I could either move in when it was done, or sell it and use the money to get a better place. Then this house sort of fell into my lap."

"Are you thinking of houses because you think you'll be getting married soon, Kevin?"

"Ha ha, not soon, but some day. First I have to meet the right girl," Kevin said.

Though Daniel was surprised by this statement, he acted nonchalant about it. "Yeah, first things first," he chuckled. "Hey, I was wondering if you could show me the rest of the house and all the work you've done on it."

"Sure, let's go."

Ellie was really happy the darkness protected her. No one could see her expression. No one could even see her! She was glad because she didn't feel like talking to anyone but Sarah now. She found Sarah still talking and laughing with eleven year old Cindy.

"Hi Ellie. Cindy was just telling me the episode about her dog running away yesterday."

"Yeah, she told me about it earlier. That was pretty funny," Ellie managed to say.

"Oh by the way, Ellie," Sarah said, "I just wanted to let you know that my brother found that missing queen from his chess set."

"Oh that's interesting," Ellie said. "I mean that's good. It's hard to play chess without the queen."

Ellie and Sarah shared a brief exchange of knowing facial expressions. "Um, how long can you and your dad stay?" Ellie asked.

"He told me to get ready to leave, so actually I'm just waiting for him to come out of the house. Too bad it'll be so late when I get home. Will you be at school tomorrow morning?"

"Unfortunately, yes, for my early class."

"Great, I'll be coming in to sign up for my fall classes. Want to meet for lunch?"

"I'll be through with my class at 10," Ellie replied. "Want to meet for breakfast?"

They both laughed because they knew. Tomorrow would be the important "talk." And breakfast was better than lunch, at least two hours better!

Ellie endured the civilities of staying till the end of her party and saying good bye and letting everyone say good bye to her. Kevin, Candace and Ben stayed late to clean up.

Ellie excused herself graciously. "Thank you all so much for all you did to put this party on. I'd stay and help you clean, but I'm so tired and I have my early, early class tomorrow morning."

"Don't worry," Ben said. "You're not expected to clean up after your own surprise party."

"Thanks so much again," Ellie said. Everyone hugged her, including Kevin.

She walked alone to her car.

Chapter Thirty-One

ELLIE WAS FEELING LOW that night and the following morning. She planned to get up at 6 and go for a prayer walk, but when the alarm went off, she changed her mind. She was tired and depressed. When she finally got ready for school, she was upset with herself for not waking up earlier. Of all days, today she really needed the encouragement she usually got from her prayer walks.

It wasn't easy to pray in the car. Rush hour traffic into the city demanded her full concentration. She had a ten minute walk from where she parked to the education building, so she prayed. But she didn't feel like she made much headway. She didn't even know what to say. She didn't know what to ask and she didn't know how she felt or how to put it into words. She just said, "Oh Lord, I'm so sorry for not making more time to talk to You. Please just help me. I don't know what to ask for."

Just saying those words made her choked up and starting to cry, but she didn't have time to allow that. She swallowed hard, wiped her eyes, headed to the water fountain, then the bathroom, then her class. In class Ellie was revived. The professor chose to talk about the advantages and disadvantages of group homes for the mentally disabled. She called on Ellie for her input a lot.

Ellie was glad she completed her paper, because now her thoughts about the issue were well organized. She was able to talk about the tell-tale signs of institutionalism on Angel: the sack dresses, the fears, the running. She also shared the hard aspects of group homes for both the residents and the staff. She talked about the advantages of getting attached to the children and the children to the staff, then the hardship that could ensue because of changes, transfers, people quitting, and so on. Everyone was very interested. The professor mentioned that Ellie wrote a paper on that topic. She then asked Ellie to share her example of how taking Benton out led to her change of topics.

"I didn't even think of the fact that Benton was black and I was white," Ellie said. "But when I heard some comments, I realized a lot of the stares were because of that, and not because of Benton's disability."

A black girl raised her hand and said a similar thing happened to her when she took out a little Down's syndrome girl who was white. The discussion got very interesting. The professor decided to have each student share the results of their research with the whole class the following week. Ellie left class feeling a lot better. She prayed, "Thanks, Lord, for making class so interesting today. I really needed that."

She started remembering that God had good plans for her life. If He answered her prayers about Kevin, He could answer her other prayers too. She was eager to meet up with Sarah and hear if God had indeed confirmed the answer like they asked for.

"Sarah!!" Ellie yelled when she saw Sarah outside walking towards the cafeteria.

"Ellie!!" Sarah yelled back and ran to meet her.

"So glad you're here early! My class just got out. It was so interesting. I'm so glad Candace suggested I change the topic of my paper!" Ellie blurted out.

"I don't know what you're talking about," Sarah said. "Do you mean the paper about your outing with Benton?"

"Yeah, but I can tell you more about that later. Let's sit at that booth way over there, and you can tell me what happened when you asked Kevin that question."

"Ok," Sarah said. "Do you mind if I get myself a glass of orange juice first?"

"Sure, maybe I will too."

They both waited to talk till they were at their booth. Sarah began, "So I'll just start, ok?" Ellie nodded and Sarah continued. "Well, right when everyone was going outside, when the wind started blowing and everything, I stayed in to shut off the fans. Kevin was just getting himself another glass of root beer, so we were the only ones in the house then. I went into the kitchen and said, 'Hey Kevin, is there any ice cream in the freezer there? You did promise Ellie ice cream today didn't you?'

"Kevin said, 'You're right! I should have gotten ice cream.' Then I said, 'I'm sure Ellie wouldn't mind if you took her out for ice cream a different day.' Then Kevin said, 'I have a better idea. I'll not only get Ellie ice cream, I'll bring a box of cones and a couple tubs of ice cream to the oneg this week! That way everyone who comes to Broken Wall can get some too! Maybe you'd like to visit next Saturday, Sarah.' "

"Oh brother," Ellie said. "Leave it to Kevin to change the conversation from getting ice cream with me to inviting you to Broken Wall."

"That's true. Typical Kevin-style," Sarah agreed.

"He sure thought up a good option fast, I mean instead of taking me out for ice cream. What a clever idea, and what a revelation too. I think God answered our prayers, Sarah," Ellie said, not trying to hide her sadness.

"But Ellie, we prayed for a confirmation, remember? Don't jump to any conclusions yet. Maybe Kevin really thinks you'd like it better if he got ice cream for all your friends at Broken Wall," Sarah said optimistically.

"Sarah, I got the confirmation. I didn't tell you what I heard yet."

"What do you mean? Tell me!" Sarah insisted.

"Ok. I was outside talking to Connie, and then she had to leave. Kevin and Daniel were talking and I was debating about whether to join them or not. So I just stayed where I was, close to your garage. It was pretty dark, so they didn't see me. Then I heard their conversation. Daniel was asking Kevin why he wanted to buy a house and fix it up. He asked Kevin if he was thinking of getting married soon. Kevin just laughed and said he hopes to get married someday, but first he has to meet the right girl."

"Oh no," Sarah said, not knowing what to say afterwards.

"Yep," Ellie assented to her silent look.

"Hmm," Sarah replied. More silence.

"I know," Ellie responded.

"Yeah," Sarah agreed.

"So what do I do now? I think it's pretty clear that God answered our prayers, don't you?" Ellie asked.

"Yes, I think so. He even confirmed it, with what I heard and what you heard. I think it's good to know, Ellie. You've been frustrated on and off with Kevin for over a year already. So now you can get on with your life."

"Thanks Sarah," Ellie said sincerely yet gloomily. "Do you think there's hope for me to meet somebody else?"

"Of course! And I think it'll be much easier now that you know the truth about Kevin. Was it a big shock to you, Ellie?" Sarah wanted to know.

"No, I think I knew it all along. And when I really prayed, I think God was showing me even before we heard anything. So you're right. It is a good thing. I believe it. It's just hard to feel happy about it right now though," Ellie confided.

"I know. So what do you think you should do? Tell Kevin you don't want to hang around so much anymore? Or just kind of gradually back out and do less and less with him? Or what?"

"That's a hard question. I don't really want to confront him. But on the other hand, how can I just suddenly back out and not help him and not ride with him to services with no explanation?" Ellie asked.

"I guess you can make up truthful excuses of things you have to do, which would be real things," Sarah suggested.

"That sounds like the easiest way. I hope he gets the hint though," Ellie said.

Ellie and Sarah parted, with no real plan agreed upon for the next step. Sarah promised to pray for Ellie, and for that, Ellie was grateful. Ellie also agreed that Sarah could tell her parents and then they could all pray for Ellie. Ellie needed all the prayers she could get.

When Ellie got home, Daniel was there. He went out of his way to be nice to Ellie. Ellie could tell he was shaken up by Kevin's response too.

"Thanks for being so nice to me Daniel. I know the reason behind it," Ellie informed him.

"What do you mean? Can't I be nice just because I'm your brother? I thought I was always nice to you," Daniel tried to convince her.

"I overheard your conversation with Kevin last night," Ellie blurted out. "I was by the garage with Connie and she left, so I was actually wondering if I should join you and Kevin. Then I started hearing your conversation."

"Oh no," Daniel said. "What did you hear?"

"I heard that Kevin wants to get married someday, when he meets the right girl," Ellie said.

"Yeah, I was shocked by that too, Ellie. I really thought he had met the right girl, YOU!"

"Thanks, Daniel. But one thing you don't know is that I prayed that God would give me a confirmation that night of whether or not Kevin really liked me in that way or not."

"You've got to be kidding!" Daniel exclaimed.

"No, Sarah and I prayed all that day and the day before about it. We even had our own plan to uncover the answer," Ellie explained. She told Daniel about the ice cream question plot and the results. She also explained that she didn't want to assume anything if it wasn't true, so they prayed for confirmation.

"No way!" Daniel said. "Amazing. And it seems like God used me as part of the way to answer your prayer! You really got the confirmation!"

"So now the question is what do I do? Just gradually back off from doing so many things with Kevin?" Ellie asked.

"No, you have to tell him. How can you just stop going to help him mow? How can you keep saying you don't need a ride when you both go to the same church? I think he has to be told."

"I think you're right, but I hate to do it," Ellie said.

"I have an idea. I'll do it for you," Daniel offered.

"That's so nice of you, Daniel," Ellie said, with tears in her eyes. "But I think this is something I need to do myself. Otherwise when I see him next it'll be so awkward. I won't know how to act."

As it turned out, that very evening Ellie used her own phone to call Kevin. It wasn't exactly the type of late evening phone call her parents envisioned when they got her the phone.

"Hi Kevin. Are you busy now?" Ellie asked.

"Not too busy. Hi Ellie. What's up?" Kevin asked, unsuspecting.

"Well, first I wanted to thank you for helping set up that surprise party for me. It sure was nice. I can't believe all the people that showed up!"

"It was a good turnout, wasn't it?" Kevin agreed. "But I didn't do too much. Candace and her daughter were the main movers and shakers."

"That's what I heard," Ellie said. "And the house is looking really good. You're doing a great job on it."

"Thanks. I kind of enjoy that type of work. Mr. Kirby seemed pleased when he saw it yesterday."

"That's good. But I wanted to tell you I probably won't be coming to help you mow too much anymore."

"Sorry Ellie, did I work you too hard?" Kevin was concerned.

"No, I wanted to do it. But after the neighbor made that statement about me being your girlfriend, it made me start thinking. I think we better not do too many things together, otherwise other people might start thinking that way." It was hard for Ellie, but she was satisfied with the way her words were flowing.

"Um, I don't think it matters much what other people think," Kevin said, sounding a bit unsure of himself.

"Well, I think if we're really not boyfriend and girlfriend, we probably shouldn't do so much together anyway. That way if somebody was interested in one or the other of us, they would think we were already matched up," Ellie said, a little stumbling, but pretty coherent for the nervous state of mind she was in at the moment.

"You've got a point there," Kevin said. "I hope we can still be friends though."

"Sure," Ellie said. "Just like the song says, friends are friends forever if the Lord's the Lord of them."

Kevin laughed. Ellie was relieved. Then Ellie quickly changed the subject.

After talking a bit about Kevin's job and Ellie's GED work, they hung up. Ellie had a feeling of peace. She was low, but she was content. She wanted to call Sarah, but she didn't even seem to have the emotional energy to talk to Sarah tonight. She prayed and went to bed.

Chapter Thirty-Two

ELLIE HAD WRITTEN OUT a scripture verse that she taped on the side of her dresser. She wrote it out over a year ago. It was from Psalm 27: "I had fainted unless I had believed to see the goodness of the Lord in the land of the living. Wait on the Lord, be of good courage, and he shall strengthen thine heart, wait, I say, on the Lord."

That verse helped her so many times when she was hopeful and not hopeful about Kevin. She especially liked the part that said "in the land of the living." She knew she'd see God's goodness in its fullness after she died. What she really needed to remember was that she could expect to see His goodness in her life right now, in the land of the living. She felt that she, like David who wrote the psalm, would have fainted, given up, if she didn't believe that. And now that her dreams about Kevin were turned upside down, this verse really helped her to keep up her courage.

She recited the verse out loud as she continued packing her suitcase. God had really carried her through the past several weeks and this weekend she was very excited about going to the Messianic Jewish weekend conference downstate. She realized how far she had come from her initial stage of shock, disappointment and confusion after giving up her dreams about Kevin. She was grateful for all the love and support she got from the Lord and her friends that helped bring her to this point.

Her talks and prayers with Sarah helped her tremendously. Also, she and Connie were becoming better friends and started meeting together a little before each Tuesday night Bible study. They usually walked around the block where Broken Wall met and prayed together for God to guide each of them to the Godly husband He had for them. Praying aloud together with Sarah and now also Connie helped bolster her faith that God was really hearing and would really answer.

Ellie's prayer walks in the morning became a steady habit again. She was actually starting to feel God's goodness and presence in her life again. Reading *Appointment in Jerusalem* during those weeks really really helped her too. When she saw how God worked in the life of Lydia Prince, a Danish school-teacher in the 1920s, she found her own depression lifting. Ellie had faith that God would help and guide her, just as He did in the true story about Lydia.

Her work and school decisions also kept her from sulking. She completed her commitment of teaching the GED class for the rest of the semester, but decided against signing up for it again in the fall semester. She wanted to devote more time to her studies as she continued to work full time toward her master's degree.

She did find a small position to replace the GED job. It involved teaching a class only one evening a week. It was a cooking class for mentally challenged adults living at a nearby mental health institution. What a pleasure it was for her to teach those students. They didn't criticize her. They loved everything she did and all the foods they made. They came with a couple of care-givers from the institution where they lived, so there were plenty of helpers for clean-up and food prep. It was just enough of a job to help Ellie feel like an adult, contributing something to her own education, yet giving her the time she needed to take a full load of classes.

Then something special happened that surprised Ellie. The high holy days arrived. The delight Ellie felt in celebrating them for the first time was an unexpected joy. Feast of Trumpets, Yom Kippur, Feast of Tabernacles…Ellie wondered how this rich heritage could have been hidden from her for so long.

The singles group at Broken Wall had many gatherings during these feasts. Some of them started a tradition of hanging around the synagogue all day between the morning and evening services. They talked, prayed, walked and ate (or fasted) together. It was a real bonding experience.

There were changes occurring in the lives of these people too. Connie's sister Bonnie started attending regularly. Bill seemed like he was getting interested in Connie. Ben and Candace broke up.

It turned out that Candace had a more complicated story than Ellie originally thought. Candace had another older son who lived with her first husband. Since her second divorce was still pending, Rabbi Weisman counseled Ben that it was not a good time to date Candace.

Broken Wall also went through some changes. Saturday morning services had been replaced by Friday evening Erev Shabbat services. Another innovation was the addition of a weekly Sunday morning service. Many people who liked attending and learning about the Jewish roots of their faith were used to going to Sunday services. And the singles started a sort of pattern of going out to lunch together after the Sunday morning services. It was a lot of fun.

However, one of the most rewarding things that happened in those months was that now Daniel was coming to Broken Wall Bible Studies. Ever since he heard about God answering Ellie's prayers so specifically on the day of her birthday party, he was hooked. He had been searching for the truth about God for quite some time, but didn't share it with anyone. He began talking more and more to Ellie after her big let-down with Kevin. Daniel thought he was doing it for Ellie's sake, but he ended up getting so much out of it himself. Those talks actually helped both of them so much.

And now here was Ellie preparing for a Messianic Jewish conference weekend at a resort downstate. She would be driving with Connie's sister Bonnie, while Connie drove with Bill. Ben would be picking up a friend who lived halfway between here and there. Kevin thought he might be able to come for one day of the four day event, but he wasn't sure. He offered to drive Daniel down for the day, if he was able to get off work.

Ellie, Connie and Bonnie roomed together. They had a small room with two bunk beds in a pretty rugged and small cabin. Though the accommodations were a bit of a disappointment, the natural splendor of their surroundings as well as the weather couldn't have been improved upon.

"I'm so glad we're here," Bonnie said. "I thought we might not make it!"

"Oh no, I thought the ride was a little bumpy. But I didn't know anything was wrong," Ellie said.

"Yeah, how did you manage to sleep?" Bonnie said.

"I guess I was pretty tired. I stayed up pretty late finishing my research paper and getting my supplies ready for my cooking class on Monday," Ellie explained.

"Well, I didn't want to wake you, but something's definitely wrong with the car. It got worse and worse the farther we drove. I'll have to take it in somewhere as soon as possible."

As Ellie unpacked, Bonnie left their cabin looking for someone to advise her about her car. She came back greatly relieved.

"Ben said he'd find out where the closest repair shop is and he'd follow me there. Can you ride with me, Ellie? I'm a little scared to be in that car by myself now."

"Sure," Ellie agreed.

Ben had a friend in his car too. Mark was the friend that he picked up on the way. He was a very chubby fellow, not too popular, who loved coming to Messianic Jewish conferences. Ben met him at another conference and so Mark called to ask Ben if he could hitch a ride with him to this one.

Ellie was pretty impressed with Ben. He was so willing to help, first Mark, then Bonnie. He was very sincere about his faith. Ellie felt something happening in her heart toward Ben. She had a good time with all her friends that weekend, but she found herself observing Ben a little more than usual.

When she got home, Daniel was the only one in the house.

"Oh Daniel, you and Kevin missed a super conference!"

"You'll have to tell me all about it sometime," Daniel said. "But Doug's coming to pick me up for a movie in ten minutes, so just tell me one thing that stands out to you."

"Well, one thing that stands out is that I think my heart is turning toward Ben."

"Really? You're gonna marry him," Daniel jokingly predicted.

"What?!" Ellie said.

"Yep, don't ask me how I know. I just have this feeling. I know Ben is looking for a wife and wants to get married. As for Kevin, well, I don't think he was."

Ellie chuckled. "I knew I shouldn't have told you anything like that!"

But as she went on unpacking, Daniel's statement stayed in her mind for a long, long time.

Part Three: Fulfillment

Delight thyself also in the Lord; and He shall give thee the desires of thine heart. — *Psalm 37:4*

Chapter One

ELLIE GOT TO THE RESTAURANT FIRST, hoping Sarah wouldn't be too far behind. Sarah was already into her second week of fall semester at the city university, and Ellie was meeting her close to campus for lunch. Ellie planned this fun outing with Sarah when she found herself off of work for a whole week! After she graduated, Ellie began working at the Monroe Avenue Workshop for Mentally Challenged Adults. And this week they were closed for a week of renovations.

Ellie chose a nice booth by the window and started perusing the menu, in between frequent glances out the window in the hopes of seeing Sarah. Ellie couldn't wait for Sarah to arrive. Catching up on the news from each other's lives in person was so much more fun than doing it over the phone.

Soon Ellie stopped looking at the menu and just stared out the window. She was beginning to worry about Sarah. Her class should have ended more than a half hour ago. Maybe she shouldn't have suggested this restaurant. Maybe they should have met at the campus cafeteria. Ellie felt responsible because she kind of took it upon herself to keep stretching Sarah to go beyond things she was familiar with. She felt sorry for Sarah being in such a protective and rather restrictive home. So she suggested this restaurant, knowing full well that Sarah had never ventured off campus before. Sarah commuted to school on the train and got off at the stop that was practically next door to the education building where she had most of her classes.

Ellie didn't think this restaurant neighborhood was very dangerous in the middle of the afternoon, but now she was beginning to wonder. She hoped Sarah wasn't mugged. In the midst of her musings, the bell on the door jingled and Ellie looked up. It was Sarah!

"Sarah, over here!" Ellie called out. Sarah saw Ellie, smiled, and walked over.

"I'm so glad you made it here, Sarah," Ellie said with genuine relief. "Did you find the place ok? Did you get lost? Were my directions good?"

"Yes, yes and yes. I'm here now, so I did find it. And your directions were good. But I didn't see that dress shop where you told me to turn left. Eventually I asked somebody where the dress shop was and it turned out that I just went two blocks out of my way."

"Great! Thanks for agreeing to this lunch, Sarah. It's so nice to be together again."

"It sure is!" Sarah said. "This is a really cute restaurant and the food sure smells good. I love Mexican food! How did you ever find out about it?"

"During my last semester one of my classmates suggested we meet here and brainstorm about a team project we had to do."

"Oh, I kind of remember you telling me about it," Sarah said. "I'm so glad you have the week off. This is so fun!"

"For me too! I sure miss talking to you in person these days," Ellie said.

"I agree. There's nothing like talking in person! I'm glad you graduated and all, and glad you got that job at the workshop too. Yet I still wish you weren't finished with school."

"It sure worked out great for a while though," Ellie said. "I think we both needed that year to talk. It was a hard year for me and I think, with your family moving, it was a hard year for you too."

"It was, but guess what? Maybe we *will* be seeing each other more often again. My father finally agreed that it would be ok if I wanted to try out your congregation sometime."

"That's great, Sarah!" Ellie exclaimed. "I was hoping you'd be able to come someday. Actually, I've been praying that for quite some time now."

"Really? Thanks a lot, Ellie. How are things going there at Broken Wall these days? I want to hear all about it after we place our orders."

Ellie ordered the chicken tostadas and Sarah chose the beef tacos. They were both enjoying the homemade corn chips and salsa on the table already.

As they munched Ellie began, "Let's see, when did we talk last?"

"We talked briefly on the phone about a week ago, but we didn't really talk-talk since you came over for Sunday dinner about six weeks ago," Sarah lamented.

"That's right. It's been quite a while since we really talked. I'm so glad you can come to Broken Wall, Sarah. I really want you to see for yourself what it's like. And Sundays aren't easy for me to get to your place anymore, because I don't want to miss out on the singles fellowship at Broken Wall. You remember how I told you that we all go out to a restaurant for lunch after the services?"

"I do remember. That must be so nice," Sarah said. "Did that couple ever get married, the one with the guy from Israel and the girl from Indiana?"

"They did, just last week. They got married in a nice ceremony right before the Friday night Sabbath service. Then they both stayed for the service in their wedding clothes and all. It was pretty amazing to see Kathy in her wedding dress during the Shabbat service, singing and worshiping the Lord with her hands raised."

"That's neat! Was her dress fancy?" Sarah asked.

"Far from it," Ellie explained. "Her dress was white and it was nice, but it wasn't a gown. And she had a little veil too, but it wasn't exactly a wedding veil. And for flowers, they bought a lot of really colorful and realistic looking artificial flowers from the craft stores. She did carry in a bouquet of real flowers that somebody brought from their garden."

"That's cute," Sarah commented. "When are they planning to move back to Israel?"

"In about six months," Ellie answered. "That's why they had such a simple wedding. They're trying to save money for when they go back. They found a great place to stay in the meantime. Somebody needed a couple to house-sit their house for several months, so Kathy and Asher get a whole house to themselves! It's all furnished and everything and they don't have to pay anything," Ellie explained.

"That's incredible! I hope I get to meet them soon."

"You will, I'm sure. And you'll be able to see some of the people you met a while back at my surprise birthday party."

"I know," Sarah said. "Is anything new happening there?"

"One new thing is that I'm working at the book table these days. Rabbi Weisman wanted two people to work the book table, so Ben asked me if I would volunteer to help him with it."

"No you didn't tell me. How is that going?" Sarah wanted to know.

"I'm enjoying it. I'm happy to be there and tell people how much different things cost and stuff. It's nice to meet and talk to some people I haven't met before. You know how that is. You get in the rut of sticking with the people you know and are comfortable with and never get around to meeting the new people."

"Sure, that's natural," Sarah said.

"So I answer questions and sell things, but I don't like to talk things up. I figure if somebody wants a book or a Star of David necklace or something, they'll get it. If not, I'm not planning to talk them into it. But Ben! He's a born salesman. It's not like he's trying to make money or twist their arms or anything. He so believes in what he's doing, that's what drives him. He says more people need to get good books and read them. And more people need to advertise their faith and wear a pin or necklace that can cause people to ask questions or see where they stand. He's so adamant about it. I believe those things too, but I'm not so enthusiastic… or bold. He really talks things up. And a lot of people seem to need that extra push to buy something, it seems, because after they hear his spiel, they do!"

Sarah laughed. Then Ellie handed Sarah a little bag. "This comes from the book table, Sarah."

"Oh boy, I hope it's what I think it is. It is! Thanks! I wanted to read *Appointment in Jerusalem* ever since you first told me about it," she told Ellie.

"I wanted to give you a copy for your birthday, but we were out. Finally the new order came in. I'm just, let's see, about six months late."

"Thanks Ellie. I really appreciate it!"

Sarah used up their last napkins to wipe off her hands before opening her book. They had to flag down the waitress to get more napkins. It was a delicious, but very messy meal.

"Does this remind you of dinner time at Monroe Center, Ellie?" Sarah asked.

"Not until right now," Ellie laughed. "I'm sure glad I'm working at the workshop now, though. Monroe Center was nice at the start, but now that they changed it all around, I don't think it's that homey anymore."

"I know," Sarah agreed. "I think that's terrible that they moved all the low level kids together and all the blind kids together and all the high level kids together. It's not like a real family there anymore. And then when you told me about your co-workers using drugs right on your shift! That was the straw that broke the camel's back. When I told my parents that, they told me to call and kind of resign from my volunteer work right then and there!"

"I remember," Ellie said.

"So how is your new job of teaching at the workshop going?" Sarah asked

"It's going pretty well. Most days I teach a few classes on telling time, reading signs and basic things like that. But some days when they're short-staffed, I actually work on the production floor and help supervise the clients. I kind of like the variety. And sometimes, if a company needs an order fast, the staff even has to pitch in and help. A couple of times last month we all had to work overtime to assemble and then shrink-wrap toy airplanes. I mean, I wouldn't want to assemble airplanes and shrink-wrap packages all day, but it is interesting to do every now and then. It helps us relate to what our clients, you know, my students, have to do every day. So all in all, I'd say it's a pretty interesting job, although sometimes I'd say it's too interesting."

"In a good way or a bad way?" Sarah wanted to know.

"Well I was thinking of the time when one client got so upset he threw a chair. It was scary. The guy who did it was this good looking guy in his twenties who was in the military for two years and married. Then he was in an accident and had severe brain damage. Now he's very mentally challenged. I think his wife divorced him too."

"That's really sad, to have had a normal life and job, and then to have to start all over again," Sarah said.

"I know. I really feel sorry for him. I don't even know if he remembers he was married before. But I think in his spirit he knows there's more to life, but can't figure out what happened. Even so, he does get on my nerves at times. He tries to act so cool. Sometimes he's so contrary and doesn't feel like working, so he just talks and talks and talks. A lot of our clients are not the most diligent workers, but that's easy to understand. I know how boring it can be, just weighing and boxing nails, or folding airplane wings all day, every day."

"I know I wouldn't enjoy that! That's so nice you get to teach some classes and provide some variety in their days," Sarah offered.

"You're so encouraging, Sarah!" Ellie said. "I really miss you. So tell me, how is it going for you?"

"Pretty good, I'd say. I like all my classes this semester. But I guess the biggest new thing is that I finally started going to the youth group, or rather the college group at our new church."

"That's interesting," Ellie commented. "I wonder why you didn't start going earlier, since you've lived in your new place for almost a year now?"

"Good question. I'm not sure myself. I guess it was a little intimidating to me, not really knowing anybody in the church very well yet. But finally I was getting desperate for more friends and fellowship. So anyway, I started going about two weeks ago and I'm liking it."

"I think that was a good decision for you, Sarah. Tell me about it. What do you do there?"

Ellie and Sarah talked and talked and had a delightful time catching up on each other's lives. But so far Ellie didn't bring up the thing, or more accurately the person, she really wanted to talk about. She wondered if she waited too long and if it was too late now.

"Sarah, do you have any more classes today?" Ellie inquired.

"Nope, I'm through for the day. I'm planning to take the 2:30 train home. Mom is picking me up at 3:30. What time is it now?" she asked.

"It's just 1:30. Why don't we walk to the train station together and we can talk more?" Ellie suggested.

"I'd love to," Sarah agreed. "We have almost a whole hour!"

Ellie didn't beat around the bush. "You remember Ben, right? I already told you about working with him at the book table."

"Of course. I talked with him at the party, remember?"

"I guess my mind was on something else the day of that party," Ellie confessed.

"That's an understatement," Sarah laughed.

Ellie continued. "Well I really think Ben's a nice guy. And I think he might be interested in me, but I'm not sure."

"This is funny, Ellie. It reminds me of what the people said at the wedding in Cana, after Jesus turned the water into wine, 'Why have you saved the best wine until the end?' And I'm wondering why you saved the most stimulating, exciting topics until the last hour of our time together?" Sarah asked.

"I wasn't sure I wanted to talk about it much, and I didn't know if you'd be interested," Ellie replied.

"What?! Ellie, have you forgotten all about my personality already? Don't you remember how I used to love hearing about how your relationship with Kevin was going all the time?"

"Thanks Sarah. But actually I do remember our conversations and I also remember how it turned out. And I was thinking that maybe I talked about it too much and didn't pray about it enough or act on it enough or something. Anyway, I don't want this relationship with Ben to end up the same way. What I mean is, I feel so witless and adolescent about how it took me so long to figure things out about Kevin. And it was all pretty apparent right from the start."

"But Ellie," Sarah encouraged her, "it wasn't so obvious. Don't you remember the double signals you were getting from Kevin?"

"True, but when I was re-thinking about that, I realized I was doing a double standard thing myself. I was taking all the positive signs whole-heartedly and I was overlooking or excusing or explaining away all the negative signs."

"Hmm, maybe so. But don't be so hard on yourself. Don't you think talking it out helped?"

"You're right, Sarah. It sure did. I don't know what I would have done without you to talk to. I know it helped. So maybe it's good to tell you a little of how I'm feeling about Ben. You're sure you don't mind hearing about it?" Ellie asked again.

"Ellie!" Sarah admonished.

"Ok. Well you know how we have a whole lot of group get-togethers with the Broken Wall people for prayer meetings and outings and things like that. And now Ben and I also share the book table ministry. But we don't do much else by ourselves, I mean with just Ben and me. At least it doesn't start out like that. But sometimes when different people leave different events, the two of us just so happen to end up being left together by ourselves. It seems like we both enjoy those times a lot and have some real good talks. And…" Ellie stopped herself. She decided not to share her next thought with Sarah.

"And??" Sarah asked, trying to spur Ellie on to continue.

"And, um, you know, a lot of the same old stuff that happened between Kevin and me. I just don't want to make the same mistake. So anyway, I'd appreciate your prayers."

"Sure. Actually, I kind of already knew you were getting interested in Ben. Whenever you would tell me about Broken Wall news, Ben would usually be in the forefront of your interesting anecdotes."

"Anecdotes!" Ellie laughed. "That's an interesting way of phrasing it."

They reached the train station and sat on the bench till the train arrived. Ellie shared more, but she didn't share everything on her heart. She kept her deeper ponderings to herself. The train arrived and they both agreed that they should get together more often than once every six weeks.

Ellie realized just how helpful it was for her to share with Sarah. She smiled as she headed toward the parking lot where her car was parked. Suddenly she thought she heard someone call her name. She turned around and looked. It was Kevin.

"Kevin, what are you doing here?!"

"I can ask you the same question," Kevin replied.

"I just walked Sarah to the train station. We met for lunch."

"I wish I'd known," Kevin said. "I just got out of a tax-law seminar from work. Now I'm heading to a place to mail this package. And guess what it is."

"I have no idea," Ellie said.

"It's the extra set of keys I have from the Kirby house. I'm done with my different renovating jobs there and the house was just turned over to the real estate company. So now I'm putting the keys in the mail. If only I knew Sarah would be here, I could have given the package directly to her," he said, hoping for a little sympathy.

"I'm so sorry," Ellie began.

Kevin laughed. "Sorry, I didn't mean to make you feel bad, Ellie. It's not your fault."

"I know," Ellie said, a little embarrassed that she so easily fell into the trap of pitying Kevin. "I had the week off from work and Sarah was back at school, so I thought it would be nice to have lunch with her."

"Sounds like a pleasant thing to do on your day off," Kevin said.

"It was." Then Ellie brought up a new topic, "I haven't seen you lately at Broken Wall. Are you coming back?"

"I hope to," Kevin said. "I've been racing around lately, trying to finish up work on the Kirby house so I can start the rehab on the house I just bought."

"You bought a house?" Ellie was surprised.

"Yes I did. It's a little farther out than I was originally planning, but it's a great fixer-upper. It's on the border of the western suburbs and the countryside," Kevin explained.

"Oh that's a really nice area. But I hope you still give yourself time to go to some congregation regularly," Ellie said.

"You sound like Ben now," Kevin joked. "I know I should and I plan to get back to it. I really do."

They talked very amicably until Ellie had to turn off toward the parking lot. Ellie felt just a little bit unsettled after that surprise encounter. But she thought she handled it well and was glad she and Kevin could still be friends.

Chapter Two

SATURDAY AFTERNOON FOUND ELLIE getting ready to go to Ben's house. At the Friday night service there was so much talk about the terrorism going on in Israel, that Ben suggested a prayer meeting. Many of the young people had been enjoying snacks and conversation together at the oneg after the service, so Ben invited them all to his house the next day. Joanne suggested everybody bring a dish to share for a pot-blessing meal after the prayer meeting.

Ellie liked the phrase "pot-blessing" instead of "pot-luck." But her brother always made fun of it, so Ellie watched her words and didn't say it around him. She didn't care for his teasing, though in all other ways he was a great brother. He wasn't a believer yet, but he was coming around slowly but surely to faith in Yeshua. Ellie even thought there was a chance that Daniel might believe already, but was just too shy to reveal it yet. She did know that he still felt uncomfortable in praying out loud because he told her that himself. He said that was why he didn't attend prayer meetings. He liked the Sunday services though. Often, though not always, he would attend the service and then join the restaurant crowd afterwards.

Daniel wasn't at home when Ellie was preparing her contributions for the pot blessing meal. She made a big batch of popcorn with her special blend of salt and a smoky flavored torula yeast sprinkled on top. Everyone seemed to like it a lot, contrary to Daniel's expressions of disgust whenever he saw her sprinkle the torula yeast on perfectly good popcorn. She also made her special drink, apple juice tea, with frozen apple juice and gentle orange herbal tea. And she made five tuna salad sandwiches and cut each one into 4 triangles, making 20 little hors d'oeuvres.

Joanne, Connie and Bill were already at Ben's house when Ellie arrived. They all greeted each other with a hug. It always seemed to Ellie that Ben's hug was the warmest. In a little while Bonnie arrived and five minutes later Ralph joined the group. After a half hour or so of friendly conversation, Ben began the meeting. He reviewed the latest news he heard about the situation in Israel, and then they all sat in a circle on the floor and prayed. Ben sat next to Ellie. Some people had their eyes closed and some didn't. The prayers were really heart-felt and they ended by holding hands and singing together Hinei Ma Tov, which means how good and pleasant it is for brothers to dwell together in unity. When they ended, Ben gave Ellie's hand a tender squeeze. He did that often. That set Ellie's mind to wondering if he was interested in her, because she was indeed growing in her fondness for Ben.

They ate and talked until Bill suggested they play the dictionary game. He explained, "One person picks a word from the dictionary that he thinks no one has heard of. He tells everyone the word to make sure it's new to everyone. Then everyone writes down a definition that sounds like it could be the real thing. When all the definitions are turned in, the leader reads them along with the real definition mixed in. People then vote for the definition that they think is the real one. Whenever someone votes for your definition, you get a point. And if you vote for the real definition, you get a point."

"That sounds like fun," Ben said. "Let me get out some paper and pencils."

"Don't forget the dictionary," Connie called.

The game, the prayers, the fellowship… Ellie couldn't have asked for more. The food too was extraordinary—especially the Israeli hummus, falafel and pita bread that Joanne brought. That was sure nice of Joanne to go through all that trouble and bring all that food. But then again,

Ellie wondered if Joanne had an ulterior motive. Before she left, Joanne told Ben she would be at the university where he worked on Monday morning for a seminar. Ellie eavesdropped as that whole little interaction was taking place.

"I'd like to invite you to breakfast, Ben, my treat," Joanne said. "Your school does serve breakfast, doesn't it?"

"Yes it does. My co-workers are forever carrying in plates with eggs or bacon or sweet rolls. So yes, I'm sure they serve breakfast. And yes, that would be nice to meet for breakfast, Joanne. What time will you be there?"

"I have to be there at 10 o'clock, so we can meet at 9:00 or earlier if you want," Joanne offered.

"9:00 is fine. I don't start work till 11:30 on Monday since that's my day to work evenings."

"Oh, I don't want to make you get to work so early," Joanne said.

"No problem," Ben assured her. "I have plenty of work I can do if I get there early."

When Joanne was satisfied with the plans, she gathered up her empty containers and headed out. The hour was late and one by one, the others followed suit, except for Connie and Bill who left two by two. As had been happening a lot lately, Ellie and Ben were the last ones there.

"Wasn't that interesting what Joanne was telling us about Hanukkah?" Ellie asked Ben.

"I'll say. Sounds like she comes from a great family," Ben said, making Ellie even more suspicious that not only did Joanne like Ben but that he liked her. But then he surprised Ellie by asking, "So Ellie, tell me how your family celebrated Hanukkah or Christmas."

Ellie was happy he was interested. "Ok. We decorated for Christmas, but also had a menorah up. We never even looked on a calendar to find out when Hanukkah occurred each year. We just lit the menorah every night we had our Christmas tree up."

"That's hilarious," Ben blurted out and then looked a bit embarrassed as if he might have hurt Ellie's feelings. "It's very creative really. I'm curious why you did it that way."

"I don't know. I never asked. I always thought Hanukkah was the same week as Christmas, give or take a day or two. So I didn't even think of asking. I thought it was normal. But now I have my theories," Ellie said.

"And?" Ben was probing.

"And now I think that my parents were kind of paranoid about not hurting each other's feelings. My guess is that they always tried to balance out each Christian activity with a Jewish one. That would fit with their personalities."

"Very interesting!" Ben said.

Ellie continued, "But I don't think those activities were really Christian or Jewish. There was no real belief behind them, no meaning attached to the lighting of the candles. And though my mom did believe in Jesus, we really just celebrated a secular Christmas with presents and a tree. When we were really small and my dad was at work, my mom would play Christmas music. I thought that was great. I really loved those songs. But when we got to be school-age, she didn't do it anymore. I think that was because dad would be coming home soon after us and my mom knew we didn't have any Jewish music to play to balance it out."

"That's pretty sad, isn't it?" Ben said. "My family was similar in a way. I mean similar in the respect of just celebrating a secular Christmas. It was kind of a family day, a day of giving gifts to your loved ones, getting together with relatives for a nice dinner and things like that. In fact one year I opened my gifts on Christmas morning even before my parents woke up. How's that for concentrating on the gifts more than the real meaning of the day?"

Ellie laughed as Ben continued. "Then when I opened up my Robby the Robot, I was so excited that I went outside with him right away. I made him walk to my neighbor's house. When my parents woke up they didn't even know where I was!"

"Oh no," Ellie chuckled.

"And as for Hanukkah… well, we had my grandmother's menorah on one of our dressers all year long. It just seemed to be treated like one of the neat heirlooms from the family in Brooklyn. That was my father's family. He passed away when I was younger, but even when he was alive, I never remember us lighting it or celebrating Hanukkah."

The conversation flowed from one memory to another and finally ended up with both Ellie and Ben sharing what they would like their celebrations to be like when they had their own families. As Ellie prepared to leave, Ben proposed an idea.

"Hey Ellie, how about the two of us going to one of the Jewish bookstores downtown tomorrow after the Sunday service? We can get more supplies for our book table. And beforehand, we can go to one of the authentic Israeli restaurants nearby. What do you think?"

"Hmm, let me think about that," Ellie said.

"While you think, I'll go move my car into the garage. I had my car on the other side of the driveway earlier, so I could unload some of the book table supplies I brought home to price and label. But Joanne came so early, she parked in front of the garage before I got my car put away."

Ellie was glad she had a little time to think. Ellie recollected how Joanne arrived early and brought all that special homemade food. Should she just be happy Ben invited her and not Joanne to the outing on Sunday? Or should she risk missing that chance of finally doing something with Ben alone and actually ask the question she was thinking of asking? Dinner together at an Israeli restaurant, just the two of them, and picking out supplies together at the bookstore …it sure sounded like fun! But then again, was she making more of the outing than Ben intended? They knew each other for way over a year and yet Ben showed no signs of being interested in Ellie any more than any other friend, like Joanne. Yet Ellie knew that her own heart started opening up toward Ben about ten months ago after that wonderful conference.

It was almost a year since he broke up with Candace and she broke up with Kevin. Though Ellie and Kevin were never really going together, in her heart she broke up with him all the same. Ben should have been ready for another relationship by now if he was really interested in her. And today she heard Joanne invite Ben to have breakfast with her at the university where Ben worked. Yes, she thought after reviewing the facts, it was about time for the question. She didn't want to repeat history.

"So did you decide, Ellie?" Ben asked as soon as he came back in.

"Your plan sounds very inviting, but I think I better ask you a question first," Ellie replied.

"Oh?" Ben waited.

"Um, are you interested in me seriously, or would you say it's more like a casual friendship?" Ellie courageously asked.

Ben was taken aback. "Hmm, well, I guess I'd say it's more of a friendship."

"Oh ok," Ellie said slowly. "I mean that's fine. But then I think I better not go with you on that fun excursion tomorrow."

"Why not?" Ben asked.

"Well, I might start getting feelings for you that aren't mutual, you know?" Ellie's heart was exposing itself a little and Ben could feel it. He didn't really know what to do about it.

"And I think maybe we better not pray next to each other either, because I was getting a little bit mixed up, wondering if you were interested in me," Ellie nervously revealed. Her voice was timid. She was even shaking a little as she said it. But her resolve was firm.

"Oh … hmmm…" Ben was at a bit of a loss for words. Finally he stumbled, "Sorry to hear that. I hope we can still be friends."

"Of course," Ellie answered. They both stood in awkward silence. Ellie raised her eyebrows and her shoulders, as if to say *Well now what?* But the silence prevailed a little longer.

"Well I better go," Ellie finally said.

"Yes, I guess it's getting late. It was a nice day. Can I hug you good-bye?" Ben asked.

"Um, probably not," Ellie replied.

They said their good byes and Ellie headed home. She needed to get gas, so she stopped five minutes away from Ben's house at the gas station. Her hands were shaking when she took out the pump. Her eyes were tearing up. And when she got back in her car, the tears started falling. She hoped God was collecting her tears and would answer her prayers soon for a Godly husband.

Chapter Three

THE SUNDAY MORNING SERVICE at Broken Wall was as lively as ever and as anointed with the presence of God as so many of the previous services. But Ellie didn't feel the deep joy she usually felt there. She went up for prayer at the end of the service, and labeled her need as another "unspoken request." The prayer that Pastor Weisman prayed must have been inspired by the Holy Spirit, because it just hit the spot. She could feel God's presence and was reassured with hope again that He would answer her prayers one day.

Ben did go to the city bookstores that day, so he wasn't at the usual restaurant gathering. Ellie realized it wasn't so much the great group of people that gave her such joy in fellowship, it was Ben. She saw that when Ben wasn't there, the fellowship wasn't as exhilarating to her.

She made it through Sunday keeping her feelings to herself. Daniel came with her to the service, and she derived satisfaction in her soul from that. It was also a pleasure to see him enjoying the restaurant fellowship afterwards.

The melancholy mood was still hanging on to Ellie on Monday morning as she prepared for work. Seeing her students at the workshop snapped her back to life again. She had a good lesson planned, and plenty of other work to do in her planning period at 11 a.m.

As she was working on the individual educational progress reports for each client, Ellie was surprised to see Carmen walk into her office.

"Ellie, there's a phone call for you."

Ellie was worried and anxiously followed Carmen to the telephone. Her first reaction was fear that something happened to one of her family members. She hardly ever got a call at work.

"Hello?" Ellie said apprehensively.

"Hi Ellie," a familiar voice said. It took Ellie by surprise and she actually needed a few seconds to process it. It startled her to hear a voice she wasn't expecting to hear.

"Oh hi, Ben," she said, still unsure of what was happening.

"You said you had planning time at 11, is that right?"

"That's right. I'm surprised you can remember that!" she said.

"I remembered," Ben assured her. "I actually wanted to call you as soon as possible and tell you I'm changing my answer," Ben said.

"What do you mean?" Ellie asked.

"I mean, yes, I am interested in you seriously, Ellie."

"Oh," Ellie said, her face turning red and her heart starting to beat faster.

"I know you can't talk there at work, but could you call me when you get home?"

"Um, sure, but isn't this your day to work the evening shift at the college?" Ellie asked.

"Yep," Ben answered. "But you can call me at work. I can talk a little while. That's nice you remembered it was my late night, Ellie."

"Yeah," Ellie laughed. "Well, I better go. Thanks for calling."

"Thanks for answering," Ben said. "Bye."

Carmen asked, "Is everything all right, Ellie? You look a little shaken up."

"Yeah, just some stuff from people at our church," Ellie managed to explain.

Ellie went back to her IEP reports and filing. Once again, Carmen walked in.

"Hi again, Ellie. I just got off the phone with Eddie Ford's family. They're moving and he's leaving our workshop."

"Oh no, not Eddie!" Ellie said.

"I feel the same way, Ellie. Eddie loves it here so much. I feel sorry for him."

"Maybe they'll change their minds," Ellie wished out loud.

"I hope so," Carmen agreed. "It would be a little longer drive for them, though I think it would be well worth it for Eddie's sake. But for now, I need his IEP. I need to mail it out this afternoon. Did you do it yet?"

"Yes, I just did Eddie's. Let me get if for you," Ellie said as she walked to the files and looked under F. It wasn't there. "I'll bring it to you as soon as I find it," she told Carmen.

Ellie knew she was doing her work with half her brain ever since Ben called. But she knew she put Eddie's IEP back in the files. Why it didn't appear under the F's, she didn't know. She remembered the black smudge on the tab of Eddie's folder, so she skimmed through the whole alphabet of files and found one with such a smudge under the R's. She pulled it out and was happy to find out it was indeed Eddie's. She walked over to Carmen's desk and handed her the folder.

A minute later Carmen came back. "Ellie, the last page is missing."

"Oh sorry," Ellie said. "I'll find it."

Ellie was so embarrassed. She tried to re-trace her steps back to when she worked on Eddie's report. She knew she was holding it when she went to receive the phone call. Then she went to the bathroom. She went back to the bathroom to check and sure enough, there it was on the counter above the sinks. What a relief! She heard stories of other people doing goofy, absent-minded things when they were in love. And now it was happening to her! Leaving a confidential paper like that in the bathroom! She scared herself into snapping her brain back into work-mode.

Chapter Four

ELLIE CALLED BEN BACK when she got home from work.

"Hi Ben, do you have time to talk now?"

"Sure, I started work early today, so I can afford to take at least ten minutes to talk. It's not much, because we're not allowed any personal calls beyond ten minutes. But at least we both have a semblance of privacy," he explained.

"Yeah, that's true. I didn't have any privacy at work, as you can probably imagine."

"That's what I thought. But I really wanted to give you that message right away. I've been thinking about it all day Sunday, not to mention Saturday night and Monday morning."

"Really?' Ellie asked.

"Really," Ben assured her. "I prayed about it and thought about it and realized I *am* seriously interested in you, Ellie. Your question came to me so unexpected. I didn't know what to say, what to think."

"Sorry," Ellie apologized.

"No, I think I needed that question to wake me up. I've been enjoying all these times of fellowship lately, but you're the main reason why," Ben said. "I think it's good that we both get to know each other better and maybe start to officially go together."

"Really? I think that would be good too," Ellie said.

"How about if I give you a ride to the Bible Study tomorrow?" Ben offered.

"It's kind of out of the way for you, isn't it?" Ellie asked.

"Not that much," Ben reasoned, "and it would be fun."

So on Tuesday evening Ellie was watching for a bluish-greenish car instead of a small white one.

Chapter Five

BEN STILL PLAYED in the music group at Broken Wall, but during the sermon times he could be found sitting with Ellie.

On Saturdays Ellie and Ben would get together at Ben's house in the afternoon. They would go for walks, make dinner together, pray, read, talk, and get to know each other more.

Ellie kissed a boy for almost the first time on one of those Saturdays. Ellie was really sorry it couldn't be the first time, because of that dreadful experience she had in college.

"Tell me again what happened," Ben requested.

"Ok, if you're sure you want to hear it," Ellie warned. "One of my girlfriends at school asked me to double date with her and her boyfriend. I was supposed to be teamed up with his roommate. I naïvely agreed."

"I don't think I ever went on a blind date," Ben said.

"You're lucky," Ellie assured him. "Anyway, Sandy's boyfriend picked us up in his car, and I sat in the back seat with Cliff, my so-called date. Sandy and her guy were in the front seat obviously. And guess what we did?"

"Go to a movie?" Ben guessed.

"No, we just went somewhere and parked. Then Sandy and her boyfriend dived down in the front seat and were no more to be seen. There

I was in the back with Cliff. I sure didn't want to dive down with him. I didn't know what to do. So I just had to think fast and start asking him question after question," Ellie said.

"That's terrible! How awkward! What did you talk about?"

"All I remember is that I asked him about his classes and how many brothers and sisters he had. Funny that I remember that and not much else. I think I tried to block that time out of my memory. But one thing I still remember. When they dropped us off again, I thought it was my duty to kiss him. I thought that was just standard operating procedure with dates."

"Oh no," Ben said with a sad expression plus a quiet laugh.

"Yes, it's pathetically funny," Ellie agreed. "I had no moral teachings up to that point in time on dating and kissing. I had no one to talk to about it, except my roommate, who wasn't too experienced herself. And guess what her advice was?"

"Tell me, what advice did she give you before you went on that date?" Ben said.

"I meant her advice after the fact," Ellie corrected.

"Oh," Ben said. "Tell me about it."

"When I got back and told my roommate about the terrible experience I just had, she was determined to protect me. She actually decided that she would answer the phone all the next day, because we assumed he would call me. And sure enough, he did call. Naturally he asked for me, and she said I couldn't come to the phone because I was in the bathroom vomiting. That was her way of handling it. We laughed and I thought there had to be a better way, but I couldn't figure out any. Then Cliff called again the next day and I was so glad she answered the phone again. And again she told him I was in the bathroom vomiting. Then, as you can probably guess, I never got another phone call from Cliff."

"What a sad story," Ben said.

"I know. I felt sorry for him in a way, but I had to protect myself."

"I know, I don't blame you," Ben said. "I had my own share of bad experiences too. But maybe I'll tell you about them some other time."

"Ok. But I just wanted to tell you that I consider your kiss to be my first real kiss."

"Ellie, that's so wonderful," Ben said.

They hugged each other warmly and then Ellie drove home. She was happy.

Chapter Six

ANOTHER SEASON of the high holy days was upon them, and Ben and Ellie both took time off from their jobs. They spent the days with the usual crowd at the congregation, talking, praying, going for walks, playing music, eating, or in the case of Yom Kippur, fasting. Debbie, who just started coming to Broken Wall, knew many of the Israeli dances, and she began to teach them to the singles group. What a delight those days were.

The Feast of Tabernacles was celebrated with palm branches being waved before the Lord. After the service, the young people who stayed played tapes of Messianic Jewish songs and danced with the palm branches in their hands. It felt like a taste of heaven. And when they found an extension cord that reached to the outside, they moved their boom box and dancing to the outdoors on a perfectly glorious fall day.

However, Hanukkah wasn't so happy. Ben was expected to visit his mother and relatives who lived seven hundred miles away. Hanukkah and Christmas fell on the same week, so Ben would be going to a Christmas Eve service where his cousin's children were in a play. Then they would be opening presents on Christmas morning. Ellie wrapped some presents for Ben to take with him and open when he was there.

When he got home, Ben told Ellie, "That present you sent was amazing. I took it to a corner to open it, when the kids were opening their toys and putting batteries in and all that. And then I found it, the little red construction paper heart that said *my heart*. I guess you meant that you gave me your heart," Ben concluded.

Ellie nodded.

"It was the best gift I ever got."

Ellie and Ben spent more and more time together. Ellie kept thinking the subject of marriage would come up soon, but it just didn't seem to. Winter led to spring, and spring brought another Passover. Ben's mother came into town for Passover and Ellie met her for the first time. They liked each other.

Finally spring led to summer. Ellie's mother, who normally didn't talk too much to Ellie about boyfriend type things, decided to venture onto that topic.

"Ellie, maybe you're spending too much time with Ben. I think you should do some things without him. Make him jealous," she said.

Ellie laughed. "That's a little under-handed mom, isn't it?" she asked.

"No, I think it would be good. I think Ben's taking you for granted."

So Ellie took her mother's advice, and when Bonnie was putting together a girls' outing to the beach the following Saturday, Ellie agreed to go.

Chapter Seven

IT WAS A PERFECT DAY for the beach, with the temperature in the 90's. Bonnie, Debbie, and Ellie met in the parking lot at Broken Wall early in the morning. They packed their blankets, lunches, and themselves into Bonnie's unique old convertible. They couldn't talk much because of the noise the wind was making. With the sun, wind and speed of the car, their hair blowing all over the place, and their sun-burned faces all smiling, this hour-long ride did turn out to be very therapeutic. No one had to worry about how their hair looked or how red their noses were getting from the sun, because there were no guys around to see them.

The beach itself wasn't as exhilarating. Bonnie had a good book and Debbie took a nap. Ellie tried to read, but she couldn't concentrate. There were books that were so good you couldn't put them down and there were books that weren't so good. Ellie had the latter. She took a walk and collected some shells. She was looking for a special shell for Ben. So much for getting away from Ben for the day, she thought to herself. It was a long day. She hoped it would prove effective, like her mother said.

All three girls went swimming in the lake for a while and that part was refreshing. Ellie always preferred being in the water to lying on the beach getting a sun tan. But Bonnie and Debbie didn't want to stay in the water too long. Ellie knew it wasn't safe to go in alone, and it wouldn't have been fun to be alone out there anyway. They ate their lunches, and then took a walk up one of the sand dunes. That was fun. Ellie saw a whole lot of people eating ice cream bars from the ice cream vendor. The ice cream looked so good to her, but she knew she better not. She already ate a sort of sweet but healthy lunch, peanut butter and jelly on homemade bread plus an apple. But she also ended up eating a bunch of potato chips from the huge bag that Bonnie brought with her. She regretted it later, when she broke out a little on her nose from the greasy chips. She hoped she would be blessed for honoring her mother and going on this trip. She so missed spending all her free time with Ben.

Ben called her when she got home. "How was your day with the girls?"

"It was pretty nice," Ellie said. "The weather sure cooperated."

"Yeah, I heard it was 94. It must have been fun riding in Bonnie's convertible."

"It was! That was almost the best part, with the wind blowing and the sun shining. I just closed my eyes and enjoyed it."

"Great!" Ben said. "Sometimes I like to pretend my car's a convertible and roll down all my windows. I've done it in the winter, leaving the heat on high the whole time." Ellie laughed. "I know that's not like my frugal ways, but it sure is fun once in a while. We should try it together sometime."

"Sure," Ellie said, thinking in back of her mind that she didn't really want to try it. Having her hair blowing all around and going crazy was fine and fun with the girls, but she didn't care to repeat the experience with the guy she was going with.

"So how was your day?" Ellie was curious.

"I slept in, prayed of course, and then caught up on a lot of reading I wanted to do. Oh, and Joanne called and told me about another seminar she'll be attending at the university on Monday. She suggested we meet for breakfast again."

"Oh, so did you agree?" Ellie asked, trying to sound casual.

"I told her I had to take my car in on Monday morning, so I wasn't sure," he explained.

"So if your car is ready in time, would you meet with her?" Ellie wanted to know.

"I guess so," Ben answered.

"Well I guess that's up to you," Ellie said.

"It sounds like you have an opinion on the matter," Ben ventured.

"I mean, if you feel like you want to do it, that's fine. It's up to you. But I'm not really comfortable going out with somebody who also does things with other girls. So I would be kind of hurt. I know it's a bit extreme but that's how I am. I know it's becoming more common to do things like that these days. But I still don't like it," Ellie said.

"That's very interesting," Ben said. "I sure don't want to offend you. And I still want to be on track with our relationship growing and all."

Ellie was relieved, though she didn't say anything right away. A brief pause of awkwardness ensued.

"Did you ever realize that Joanne might like you?" Ellie finally asked.

"No, I never thought about that," Ben admitted. "You think so?"

"I don't know, but she does show up at your house earlier than everybody else whenever you have a get together," Ellie said.

"Hmm, that's true. It might mean something and it might not," Ben reasoned.

"That's true. But then again, I'm a girl and I kind of read things into behaviors like that," Ellie said.

"Oh," Ben paused and reflected a few seconds. Then he added, "So you think your women's intuition is telling you Joanne likes me?"

"I think there's a good chance of it but I'm not sure."

"I'm glad I gave her a true excuse this time. Next time I'll be more watchful," Ben promised.

"Thanks," Ellie said.

"No problem," Ben assured her.

They talked and planned out their Sunday, with Ben picking Ellie up early so they could go to the Broken Wall Sunday School class. Kathy's husband would be teaching Hebrew in Sunday School for the next several months before he and Kathy moved back to Israel.

Chapter Eight

SUNDAY WAS A DELIGHTFUL DAY with a magnificent service, as Ellie had become accustomed to. A sweet time of fellowship at the local deli followed. The only sad part was when Ben reminded her about his upcoming trip to Israel.

"I knew about it," Ellie said, "but I forgot it was coming up so soon."

"At least I'll be here at Broken Wall for the Rosh Hashanah and Yom Kippur services," Ben encouraged her.

"And you'll be in Israel for the whole time of Feast of Tabernacles?" she asked.

"Yes, which means we'll be leaving two days before the feast and coming home two days after the feast."

"That's a long time," Ellie sighed.

"I know. I signed up for the trip a little over a year ago, remember?"

Ellie remembered. She and Ben weren't going together yet.

"And Connie signed up before she started going with Bill," Ellie said.

"That's true," Ben remembered.

"So tell me what the trip involves," Ellie requested.

"I'd be happy to. The International Christian Embassy in Jerusalem hosts the event, and each night there's a big service with excellent musicians, speakers, dancers…oh, and there's a big parade the first day. A lot of the local Israelis gather every year to watch the parade. It's a great testimony to them, about how Christians and Messianic Jews from all around the world love Israel."

"Oh that sounds wonderful. I wish I could be there. But I couldn't afford it anyway. And it's too late even if I wanted to go."

Eventually Ben changed the subject, and he and Ellie shared news with each other about the various happenings at their workplaces.

Monday at the workshop held a nice surprise for Ellie. Kathy came to apply for a job. Ellie knew about it, but it was still a nice treat to actually see a fellow believer at her work place.

Kathy and her husband had to postpone their trip back to Israel because they still didn't have the funds they needed. Asher started catering Israeli food from their home and Kathy hoped to get the temporary position of social worker at the center. Ellie told her about the opening since she knew Kathy had her degree in the social work field. After Kathy left, Ellie's boss called Ellie into his office.

"We need a social worker to start as soon as possible and your friend Kathy gave your name as a reference. Can you tell me a little bit about her character?"

With Ellie giving Kathy rave reviews, her boss decided to hire Kathy and have her begin work the following day. How comforting it was to Ellie to have a fellow believer working with her at the workshop every day. Their jobs didn't intersect very much, but their lunch hours did.

This job suited Ellie well. She felt like she was doing a better job of teaching than she ever did in the school system. She wasn't where she wanted to be yet, but she was getting better. In her early days of teaching, her standard operating procedure was to portion out her good ideas to have enough to last for the week. But now she was not so frugal with her ideas. She spent them more generously, because she trusted the Lord to keep inspiring her with more. This day she brought an alarm clock with big numbers on it. It had an easy to work dial to set the time and the alarm setting. Ellie used the alarm clock in all five of her classes that day, teaching the students more about recognizing time, and also teaching them how to set the alarm. They loved this exercise and even more, loved hearing the alarm go off. They got a little too rowdy with their enjoyment and Ellie had a hard time reining them in. But her second good idea, which she planned for the same day, was a Godsend.

She had a new flannel-board, new to her and the students, but actually a hand-me-down from Sarah's childhood Sunday School class. Just like Ellie enjoyed the flannel board when she was in first grade, so her twenty and thirty year old students enjoyed it now. They settled down when she brought this new "toy" out. Ellie let them move the characters and props around according to the activity the characters would be doing at different times of the day.

"Ok, I set the clock for 8:00 in the morning. That would be the time to get ready to go to the workshop. Who wants to put the boy's and girl's jackets on them?"

Almost everyone answered at once. Some raised their hands, others shouted out their answers, and some even started walking up to do it. Ellie turned the flannel board backwards and had the students quiet down and go back to their seats. Then she told her class everyone would have a turn. She got to practice her whole lesson five times, with each of her five classes, varying only slightly depending on the level of her students. By the fifth class, she finally mastered it. She saved the wild alarm clock fun for the end of the class and began with the flannel board. And she didn't ask who wanted to participate. She just told her class that they would all get a turn.

Ellie felt good about her week. She felt like she taught her students something substantial and kept her classes in reasonable order. She hoped this pattern would continue.

Chapter Nine

THE HIGH HOLIDAYS rolled around again. Ellie thought it was so ingenious of God to institute these feasts which came around again and again each year. What a joy, what things to learn, and what new things each year brought!

This year Ellie fasted the whole day of Yom Kippur, the first time in her life she ever fasted so long. It was easier to do with the group of young people at Broken Wall than it would have been to do it herself. They had things to do all day long, which distracted them from thinking about food the whole time. They prayed, they talked, and they walked. Ellie and Ben took a walk together with two borrowed umbrellas in the sixty degree misty-rainy day. It was invigorating.

When it came time to break the fast with a shared meal at sundown, Ellie was starving. More and more people were arriving with mouth-watering aromas coming from their pots and casserole dishes. It was the first time Ellie remembered Pastor Weisman going on a bit too long in his prayers. She was ready for a brief prayer and then the meal. But he prayed about fifteen minutes and then handed out a page of liturgy for everyone to read together. It was all good stuff, but Ellie was too hungry to be very spiritual. She tried to convince herself that if she could wait all day to eat, another twenty minutes shouldn't be so bad. But it was still hard. When the meal time finally arrived, just about everything Ellie put on her plate tasted like a prize-winning recipe.

In two days Ben had to leave. He and the group from Broken Wall along with a group from another nearby church were scheduled to meet at the airport for the flight. First they would fly to New York City, then to Israel. Ben asked Ellie if she would like to drive him to the airport.

Of course Ellie said yes. They talked, they laughed, they got serious again, they prayed together, and before they were hoping, they were there. Ben kissed Ellie goodbye, and then he had to quickly jump out of the car. A very rude airport security woman was rushing the drivers to move along as soon as their passengers disembarked.

Ellie tried to enjoy the Feast of Tabernacles and tried not to worry about Ben's safety, but she wasn't always successful. When Carmen at work found out that Ben was going to Israel, she gave Ellie an interesting prediction.

"I think Ben will ask you to marry him when he gets back from Israel. He'll be missing you like crazy. Let's see, how long did you say he'd be gone?"

"Twelve days," Ellie said.

"Yep. That's a good long time," Carmen said. "Mark my words."

Chapter Ten

ELLIE DID MARK those words in her mind and her heart. That prediction helped her get through those twelve days of missing Ben. Work, Bible studies, services and fellowship at Broken Wall helped immensely. But the Feast of Tabernacles surprise helped the most.

Up to that point, Sarah had just visited Broken Wall for one Sunday service and the traditional restaurant follow-up. She liked the service and she liked the people, but still felt a little too shy and unfamiliar with everyone to really enjoy herself. Ellie and Ben tried to make her feel welcome, but since Ellie was with Ben on that Sunday, she didn't feel as close to Sarah as she used to feel. Sarah hadn't been back since. Ellie felt that it was somehow her fault, even though their friendship continued with many good talks on the phone.

When Sarah called and asked if she could join Ellie for the Feast of Tabernacles weekend, Ellie was taken aback. What a welcome surprise that was to her and she heartily agreed. Sarah's parents would drop her off at Ellie's house on Friday at 6 o'clock. She would leave her overnight bag there and then she and Ellie would drive together to the Friday night service. The service was scheduled to be held outdoors, in the giant sukkah that the young people built the weekend before. Ellie didn't help with building the sukkah, since that was the day she drove Ben to the airport.

"What's that word you're saying?" Sarah asked Ellie.

"It's sukkah, s-u-k-k-a-h," Ellie spelled out. "It means a booth or a temporary dwelling. God gave the directions for the Feast of Tabernacles in Leviticus 23. He tells everyone who is 'Israelite-born' to live in booths for this whole feast, so they can remember God's provision for them when they left Egypt."

"That is so neat!" Sarah said. "I always loved holidays, but these Bible holidays are ones God Himself put together. It must be so great to celebrate them!"

"It is!" Ellie said, making herself excited for the first time since Ben left. "And God says to rejoice before Him with branches of palm trees and willows and goodly trees. It's really amazing to sing and wave palm branches. It feels like that's what worship is supposed to be!"

"I can't wait to do it," Sarah said. "Where do you get palm branches?"

"Actually Ben and I were responsible for that this year, since we do the book table. We ordered them from a local florist," Ellie said.

When Ellie and Sarah first arrived at Broken Wall that evening, the sights and sounds were fascinating! There were Christmas lights lit up all around the giant sukkah. Some very tall logs served as posts on four corners with two more in the middle. More logs, a little skinnier, were tied and crisscrossed around the sides and tops. And branches with lots of leaves made up the roof. Outside of it there must have been about twenty lit torches. The yard was ablaze with light and color and the sounds of people talking and musicians practicing. When the service started, everyone was given a beautiful green palm branch to wave.

"These are like fresh branches from a real palm tree!" Sarah exclaimed. "My church gives out a different kind, more beige and dried, on Palm Sunday."

Ellie just smiled in response, since the praise and worship was already beginning. She and Sarah waved the branches and sang with gusto. Soon Daniel surprised them and sat in the empty seat next to Sarah. Someone gave him a palm branch, and that was what motivated him to finally stand up and get involved in the joyful worship himself.

The service was a little bit different than usual. Pastor Weisman gave a very very short message, no more than five minutes, telling everyone the purpose of this feast was to rejoice before the Lord for seven days. He said they would devote the rest of the service to music and dancing and worship and praise, and if anyone wanted prayer at any time, they could come up to the front.

Sarah wanted to learn the dances and Daniel decided he would take the plunge too. It was dark enough outside, with just the holiday lights and the torches, so no one would feel too embarrassed if they made mistakes. What fun they all had!

Though Ellie's joy was high, it wasn't full since she missed Ben so much. But what better friends to have with her on a festive night like this than her best friend Sarah and her only brother Daniel.

When the service ended, snacks were set up inside the sukkah on two giant picnic tables. While some people ate, other people kept dancing. Someone brought out a boom box and some tapes to play so that the musicians themselves could rejoice in the dance. The celebrating went on till 11 p.m. Daniel left at 10, since he had to be at work early the next morning. Ellie and Sarah stayed till the very end.

Ellie enjoyed talking with Sarah as they lay in bed that night.

"Ellie, I can't believe how much fun I had tonight. I love these feasts! I want to go to Broken Wall all the time!"

"Maybe you can," Ellie said a little uncertainly.

"That would be amazing. My parents are coming around, letting me do more on my own these days. If Broken Wall or your house were closer, I think it would be possible. But to drive over an hour, and with only one car in the family, it makes it very involved. Besides all the logistics, it also involves not going to our family church and the youth group on Sundays or else driving in the heavy Friday rush hour traffic and driving home late at night."

"That's true," Ellie said. She tried to say it as if she was greatly disappointed, but in reality, she was relieved. Ellie was glad it was dark so Sarah couldn't see her expression. She felt so selfish. Though Sarah was her best girlfriend, she wasn't sure she could give Sarah much close attention if she did come regularly, especially when Ben would be back in town. Maybe she could, but then again, maybe she couldn't. She wrestled with her conscience in thinking about this possibility and was glad it was just a theoretical issue right now and not actually happening.

They finally fell asleep at 2 o'clock, and slept in till 11. The girls took a prayer walk together when they woke up, and then made themselves a late breakfast/early lunch type meal. They made omelets with lunch meat, cheese, green peppers and onions. Instead of toast they had Ellie's mother's homemade bread with butter and jelly.

After their meal, Ellie wanted to play some tapes for Sarah. "Most of the single people at Broken Wall have heard these tapes and we all really love them. This will actually be the third time I'll be listening to them," Ellie explained, "and every time I listen, they help me so much."

It was a two tape series called "Let God Choose Your Mate." The speaker was the same man who authored her new favorite book, *Appointment in Jerusalem*. Ellie got an extension cord and they put the tape player outside right next to the swing in Ellie's yard. God blessed them with a gorgeous day. They swung and listened and shut off the tape every once in a while to make some comments.

"I love it!" Sarah said.

At 4 o'clock the young people were gathering at the giant sukkah for a pot blessing meal and more dancing and rejoicing before the Lord. Sarah's parents were scheduled to pick her up at 6 o'clock. At Ellie's suggestion, Sarah called and asked her parents if they could pick her up at Broken Wall instead.

"What did they say?" Ellie asked.

"Yes!" Sarah exclaimed. "Oh Ellie, this weekend just hit the spot for me. It was just what I needed."

"Really?" Ellie asked.

"Yes, really! That tape, that message, it was so encouraging. I've been praying for the right mate for years and sometimes it gets so discouraging when I don't see anything happening."

"I know what you mean," Ellie said. "Like all those weeks and months I prayed for a Godly mate and I thought it would be Kevin. I remember the hope, the discouragement, and the confusion as I prayed and prayed and believed and doubted and prayed and believed and doubted. That was sure a hard time in my life!"

"I love talking to you, Ellie. You put things in words that I feel too. It makes me feel not so alone," Sarah said.

Ellie felt real love in her heart for Sarah again, just like the old days when Sarah was there for her so much. Ellie was very frustrated with herself for feeling relief that Sarah couldn't come too often to Broken Wall.

"Oh this boy thing isn't easy, Sarah," she said. "I guess God puts this desire in us and it's good. But then we mix things up with doing things the wrong way and not thinking right and wondering and oh, I don't even know what I'm saying."

"No, you're making sense to me," Sarah assured her.

"Well, now I really think Ben is the one for me, but still no talk of marriage on his part. I keep wondering if history is about to repeat itself, like with the Kevin thing."

"I don't know. It doesn't seem the same to me. It really seems like Ben is interested in you."

"I know. I think so too," Ellie answered. "And Carmen at work said she thinks Ben might ask me to marry him when he gets back from Israel."

"Really?! Do you think he will?" Sarah asked.

"I don't know. But it's the first time he'll have been gone so long since we've been going together. Maybe he'll realize how much he misses me. Maybe God will speak to him in Israel," Ellie said.

"Hey yeah. Maybe he *will* hear God's voice more clearly in Israel!" Sarah agreed.

Sarah packed her things while Ellie made a big bowl of tuna salad for the pot blessing meal. She packed a loaf of whole wheat bread and a bag of apples. They loaded their stuff in the car and were about to drive off, when Daniel pulled up behind them.

"Where are you two off to?" he asked.

"There's a pot blessing at Broken Wall and more dancing and stuff going on for the Feast, starting at 4," Ellie explained.

"Hey, maybe I'll take a shower and come there too. Do you think it'll still be going on at 6?"

"Sure, but Sarah will be leaving at 6. Her parents are picking her up there."

"Oh, I think I'll be there around 5 anyway," Daniel said.

"That's neat, Daniel," Sarah said. "I'm glad you'll be coming."

Daniel just smiled and ran in the house.

Ellie and Sarah both smiled to themselves, but didn't tell each other what they were each thinking.

The pot blessing meal didn't start till 5 o'clock, with people just drifting in between 4 and 5. Ellie, Sarah, Daniel, Bill, Joanne and Bonnie all sat together. They ate and talked and then Daniel surprised them all by coming out of his shell and saying, "Hey, it's quarter to six! We have to do at least one dance before Sarah has to leave."

Their whole table got up and put on the music. More people joined them when they started dancing. And when Sarah's father and brothers came to pick her up, they stayed and watched for fifteen minutes.

"What a sight!" Mr. Kirby said. "Now this is what I call celebrating!"

Sarah was very sad to leave, but also very glad her father got to see the dancing and approved. Then when Daniel came over to say good bye and walk with them to their car, Sarah wasn't so sad anymore.

Chapter Eleven

THE REST OF THE TIME that Ben was in Israel dragged on. Ellie used one of those evenings to shop.

On the day of Ben's return, she eagerly put on the new outfit she bought just for the occasion. She carefully ate her lunch at work without getting any stains on her new blue and white shirt. Ben was very happy to see Ellie and so appreciative that she drove to the airport to pick him up, even though it was rush hour.

Ben told Ellie how blessed he was to be in Jerusalem and what a good time he had. When they got to his house, Ellie was hoping for more personal-type conversation. Ben, however, continued spilling out anecdotes about his trip with great exuberance. He told how anointed the services were, how inspired the messages were, and how impressed he was by the music.

"They could have been a professional orchestra," Ben raved.

"Wow," Ellie said, trying to empathize with his joy and enthusiasm.

Finally he asked how her Feast celebrations were. Ellie told him about the Broken Wall gatherings during the Feast and especially emphasized the great time she had the weekend of Sarah's visit. She wanted to show him that she too had a lot happen that was wonderful and blessed. However, she decided not to tell him how much she missed him even during that delightful weekend. And she didn't tell him how she thought of him all the while she and Sarah were listening to the message *Let God Choose Your Mate*. She didn't tell him how she prayed for him and worried about him almost non-stop all the time he was gone. What she did tell him was that she was very happy he was home. After she told him, he reciprocated the sentiment.

Then Ben kissed her longer than usual. She felt comforted. Ben did indeed love her. Though he didn't say it outright with words, he did convey his love for her in other ways. The tender touch of the man she loved made her forget her disappointment at the way their previous conversation had flowed. Ellie stayed at Ben's house a little later than usual, especially for a week night when she had to work the next day. She was thoroughly enjoying the closeness to Ben. She didn't know if it was right, but she didn't want to examine the rightness of it just yet. She left feeling reassured that Ben did love her and miss her, though they never really got back to talking.

As she began driving home, she began feeling rather downcast again. Why did Carmen have to make that prediction? Why did Ellie have to get her hopes up like that? Ellie was angry. Carmen was wrong. There was still no talk of marriage. Now that she was apart from Ben and could think objectively again, the frustration she had about their earlier conversation returned. She kept replaying the tape of Ben raving about his trip but not about missing her.

Ellie felt something happening in her heart after that evening of Ben's return from Israel. She felt a sort of cooling in her feelings toward Ben, but not all the way and not all the time. She couldn't explain it very well. She was very frustrated with him for not making any commitment to her. At the same time she understood that putting feelings into words was not as easy for Ben to do as it was for her. And she still loved him dearly and wanted to continue on "as before," even though she didn't feel "as before." She sensed that Ben really loved her too. So she hoped and she prayed.

However, her prayers felt more hindered than usual. Her worship at the congregation was also affected. Ellie was pretty sure it was because she and Ben were getting closer than was right, especially since she was so ambivalent about their relationship. All the sensations of being close to a man, of being in love, albeit a confused kind of love, were so new to her. She thought maybe she was just feeling things more deeply because it was the first time she was ever physically close to a guy. Maybe there was nothing wrong with how close they were getting. She was confident that she, as well as Ben, would never get that close physically as to violate the definite cut-off point. At least she thought she was sure they wouldn't. So she decided to keep enjoying the closeness and keep praying at the same time for God to guide them into what was right. Maybe this dry period of prayer was just one of those dry times that come to every believer once in a while.

Ellie continued her habit of spending all her Saturdays with Ben, sitting with him at services, and going on occasional dates to fun places. She described herself to Sarah like a bottle of sweet and sour sauce, because she was like a person who contained two opposites. She still felt a type of coolness in her mind and attitude toward Ben, and at the same time, felt more love and warmth when they were together than ever before. Praying, thinking, hoping, rationalizing, believing, wondering, doubting… they were all part of the picture right now. And Ellie chose to just keep on keeping on with the relationship.

One event that loomed on the horizon greatly influenced her decision to not give up on Ben. She was really looking forward to the fund-raiser dance from work that was only two weeks away. It would be her first real "dance" with a boy.

But two weeks don't occur in a vacuum. Ellie was to experience more ups and downs in her relationship with Ben during that time. And they both happened, the ups and the downs, in the same day.

Chapter Twelve

ONE DAY BEN TOLD ELLIE that Joanne invited him to her house to see her father's old clarinet. Ellie was alarmed.

"I wonder what made her think of that," Ellie said.

"She was just telling me what a great clarinet player I was, and she asked me how long I had my clarinet. So I told her about the one I had in elementary school. Then I told her how my parents bought me this one, a professional…"

"Oh, and so then she started telling you about her father's clarinet?" Ellie interrupted.

"That's right. She said it sounded like her dad's clarinet might have been a low quality one like my elementary school clarinet was. She wanted me to see it. She said maybe her father could have done better if he had had a better instrument. Apparently her father aspired to be a great musician, wanting to audition for positions in professional orchestras and all. But he never had an open door, as she put it."

"Interesting," Ellie said, "so what did you tell her?"

"You'll be proud of me Ellie," Ben smiled.

"What?" Ellie asked.

"I asked her if you could come with me," he said.

"You did?! That was sure nice of you!" Ellie said. "So what did she say?"

"She said sure."

To hear Ben taking her advice and being on guard with Joanne was reason enough to rejoice. But to also hear that he asked if Ellie could come too, that was like a breath of fresh air, kind of like fresh warm air blowing in and taking away the coolness from Ellie's confused heart.

The trip to Joanne's house proved to be an enjoyable outing on their next Saturday together. Both of Joanne's parents were home and her father talked to Ben a long time about clarinets. Joanne showed Ellie her room in the meantime. She pointed out which books on her bookshelf were her favorites. Ellie wrote down a lot of the titles, because they sounded great to her too.

Then Joanne's mother made lunch for everyone. She made chicken matzah ball soup, which would have been a treat in itself. But she also shredded the chicken from the soup and combined it with onions, peppers and barbeque sauce. She served it on bakery buns. It was scrumptious!

On the way back to Ben's house, Ellie and Ben talked about Joanne and her parents. They both liked them a lot.

"Joanne was so nice to me," Ellie said. "She probably didn't have any ulterior motives toward you at all. She probably just believes the things most people of today believe."

"Which is?" Ben asked.

"Oh, that having lunch or breakfast with another co-worker or fellow believer is just fine, whether it's somebody of the opposite sex or not," Ellie answered.

"Maybe so," Ben said. "But from the way her father knew so much about me, I kind of wonder if your first impressions were more accurate."

"Really?" Ellie asked. "Why? What did he say?"

"He just kept telling me how many things I have in common with Joanne—my love of music, my interest in cars, my …"

Ellie was startled. "I didn't know she was interested in cars."

"Yeah, she was talking to me a long time about my car when she came early to the prayer meeting."

"You never told me that," Ellie teasingly accused.

"I never thought too much about it—before just now, that is," Ben patiently explained.

"What else did Joanne's father say?" Ellie wanted to know.

"He said Joanne is always bringing home something or other from that book table of mine. She told her dad she can't resist my sales pitch. Then he laughed and said I was probably as good a salesman as he was in his early days."

"Wow, that sounds like either she really is interested in you or else that she tells her father everything she does."

"Or both," Ben laughed.

They both concluded that Joanne was a lovely person and a great friend, but Ben better not give her any double signals.

"And believe it or not, I don't think I'll give her even one more convincing sales pitch for one of our products."

"Now that is hard to believe, coming from a natural born salesman like you. But I do believe you," Ellie said, half joking and half serious.

After a bonding experience like that, Ellie was ready for more wonderful conversations with Ben the rest of the day.

But a subject came up that she wasn't prepared for.

Chapter Thirteen

"THAT'S SURE NICE that you have your own house, Ben," Ellie said as they pulled into his driveway.

"I know," he agreed.

They were inside the house now. After almost an hour drive, Ellie didn't want to sit down and talk just yet. She suggested they wash the dishes together. Ben usually left his Friday dinner dishes till Saturday afternoon, unless he had a group of people over. He didn't try to impress Ellie any more. She knew his habits and he knew she would be happy to help.

"I was surprised it took an hour to get home from Joanne's place," Ellie said. "I guess you live a half hour south of Broken Wall and she lives a half hour north of it."

"With a lot of traffic lights in between," Ben added.

"How long have you lived here?" Ellie asked.

"I bought the house from a professor at the university where I work about six years ago. But then I went into joint ownership of the house with the woman I lived with. I guess I lived in this house with her and her son for almost two and a half years."

Ellie knew about Ben living with his girlfriend in the past, but was surprised to hear it was this very house and it was that recent. She was also surprised he shared ownership of the house with the woman. And she was hearing for the first time that a boy lived here with them. She felt energy draining out of her body then, and she felt herself getting a little weak in the knees and limp feeling. It almost seemed like the blood, the life, was draining out of her body. The thought that Ben was almost sort of married and had a previous family was so disturbing.

When Ellie didn't say anything right away, Ben thought he better explain.

"I met her and began living with her way before I became a believer. And by the time I realized it wasn't right, when my faith finally caught up with my lifestyle, I was in this joint ownership deal. I told her I wanted to get out of it, but she wouldn't let me. She didn't want to leave. She said it was her house too."

"Oh," Ellie managed to say.

"I finally got the name of a good lawyer who was a believer, and he and my mother helped me out. My mother helped me come up with the money to buy her part of the house and then agreed to loan her some money so she could buy a townhouse nearby. Then I finally got the deal closed and the documents processed, putting the house in my name only. Believe me, it was a very arduous and unpleasant ordeal."

Ellie wasn't too interested in the money details, though she was impressed that Ben's mother was such a big help. What Ellie was still fixated on was the thought of the woman and her son living with Ben in this very house.

"I'm surprised you had her boy living here with you," Ellie said. "It makes me feel weird, like you had a son and a family before. I'm a little shaken up."

"Sorry about that," Ben said. "I was never that close to the boy, though I tried to be a good friend to him. And when I knew it was wrong, what I was doing, I suggested we live in different areas of the house."

"That's good," Ellie said. "How long did it take you to realize that what you were doing wasn't right?"

"A pastor friend told me once that I needed to wake up and get out of that relationship immediately. That's what made me start taking it more seriously. But it took a while before I had the strength to actually start the whole process. What a mess I made of my life, Ellie. I'm so sorry."

"I think I need to be alone awhile," Ellie said. She went to the bathroom and closed the door. She looked at her face in the mirror. She looked pretty distraught. She splashed cold water on her face to revive herself. Then she went to the living room and sat on the couch and prayed silently. Ben gave her the space she needed to be alone.

Ellie thought a lot of thoughts in that time. Would she be comfortable going with a guy who was sort of like married before? Would she feel right about marrying such a guy some day? That's not how she ever imagined it. Even though she had a lot of doubts and misgivings, she still loved Ben and didn't want to lose him. She loved the Messianic Jewish lifestyle they were both living out now. She trusted his faith to be real as she had seen ample evidence in the way he lived and prayed. She loved his spirit and his kindness. She was already envisioning this house being Ben's and her house one day. She really thought they'd be getting married one day soon. But yet it hadn't happened. They had known each other quite long and still no talk of marriage. But some day, she always thought.

Now it all seemed to change. How could she reconcile his past? How could she live with that knowledge and pretend everything was ok? She couldn't. It was too distressing. She really always wanted somebody pure, who never loved anyone else. She did manage to get used to the fact that Ben had other girlfriends and he even lived with one of them for a time. But living in this very house? And just a few years ago? And with a child?? That was hard news to process, hard news to bear.

Ellie was having trouble breaking through the barriers of her own mind and thoughts to hear from God in prayer those days. She was still in a befuddled state of mind when Ben asked her if she was hungry.

"My appetite sort of left me after you told me all that stuff," Ellie said. "Maybe I should just head home now, and we can talk more tomorrow when you pick me up for services." They kissed goodbye, but it wasn't too long. Ellie's heart wasn't totally in sync with Ben that evening.

Sunday dawned bright and sunny. Ben picked Ellie up for services, as had become their usual custom. Ellie and Ben were friendly with each other and they wanted to be with each other, but each was a little uncertain of where they stood. After the service and the restaurant outing, Ellie told Ben she better go home soon, as she had lesson plans to get ready for the next day at work. Ben said he could drop her off and then he would go home and wash his car, making good use of the sunny day. They parted a little stiffly again.

Chapter Fourteen

ELLIE WAS GLAD her work at the center was so interesting that month. It made it easier to persevere through those hard and uncertain days, wondering just where her relationship with Ben was headed. They both agreed that they should stay together, but Ellie was still wondering if that was the right thing to do. She had been so looking forward to going to the Monroe Center Dance with Ben that she wanted to put all her ponderings on hold for a time. She just wanted to enjoy the experience.

The annual fund-raiser dance was always scheduled for November. It was a dinner dance that staff and parents of the clients were expected to attend. The tickets were $30 a person. Ben bought two tickets.

Ellie's classes at the workshop moved into decoration mode weeks before the event. Ellie loved thinking up ideas. She discussed them with Kathy over lunch one day.

"I wish I was a better artist," Ellie confessed.

"What is it you want to do?" Kathy asked.

"I was thinking… Wouldn't it be neat if I could get a roll of white butcher paper and somehow sketch scenes of our clients working here? Then my students could paint or color them."

"That's a great idea Ellie," Kathy encouraged her. "I have a feeling that if you had that idea, you must be capable of doing it."

"Not really. My art ability is really lacking. I'd say I can draw like maybe a ten year old. But then I was thinking that maybe a childish drawing wouldn't be so bad, because it would look like my students did it."

Kathy laughed. "I think you should do it then!"

"But the problem is, how would it turn out if I had to make giant people and everything big like for a banner," Ellie thought out loud.

"My husband is a graphic designer, Ellie, remember?"

"You mean he can help me?" Ellie asked.

"Sure, Asher is also a great artist. Did you know that?"

"No I didn't know," Ellie said.

"Here's an idea! Why don't you just make your sketches on normal paper and I'll give them to Asher. He can re-do them however he needs to, feed them into his computer program and enlarge them. Then he can get them printed out at the print shop as a banner."

"That would be great! Do you think he would mind?" Ellie asked.

"I don't even have to ask. I know he'd love to help out," Kathy said.

When the banners came back, they were just what Ellie was hoping for. They looked like giant pages from a coloring book. Ellie's idea was for her students to color the posters using crayons and markers. The banner with the huge letters spelling Monroe Center Workshop was the only banner which she allowed them to paint. The block letters would be easy to paint with big brushes.

The students loved using the paints and paint brushes, but the clean-up was quite messy. Ellie also had to watch the students very carefully to make sure none of the paint bottles spilled over. She only allowed her highest level class to do the painting. The other students worked on the other banners, fighting a little at the start for who would be coloring what. The students loved this project. There was enough work on the banners to keep all the students from her five small classes busy for many days. While they worked, they talked and joked and Ellie had as much fun as any of her students. She actually hated to see it end. When Ellie realized they would be finished with the banners way ahead of schedule, she sketched out two more scenes. These were more fun and light-hearted, with pictures of her students coloring, laughing, snacking and goofing around. As expected, these turned out to be their favorite banners. Some things came out looking a bit goofy, but the overall effect was great. The chatter and banter during this project was so jolly. Ellie listened closely just for the fun of it but also to catch things before any mischief emerged.

"You better not color my face green," Terrence yelled out.

"Oh so you don't like green?" Ricky said. "How do you like orange?"

Amid much laughter, Ellie had to intervene and threaten to take Ricky off the project if he wouldn't cooperate.

"Please let me paint the potato chips purple," cute little Michelle (who was twenty-seven years old) begged.

"Let her, let her," all her friends begged Ellie. Michelle was as sweet as she was cute. Everyone loved her.

"Ok, would everyone be ok with seeing purple potato chips on this banner?"

"Yes," they all shouted. So Ellie concluded that in this case purple potato chips would be all right.

"Ok, just don't get carried away. A joke is funny if it's just one joke, but if you end up coloring everything an odd color, it's not funny anymore," Ellie said.

The students didn't understand why it wouldn't be funny anymore, so Ellie had to think of several examples to tell them. They finally seemed to grasp it and laughed hilariously as all the potato chips turned purple.

Ellie's boss thought her ideas were great. And the volunteer work that Asher did on the project really impressed the Center. From then on, they gave Asher various graphic design projects to do as a paid free-lancer. Ellie felt happy that her idea had such great results.

Chapter Fifteen

ON THE FRIDAY EVENING OF THE DANCE Ellie kept asking herself, *Is this actually happening to me?* It was her first dance with a date. She never went to any of the proms or other school dances. Whereas some of her classmates went as a group to the prom, without a specific date, Ellie never did that. In fact, she didn't even know people did that sort of thing, going to the prom even without a boyfriend.

As she was getting dressed for the dance, she thought about all the other wonderful Friday evenings when she would be getting ready to go to the Shabbat services at Broken Wall. She actually would have preferred for the dance to be scheduled on a different day, but it wasn't. However, it wasn't just Ben and herself who would be missing the service, it would be Kathy and Asher as well.

Ellie looked at herself in the mirror after she put on her new dress. She shook her head in amazement as she reflected on the fact that it was actually her mother who bought her this dress.

"I just can't find the right thing to wear for the dance," she lamented one day after an unsuccessful shopping excursion.

"I'm going shopping tomorrow," her mom said. "I'll keep my eyes open for you."

"Ok," Ellie said, not sure if she should tell her mother not to bother. She knew it wasn't likely that her mother would find something that she liked. And what if she found something and Ellie didn't like it? She thought she better speak up.

"But mom, I'm not sure you really know what I would like," she gingerly said.

"Well if I find something and you don't like it, you can always return it."

"That's true. Thanks Mom. But don't go out of your way or put a lot of time into it."

Ellie was pleasantly surprised when her mother showed her the dress. She didn't know if it was because she had been praying for the right thing to wear for the dance or if it was because God wanted to show her something about her mother. But whether it was by chance, by God's intervention or by the fact that Ellie's mother knew a lot more about her than she thought she did, Ellie knew her mother had found the perfect dress for the occasion.

The dress was cream-colored and made of lightweight, flowing cotton, yet it wasn't see-through. The length was a little below the knees. It had three quarter length sleeves. It was dressy but not too formal and it was just very cute. It fit Ellie beautifully, besides having the added benefit of being so comfortable. The only thing she'd have to watch out for was to keep it clean while she ate. So many of her nice tops were ruined because of a stain getting on them from something Ellie ate or from a little mishap at work. Ellie had a hard time staying neat for any length of time, especially with skirts slipping down and blouses coming un-tucked. Dresses were definitely easier for her to wear.

For a finishing touch, she bought a hair clip with a tiny realistic-looking silk lilac attached to it. She clipped that onto one side of her hair. She looked just like she was hoping she'd look. She didn't normally wear perfume, but she did buy some oil of lilac that a fellow co-worker was selling. As a finishing touch, she dabbed a little on her wrists.

Ben told her she looked beautiful. He brought his camera and asked Ellie's brother if he would take a picture of them before they left. Ellie's parents were watching too, and it was hard for Ellie to act natural. But after Daniel took two pictures with everyone watching, the phone rang and both parents left the room. Ellie asked Daniel to take another picture after her parents left, when she could feel less awkward. He took the picture and then they left.

Chapter Sixteen

CARMEN SEATED ELLIE AND BEN at the same table as Kathy and Asher. Also seated at the same table were the parents of Gordon and the parents of Shelly, both of whom were Ellie's students. It was a very friendly group.

Ben had an idea when he noticed that a glass of red wine was set out for each person at the table. "Would anybody mind if we said the blessing over the wine? It *is* the start of the Sabbath."

Ellie felt uncomfortable. What would the parents think? She wished Ben didn't say that.

"Great idea," Kathy said quickly. "Do you mind?" she addressed Gordon's and Shelly's parents.

"Uh no, of course not," they said a little clumsily.

"Would you like to do it, Asher?" Ben asked.

Asher didn't answer. He just lifted the glass and everyone followed suit. Then he began the chant in his rich Hebrew tenor.

"Baruch Atah Adonai, Elohainu Melech Ha Olam, Bo-rei pri hagafen."

He added the English afterwards, though with a thick Hebrew accent. "Blessed art Thou, O Lord our God, King of the universe, Who creates the fruit of the vine."

"That was beautiful," Shelly's mother said.

"You sounded so authentic," Gordon's father said. "What language was that?"

The conversation flowed beautifully after that, about Hebrew, then Israel and Asher and Kathy's upcoming move back.

Ellie felt bad that she was so concerned about what people would think. Now she was glad Ben made that inspired suggestion.

Ellie and Ben danced a little. They sat out for a whole lot of the songs they didn't like. But for the slower love songs it was a real treat to dance together. Ellie was taking it all in. She was enjoying herself very much. Even though her questions weren't really settled, she did know that she didn't want to give up on Ben quite yet.

When Ben dropped her off at home, they kissed a little too long in the car. Ellie walked in to the shock of seeing her mother, who was still up. She really hoped her mother didn't see them in the car so long.

"Did you have a good time Ellie?" her mother asked.

"Yeah it was really nice," she answered simply.

Then they both went to bed.

Chapter Seventeen

SATURDAY MORNING FOUND ELLIE sitting in bed talking on the phone to Sarah.

"I hope I didn't call too early," Sarah said hesitantly. "I imagine you were up late at the dance."

"No, this is perfect," Ellie said. "I was still in bed, but with my eyes opened and my mind spinning."

"Oh good! I hope you feel like talking a little."

"Yeah, a little to anybody else, but a lot to you, Sarah," Ellie said.

"Thanks," Sarah replied.

"It was a great time, Sarah. I never really went to a dance with a boy before."

"But you have all those feasts with dancing at Broken Wall," Sarah reminded her.

"I know. Those are great. But last night was a different great. It was like something that seemed like a milestone in my life. It was like in this old movie that's one of my mother's favorite movies. It's called *The Bells of St. Mary's*. Did you ever see it?"

"No, do you think I should?" Sarah asked.

"Oh yes! It's really good. There's this one scene where this girl who just graduated eighth grade is talking to the nun who taught her. The girl is so grateful for all the nun has done for her, because she came from a broken home and her mom had all these boyfriends. So the girl came to live with a wholesome family right across from the Catholic school and the convent. When she was about to graduate, she was afraid to leave and go back to her old home. So she told the nun that she wanted to stay and become a nun."

"I don't understand. Did the dance make you realize you don't want to be a nun?" Sarah joked.

"No, but the thing the nun said next is the quote I wanted to tell you. But first I had to give you the background. The nun reassures her that now her parents are back together and things will be different. The girl still wants to stay with the nuns she has come to love. So she says again, 'But it's true, sister. I really do wanna be a nun like you.' Then the nun she is talking to makes this neat statement:

"'No Patsy, you don't cry and say "I wanna be a nun like you," just because you don't want to face what you're afraid of in the future. You're young. You need to experience high school. Those are the days…your first football game, your first boyfriend, your first dance! No, you can't give those things up without knowing what they are…'

"So anyway, what I meant to say was that the way the nun said 'your first dance' was making it seem like it was a really big thing. She made it seem like it was sort of a milestone in life, a rite of passage. Do you know what I mean?"

"Yes I do! What a nice way to think of that," Sarah said.

"And if you really saw the movie and heard the quote for yourself it would be even more meaningful. So anyway, at different times throughout the evening I would think of that. I would think *I'm at my first dance.* I'd think *I can't believe it… I'm actually at a dance with my boyfriend.*"

"Oh Ellie, I'm so happy for you. I'm so glad you and Ben found each other."

"Thanks, Sarah, but for all that good stuff I just told you, I'm still struggling," Ellie told her.

"About what?" Sarah was surprised.

"The same thing I told you about before. I still think about it. Sarah, it's still so hurtful whenever I think about how Ben was living in his house with another woman and her son. It's really hard," Ellie confessed.

"I didn't know you were still thinking about it so much," Sarah said. "Have you prayed about it?"

"I've been trying, Sarah, but it seems like I'm not getting through. When I used to pray, I'd get such peace afterwards and I'd know, I mean I'd really know that God heard me and He would be moving in this situation. But lately I'm not getting through. That peace and reassurance isn't coming."

"Have you talked to your pastor about it?" Sarah asked.

"Oh no, I'd be too embarrassed! You're about the only one I told, you and God, oh, and of course Ben."

"So did it spoil the whole dance event for you?" Sarah asked.

"No, not completely, just a little. I do know I still love Ben, but I'm not sure how much. And another thing, Sarah, I think Ben and I are getting too close physically."

"Oh," Sarah said a little uncomfortably. "If you want to tell me anything, you can," she offered. Then she quickly added, "But you don't have to."

"Thanks Sarah. I won't go into detail, but let me just tell you that last night when Ben dropped me off after the dance, we kissed a little too long in the car. I had no idea my mother would still be up, but when I came in I was shocked. She was still up. I know she wasn't looking out the window and probably didn't even hear us pull up. So she most likely didn't know how long we'd been out there, but I was still so embarrassed when I came in."

"Oh," Sarah said again.

"I know this conversation is not really up your alley, Sarah. Sorry to bother you with it. I'm not even sure that what we're doing is wrong. I do know what would be wrong to do, but I'm not sure where to draw the line of what's ok and what's going too far."

"Well, as you said, this isn't familiar territory to me, but it seems like if you were embarrassed, maybe it was your conscience trying to tell you something," Sarah said.

"Hmm, maybe you're right," Ellie agreed. "I don't know. But who knows? I was embarrassed when Daniel was taking a picture of Ben and me in front of my parents and I know *that* wasn't wrong."

Sarah laughed. "That's true but just be careful. Our emotions and thoughts can play tricks on us. I'll be praying for you, Ellie. And keep on praying yourself. Sometimes we do go through these dry times and we can't sense God's presence. But He's still really there. We just have to persevere and keep on praying."

Then Sarah very tentatively added a thought. "I just heard a teaching on the radio, about several reasons why God doesn't seem to answer our prayers. One reason the preacher mentioned may pertain to you or it may not. So I don't know if I should say it."

"Go on and say it," Ellie urged.

"Well, you said you don't know if you and Ben are doing anything wrong or not, so I don't know. But if it is your conscience telling you to be on guard, that could be the reason you're not hearing from God. The scripture from one of the psalms he quoted said that if you regard iniquity in your heart, the Lord will not hear you."

"Hmm," Ellie replied, afraid to admit how hard that scripture hit her.

"So anyway, Ellie, just don't give up praying," Sarah encouraged.

"You're right," Ellie said. "I won't."

"I have one more suggestion," Sarah said. "What you're remembering about Ben and his old girlfriend was in the past. We all have things in the past we wish we didn't do. Maybe you should just forget about that."

"I'm trying to," Ellie admitted. "But it's still not easy to do. Like remember when Pharaoh asked Moses to pray to God that the plague of frogs would stop? Moses did pray and God answered and the plague of frogs stopped. But still there were all these piles of dead and stinking frogs to get rid of all over the land. It's like God answered the prayer, but the results or the repercussions of the plague still had to be dealt with."

"That's a great way to understand it," Sarah said. "Like even if a sin is in the past, you still have to deal with the effects it has on the present. That was sure a funny example you gave though. I guess you just heard a teaching on Exodus lately. I wish I knew more about the Old Testament."

"Yeah, the Old Testament is sure interesting and so helpful in all these real life situations," Ellie said. "But back to the main subject.

I'm pretty sure Ben wants to marry me, but still nothing has come up." Ellie said.

Eventually Sarah shared with Ellie her desire to have the right guy come into her life too. They hung up, each feeling comforted with the other's friendship, understanding, and encouragement.

Ellie got out of bed and got ready for another Saturday with Ben. But first she got out her concordance and looked up the scripture Sarah mentioned. She found it in Psalm 66: "If I regard iniquity in my heart, the Lord will not hear me."

Chapter Eighteen

THIS SATURDAY AFTERNOON, Pastor Weisman would be leading a Bible Study for the singles. Ben picked Ellie up and they headed to Broken Wall.

The lesson that was taught was on the Holy Spirit. Pastor Weisman was saying how the Holy Spirit was gentle, like a dove. A dove gets easily scared away. We have to strive to keep our conscience pure, so we don't scare the Holy Spirit away. He said that if we ignore the promptings of our conscience, we start hardening ourselves and we get callous to what God is trying to tell us. If we listen to the little things God is telling us or correcting us about, He'll be able to trust us to reveal more things.

Then he had people get together in pairs with someone of the same gender to pray about or discuss ways each person has gotten promptings from their conscience. It could be from the past or the present, and it could be examples of things the person handled the right way or the wrong way. He encouraged the group by saying we can even learn a lot from our own or others' wrong ways of handling things—as much as we can learn from examples of right ways of handling things.

Ellie purposed in her heart that if she was paired up with Connie or Bonnie, she would share the confusion she felt about her and Ben's getting too close. She needed someone else's advice as to whether she was just over-thinking things or if her conscience was really trying to warn her about something. However, Bonnie and Connie teamed up together and Ellie's partner was a new woman that Ellie didn't feel comfortable baring her soul to. So she let her partner talk and she listened and gave feedback, as best as she could. Her whole mind wasn't on that conversation, though. She kept thinking of the teaching she just heard and the scripture Sarah mentioned: "If I regard iniquity in my heart, the Lord will not hear me."

As she and Ben drove back to his house after the meeting, they talked about the message. Ellie began.

"Ben, I think my conscience is bothering me a little and I've been ignoring it."

"Really?" Ben asked. "Do you feel comfortable sharing it with me?"

"I think I should because it's about us. I think we're getting too close physically especially since we're not really sure where this is going. I mean, even if we were sure, it still might be too close. I don't know. But now everything is a little more precarious because I don't even know what I think or what I'm supposed to think or what God thinks about what you told me lately about your old girlfriend."

Ben listened, but was quiet. Ellie waited. She knew Ben took longer than she did to process things before he spoke. At last he said, "I think you're right, Ellie. We should back up. We should pray about our relationship. And maybe I should drop you off early tonight and we should take time to think and pray on our own."

"That might be a good idea," Ellie said. "Maybe we should just pray in the car now and then you can take me home."

Chapter Nineteen

ELLIE WAS SHAKEN UP, wondering just where this whole relationship would lead. It was sad being home alone on a Saturday evening. She missed Ben terribly, but she was glad that nobody in her family was home now. If her parents or brother were there, she'd have to explain why she wasn't with Ben as she usually was on a Saturday night.

Ellie started out by trying to pray and read the Bible. She did it, but didn't feel like she connected. Then she made herself a nice supper snack of granola with banana and some toast with peanut butter. After that, she didn't know what to do with herself. She didn't want to watch TV. She sort of gave it up a while back. She wasn't in the middle of a good book and didn't have an idea for another one to start. She ended up wandering around the house till she spotted a gift catalog on the living room couch, along with the pile of the day's mail. She decided to browse through the catalog and get ideas for Hanukkah presents for Ben. She wanted to get him a gift for each night of Hanukkah, which meant she'd need eight ideas. She did have a couple of ideas already, but it would be fun to look for other little things he might need that would be just plain fun to give.

As she leafed through the catalog, smiling at some of the cute items, a sudden feeling of fear hit her. *What if she and Ben broke up before*

Hanukkah! She couldn't enjoy perusing the catalog any more. That fear gripped her and hung on. She was finally motivated, almost driven, to pray again and this time she prayed with tears, from her heart.

She loved Ben, she loved him a lot, but she was so confused. She loved him a lot, and it seemed like he loved her. But why did he never bring up marriage? He was sure nice about the trial they were going through right now, giving her the space and time she needed to figure out how she really felt. He still wanted to be with her, even agreeing that they should back up in their physical closeness. That was a big relief to her. She was starting to feel clean again. She realized she knew all along that what she was doing was wrong.

She prayed out loud and she thought out loud and she wondered out loud. She had so many questions. Why oh why didn't Ben bring up marriage? And if he ever did, what should she do? Could she ever forget that he lived with another woman and a child in the very house they would be living in? She cried, she prayed, she prayed in the spirit, read some psalms, and tried to listen. She desperately needed to hear from God.

And this time she actually felt like she was breaking through! She didn't know what the answer would be, but she felt genuine relief from the burdens on her heart. She somehow knew that God heard her. She was able to sort out her feelings and put things in words with a stumbling but deep honesty. She knew God would answer the cry of her heart for a wonderful Godly husband someday. Maybe it would be Ben, maybe not.

She hoped it would be Ben, but she still wasn't sure. But she knew God heard her and she was determined to trust Him. She was scared, but she knew God had the best in mind for her.

Ellie wanted to make herself a piece of toast, but just as she came out of the bathroom, she heard her parents' car pull up. She quickly made her way back to her room, shut off the lights, very quietly got into her pajamas, and got into bed. She didn't want to risk a conversation with her parents tonight. She was emotionally drained.

She heard her mother's footsteps coming close to her bedroom door. It was unusual for the door to be closed if Ellie wasn't home, so her mother knocked lightly on the door. Ellie closed her eyes and pulled up the covers. Her mother gently opened the door, peeked in, then just as softly closed the door again.

"Ellie must have gotten home early tonight," she heard her mom tell her dad.

"Maybe Ben is picking her up earlier than usual for church tomorrow," her father replied.

Ellie lay in bed a good hour before sleep came to her that night.

Chapter Twenty

SUNDAY MORNING FOUND ELLIE watching out the window for Ben's car to pull up. She walked out to meet him right away, before he had a chance to knock on the door and wake everybody else up.

"How was your time of praying, Ellie?" Ben asked.

"I was about to ask you the same question," Ellie said. "Can you go first?"

"Well, I think God still wants us together, and I think we have to hold back from being too close with our physical affection."

"Really? That's what I was hearing too. What a relief that we both feel the same way," Ellie said.

"I'm so glad to hear that, Ellie," Ben said. "So are we back on track now in our relationship?"

"Well, I'm still waiting for God to give me peace about the part of your life you told me about recently. It's still pretty troubling to me," Ellie admitted.

"I prayed for that too," Ben admitted. "Maybe the sermon will help today. I wish I could do something to help, but I know it has to come from you and not me."

The sermon was inspiring, but it didn't speak on any issue that would apply to Ellie's question at the moment. Ellie went up for special prayer at the end of the service. She felt clean again, with her and Ben's new resolve about not getting too close physically. She felt brave enough to be a little more specific in her prayer request, asking Pastor Weisman for prayer about her and Ben's relationship. She didn't say too much beyond that, but at least she felt it was a step beyond calling it an unspoken request.

After the service, Ellie and Ben headed to Ben's house. The wonderful deli they used to meet at for lunch closed down. That was a big disappointment to the Broken Wall regulars, but on that particular Sunday Ellie was content it would just be Ben and her.

Ellie and Ben were both pretty good cooks, so together they whipped up a Chinese stir-fry for lunch. The only place where they had a slight difference of opinion was when it came time to take the meat out of the pan. Ellie wanted to make sure the meat was cooked sufficiently. Ben wanted to take it out at the first sign of done-ness.

"But it's dangerous to eat meat that's not cooked all the way," Ellie tried to convince Ben.

"But Ellie, look, this meat is cooked all the way," Ben said. He took a piece out of the pan, cut it in half and gave Ellie a taste.

"I guess so," Ellie hesitantly agreed.

They ate and talked and were freely enjoying each other's company again. But somehow the old subject came up again. Ellie couldn't even remember what triggered her question, though she did remember it was her fault it was brought up again. When Ben was giving his explanation, Ellie's hands started getting cold and her face started getting a frozen-like expression. It was still so hard.

"Ben I'm sorry, but it's still so hard for me to think about that," Ellie said. "Maybe I shouldn't have asked anything more about it."

"That's ok, Ellie. Ask me what you need to ask me. Take your time in sorting through it all," Ben said.

"Thanks. Do you mind if I take a walk for a few minutes by myself?" she asked.

"Sure, I'll start the dishes," Ben said.

Ellie went outside and began praying. It was invigoratingly cold, but the air smelled so fresh, just like the fresh air smell of a snowy day. Cold or warm, she still loved praying outside as she walked. She cried out to God and again she felt relief, like God heard. She felt comforted. She still didn't know the answer, but she felt better. She came back inside the house, where the warmth felt great.

"I'm back," she said. "I think I'll sit down for a while and read the Bible."

Ben was still working on packing the Chinese leftovers and washing the dishes, including the dishes from his dinner the night before. Ellie took up her Bible and wondered where to read. Where was there a story with pertinent things to what she was experiencing? She didn't know, so she just opened her Bible and started reading. She happened to open it to Isaiah 43. This is what she read:

"Remember ye not the former things, neither consider the things of old. Behold, I will do a new thing; now it shall spring forth; shall ye not know it?"

Ellie was astounded. Was God speaking to her?! Did He guide her to open the Bible to this exact page? Did He cause her eyes to be drawn to those particular verses? It was so fitting, so relevant to her situation at that very particular moment. She re-read it. "Remember ye not the former things, neither consider the things of old." She thought about that a while. Then she read the next part. "Behold, I will do a new thing; now it shall spring forth." Was this relationship with Ben the new thing that God Himself was putting together? Was God Himself telling her not to dwell on Ben's past?

As Ben was quietly and nervously finishing his work in the kitchen, Ellie walked in with the Bible.

"You'll never believe what verse I opened to," she began.

"What?" Ben asked, greatly encouraged by Ellie's change in voice and demeanor.

"Well, I was trying to think of a Bible story or passage that would be helpful for me to read now, you know, something that pertained to relationships or something. But I couldn't think of any. So I just opened the Bible randomly and my eyes fell to the bottom of the page at this exact verse. It's in Isaiah 43. Listen. "Remember ye not the former things, neither consider the things of old. Behold I will do a new thing; now it shall spring forth; shall ye not know it?'"

"Wow," Ben said. "Thank you, Lord! Thank you, Ellie! Will you give me another chance?"

"Yeah I think so," Ellie said.

They both laughed. The tension was relieved. They sat down and talked.

Even though all her sadness didn't leave at once, even though the thoughts of Ben's past still bothered her lot, she believed God wanted her to forget it. She believed God wanted to give her hope again, that He was doing a new thing right now, putting Ellie and Ben together.

Ellie and Ben had a great time the rest of the evening. Ben drove her home before it got too late, and they gave each other a very modest and heartfelt hug and kiss. Ellie went straight to her room and cried. She was happy again.

Chapter Twenty-One

HANUKKAH CAME EARLY THAT YEAR, right after Thanksgiving. Ellie was pre-occupied with thinking of and shopping for a few more gifts for Ben. They would still be having Hanukkah together! When she finally had all eight gifts, she wrapped them and decided to think of a scripture clue for each one. Ben would have to read the clue and then try to guess what the gift was. Her favorite gift was a new stand for his clarinet. Ben's old clarinet stand got lost somewhere the previous month. She chose the verse from Timothy to go with it. "Neglect not the gift that is in thee."

Ellie wanted to celebrate Hanukkah at work and tell her students about it. She wanted to bring a menorah to work and light the candles with her students. But she found out that fire regulations wouldn't allow her to do that. So she just concentrated on making Christmas decorations with her students and putting in little plugs of its real meaning wherever she could.

Ben had a party at his house on the fifth night of Hanukkah. It was a Sunday, so after the service both Ellie and Ben went straight to Ben's house to prepare. They guessed that with fourteen guests, and each guest having about four latkes, they'd need to make about sixty.

"Good thing we started when we did," Ellie said. "Everything seems to take longer than you'd think."

By the time they were frying the last dozen pancakes, the batch of batter had turned black.

"My mother used to make potato pancakes when I was small, but she never made this much. I guess these shredded potatoes were sitting around too long in the bowl and they got oxidized. I never thought about that!"

"Well that makes two of us," Ben said. "But who cares how they look? They'll taste great!"

"They better, with all those fried onions and potatoes in them!" Ellie agreed.

They also cooked up two dozen hot dogs, first boiling them, then frying them in a little bit of oil. After all, a holiday that celebrates the miracle of the one day's supply of oil lasting eight full days needs lots of fried foods on the menu.

The traditional apple sauce and sour cream to eat with the latkes were more than they needed, as they bought three jars of each. Then Bonnie brought over one jar of each and Joanne brought over three more apple sauce jars, along with a huge salad and a pot of chicken soup.

The food feast was wonderful, but the songs were even more fun, and the dancing was the most fun of all. Gifts were exchanged and hot chocolate and tea were made to go along with games and conversations. It was 11 o'clock when the last guest left. Joanne was the last guest. She was nice enough to help with the clean-up, though Ellie would have preferred to do the clean-up with Ben alone. She wanted the party to end earlier so she could give Ben his clarinet stand.

"It's so late, should we still exchange our gifts?" Ellie asked Ben.

"Sure, how long can that take?" Ben said. "Besides, tomorrow there'll be more gifts to open."

"Good," Ellie said. "I can't wait for you to open this."

Ben read the clue. "Neglect not the gift that is within thee." He misunderstood and thought it was referring to the gift inside the box, not the gift of his musical talent.

"Hmm, so it's something I can't neglect. Maybe it's some dish cloths, so I don't neglect doing the dishes and just leave them till you come over."

"No, that's not it," Ellie laughed. After a few more wrong guesses Ben just opened it.

"A clarinet stand! Great! Where did you get it? Thanks a lot!!"

"There's a new music store in the plaza on my way home from work," Ellie answered.

Then Ben gave Ellie an envelope with a card in it. "This has a clue for you," he said.

She opened the card and it had a quote from the Book of Ruth. "Sit still, my daughter, until you learn how the matter turns out, for the man won't rest 'til he finishes the matter today."

Ellie's face turned red and her heart started beating fast. Goose bumps were popping up underneath her sweatshirt. Her eyes were starting to tear up. She knew that was the passage where Naomi was telling Ruth that Boaz would not rest till he gave her the answer of whether or not he would marry her.

Ellie gulped and said out loud, "Does this mean what I think it means?"

Ben said, "I think so. Ellie, will you marry me?"

Ellie immediately, straight-away, directly said, "Yes." Then she added, "I'm so scared."

Ellie was in shock. The thing she waited for almost her whole life long had finally happened. She knew she would say yes, but she didn't know how scared she would be, realizing her life would change forever. She thought she was ready for Ben to ask her months ago, even a year ago. Now she knew maybe she really wouldn't have been ready then. She was happy, so very, very happy. But she was also kind of numb, with the feeling of shock and surprise. What a day! What a Hanukkah!

They hugged and they kissed, but not too long. Ben sent Ellie home before she got too tired. And Ellie got home safely, driving most of the way on auto-pilot.

Everyone was sleeping when she got home, but she went and knocked on her parents' bedroom door. "Can I tell you something?" she called out.

Ellie's mother got up and was quite alarmed. She thought someone had gotten hurt. "What happened?" she asked.

"Mom, Ben asked me to marry him," Ellie said.

Daniel heard and her father heard and everyone got up and congratulated her. Everyone seemed to get a second wind after the news so Daniel began putting bread in the toaster and Ellie's mother poured four glasses of orange juice. After hearing all the facts and all the feelings and all the extraneous events surrounding Ellie's evening, four very happy people went to bed, along with one very happy man who lived in his own house in a nearby town.

Chapter Twenty-Two

THE REST OF THAT WEEK went by in a fog for Ellie. She stayed in the state of a good but numbing shock the whole next day. She told the good news to the people she worked with and received many congratulations. She was so happy in her mind and her spirit, but she still couldn't feel it in her body. Maybe this was what a drunken stupor was like. Finally in the evening after work, as she drove to Ben's house, her body was snapping out of the shock and getting with the program—excitement!

"How long do you think we should wait?" Ellie asked.

"I called my mom last night after you left and she was so happy for me! But she asked if we could schedule the wedding for a warmer month," Ben reported.

"Oh no, I'm so excited, I don't really want to wait till summer! Let's think. Let me look at your calendar… Spring starts in March. March 1 is a Saturday, how about March 1st?"

Ben thought about it. "Hmm, March 1. Let's see, that's 3-1. Hey, that would be a great symbolism! The three in one God and also God making you and me and Him into a three-fold cord! Yes, I like it, except for one thing! It's on the Sabbath and it's traditional not to get married on the Sabbath."

"How about if we have the ceremony after sundown? It still gets dark kind of early in March."

"That's true. That's a good idea," Ben agreed.

"You should call your mother and make sure she's ok with that date," Ellie encouraged him. "I think you should call her now!"

"Ok," Ben laughed.

He did and she was able to be persuaded. It was all approved for March 1.

"Ellie, I'd like to get you an engagement ring," Ben said later.

"That's nice of you," she said. "But I don't really need one. Diamonds are so expensive. A wedding band will be enough for me."

"True, it's not really needed. It's not what you would call essential. Yet it would be nice. It's like a seal. Like the Lord sent the Holy Spirit as a seal to show He's coming back one day. It's like the sign that we're promised to Him. And my gift of an engagement ring for you would be like a seal that you're promised to me. It shows that you're taken. You're not available anymore."

"That's neat. I never thought of it like that before. Yeah, it would be really nice to have an engagement ring."

"My mother was telling me that my cousin just got engaged. She was telling mom about a great place to go for ordering a diamond."

"You mean in Virginia?" Ellie asked.

"Yes, and my mother asked if you and I could come to Virginia for some of the days of our Christmas vacations. She said she could pay for your plane fare."

"Really?!" Ellie said.

"That's what she really said!"

"Wow, I can't believe all this is happening to me!" Ellie said.

"And my mom said she has two small diamonds from a brooch that my grandmother from Brooklyn gave her a long time ago. If we want, we can use those two diamonds in the ring," Ben suggested.

"Wow that would be special!" Ellie said. "Diamonds that belonged to your grandma! I'm really excited to go to your old home with you, Ben! That'll be so fun and interesting!"

"Me too!" Ben said. "Did you tell Sarah yet?"

"No, I didn't have time. I got home late and stayed up really late talking to my family,"

"I can understand that," Ben laughed.

"Then I went to work this morning and came here as soon as I could," she said.

Ben just laughed. "Do you want to call Sarah from here?"

"Sure! But first I wanted to ask you something. Do you think it would be ok to ask Sarah to be my bridesmaid?"

"You mean your maid of honor?" Ben asked.

"Yes, in fact, I always thought that at my wedding I would just want one bridesmaid. What do you think of that idea?" Ellie asked.

"Fine with me," Ben said. "Who would I ask?"

"Well, I know it's really the man who gets to ask his best friend, but since you're getting to know Daniel more now and since he is my only brother, I was wondering if you could just consider the idea of letting him be the one," Ellie asked.

"That sounds great to me," Ben said immediately. "But I probably should pray about it before we ask him."

"Sure," Ellie agreed. "The reason I asked all this now is because I thought I could call Sarah and tell her I have a favor I want to ask her. Then I'd ask her if she could be my bridesmaid."

"Ok, but only if you do it right here and right now. And hold the phone away from your ear when she answers so I can hear the screaming," he said.

"Ok, here goes…" "Hi Mrs. Kirby, is Sarah home?"

"Oh hi Ellie. Yes, she's in her room doing some reading for school. I'll get her. How are you doing?'

"I'm doing fine, thanks."

Sarah was quick. "Hi Ellie! Nice to hear from you. You don't usually call on a Monday night. What's up?"

"Well, I have a favor I wanted to ask you," Ellie said.

"Sure, what is it?" Sarah answered.

"Will you be my maid of honor at my wedding?"

"You mean you want to be prepared in case Ben asks you? Do you think he's getting close?"

"Sarah! He already did! And I said yes!"

"AAAAAHHHHHHHH!!!!!!!"

Ben and Ellie listened with the phone away from their ears. They heard more commotion, then voices of her mom, her brothers, and her father.

"What's wrong Sarah?... Mom, what happened?... William do you know what happened? …I was in the basement, what happened?"

"Tell them Ellie," Sarah said.

"I'm engaged," Ellie shouted into the phone. She and Ben totally enjoyed hearing the comments of surprise and rejoicing coming from the other end of the line.

Ben began to prepare dinner and gave Ellie time to talk to Sarah privately. They ended their happy discussion with the agreement that Ellie and Sarah would get together in person sometime during Christmas vacation. Then Ellie could tell Sarah all about her trip to Ben's childhood home and update her on all the developing wedding plans.

Chapter Twenty-Three

WEDDING PLANS WERE BEING DEVELOPED right and left, here and there, daytime and night-time during the next several days and weeks. Debbie from Broken Wall suggested having Israeli dancing at the wedding. Ellie thought this was a great idea, that is, until she heard that Debbie was not just thinking of the reception. She was suggesting dancing as part of the actual ceremony.

"That's kind of unusual. I don't know how that would be. I might be scared to do something that different," she told Debbie.

"Let me tell you my idea" Debbie said, not giving up. "We can have some dancers come in to start the ceremony, dancing down the aisles and then finishing up when they're in front. This would be before Ben or you make your grand entrance."

"Hmm," Ellie mused. "Let me think about it."

"And then the dancers can come out at the end of the service again, with you and Ben joining them and dancing down the aisles." Debbie was excited.

"Hmm… I did see a Christian wedding once where the bride and groom kind of danced or more like skipped down the aisle at the end. That was an astonishing sight to see, but I remember really liking it. It was so happy, so different."

"So do you want to consider it?" Debbie asked.

"Let me talk to Ben about it," Ellie concluded.

As the dancing idea was working itself into Ellie's heart, other ideas were coming fast and furious. One unseasonably warm day, as Ellie drove past some farm fields to Ben's house, she was listening to a Christian radio station. All of a sudden, at the exact time that the words "to God be the glory" were sung, a huge flock of birds that were feeding in the field rose up together, as one, into the air. It was amazing. It was like God choreographed that scene to happen just at that moment as a special gift to Ellie. It actually brought tears to her eyes, it was so grand and such a gift from God to see. She started thinking about the power of music to elicit emotion.

Her mind immediately started connecting these thoughts to her wedding day. One song she was considering for the wedding played itself out in her mind as she imagined the whole scene choreographed before her. She would be walking down the aisle with her father while the music group sang Sabbath Prayer from Fiddler on the Roof. The words seemed so appropriate for a bride. She reminded herself of them as she sang out loud. "May the Lord protect and defend you, may the Lord preserve you from pain…may you come to be in Israel a shining name.…may God bless you and give you long life, may God make you a good mother and wife…" She loved it! She couldn't wait to tell Ben the idea.

Ben didn't object. He loved the idea too, and he was brimming with ideas of his own. "I've been reading this book on Jewish wedding traditions," he told Ellie.

"That's interesting," Ellie said.

"One thing I found out was that it's traditional for the man to wear a long white robe called a kittel for his wedding day."

"What? I can't really picture it. But it seems kind of odd, doesn't it? I think it would be a little too strange for this day and age, don't you think?" Ellie asked.

"It's not done too often I guess," Ben said. "But I'd like to do it. It says the white robe is the same one that's worn by the service leader for Passover services and Yom Kippur. It's also the robe the person is supposed to be buried in when he dies."

"Oh no, I think that sounds a little too weird to me," Ellie said.

"Give it a chance, Ellie. Let's think about it and pray about it," Ben pleaded.

"Ok," Ellie agreed. She realized she owed it to Ben to at least consider it. After all, he agreed to almost all the ideas she suggested.

"I've been reading this other book by a Jewish believer," Ben continued. "It's about how the Jewish wedding traditions perfectly portray Jesus coming back for us, His bride."

"What do you mean?" Ellie asked.

"It said that in the ancient Jewish wedding traditions at the time of Jesus, the groom would first propose. Then he would go back to his father's house and start building a home for himself and his wife. When it was done, he would come back for his bride. Nobody knew when that would be except the father, because the father has to tell his son when he approves of the house. However, in those days people had a good idea of the general time frame, as it usually took about a year," Ben explained.

"Wow, that *is* amazing," Ellie agreed. "So much like when Yeshua comes back, nobody knows exactly when except the Father. And we know the general time frame, like what things will be happening on earth before He returns, but not the exact day or hour."

"Yes," Ben went on, "and then when the bridegroom comes back, he comes back with a bunch of his friends. They make a lot of noise to wake up the bride and her friends, because it usually happens at night. And they blow the shofar and shout something like, 'Behold the bridegroom cometh!'"

"Wow, that's like Jesus coming back with the sound of the trumpet! And it reminds me of the parable of the ten virgins who waited for the bridegroom with their friend who would be the bride. Five of them had oil for their lamps and five didn't. And they didn't know exactly when the bridegroom would be coming, but they had to be prepared."

"Yes!" Ben was enthused and continued. "Jesus used parables about the Jewish wedding traditions a lot. The parallels to His coming back for us His bride are so uncanny. I think God wanted us to see this! He wants to show us that Yeshua will really be the bridegroom coming back for the bride, and just like in Revelation, we'll have the great wedding supper of the Lamb! Ellie, I hope you agree. I really want to have a feast for our wedding supper, not just some cake and punch and stuff. I want it to simulate the marriage supper of the Lamb."

Ellie laughed. "Of course I want that too! I just take it for granted that that's what a wedding is supposed to be. I'm used to the weddings of my cousins on my mother's side of the family. They're big Polish weddings with a bunch of delicious food! I've hardly been to any cake and punch weddings, except for one friend at college. But of course I always wanted my wedding to have the traditional big generous delicious meal for everybody."

"Great!" Ben was excited. "We can have some Polish food, like the pierogis your mother makes, and some Israeli foods too. Maybe Asher and Kathy can make some hummus and we can buy some pita bread and stuff."

"And of course we can have the chicken and beef like most weddings have," Ellie said, joining in the fun. "But I don't know who can make the pierogi. They're complicated to make and to make enough for a big crowd… How many do you think we'll have at our wedding?"

"I don't know. We'll have to start writing down who we want to invite."

When Ellie told Carmen at work about the plans, she was very happy for Ellie.

"Ellie, I really think God must be in this for you. It's not very common to hear good reports like yours about wedding preparations. So many people I've known have a lot of tension during this planning period. But for you and Ben to be in such agreement is a pretty exceptional thing. You know some of your ideas are a little outlandish, don't you? And yet both of you are ok with them? That's like a little miracle," she risked saying.

Ellie made a silly expression and said, "I know. I guess they are pretty unconventional. I'm surprised I'm even telling you about them and not being embarrassed or shy about it."

Carmen got very sincere and said, "Oh please don't take it to mean I don't think those are great ideas. They *are* weird but they're wonderful! I can't wait to see the real thing! Will you be inviting a lot of people from the center?"

"I don't know. I'd like your opinion. What do you think we should do?" Ellie asked.

"Well, when Janice got married, you never met her but she used to work here, she posted an open invitation to the staff and parents and clients. She just made a flyer and put it on the bulletin board."

"Really? About how many people came from the center?"

"I'd say about ten of the staff and four or five of the clients with their parents."

"That sounds like a great idea," Ellie said. "I'll talk to Ben about it."

But before Ellie even had a chance to bring that idea up to Ben, she had another idea to share when she called him after work.

"Are you ready for another idea?" Ellie asked.

"Yes," Ben said wondering.

"What if we had someone blow the shofar before you come out and then maybe you and whoever is your best man can come out, and maybe the other guys who will be holding the chuppah poles. And you can all be holding candles and march down the aisle…"

"Candles," Ben said. "Yes, that would be like coming for the bride at night. And maybe we could somehow incorporate lighting the seven-branched menorah that's at Broken Wall."

"That's just what I was thinking!" Ellie almost screamed.

"Really?" Ben asked.

"Yeah, you know how some people have a unity candle they light? I was thinking if we have six people we can light the menorah, each person lighting one branch and then you and I can both light the top one together and blow out our own candles. I've counted and with you and Daniel and the four guys who will be holding up the chuppah poles, that's six. Then there'll be Sarah, with the seventh candle. Well, actually Sarah will be six, and you and I together will light the seventh and then blow out our own."

"That would work! Hallelujah! I love that idea!"

"And having the wedding at sundown when it's dark would work out perfectly for coming in with candles," Ellie added.

And so more and more ideas flowed and were incorporated into the wedding.

Ellie had no success in finding an appropriate wedding dress at the bridal shops. She thought maybe she should just have a dress made by a friend from Broken Wall who was an accomplished seamstress. So with that idea floating around in her brain, along with a heart full of so many more thoughts, emotions, lists, fears, and ideas, she and Ben flew out to Virginia.

Chapter Twenty-Four

THE TRIP REALLY HELPED ELLIE in more ways than one. At least she didn't have to worry about Ben's safety on the airplane, because she would be with him! Better to be there with Ben than worrying back home.

Ben's mom was friendly and excited. She offered to show Ellie the house, but Ben wanted to give her the tour himself.

It was a simple house with simple furniture. Most of it was stuff from when Ben was a kid, like the funny red swivel chair in the living room. The stereo and coffee table were typical 60's style, smooth and kind of plain. The kitchen was small. In fact all the rooms on the main floor were small. The stairway to the upstairs was narrow and steep. It was really sort of an attic, but the one room that converted into a guest bedroom up there was nice and big. And that's where Ellie got to stay. The walls were wood paneling and it reminded her of a vacation cabin. It was a nice roomy place to pace around and pray and think. Ben stayed in his old bedroom downstairs, which seemed pretty tiny now that he was a grown man.

They visited relatives, visited bridal shops, prayed together and read the Bible together. They took daily walks and talked and brainstormed continuously.

"If our wedding is supposed to be a picture of Yeshua coming back for his bride, wouldn't it be nice if I got linen material for my wedding dress?

It would be like in Revelation 19 where the bride is dressed in linen," Ellie thought aloud.

"Ellie that would be so wonderful! And if you agree on the kittel idea, I can have a kittel type robe made for me out of some linen material too," he said very enthusiastically.

Ellie was softening to the idea of a kittel, even though she was still a little afraid of the strangeness of the whole thing. How would it look and what would people think? But Ben was so supportive of all her ideas. And now this linen thing, with Ben's kittel being made of linen, made it seem like the right thing to do.

In the course of the week there, Ben's mom said she and Ben's aunt could make the kittel if Ben and Ellie found a pattern and the linen material. So Ben and Ellie bought a pattern for a man's robe at a fabric store in Virginia the next day. At the same time, Ellie found a pattern she could use for a wedding dress. It was really a pattern for a hippie-style flower child sort of long dress, but when it would be made in all white linen, Ellie was sure it would make a beautiful wedding gown. They ordered the linen, which would have to be shipped from New York, and were that much closer to the wedding preparations coming together.

On the Sabbath, Ben and Ellie went to the Messianic Jewish congregation about an hour away from his mother's house. It was remarkable that all of a sudden Messianic congregations were popping up all over the country. At the end of the service, while the last worship songs were being sung, the leader invited people to come up for prayer. Ben and Ellie went up for prayer for their upcoming wedding and marriage.

"Do you recognize the elder who is praying for people now?" Ben asked Ellie.

"No, not really," Ellie replied.

"He's one of the musicians whose music we've learned at Broken Wall," Ben told her. "We've been dancing to the tapes he and his music group have made."

"Really, that's him?!" Ellie was impressed.

"Let's go in his line," Ben said, as there were three other elders up front praying for people.

When it was their turn, Ben asked, "Can you pray for our upcoming wedding and marriage? And also, would your music group be able to come out for our wedding and play at our reception? It's going to be on March 1st."

Ellie was surprised Ben was asking this without talking to her about it first. Not that she didn't think it was a great idea!

"Sorry, my wife is expecting a baby around then, so I know we won't be doing much traveling. But I'd be happy to pray for you," he said. The words he said as he finished his inspired prayer stayed with Ellie and Ben. "…and Lord, I pray that Ben and Ellie's wedding celebration would be like a Feast of Tabernacles celebration…"

On their way home, Ellie and Ben talked excitedly about how their wedding could be like the Feast of Tabernacles. They agreed then and there that they would tell Debbie yes to the dancing idea. That was so important to the Feast. And they could go to the Jewish bookstores and buy some Feast of Tabernacles decorations. Ellie remembered seeing garlands of colorful fruit and leaves strung from the ceiling of the store at the time of the fall feasts. She thought they would add a real festive flare to the hall they would rent.

The engagement ring was ordered on the trip too. The diamond dealer seemed to be as honest and helpful as Ben's cousin led them to believe. He measured Ellie's finger and would be mailing the ring to Ben's house when it was finished. One diamond for the center would be coming from Israel and the other two small diamonds from Ben's grandmother, not exactly matching but close in size to each other, would be set on either side of the diamond from Israel.

Chapter Twenty-Five

TWO DAYS AFTER ELLIE AND BEN returned home from Virginia, Sarah came to spend the night with Ellie.

"So nice to see you, Sarah! I have some good news to tell you!" Ellie exclaimed.

"What? Tell me," Sarah said.

"Well, actually two surprises, at least two things you don't know about yet but I think you'll be happy to hear," Ellie told her.

"What?" Sarah demanded.

"One thing is that Ben picked out his best man, the guy you'll be standing up with. And it's somebody you already know."

"Whew, that's a relief. Did you know I was a little worried about that?" Sarah asked.

"I didn't know for sure, but I figured you would be. I mean I would be if it were me. So it's gonna be Daniel!"

"Daniel! Wow, that is a surprise. That sure makes me happy," Sarah said, trying not to show just how happy it actually made her.

"And the other surprise is that we arranged an afternoon of dancing tomorrow."

Sarah's eyes lit up and her expression seemed to tell Ellie to go on with the details that she couldn't wait to hear about.

"We'll all meet at Ben's house. It's actually closer to the expressway for when your dad comes to pick you up. And we'll practice a few of the dances we'll be doing at the reception. Debbie said that if several people know the dances really well, it will be that much easier for others to join in. That way there should always be some people who know the dances close to the new people, and then they can follow along without messing up the whole dance too much."

"Oh boy, I'm thrilled! Who'll all be there?" Sarah wanted to know.

"Daniel for one, and also Debbie. Those are the for sure people, along with you and me and Ben. But most likely Connie and Bill and Bonnie and Joanne and Ralph will join us," Ellie explained.

Ellie and Sarah were busily getting ready to leave for the Shabbat service when Daniel zoomed into the house.

"How did you get out of work so early tonight?" Ellie asked.

"Actually, I was just scheduled to work till 6 o'clock today. I came straight home and here I am! Hi Sarah," Daniel said.

"Hi Daniel," Sarah replied.

"Am I in time to catch a ride with you two to Broken Wall?" Daniel asked.

"If you can get ready in ten or fifteen minutes," Ellie said.

"I can," he replied.

Ellie and Sarah looked at each other and smiled. "He seems determined to go with us," Ellie said.

"That's good, right?" Sarah asked innocently.

"Of course it's good. I'm always glad when Daniel comes. But it seems like when you're here, he's a little more motivated," Ellie revealed.

"Really?" Sarah asked, very pleased to hear that bit of information.

The car ride, the service and the fellowship were all so very good. They were all tied in Sarah's estimation, but the service and fellowship where Ben was present won out in Ellie's appraisal of the evening. The girls didn't get to talk too much about the wedding details on Friday night, because Daniel hung around with them till midnight. By then they all decided to go straight to sleep.

"We can talk more in the morning," Ellie apologized. "Sorry we didn't have much of a chance this evening."

"Sorry?! No need to apologize. It was a wonderful evening. I wouldn't have changed anything about it," Sarah explained. They both went to sleep smiling.

Daniel was up early on Saturday to go to his part-time job at the sports store. He traded with a co-worker, who agreed to let Daniel work his early shift while he would work Daniel's afternoon hours. That way Daniel could have the afternoon free to go to the dance practice.

Chapter Twenty-Six

ELLIE'S MOTHER HAD PANCAKE BATTER waiting for the girls whenever they woke up. Then she and Ellie's dad left to do their usual Saturday errands and grocery shopping. The girls had agreed to go on a prayer walk first thing in the morning, so by the time they were ready for breakfast it was 11 o'clock. The house was pleasantly empty except for Sarah and Ellie.

"This is fun," Sarah said, "talking about your wedding and eating fresh pancakes with maple syrup."

"I'll say," Ellie agreed. "And there's so much to tell you. Let's see. You already know about the dancing at the ceremony and at the reception. At the end of the ceremony, Ben and I will join the dancers and dance down the aisles to make our exit."

"That'll be incredible. Are you nervous about it?" Sarah wanted to know.

"A little. I don't catch on to these dances real fast, so Debbie showed me the dance we'll be doing and I've been practicing it in my room every day, at least ten minutes or so."

"Will that be one we'll be doing tonight?" Sarah asked.

"You mean this afternoon?" Ellie asked.

"Yeah," Sarah corrected herself. "Too bad I can't stay later into the evening. One of these days we'll be getting a second car and then Dad said I'll be able to drive myself down here."

"That'll be great," Ellie agreed. "But before my parents come home I should tell you about one hard decision we had to make. At first Ben and I didn't want any liquor at the reception. But my mom said her relatives wouldn't even want to come if there wouldn't be any liquor served. So we talked about it and realized even Yeshua turned water into wine for a wedding celebration, so there's nothing unscriptural about it."

"That's true. I never thought of that," Sarah said.

"And another thing you haven't heard about yet is that we found a band to play the music. Remember how I told you that we were prayed over and the guy prayed that our wedding would be like the Feast of Tabernacles?"

"Yes I remember. The Feast of Tabernacles was so joyful, I don't see what better model you can have for a wedding celebration," Sarah said.

"I know. It was an inspired suggestion. Anyway, we remembered about this Mexican church in the city that loves Israel and prays for Israel and celebrates the Feast of Tabernacles every year. They have excellent musicians and we decided to go there and ask if their group could play for our reception. And they said yes!"

"Wow, that'll be different. What sort of music will they play?"

"A variety. I want some polkas for my Polish relatives and a lot of the Jewish and Messianic songs for my Jewish relatives and Messianic Jewish friends. And of course some waltzes and love songs. But I did tell them I didn't want things like the polkas with words like 'I don't want her, you can have her, she's too fat for me' and things like that. And no songs about a love that failed. We gave them so many directions and suggestions, I just don't know what they'll do and how they'll do it! But we both trust them a lot and believe they'll do a great job."

"Wow, it's all so fascinating. Anything else you forgot to tell me?"

"Oh yeah, I meant to tell you a real good development. Remember I told you that I thought Ben and I were getting too close at one point?"

"Yes," Sarah said thoughtfully, getting more serious all of a sudden.

"Well, ever since we got engaged, in fact, even a few weeks before we got engaged, we started being not so close that way anymore. It feels so good."

"That's great. Did you two talk about it or did it just naturally happen or what?" Sarah wanted to know.

"We talked and things happened and we prayed. Hey, maybe you were praying too," Ellie just realized.

Sarah confessed, "I was."

"Thanks, Sarah. In fact, I told Ben we better practice how we're going to kiss in public. That'll be new to me, kissing with everybody watching. So we've been practicing. I told Ben we should start with a hug to make us more comfortable and then he can kiss me."

"That is so cute!" Sarah said.

"And it won't be a long sensual kiss either. I hope you know that," Ellie said.

"Yeah, I figured," Sarah answered.

"Well, I can share a few more things, that is, if you're still interested."

"Great. So what about the food and the place?" Sarah asked.

"My uncle's restaurant agreed to cater the food. It'll be the standard wedding fare, chicken, beef, gravy, mashed potatoes, green beans and stuff like that. And this lady from Poland that my mom knows is making a couple hundred pierogi. Kathy and Asher are making Israeli salad and hummus. And we were able to rent the American Legion Hall right down the street from Broken Wall for the reception."

"You're making my mouth water. What about the wedding cake?"

"Ben had a friend at work who got married and he said the cake was delicious. So we got the name of the baker and he'll be making our cake. There'll be a Star of David and a cross on the top."

"Stop already!" Sarah joked. "It's too much. I'm getting so tired of hearing myself say the same words over and over, wow, great, exciting! I just can't believe how you've thought of all these things. There are so many parts to this wedding. I hope you can pull it all off without any hitches. The ceremony itself sounds so beautiful, with the men marching in with the shofar blowing and carrying candles."

"Oh, and did I tell you what song we'll be doing when Ben and the men march in?" Ellie asked.

"No, what song and will this be the Mexican band?"

"No, it'll be our Broken Wall music group, minus Ben of course. But this song will be Od Yishama, about the sound of joy of the bride and the bridegroom in Jerusalem. And Kathy and Asher will be singing it as a duet."

"I can't wait. But then again, I can wait. More dance practices and rehearsals! This preparation time is so much fun too. It'll be hard to get back to normal after it's all over," Sarah said.

Ellie felt sorry for Sarah. She knew that her own life wouldn't be going back to normal after the wedding, but she knew Sarah's life would. But then again, Sarah's family was getting a second car and maybe she'd be able to get out more. And maybe very soon God would satisfy the desires of Sarah's heart too. And maybe God would satisfy the desires of Daniel's heart at the exact same moment.

Chapter Twenty-Seven

AS HAPPENS OFTEN IN LIFE, the day that seemed so far away, that long awaited special day that seemed like it would never come, it finally surprises you and comes! And so it happened for Ellie. One day she woke up and it was actually March 1, her wedding day!

She wasn't able to sleep very well, but she did manage to stay in bed in a prone position with her eyes closed for several hours during the night. She would doze, think, get excited, get scared, pray, doze again, dream a little and eventually wake up and begin the whole process all over again. But when the sun came up, Ellie was up with it.

Ellie got an unusual gift from someone at her bridal shower. An older woman at Broken Wall gave Ellie a coupon for a manicure on the day of her wedding. It was from a beauty shop just two blocks away from Ellie's house. So Ellie took her prayer walk and then stopped at the beauty shop before heading home. She got her fingernails, which were not very long, painted with ivory nail polish. She asked about toe nail polish, but they didn't do toes. They did sell her the rest of the bottle of matching polish, and Ellie went home and painted her own toe nails. This was the first time in her life that she ever put fingernail polish on her toes, but since she'd be wearing white sandals, she thought it would be a nice touch.

"Ellie, I was worried about you," her mother greeted her. "You were gone so long on your walk!"

"Sorry Mom. Remember I told you someone gave me a coupon for a free manicure today?"

"That's right," her mom answered. "I did forget. Ellie, I'm so excited for you and so jittery. Do you want to eat breakfast?"

"No, I don't think so," Ellie answered. She didn't tell her mom the reason, though. Ben was so excited to do as much as they could the traditional Jewish way, and fasting on one's wedding day until the bride and groom shared their first meal together as husband and wife was one of the customs he read about. Ellie wasn't as zealous for all the suggestions in the book as Ben was, but she did love the parts that symbolized the story of Yeshua coming back for His bride. However, she did believe strongly in the idea of praying and fasting for different important situations in life. And what could be more important than a person changing his whole role in life and getting married? So she readily agreed to the fasting and prayer idea. And how hungry could a girl get on her own wedding day, Ellie wondered. She figured she wouldn't be able to eat much anyway.

"I don't blame you," her mom said. "I don't think I was too hungry on my wedding day either."

"Mom, Ben and I decided that I could take a lot of my clothes and things to his house this morning. My wedding dress and veil are there already. I won't get dressed at his house. We'll be heading out to Broken Wall early this afternoon and I'll get dressed there."

"If that's what you want," her mother said. "You know it's traditional that the groom doesn't see the bride until she comes up to the altar to meet him."

"I know, mom, but we're not really going by those traditions. Ben is reading this book on Jewish traditions and we're doing a lot of those, especially the ones that point to Jesus."

"I think that's so nice that you're incorporating both your Jewish heritage and your faith in Jesus into this wedding," her mom said.

"But mom, of course I would. You know that's so dear to my heart, that's the core of my being now, my belief in God!" Ellie said, getting a little frustrated with her mother's lack of understanding.

"I know, Ellie. You really have become a good religious girl. We're so proud of you. And you're honoring your father's faith and my faith too," her mother naively said.

"Thanks mom. I know I should have shared more with you as we were planning this whole thing. Sarah shares so much with her mother and father."

Ellie's mother was very loving and accepting, though she didn't understand Ellie's faith and beliefs much at all. "I know that's what Sarah does, Ellie, and I think that's great because her parents were her teachers too. But our family is different. You went to school and learned how to think for yourself. I'm so proud of you for planning this unusual and creative wedding."

"Thanks mom," Ellie said. "I love you!" Then she kissed her mom and her mom started crying.

"I'll miss you, Ellie. I know we didn't talk that much, but I just loved having you home! I love you so much. I'll miss you, Ellie."

Now Ellie started crying. "And I'll miss you too, Mom! But Mom, I'm so happy. The dream I've dreamed about for so much of my life is coming true!"

"I know," her mother said, as they both hugged each other and started crying even more.

Ellie kept the interchange with her mother in her mind and heart for a long time. She started packing all the clothes she would need for her first few weeks with Ben, including the things she'd need for their honeymoon in the mountains of North Carolina. She had most of the stuff on one side of her closet already, and all she had to do was pack them into her car. It was a nice mindless task that she could do while giving her mind and heart the freedom to think about all kinds of things. Memories of the past, visions of the future, but mostly thoughts about the present…this very day…her wedding day!

Chapter Twenty-Eight

ELLIE TOOK A BATH at Ben's house and submerged herself as completely as she could in the tub. Ben suggested she do that, to make it more like the traditional mikvah Jewish women would go through in Yeshua's time as they ventured on to a new phase in their lives. After the bath, Ellie usually set her wet hair with a few rollers for an hour or two. But because she didn't want Ben to see her with rollers, she didn't do this. She hoped she'd look good on her wedding day anyway, even though she thought her hair would behave better if she had used the rollers. She thought she might be the only girl who ever skipped making her hair a big priority on her wedding day. But she knew Ben liked her hair just plain and straight, so that's how she wore it.

As Ellie and Ben arrived at Broken Wall, some of their friends were there already, waiting to help however they could. The flower lady was there too, setting up the flowers and the runners. Ellie was eager to see how the headband of real flowers turned out. She wanted to wear real flowers in her hair and use the headband to help hold down her veil. Ellie had explained to the woman from the flower shop that she just wanted flowers on the bottom of both sides of the headband, but none in the middle. She knew she would look ridiculous with flowers sticking straight up on top of her head.

Ellie carefully removed the plastic protection around the headband. She almost panicked. It was just the way she didn't want it! Providentially

Sarah arrived right before she opened the package. Sarah re-assured Ellie that they could fix the problem easily, by removing all the flowers except for the bottom ones. They worked on it together and found it wasn't so easy but at least it was do-able. Ellie tried it on with the veil and was so relieved that it looked good. She needed more bobby pins, but she only had a few black ones in her purse. Bonnie volunteered to run to the drugstore to buy some white ones. What a blessing to have so many people to help.

"Let me help you with your make-up," Joanne offered.

"I already have it on," Ellie told her. "I'm just wearing eye-liner and a little powder and blush."

"Oh," Joanne said, not really agreeing but accepting Ellie's wishes.

"I don't really want to look different than I usually look," Ellie explained. "Besides, I like the natural look."

Joanne didn't say too much to object, but her lack of enthusiasm caused Ellie to wonder if she looked all right. Good old Sarah re-assured her again.

People started arriving. Ellie couldn't get over the fact that people were coming out just for her sake! So many people flying in, so many people buying new outfits! It was overwhelming that she was the cause of it all. It was kind of scary, until she convinced herself that everybody loves to celebrate and loves an excuse to do it. That way she didn't feel so responsible for everyone spending all that time and money to be here just for her sake, and of course Ben's too.

Finally she was all ready. Pastor Weisman came downstairs to the room where she was waiting. He would do the traditional blessing over Ellie before she covered her face. Ellie bought some beautiful white tulle and lace material to drape over her head and face as she walked in. As Pastor Weisman prayed Ellie felt the Holy Spirit's presence and all of a sudden felt a kind of supernatural peace come over her. She wasn't nervous or jittery or anything. She was more at peace than she was the night before when they were just practicing!

Sarah and Ellie walked up the stairs together to wait in the foyer until it was time to walk in. By now the whole building was packed and the music team was playing the prelude music, some of Ellie and Ben's favorite worship songs. The Broken Wall people knew these songs and were singing so passionately. What a thing for Ellie to hear! How could she wait? It was so perfect.

Ellie and Sarah waited together with Ellie's dad. The dancers were there too, about ready to dance down the aisles as soon as they heard their cue.

"They look so pretty, don't they?" Sarah asked Ellie.

"Yeah, they sure do." Ellie's answer was short and sweet. She couldn't concentrate too long on any one thing except the fact that she and Ben were about to get married.

Sarah made a few more comments to pass the time, but Ellie just smiled in response. Sarah was quite impressed at the amazing job Debbie did in piecing together such nice matching outfits for the girls—white skirts with blue ribbon trim, white blouses, blue vests, and a matching blue scarf for their heads. They looked like some version of Polish or Jewish folk dancers. The men dancers looked good too of course, but you wouldn't exactly refer to them as "pretty." They wore white slacks and shirts with blue vests.

The prelude music just ended and suddenly the music group changed gear. They began playing *O Come Let's Sing, Let Us Rejoice.* **That was the cue!!** The ceremony was starting! The dancers entered, dancing, playing tambourines, and smiling, smiling, smiling. Ellie's heart was overwhelmed with happiness.

After the song, the dancers took their places in the front pew and Pastor Weisman began by welcoming everyone to the marriage ceremony. He gave a brief description of the way the Jewish wedding traditions point to Jesus coming back for His bride. At the very end, right on signal, the lights were cut off and the pastor said, "And when Yeshua returns, we'll hear the sound of a shofar and a shout."

After those words Daniel boldly shouted out, "Behold the bridegroom cometh!"

Ellie was so proud of him! Then Ben blew the shofar, and he, Daniel, and his four chuppah bearers marched in. It was beautiful with the lights off and the men holding their candles coming down the aisle. All the while Kathy and Asher's lovely harmony of *Od Yishama* was wafting through the air. When they got to the front each of the men put their candle in one of the openings of the seven branched menorah, except for Ben of course. Ben held on to his candle and took up his post watching and waiting for his bride.

Finally the music team played an instrumental version of *Sabbath Prayer*, changed to *Wedding Prayer*, and Sarah walked in. Ellie trusted Sarah and had given her free reign to choose any dress she wanted to wear. Sarah chose a gorgeous yellow dress that came just below her knees. She walked in very gracefully, lit the sixth candle, and joined Daniel and the chuppah bearers on the raised platform.

Then the singers began singing and the instrumental turned into a song with words. "May the Lord protect and defend you..." Ellie and her father began walking down the aisle. Ellie was beaming. She saw all the people rising and gazing at her and her father. She was balancing the candle, trying to hold it far enough away from her veil. And as she reached the front, her father very skillfully removed the veil from her face without getting it near the flame, folded it quickly over his arm, and kissed his daughter. Then he shook Ben's hand and left his daughter in Ben's charge. Ellie and Ben climbed the two steps onto the raised platform and lit the center candle with their two candles. They blew out their individual candles and walked up to the chuppah.

The vows, the prayers, the songs, the signing of the Ketubah/wedding covenant...it was all so magnificent. Pastor Weisman ended the ceremony with the words, "Now with the authority given unto me by the Messiah of Israel, I declare that Ben and Ellie are now husband and wife, in accordance with the ordinance of God and the laws of the state of Illinois. Whom therefore God hath joined together, let no man put asunder. Ben, you may now kiss your bride." Ellie and Ben did it as they had practiced, starting with a little hug and ending with a kiss. There was a lot of clapping after that precious moment, but the ceremony was not yet over.

Ben faced the audience and explained the next step himself. "In the Psalms it says we should always put Jerusalem above our chief joy. So even on this day of our greatest joy, our wedding day, we don't want to forget Jerusalem."

Ben then had a good explanation of how breaking the glass was connected to remembering Jerusalem. Ellie was amazed Ben could be so well spoken and composed at such a time, but he was. Then Ben stepped on the glass and bang! The sound was as loud as they hoped it would be! A chorus of jubilant *Mazel Tovs* broke out from every corner of the room.

Being so overwhelmed with emotion, the final dance out of the sanctuary just hit the spot for Ellie. Dancing helped her to release all that pent-up joy and turn it into dancing energy. The dancers came up front to join the newlyweds and then they all danced around the aisles a couple of times before dancing out of the sanctuary. At the end Bonnie captured a great picture of Ben and Ellie and the dancers, facing the congregation with hands upraised and joy beaming from all their faces.

Could anything extra be added to such a magnificent celebration, Ellie and Ben wondered. They delayed a while before going to the reception. Ben's mother made some meatballs, per Ben's request, so he and Ellie could break their fast and have their first meal together as husband and wife. They had the food in a container in a small room inside the Broken Wall building. They each took a tiny nibble, but neither of them was very hungry. Finally they headed on over to their reception.

Chapter Twenty-Nine

APPLAUSE AGAIN GREETED THEM. The tables were all filled with people they knew, including a lot of the residents, staff and parents from Monroe Avenue Center. All three hundred seats were filled! Ellie's relatives who worked at the restaurant were ready to serve the food. Ben prayed.

"Thank you, Lord, for putting Ellie and me together. Thank you for the wonderful feast we're about to partake of. And thank you for this loving community that has come together today to witness and share this wonderful day with us. It reminds me of the wedding supper of the Lamb that we all have to look forward to in the future."

Then very uncharacteristically for Ellie, she reached for the microphone that Ben was holding and began to speak. "And at that supper we'll all be the bride, so we'll all be as happy as I am today!"

People laughed. The joy was super-abundant! The meal was fabulous, though Ellie just accepted this fact by faith and hearsay. She was too over-excited to eat. After the meal came the cake-cutting, which remained very simple, each one feeding the other a bit of the cake. Then the part began that is so vital to all great celebrations, the music.

The leader of the band started with an explanation. "Since Ellie and Ben didn't want a lot of secular music, we put a lot of praise songs to the polka beat. Hope you're all ready to get up and dance. And as a special treat, we brought along our dancers."

That was indeed a surprise to Ellie and Ben. Praise songs with a polka beat? Ellie wondered how their guests would react. But before she spent a lot of time worrying about that, there was something else that caused her concern… the dancers. She didn't know about that and she wondered what they were planning to do. The band began with a lively Messianic Jewish song and the dancers performed a nice line dance that everyone watched. Another beautiful Messianic Jewish song followed with another dance by the dancers, and then another one. Everyone just sat and watched.

"Oh no," Ellie smilingly whispered to Ben. For the first time that day she got quite nervous. "Everybody thinks it's a performance and they just have to watch. This isn't how it was supposed to be. What should we do?"

"Well, let's give them the example," Ben said. So he and Ellie got up and rounded up some of their dancing friends. They started a dance circle that anybody could join. People were slowly getting the idea. Next came a joyful polka. When Ellie's mother and her aunt started doing the polka, more couples started venturing onto the dance floor. The celebration finally kicked into full swing.

For one of the beautiful Messianic praise songs, Ellie started giving out palm branches to her friends. They could wave them and praise the Lord as they danced. "It sure seems like a Feast of Tabernacles wedding now," Ellie laughingly shouted to Ben, who had to strain to hear her at this loud exuberant point in the evening.

Soon more and more people were grabbing the palm branches and dancing. Even some of the relatives who already had too much to drink were grabbing the palms and dancing. Ellie and Ben were a little startled to see that, but they were glad the joy was spreading. And soon they had another surprise. They noticed Daniel and Sarah were actually doing a waltz together!

Ellie and Ben were wet with sweat, dancing their hearts out in their full wedding garb. Ben didn't have the kittel on after the service, but his long sleeve shirt and white tuxedo were plenty warm as it was. Ellie wore her beautiful long sleeve linen wedding dress and veil. She didn't want to take off her veil. She loved the look and it was just one day of her life when she would have the privilege of wearing this magnificent attire.

The spirit of the Lord seemed so present on this whole magnificent day. It seemed like the joy was contagious and everyone caught it. Ben and Ellie even forgot about having their photographer take some posed shots of them and their families. They were happy with the pictures taken as the actual ceremony was taking place but they did want some close-up shots too. So when the photographer suggested this late in the evening, even though no one was fresh as a daisy anymore, they rounded up their family for a few posed portraits. There were no blank walls at the American Legion Hall, so a navy man who was painted on one of the walls showed up as background in most of the pictures. Though they were a little disappointed that they had no good wedding portraits to choose from, they laughed about it more than fretted. And Ellie ended up enlarging Bonnie's candid shot of her and Ben with the dancers and using it as their main framed wedding picture. It conveyed the spirit of the wedding better than any other picture could have done anyway.

The evening festivities started slowing down when the band played *Let Me Call You Sweetheart*. That was the traditional song played at American Polish weddings near the end. During the song, everyone holds hands and sings the simple words as they circle the bride and groom. First the bride and groom dance together, then the bride dances with her father and the groom with his mother. After a while other people cut in. Ellie thought it was a nice tradition, but she really didn't feel like dancing with anybody else besides Ben that night. Ellie was glad when she and Ben finally had each other as partners again. It was kind of the climax of the closing scene of the big wedding celebration.

Things did indeed start winding down after that, with many people leaving. But the band still played and many people stayed and danced and danced. Ellie, however, was ready to leave. She began yearning to go home to be with her new husband. And very shortly after that, her dream came true.

Chapter Thirty

ELLIE AND BEN heard later that the Sunday morning service at Broken Wall had a "glorious afterglow following the amazing wedding celebration of the night before" according to Daniel. Ellie and Ben stayed home that morning. They were happy, they were fulfilled, and they were physically and emotionally exhausted. There were no doubts in either of their minds or hearts that this marriage of theirs was God-ordained.

"I can't believe God would give us the best wedding in the world," Ellie said with tears in her eyes.

"I know," Ben agreed and they both broke down crying, the good kind of crying.

God was good to Ellie and Ben. They honeymooned and then returned back to their new normal, working their jobs and coming home together in the evenings. They celebrated their first anniversary by going swimming together at the university pool. Ellie needed the exercise, as she was about to give birth in only a few more days.

Ellie never forgot two things about the day her first son, Joshua, was born. She wrote them down in her photo album with the baby pictures. She wrote: 'This was the hardest thing I ever did in my life." The words by the next photo were: "…and when the nurse came to bring me my baby she called me Mama. I couldn't believe it was true.

I was somebody's mama. I couldn't believe something this good could be happening to me."

It was hard but it was wonderful. Ellie had a hard labor and birth, and the doctor told her she needed a lot of bed rest. So Joshua began to sleep on his parents' bed and that's how the family bed idea was born in Ben and Ellie's family. The house was a mess. Ben tried to cook up great meals, which he did. But he wasn't so good at cleaning up the messes. He always got to them eventually, but not as quickly as Ellie would have preferred. Ben's mother flew in for two weeks to help out and she was a Godsend.

"The lines have fallen for me in pleasant places, yea, I have a goodly heritage," Ben would often quote as they prayed together. God had surely blessed their lives with His favor, and they thanked Him for it every day. Ellie was so grateful she could stay home with her baby and that Ben was happy for her to be a stay-at-home wife. But the challenges that came with this new stage of life were very present too. Learning how to care for a high-need baby, do the housework, get enough sleep, cook for Ben and herself and even talk on the phone once in a while required Ellie to do a balancing act quite often. Staying involved in the lives of family and friends took a concerted effort on both their parts.

For one thing, the fairy tale love story between Daniel and Sarah didn't play out as Ellie had hoped. Daniel really liked Sarah and Sarah really liked Daniel. But when Daniel asked Sarah to go out with him, her parents weren't too enthused.

"That's too bad," Ellie said, as she comforted Sarah on the phone. "What did they say?"

"Well, I don't know if Daniel told you anything yet. Should I start at the beginning or do you already know he talked to my dad?"

"No, I don't know anything," Ellie said. "My life is so consumed with little Joshua right now, I hardly have time to talk at length with anybody. And knowing Daniel, he probably didn't tell anyone else either. I'm sure if my mom knew, she would have told me."

"I know. Daniel is kind of shy. That's why it hurt me so much for my dad to make it so hard for him! I know it took a lot of courage on his part to actually call my dad that day. But wait, let me tell you from the beginning," Sarah said.

"Thanks," Ellie said. Just then little Joshua woke up and started to cry. "Ben, can you walk around with Joshua now so I can talk to Sarah? This is really important."

"Do you have time?" Sarah asked hopefully.

"Yes, Ben is such a good father. I know Joshua isn't hungry now; he's just really tired and fighting sleep. He'll fall asleep pretty soon after Ben walks around with him."

"Thanks, Ellie, I really need to talk to you. And I'll try to make this short and to the point. You know what a good time we had together at the wedding and the various dance practices before the wedding and the rehearsal dinner and everything."

"I know," Ellie said sympathetically.

"So after your wedding, Daniel would call me every once in a while to see when I'd be coming to Broken Wall."

"Really?! That's great! I know he must love you a lot to have mustered up the courage to do that!" Ellie said. "And now that explains the mystery. So those times you showed up at Broken Wall, and Daniel just happened to have the day off work and be there on the same day, those weren't a coincidence?" Ellie asked.

Sarah laughed. "No, not really. I loved going to Broken Wall and I would have gone all the time if it were closer. And it was so nice to be able to see Daniel whenever I went. We would talk quite a bit each time, as you probably noticed."

"I sure did notice and I've been praying for you two a lot," Ellie said.

"Thanks Ellie. Well, about three weeks ago your brother finally asked me if I would go out with him. I told him I'd have to tell my parents, because my family had planned to do this whole dating/courtship thing together. My parents wanted to be involved right from the start, and so we all agreed I'd have the guy ask my father's permission before he could even ask me out. It seemed so right when we talked about it. But when it actually happened, it felt very weird. I felt like a baby."

Ellie gave Sarah an understanding "hmm."

Sarah continued. "When I got home that afternoon, I told my parents right away that Daniel asked me out. I thought there'd be no problem. They know you and your family and have been praying for all of you for years. But I was shocked when my dad said that Daniel isn't ready for a wife yet. He's got a lot of growing in the faith, a lot of maturing to do."

"Oh," Ellie took it in.

"We had big discussions that night and the next night. Finally my father said he would give Daniel a chance. He said to have Daniel call him. So I called Daniel and told him. He was scared but really hopeful, so that made him bold. When he called, my dad told him he would consider letting me go out with him after he had several mentoring sessions with Daniel."

"What did he mean by that?" Ellie asked.

"That's what Daniel asked. So my dad told him what he meant was that he would ask Daniel what he believed about various issues. Also he'd have a kind of personal Bible Study with Daniel. He told Daniel he wouldn't even consider letting him date me till he went through several sessions with him. I guess Daniel asked him how long that would be and he said probably at least half a year."

"Oh no," Ellie said. "Daniel's faith is still a little fragile. I hope that didn't turn him off."

"I know," Sarah said, starting to cry. "But my dad said he just wanted to protect me. He said Daniel seems very nice and very sincere in his faith, but he just had to be more sure of him before he allowed us to date."

"Wow, so what did Daniel say?"

"He said he'd think about it. But since then he's never called me."

"Oh no, and he stopped showing up at Broken Wall too," Ellie informed her.

They both mourned this together, both loving Daniel and feeling deeply for the pain he was going through alone. Sarah told Ellie that she was still struggling to have a good attitude toward her parents; she said it was a real test of her faith. They hung up after talking a few more minutes.

Chapter Thirty-One

ELLIE DIDN'T HAVE too much time to devote to others, but with what little time she did have, she tried to make herself available for Daniel and Sarah to talk with. Daniel slowly got back into attending Broken Wall, and Sarah sometimes showed up there too. They were still very friendly, but now Ellie sadly noticed a new awkwardness between them. They both struggled in their own ways to figure out what the next step in their lives should be.

Ellie and Ben had their own hurdles to navigate through. The gentle parenting style they had chosen was not the most popular style of parenting in those days. They were misunderstood by many people and didn't measure up to the norm. When comments and suggestions came their way, Ellie just listened and didn't yet have enough confidence to counter the remarks. "You need to go out more often and leave your baby with a babysitter... You should close the door and let your baby cry himself to sleep, or you can take a walk and let Ben stay in the house. It won't bother him so much to hear the crying. ...Stop nursing and use a bottle. And mix some oatmeal with the bottle so it'll sit on your baby's stomach longer and he won't wake up so often."

One book they had, *Christian Parenting and Child Care* by Dr. William Sears, was a book that affirmed the gentle parenting style that they felt led in their hearts to do. It was good to find words of comfort and agreement in that book from time to time. But even more important was the fact that Ben and Ellie were united in wanting to parent this way. How Ellie thanked God for such a husband as Ben. She saw other new fathers at Broken Wall, people she had thought in the past would be gentle and caring parents. But when they had children, it turned out that they were harsh disciplinarians. It was scary to think what might have happened if Ellie had married someone like that. And how could she know who would be a good father? It was God who put Ben and Ellie together and they could feel it more and more every day.

Nevertheless, Ellie was often quite lonely. The car seat challenge made it hard for Ellie to get out too much at all during the weekdays, except for stroller trips. For some reason, Joshua hated the car seat. The telephone was helpful, but it also became a source of stress at times. Sometimes she found herself sweating profusely on telephone calls because she was so nervous trying to figure out how to break up a long conversation when she had to go, knowing that Joshua would wake up any minute and need to nurse. Sometimes she was anxious because all of her precious free time was being used up and she still wanted time to read the Bible or do the dishes or start the supper. She always liked to end her phone conversations in a kind way, but she learned that sometimes she just had to be more blunt and say she had to go.

Eventually, with much prayer and trial and error, the car seat situation worked itself out. And just in time, too, for Ellie soon had another challenge to deal with. She became pregnant again! Morning sickness took on a new dimension as she experienced it with a toddler to take care of, as well as the usual cooking, cleaning and daily life activities. But she rejoiced every day of her pregnancy regardless of how she felt, because it was another desire of her heart coming to pass. When Baby Jesse was born, another dream of Ellie's was fulfilled. She always wanted to be a "joyful mother of children," as Psalm 113 talked about. "He maketh the barren woman to keep house, and to be a joyful mother of children. Praise ye the Lord." The psalm said "children." It was plural. She trusted that when she had more than one child it would be easier and she would be even more joyful. And she was! It did take a few years for the two boys to begin to play together, but even at the start it was really fun to have a baby in the house again. Little Joshua was the best big brother ever. However, no more children followed. Ellie's and Ben's prayers and hopes for more children were not answered. So they poured themselves into raising their two boys, enjoying it thoroughly. But Ellie still found herself questioning, at various times, whether she really was a good enough mother.

Ben's office began to hire more women who were young mothers, including many who had even more children than Ellie and Ben had. Ellie felt small compared to them, because she was just staying home and raising her children. She didn't even like to visit Ben in the office very much, because she would feel so belittled. But Ellie didn't feel these feelings often. As hard as it sometimes was, Ellie was never happier. She realized that true joy wasn't when everything in her life was perfect. It was when she felt like she was in the center of God's will for her. She felt that she finally found what God made her for, to be a wife and a mother. Sometimes as she lay in bed with Ben and her two small sons, she would just open her eyes to look at each of them. Then she would smile and thank God again and again that all was right with her world.

Chapter Thirty-Two

MORE YEARS ROLLED BY and a few gray hairs actually started to appear on Ellie's head. The years had brought challenges, sicknesses, sorrows and joys, but the overwhelming sense of contentment and fulfillment overshadowed everything else.

An exciting time of the year was fast approaching—the annual homeschool science and history fair. It was one of the highlights of the school year. Ellie loved homeschooling her own children, and finally found a teaching job she cherished. The heartfelt delight she experienced on the day when reading suddenly clicked for Joshua brought tears to her eyes. He was so happy and she was even happier! Then that same joy appeared again, goose bumps, tears and all, when it happened three years later for Jesse. She figured even if she had ten kids, that happiness of seeing the day when reading finally clicked for the tenth child would be just as great as the first time!

But she also remembered the earlier years of anxiety. She had begun worrying when she found out that a couple of two year olds at Broken Wall already knew the whole alphabet. Then someone told her that their four year old daughter could already read! Yet Joshua, at age four, wasn't the least bit interested in learning his letters. Was it her fault? Was she really a bad teacher after all? She was so confused. Was she doing something wrong? She wondered if she and Ben should have allowed their kids to watch shows like Sesame Street. Would it have helped them to see the clever way a different letter was emphasized each day and repeated over and over in a fast paced eye-catching way? There were a few times when she really wished she could use the TV as a babysitter. She even gave Sesame Street a chance two or three different times. But inevitably, after only a few minutes into the show, something would come on that she objected to.

Now Ellie saw it as the hand of God protecting her and her family. Joshua did learn to read. He was smart all right. He was a real talker and a really clever and wise thinker. But for some reason he had a hard time identifying or even being interested in the alphabet until he was almost six! And reading didn't click with him until he was seven. But now at age twelve he was a genuine scholar! He was only nine when he picked up the book called *The Last Word on the Middle East* and read it straight through. Ben also read that book, but Ellie hadn't. What a feeling it was for her to realize her son was starting to pass her up in his knowledge and interest in so many subjects. She wished she could have known in advance how things would turn out. Then she could have spared herself those struggles and confusions of wondering if she was doing something wrong. But at this point in time, she did know how things worked out and now maybe she could be a help to other mothers. She could reassure them and let them know that the age a child starts reading isn't very relevant to their future skills. Why now the little girl who could read when she was four wasn't much of a reader at all.

Ellie was so glad she was able to homeschool her children. What if Joshua went to school and was labeled a slow learner at that early age? And what about Jesse and his growing passion for the violin? Would that interest have a chance to develop with a full schedule of school and homework?

Ellie's rambling thoughts returned to the present. It was time to pack up the history fair projects. Where had the years gone? Joshua just turned twelve and Jesse was eight. Sarah and Daniel were married. It seemed like only yesterday, yet their twins were almost seven. Too bad the twins got sick and their family wouldn't be coming to the fair to cheer on their cousins.

"Be sure to call me sometime this evening!" Sarah told Ellie. "Not only do Daniel and I want to know how the boys do, but Ruth and Eddie keep praying for their cousins to win first place. I'm sure a phone call would cheer them up. We all expect them to win first place."

Ellie laughed on the phone. "I'm glad you all have such confidence in them! I think they'll do great too. But this year is kind of scary. This year Jesse is old enough to be in the same category as Joshua. So they'll both be competing against each other!"

"Oh no," Sarah sympathized. "But I thought there are usually several people in each category who get the blue ribbon."

"That's true. But Jesse and Joshua are spoiled. The last few years they started awarding a purple ribbon for the highest in each category. Jesse and Joshua have each won one before and they're both aiming for another one this year."

"Oh no, spoiled already!" Sarah joked. "But spoiled in a good way!"

"I know it *is* good that they want to excel. But it'll be so hard if one of them wins and the other one doesn't. How are Ben and I supposed to react? How can we be sad and sympathize with one when the other one wants us to rejoice? I don't know how we'll do it. I'm so anxious. I know it might sound crazy, Sarah, but I get so nervous over these things. I know how much it means to the boys. We use this fair as motivation to kind of direct our homeschooling for so much of the year. It's their one chance to show off their work, to have a good reason to write very legibly, to practice speaking and explaining their works. I pray and pray that they won't get sick and have to miss it. I must be doing something wrong to get so worried," Ellie confessed.

"Well," Sarah said, "maybe you're just too good a mother. You feel too much for your kids. But I guess that's the price you have to pay for feeling their joy so much too. And if one of them doesn't get the purple ribbon it'll be a good opportunity to teach them that the ribbon isn't the important thing."

"I know that. I keep telling myself that. And we keep telling Joshua and Jesse that. But I still know it'll hit the kids hard if one of them doesn't win. You know they both want each other to win too. They feel for each other so much, and I'm sure if one won, he wouldn't be able to enjoy it that much if his brother didn't win too."

"I know. They're great kids! And I feel for you, Ellie. I don't know how I'll be. Next year Ruth and Eddie want to enter the science fair," Sarah said.

"Wow, that'll be fun!" Ellie said. "And tell Ruth and Eddie we'll really miss them being there and cheering us on. We'll take a videotape of part of the fair. Then maybe you can all come over sometime to watch it. I can make sloppy joes and buy some donuts from the bakery, just like they would have had if they'd have come to the fair."

"Thanks Ellie! That'll cheer them up a lot!"

Chapter Thirty-Three

JOSHUA AND JESSE stood guard over their projects the whole time they were at the fair. Many of the students took breaks or walked around looking at other projects. Joshua and Jesse couldn't even be cajoled into taking a lunch break until the judging of their projects was completed.

Before any judges came around, many other parents and friends stopped by and asked Joshua and Jesse about their projects.

"So why did you decide to do your project on this Polish group that helped fight the Nazis?"

"Well," eight-year old Jesse answered with a little bit of a lisp, "since I'm Polish *and* Jewish, I got interested in this when I saw a video about this Polish group called Zegota…."

After talking to Jesse, the visitor turned to Ellie and said, "My, your son is well spoken. It's amazing he even met one of the soldiers who helped liberate one of the concentration camps!"

"I know," Ellie replied. "One of my husband's friends at work told him about this man who lived across the street from him. He asked this guy if Jesse could interview him. He agreed and our whole family went to his house."

"My how interesting!" the visitor said. "What did he say?"

"He said nowadays some people are saying that the Holocaust never happened. He said Eisenhower warned his men that this would happen.

Eisenhower told his soldiers, 'Look well to what you see today, men, and always remember it. One day people will deny this ever happened.'"

"You're kidding! Eisenhower really said that??"

"Yeah, we looked it up later and found it was a true quote. And this man heard it firsthand. He said he is a witness and he could never have made that up. He said he could never make up that smell."

"The smell?"

"Yes, he said he could never forget that terrible smell."

"What an education you're giving your son," the visitor said. "Are you a teacher?"

Ellie laughed. "I was trained to be a teacher. I wasn't too successful in the classroom. But I just love homeschooling."

"You're a natural," the lady told Ellie and then left. Ellie drank up the compliment. It took years to come, but this is the place Ellie wanted to succeed, in her own home.

Joshua's project on Dietrich Bonhoeffer was excellently done as well. Joshua loved to do radio dramas, so along with his paper, which turned out to be a twenty-four page report that was more like a little book, he made a tape where he re-enacted key turning points in Bonhoeffer's life. Joshua made five extra copies of his little booklet for anyone interested and in the end, he gave away all of them and had the addresses of three more people who wanted this twelve year old author to mail them a copy.

"How do you teach such a scholar?" one man asked Ellie.

"Joshua kind of overtook me in his reading a while back," Ellie answered, "and now one of my jobs is editing and helping him to cut out some things and to actually stop writing. He never thinks his project is done. He usually concedes and comes to a stop when the deadline approaches. But he convinces himself that it's not really done and plans to write a book on the subject sometime later."

"It must be a challenge to teach him," the man said.

"It's a challenge and a delight at the same time," Ellie answered.

Ben, Ellie and the boys enjoyed the sloppy joe sandwiches they bought at the fair. They ate them along with potato chips and apples they brought from home. And they eagerly waited for the time when the winners would be announced.

Finally it was time for the history category awards. First the yellow ribbons were given, next the red, and finally the blue. Ben and Ellie were relieved when their sons' names were not announced during the yellow and red awards. And happily, Joshua and Jesse each received the coveted blue ribbon.

After all the blue ribbons were presented, the students went back to stand by their parents as everyone awaited the announcement of the purple ribbon winners. The science category was first, next was arts and crafts, and finally it was history. Ben, Ellie, Joshua and Jesse were all ears listening to the announcer.

"For the history category, ages eight to twelve, we have a tie."

Ellie started getting tears in her eyes. Could it be that the tie would be their two boys? That was too good to be true. Maybe it would be somebody else.

"It's the two brothers, Joshua and Jesse!"

Ellie was a mess. She was fighting back sobs, she was so happy. She didn't want to come across as a nut. Why should this science fair be such a big thing to her? But it was. Ben was crying too. Really crying. Joshua and Jesse were smiling and on stage holding their purple ribbons for the picture.

As if the happiness wasn't complete enough, another comment was made by a stranger as they were on their way to the car. Ben, Joshua, Jesse and Ellie were all carrying multiple boxes and bags filled with all the props from their projects. There was also a bag with four donuts, which they bought every year to eat when they got home. As they closed the trunk, the couple that got into the car next to them recognized Joshua and Jesse.

"Oh, so you're the parents of these two boys?" the older man said.

Ellie smiled and assented.

"All I have to say is that the mother of these boys," she paused, "you are their teacher aren't you?"

"Yeah," Ellie chuckled.

The lady continued. "All I have to say, then, is that you must have been cut out to be a teacher."

Ellie laughed, trying to hide the tears that popped into her eyes.

"No, I mean it," she said.

"Thank you so much for the compliment," Ellie told her. "I laughed because you made me so happy. You see, I was a teacher in the public schools before I got married. I wasn't too successful there and I couldn't control the class. So one of the teachers once told me that she thought maybe I wasn't cut out to be a teacher."

"Now isn't that something?" the kind lady said. "Maybe it was just your students who weren't cut out to be your students, and now finally you have the right mix."

The right mix... Ellie thought about that phrase. She realized it was true, it was the right mix. She was the perfect teacher for these two specific children, her own sons. Maybe she was cut out to be a teacher after all.

Epilogue

SEVERAL YEARS LATER Ellie was in the laundry room, about to do some diapers with her daughter-in-law. Joshua had married Lynn five years ago, and now they had two children, aged four and 10 months. Both children were taking naps and Ellie and Lynn had one of their rare and treasured opportunities to talk undisturbed.

"Don't you think my brother and Arlene would make a good match?" Lynn was asking.

"It sure looks like it," Ellie said, "but it seems like your brother is more interested in just a friendship with Arlene and nothing more, doesn't it?"

"I know. But she'd be the perfect wife for him, don't you think? And shouldn't friendship come first anyway? Do you think guys and girls can be good friends?"

"Lynn, that's such an age-old question," Ellie laughed. "I had to work through that question myself years ago. I remember thinking I was so smart to actually come to a conclusion one day. My answer was that no, guys and girls can't be just friends, at least not real close friends. Inevitably somebody gets hurt. Usually one person wants it to be more than just a friendship."

"But if they can't be friends, how do they get to know each other? Not everybody has such a great opportunity like Joshua and I had, growing up in the same congregation together from when I was twelve and we moved here," Lynn said.

"I know," Ellie agreed. "A lot of us homeschooling parents wanted to protect our kids from getting hurt and making the same mistakes we did. So in the process, I think we put too many restrictions on guy-girl relationships. We tried to avoid the bad things happening, but I don't think we figured out the way to make the good things happen at the same time. In a lot of these families now, they don't want to allow their girls to get to know boys, except as part of a big group or something."

"I know. My mom and I bought into a lot of those teachings too. They seemed so right when the speakers presented them," Lynn said. "But it's not working out for Jesse the same way it worked for us, is it?"

"No it isn't," Ellie said. "One problem is that this restrictive method seemed to work in many cases, so we thought it was good and hopeful. But so many of the homeschool families were big families, and boys who had sisters had a built-in system for getting to know girls pretty closely while still being protected. They got to know their sisters' friends. Yet the situation for boys who didn't have sisters was not taken into account."

"Hey, that's a real good point," Lynn agreed.

Ellie continued. "And each person is so different anyway; one method can't work for everybody. We all have to keep praying. We have to be led by the Holy Spirit and discern how God is guiding us. I think another problem with a lot of the homeschool teachings we've heard was that the speakers' kids weren't even grown up yet when they taught these principles."

"Yeah," Lynn laughed. "I wish I could hear some of them speak now, with the additional insights they have after their own kids dated or courted or got married. Maybe they wouldn't even agree with their own past teachings."

"I know," Ellie agreed. "We all fell into the trap, I think, of following a man's teaching and not being free to be led by the Holy Spirit."

"But wouldn't you think that somebody would have the answer now, I mean, these really wise people, now that they're older and have more experience…"

"Lynn," Ellie interrupted her. "The Bible tells us this is an age-old issue. Each generation has to figure it out for themselves, each individual I mean.

Remember the verse in Proverbs—I think it's in Proverbs 30. It says there are three things that are too wonderful for me and four which can't be figured out, and one of them is the way of a man with a maid."

Lynn laughed. "That's funny. You mean you can't even figure it out now?"

"No I can't. I think I know more than somebody who is young, and I think I can help and advise some of the young people I know today. In fact, I would love to do that. I did some things in my own dating days that worked and some that didn't. I made plenty of mistakes."

"You should tell me your whole story someday," Lynn said.

"I have a surprise for you, Lynn. I'm writing my story!" Ellie exclaimed.

"What! That's great! I wish you could…." Lynn began, but the doorbell interrupted them.

"Oh no, the doorbell! Run, I don't want the kids to wake up," Lynn said.

Ben was in the living room and had already opened the door. He met Ellie and Lynn at the top of the basement stairway. "Sarah's here!"

"Aunt Sarah!" Lynn exclaimed.

"I heard you and the kids were coming over. Where is everybody?" Sarah asked.

"Joshua dropped off Lynn and the kids and he left with Jesse to help some friends move," Ellie explained. "The kids are taking a nap, and Lynn is right here."

"The twins are planning to join me here when they get back from the youth group they're leading," Sarah explained. "And Daniel is coming down with a cold, so he decided to stay home."

"Too bad about Uncle Daniel, but glad the twins are coming," Lynn said.

"Sarah, you came at the perfect time," Ellie said. "Since the kids are asleep, Lynn and I were just starting to talk about the way of a man with a maid."

"You mean you're talking about girl-guy relationships?"

"Of course, and a little match-making too," Ellie added.

"Aunt Sarah, can you please tell me your story of how you and Uncle Daniel started going together? I just heard bits and pieces and I never heard the whole story. Please!" Lynn pleaded.

"I'd love to. But I don't want to interrupt," Sarah answered.

"Sarah, start talking. This is great timing, and you know we have limited time before the kids start waking up," Ellie said.

"But maybe we should go and sit somewhere other than the top of the basement stairs," Lynn suggested.

"Oh, so you don't think this is the perfect place, so we can always remember the time we talked at the top of the stairs?" Ellie joked.

"Well, I must admit it would be great to hear the story anywhere! But I still think if we sat on chairs, or maybe even the couch, it would be more comfortable," Lynn responded.

"Sure, let's go," Ellie said. "I was only joking. And since I already know most of the story, I'll go and make some tea for us."

"Thanks," Sarah said. "I guess I'll just start."

"I'm listening," Lynn assured her.

"I think Ellie told you how we were best friends and how I met Daniel for the first time at the surprise party for Ellie's birthday," Sarah began.

"Yes, I kind of remember. But don't be afraid of repeating things, because I probably didn't hear all the details and I don't mind hearing stuff again even if I already knew about it."

"Ok, well let's see, where should I start? I stayed overnight a few nights at Ellie's house when I wanted to go to Broken Wall. That's when I got to know Daniel a little better. He'd talk to us for a while in the house and then I'd talk to him some at Broken Wall. He was pretty quiet and he seemed much more comfortable talking to me at Broken Wall when Ellie wasn't around. Of course he was even more uncomfortable talking in front of his parents."

Lynn laughed.

"After a while, whenever I called Ellie on the phone and Daniel answered, he'd take the opportunity to talk to me for about five minutes or so before he'd call Ellie. I thought he was cute when I first met him, and I thought he was a very nice and wholesome guy. Eventually I realized he was even nicer than I thought and I really started liking him, you know?"

"You mean like you thought maybe he'd be the one you'd marry?" Lynn asked.

"Yes like that," Sarah agreed. "Then when I was visiting one time during the Feast of Tabernacles to go to Broken Wall with Ellie, Daniel came home from his job and saw me. He said he'd be going to Broken Wall that evening too, and then I found out he even traded shifts with somebody he worked with so he could go the next day too. And since my father was picking me up on Saturday afternoon at the congregation, Daniel did something very uncharacteristic for him. We all wanted to dance but the pot blessing lunch was still going on. So Daniel said, "We should get in at least one dance before Sarah has to leave.""

"Wow, I bet that made you feel good," Lynn said.

"It sure did. I suspected he liked me as much as I liked him, but I didn't know for sure. That day I think I was convinced."

"That's great. Then what happened?" Lynn prodded.

"Well, the next big thing was when Ellie asked me to stand up to her wedding, and she told me Daniel would be the best man. I couldn't believe it. I was thrilled. And so Daniel and I got to be closer as we got together for dance practices and rehearsals and things. And at the wedding, he even asked me to dance a regular dance, not a circle dance."

"Were your parents ok with that?" Lynn asked.

Ellie came back with the tea. "I'd like to hear this part," she said.

"My parents had to know I liked Daniel just by my actions," Sarah said. "But at that point I didn't bring it up on my own. They didn't know how fond I had been growing of him, with all the wedding preparations we were doing together. So that night at the wedding, I think they realized that Daniel liked me and I liked him. They told me later they suspected it before that."

"They did?" Ellie said. "But they never saw you and Daniel together much, did they?"

"No, not really. But remember, we were always a close family and we kind of knew each other a lot, kind of intuitively," Sarah said.

"Yeah, you were or should I say still *are* a very close and loving family," Ellie said.

"But that time of my life was one of our roughest times," Sarah confessed. "My parents and I were not on the same page and it was so hard for me to know what to do. I still visited Broken Wall whenever I could, but of course I couldn't do an overnight with Ellie anymore. So being that it was an hour drive, I didn't come out too often. Finally Daniel realized he had to do something to keep up our friendship, so he actually started to call me."

"And believe me, Lynn, that was a big thing for Daniel," Ellie chimed in.

"I knew it was a big step for Daniel, so it made me that much happier," Sarah said. "And finally the day came when Daniel asked me to go out with him to dinner. I wanted to agree right away, but my family had long-before decided that if anyone ever asked me out, I would have the guy call my father and get his permission first."

"How did you feel about that?" Lynn asked. "I know a lot of homeschoolers do that now, and that's how my family did it too. But you and your family were kind of pioneers in this homeschooling thing and not many people were doing things that way back then."

"You're right, Lynn. I was convinced that was a very good thing to do when I was younger and my parents and I talked about courtship together. But by the time Daniel asked me out, I was already twenty-three. I felt so babyish, having to tell him he had to call up my father and ask his permission."

"So did your father give him the go-ahead?" Lynn asked.

"No, well not exactly no, more like a maybe with strings attached," Sarah struggled to articulate. No one said anything. They all just waited for Sarah to continue.

There was a knock on the door and then Sarah's twins gingerly let themselves in. "Hi everybody," they cheerily said.

"Oh hi," all three ladies said, happy to see the young people, but sad to have the story stopped. Just then four year old Danny appeared sleepy-eyed at the top of the stairs.

"What's going on down there?" Danny asked.

"Oh Danny, the twins came here to see you," Lynn said. "Would you like them to read you a book?"

"Sure," Danny said.

"Danny loves to be read to when he wakes up from a nap," Lynn said.

"We'd love to," one of the twins said, and then they both bounded up the stairs to join Danny in the empty bedroom and read together.

"Whew, a little more time to finish," Sarah said. "I'll pick up my speed. So my father told Daniel that before he'd let him take me out, he wanted to have a few private Bible study sessions with Daniel. Daniel was taken aback, but thought quickly enough to ask how many. Then my dad said at least six months' worth. Somehow Daniel got off the phone gracefully. To this day, he still can't remember exactly what he said. But he was crushed. He didn't think he'd pass the test. So he thought he just better give up on the idea of going out with me. "

"Oh no, I'm glad that's not the end of the story," Lynn said.

"No, a lot of hard months followed that. I really struggled during that time to have a good attitude toward my parents, but it wasn't easy. My father kept insisting he was just protecting me. He said Daniel seemed like a very worthwhile person, he just wasn't sure Daniel was steady enough in his faith to take on a wife and a family. I went through a pretty gloomy period then, trying to forget about Daniel and do more with the singles group from our Sunday church. But it just wasn't working. I really fit in more at Broken Wall and so I tried to visit whenever I could."

"Did Daniel still go there?" Lynn asked.

"He stopped going for a while," Sarah said. "He stopped calling me too, so he never knew if I'd be there or not. But one day, after almost a year I'd say, he started going there again. I think Ellie and Ben started talking to him more at that time and encouraged him to not give up on the faith."

Ellie jumped in. "He insisted he wasn't giving up on his beliefs, he just didn't want the memories or embarrassment of going back to Broken Wall. He said so many people there knew he liked Sarah. And when it was all off, everybody knew that too. But after a while, he did go back."

Sarah continued. "And then one day, I came home from my job and overheard my parents talking. By the way, Lynn, I was working as a teacher aide. Do you know what I mean by teacher aide? Nowadays they call it para-professional."

"Oh yeah," Lynn said.

"Anyway, I worked with a class of mentally challenged middle schoolers. So I came home earlier than I usually did because it was a teacher's institute day and the aides only had to attend the morning session. My dad took the day off, to take my grandpa for cataract surgery. But there was a mix-up and my Grandpa drank a few sips of coffee in the morning. He said they told him not to drink any water, so he thought coffee was ok. But of course it wasn't and they had to postpone the whole thing."

"Oh no, that's funny, I mean terrible!" Lynn laughed.

"I know," Sarah chuckled. "But all that to say, my mom and dad were both home unexpectedly and I came home earlier than they expected too. So I overheard my parents talking. My mom was crying. I listened long enough to pick up the gist of the conversation. My mom was crying because she was heartbroken for me! She sensed my depression, even though I tried to appear cheerful and normal to them. I heard her say one statement very clearly. 'Sarah's not the same. She doesn't trust us anymore. I can feel it. She's pulled away emotionally.'

"Then my dad was saying he probably made a mistake telling Daniel no and giving him such a tough time. About this time there was another family going through a bad courtship experience. I'm pretty sure my parents heard about it too. This guy was somebody we all knew. He was interested in a girl whose family wanted to do the courtship thing instead of dating. So he complied with the family's rigid standards and was given a really hard time by the father of the girl. After a year of meeting with the father and being grilled on all his beliefs and past sins, the father finally told the guy no, he wouldn't allow him to go out with his daughter."

Ellie interrupted. "You mean that incident happened at the same time all the stuff between you and Daniel was happening?"

"Yes," Sarah confirmed. "I told you a little about it, but Joshua was a newborn and you were so pre-occupied, you probably forgot."

"I think I vaguely remember," Ellie said.

"So anyway, I think my parents were starting to see the realities of this courtship ideal. They saw that it wasn't as ideal as they thought. I didn't want to stay eavesdropping and embarrass my parents, so after listening just a little while, I quietly left the house. Then I came back in, purposely closing the door really loud and saying 'Hi everybody, they let us out early!' I wanted to warn them that they weren't alone anymore."

"Then what happened? Did your father change his mind soon after that?" Lynn asked.

"Apparently he did. He didn't say anything to me directly up to this point, except for one thing. He did ask me if I still liked Daniel. I told him I did. He asked if I ever prayed about it. I told him I did, every day. So he told me he'd pray about it too. But I never heard how God answered him. That weekend I went to Broken Wall. And guess what?"

"Daniel was there?" Lynn guessed.

"Right. And then after the service we talked and he asked me out to dinner. I told him I wasn't sure my dad changed his mind about that yet. That's when Daniel told me my dad had called him already and told him he had his approval to ask me out."

"Wow, that's amazing," Lynn said.

"And the rest is history," Ellie added.

"I can't believe all these generations have to figure things out all over again. Why can't we help each other?" Lynn asked. "You two sure had your share of relationship challenges."

"The older I get," Ellie began, "the more I see how these same questions come up over and over again. Sarah, did you know this whole conversation came up today because Lynn asked me if I think guys and girls can be friends?"

Sarah squealed. "Lynn, did you really ask that? That's what Ellie and I talked about so much before we were married! We thought we had it figured out too. And we sort of did, didn't we, Ellie, at least for our own situations?"

"Yeah, we sure thought we finally learned some things. But that's why I think each generation has to learn it all over again, because each situation is so different. Each *person* is so different," Ellie emphasized. "I know a lot of us homeschooling parents made mistakes in our dating lives and we wanted to protect our kids from making the same mistakes. So that's why we tried to go back to the old-fashioned courtship model. It was a good goal, but the specifics still need a lot of refining. And besides, these days aren't like the older days when so many people in my generation met their spouse at school. What about homeschoolers who don't have day to day contact with other young people in a school setting? Where are they supposed to meet? We can't expect everyone to find their life partner in a little pool of ten or fifteen other kids their same age range. These days the logistics are different, the temptations are different. I mean the age old temptations are still the same, but these days the evil is more available, you know what I mean?" Ellie concluded.

"But don't you think you could help other girls anyway, Mom?" Lynn asked. "I know you can't give them the *exact* answers for their own life and relationship struggles. But you can share your mistakes and good Biblical principles you've learned or something that could help them."

"I agree with you, Lynn. I think I can help and I really want to. There are so many young ladies in our congregation now that I wish I could help somehow. I'd really like to find a way to speak into their lives. That's what made me decide to write my book."

"A whole book?!" Sarah was surprised. "I want to read it!"

"Me too!" Lynn said.

And so Ellie persevered and wrote her book. It turned out longer than she expected and she wondered if anybody would like it or if it could help anybody in their lives. But even if it wasn't well-read, at least she comforted herself with the knowledge that it was useful and good to write her own story for her own children and grandchildren.

And that's what Ellie did, and that's how this book came to be. And for the most part, as you've probably guessed, I'm Ellie.

This story is based on my own life story, but events are put in a closer time frame, collapsing about twelve years of events before my marriage into a more compact three year time frame. I actually got married when I was 35. So the

blessing of bearing two sons when I was in my late thirties was a true gift from God, answering years of dreaming and hoping for a family of my own.

Ellie's religious and cultural background is more of a combination of my background and my husband's background. Some events in Ellie's life happened to other people close to me, but I incorporated them into my story, because in one way or another, they affected me and my family and I wanted to speak on that issue. All names of characters based on real people have been changed. Some characters are not based on one real person, but sort of a conglomeration of real and fictionalized people and events.

I hope this story encouraged your faith. I hope it has inspired you to keep God central in your life, even regarding jobs, dating, marriage, and child-rearing. "Trust in the Lord with all your heart and lean not unto your own understanding. In all your ways acknowledge Him and He shall direct your paths."

God's direction and guidance has helped me through so many challenges in my life. His help is real. It may not always be immediately seen or felt, but it always comes. As God told Habakkuk when he had to wait a long time for his vision to come to pass, "Though it tarry, wait for it; because it will surely come, it will not tarry."